IMPLIED SPACES

Other books by Walter Jon Williams

Novels:
Ambassador of Progress
Knight Moves
Hardwired
Voice of the Whirlwind
The Crown Jewels
House of Shards
Angel Station
Elegy for Angels and Dogs
Days of Atonement
Aristoi
Metropolitan
Rock of Ages
City on Fire
The Rift
Destiny's Way
The Praxis
The Sundering
Conventions of War

Collections:
Facets
Frankensteins and Foreign Devils

01

With long strides the swordsman walked across the desert. Gravel crunched beneath his sturdy leather boots. His eyes were dark, his nose a blade. He wore robes, very dusty, and a flowing headdress, all suitable for the high stony land on which he walked. On his back he carried a pack with dried food, a skin shelter, and a rolled-up carpet to lie on. Though the sun in the sky was small and pale, its heat still quavered on the horizon.

The land rolled in gentle hills, endless as the ocean. The soil was grey and covered with stones the same shade of grey. The air smelled of dust. There was little vegetation. The sky was cloudless and twilit, and the sun never moved.

The swordsman's blade was carried in a plain wooden scabbard covered with cracked leather. The broadsword was heavy, single-edged, broader in the foible than the forte. Its name was Tecmessa.

The man walked beside a wagon road, two dusty ruts that carried in a straight line from one horizon to the next. The iron-shod wheels of numerous wagons had thrown all the stones out of the ruts, or ground them to powder, but the swordsman found the ruts too dusty, and chose instead to walk on the stones near the road. The thick soles of his boots made this less trying than it might otherwise have been.

While the man made only an occasional detour from the road, the slim form of his companion roamed left and right of the track, as if on a series of small errands. She returned from such a side trip, and spoke.

"A spider, common and brown. And ants, common and black. The former is happy to feed on the latter."

"Anything uncommon?"

"Alas, no."

The man coughed briefly, the sound smothered by the strip of turban he had drawn over his mouth and nose to keep out the dust.

"Our trek threatens to become tedious," he remarked.

"Threatens?"

There was a moment of silence.

"Sarcasm," said the man, "is a poor companion on a long journey."

"So," said his companion, "are spiders and ants."

They came to the mild crest of a rolling hill and looked into the valley beneath. Shrubs cast a dark shadow on part of the valley floor, and the two left the trail to investigate. As they approached there was a startling clap of wings, and a flock of birds thundered into the sky.

"Quail," said the swordsman.

She turned her green eyes to him. "That implies there is enough here for quail to eat."

The swordsman raised a gloved hand to a drooping branch with long, dark green leaves. "Why don't you investigate?"

His companion darted beneath the shrubs while the swordsman looked at the branch with interest. He turned his eyes toward the ground and saw broken branches, debris, and a scattering of long brown seed pods. He squatted on his heels and picked up one of the pods. It crumbled in his hand and he extracted a pair of seeds, which he put in a pouch on his belt.

His companion returned.

"Ants and spiders," she said.

"Anything else?"

"An elderly tortoise, and a snake anticipating the birth of many baby quail."

"What kind of snake?"

"Bullsnake. Long as your arm."

The swordsmen opened his hand and let fall the remains of the seed pod.

"This appears to be some kind of dwarf mimosa," he said. "Mimosa can tolerate drought, but they're hardly desert plants. Yet here they are."

She narrowed her eyes. "Thriving."

The man looked at her. "What did I say about sarcasm?"

The pair returned to the road. No earth-shaking discoveries were made. Grey lizards the color of the desert scurried out of their way. Wind swirled dust over and around them. They paused for refreshment at a well, where they sat in the shade of an abandoned caravanserai and ate a meal of dried meat, dried apricots, and stale hardtack.

IMPLIED SPACES

WALTER JON WILLIAMS

NIGHT SHADE BOOKS
San Francisco

First Edition

Trade Hardcover:
ISBN-13: 978-1-59780-125-6

Night Shade Books
Please visit us on the web at
http://www.nightshadebooks.com

With thanks, in no particular order, and for a host of particular reasons, to Kathy Hedges, Daniel Abraham, Sage Walker, Melinda Snodgrass, Emily Mah, Ty Franck, Ian Tregillis, Terry England, Steve Stirling, Steve Howe, and Geoff Landis.

And also to Jason and Jeremy, who took a chance.

For Erick Wujcik

An hour later, traversing the bottom of another valley, they were ambushed by a troop of cavalry.

Riders came rolling over the hill just ahead, spreading out in a crescent as grey dust rose in a pall. They didn't charge, but advanced at a controlled trot. The swordsman paused and considered.

"How many?" he asked.

"Seventeen. Eleven with lances, two with swords, four with bows. And their beasts of course, some of which seem ill-natured and prone to violence."

The man frowned beneath the cloth that covered his mouth. He took a step back with his left foot and loosened Tecmessa in its sheath.

The riders came forward and drew rein about ten paces away. The leader was a massive figure, broad as a wall, with pallid skin touched with the grey dust of the desert. His eyes were an eerie gold. A few links of mail, large and crudely forged, hung from beneath his robes. He carried a long lance, and rode astride a bipedal lizard with long, sturdy legs, an occipital crest, and sharp teeth.

"A troll," murmured the swordsman's companion. "What joy."

There were other trolls among the riders. Others were humans of varied hues and genders. One woman had four arms, and carried two bows, both with arrows nocked.

"Hail, traveler," the troll said, in a voice like boulders gargling.

"Hail," said the swordsman.

The gold eyes regarded him. "Have you lost your mount?"

"I come on foot."

"You have chosen a long road to walk. Where are you bound?"

"Gundapur."

"And your business there…?"

"I have no business there, or indeed anywhere. I travel for my soul's sake, not for profit."

The troll narrowed his gold eyes. His mount hissed and bared slab-shaped teeth.

"You will find the journey dangerous," the troll said.

"I am not indifferent to danger," said the swordsman, "but I will walk the path in any case."

"Your name?"

The swordsman took a long breath, then spoke. "I believe it is customary, before asking the name of a stranger, to introduce oneself, and in such a case as this to state clearly the right by which one asks."

A puzzled look creased the troll's face.

"I perceive you are unused to the impersonal pronoun," the swordsman said. "Allow me to rephrase in the second person plural. *Who the hell are you people, and why are you barring my way?*"

For a moment the troll could not decide between anger and laughter. He chose the latter. A grin split his huge grey face."

"Stranger, you have courage!"

The swordsman shrugged. "I claim no more than the normal share," he replied.

Laughter gurgled from the troll. "I am Captain Grax," he said. "These—" Gesturing. "—are my Free Companions. We're employed as caravan guards on the route from Lake Toi to Gundapur."

The swordsman drew his feet together and offered a modest bow.

"My name is Aristide," he said. "My companion is Bitsy." He looked at the Free Companions. "You seem to have misplaced your caravan," he said.

"It's ahead, at the Ulwethi Caravanserai. We're patrolling, looking for bandits who are infesting the district." The gold eyes narrowed. "You could be a bandit scout."

"If so," said Aristide, "I'm a poor one. I'm without a mount, and I walked directly into your ambush."

"True." Captain Grax considered, his cone-shaped ears flickering. "You have seen no one on the road?"

"Nothing but ants, spiders, and the occasional tortoise."

"We'll continue on for a while, then, in case you're lying. If you are, we'll come back and kill you after we've disposed of your allies."

"Good hunting to you," said Aristide, and bowed again.

Grax and his Companions parted and rode around Aristide, on his trail. Aristide adjusted his turban and continued on his way, conversing the while with his companion.

In less than four turns of the glass he came upon the caravanserai, a blocky stone fort crouched over an oasis. Animals and people swarmed about the place, more than could be contained within its walls. A pen for extra animals had been built out of dry stone, while many brightly colored tents were pitched near the oasis. On the near side of the glittering pool, Aristide could see what appeared to be a market.

Far from moving on, the travelers seemed to have settled into this remote outpost for a long stay.

Bitsy gave the swordsman a green-eyed look over her shoulder, then slipped away to conduct an investigation.

The swordsman walked past the stone corral and a row of tents to the elaborate arched door of the caravanserai. He pulled away the strip of turban that lay across his nose and mouth, revealing unshaven cheeks and lips shadowed by a heavy mustache. He asked the guard where he could find the seneschal.

"His office is by the pool of life."

Aristide entered the great stone building and found the shrine with its menhir and silvery pool, and next to it the booth of the timekeeper, who— as the swordsman approached— turned the glass and struck eight o'clock on his gong.

The seneschal's office was behind the timekeeper's booth. The seneschal was a lean man with a sly look in his eye, and a paper-thin mustache that followed the line of his upper lip. He smelled of strong tobacco.

"You will be provided with food for one hundred and forty-four turns of the glass," he said, "and fodder if you need it. Afterward you'll have to purchase rations at the market."

Aristide wondered if the seneschal was slipping food and fodder to the market, and making a profit with the items the sultan intended he give away.

"What's causing the delay?" Aristide asked. "Is there war in Gundapur?"

"The area has been plagued by an unusually rapacious troop of bandits. The caravans have stopped here until their combined companies of guards feel equal to the challenge, or until the sultan sends a force to relieve us."

Aristide looked out the arched window of the office, at the swarm of people and animals in the fort's courtyard.

"There is a small army here," he said.

The seneschal touched the corner of his little mustache with a long finger. "The last group to leave consisted of three caravans with nearly sixty guards. They were routed. A few of the guards returned, but none of those they professed to guard."

"How many bandits were there?"

The seneschal's lip curled. "Swarms of them, according to the survivors. But of course that's what the ones who ran *would* say, is it not?"

Aristide looked at him. "They weren't orcs by any chance, were they?'

"Not according to the survivors, no."

"At least we've escaped cliché," said Aristide. "You have informed Gundapur of the situation?"

"I've sent messages. It's impossible to know if the messengers were intercepted on the way to the capital." He shrugged. "In time the government will wonder at the lack of caravans and send a force to relieve us."

"If you wish to send another message," Aristide said, "I will carry it."

The seneschal raised an eyebrow. "You will brave the bandits?"

"Bandits exist to be braved, though I will avoid them if I can. In any case, I shall accept your hospitality for a few dozen turnings of the glass, and then continue on my way."

The seneschal gave a little smile. "Is it pride or foolhardiness that causes you to make such a decision? The two often go together."

"I claim no more than the normal share of either," said Aristide.

On taking his leave of the seneschal, Aristide inquired where he could find the caravan masters. The first he spoke to was Masoud the Infirm, a lean, leathery man with long grey-white hair and a hacking cough. Masoud had been at the caravanserai for the longest amount of time, nearly three months, and had a small apartment in the building itself. Tapestries hung on the walls, and the floor was thick with carpets. He courteously offered, and Aristide accepted, a cup of tea.

"Hasn't enough time been wasted?" Aristide said. "There must be a force of sufficient size to deal with any bandits here, surely."

"Any ordinary bandits," said Masoud. "But these are a particularly vicious band. They capture whole caravans, over a dozen so far, and nothing is heard from the captives ever again. None are ransomed, none escape, and none appear in the slave markets. It is said that the bandits serve a god who demands human sacrifice."

Masoud's voice cracked on the last few words, and he coughed heavily for a few moments while Aristide politely waited for the fit to subside.

"If the bandits serve an evil god," Aristide said in time, "then fighting them will surely grant a warrior spiritual merit."

"Let the sultan's army earn such merit," Masoud said. "They could use it." Again he coughed, then wiped spittle from his lips with a napkin.

"One could earn merit also," Aristide said, "by bringing you to a physician."

Masoud offered a thin smile. "This cough has followed me, man and boy, for over forty years. The nostrums of physicians are useless, a waste of time and good silver."

"It is a waste of time and good silver to remain in this place."

Masoud coughed for a while before he answered. It was possible to believe that Masoud rather enjoyed his illness.

"I concede your point," Masoud said finally, "but there are nine caravans here, plus their troops of guards. Get the caravan masters and their guard captains to agree to any course of action, and I will applaud you."

"To whom should I next urge a common plan?" Aristide asked.

"Nadeer of the Glittering Eye," said Masoud. "He occupies an apartment across the courtyard, and a more disagreeable ogre I have never met."

Aristide thoughtfully swirled the tea in his cup. "Literally an ogre?" he asked.

"He would not be called Nadeer of the Glittering Eye if he weren't," said Masoud.

Aristide thanked Masoud for his hospitality and ventured across the

courtyard to the apartment occupied by Nadeer. Nadeer was easy enough
to find: his snores were heroic, and echoed mightily along the cloister that
surrounded the courtyard; and the ogre's great bare feet thrust out of the
apartment door, which was not long enough to hold him. Nadeer was taller
than any troll, far too large for any riding beast to carry. His skin was a
brilliant green. The thick dark calluses on the broad, paddle-like feet made
it clear that Nadeer crossed the high desert on foot, walking alongside the
camels that carried his goods.

Aristide sat on one hip before the doorway, one leg curled under him,
and began to sing.

> *"Nadeer, whose strides engross the leagues,*
> *And before whose voice the lions tremble—*
> *Let Nadeer stand in the sun!*
>
> *He whose glittering eye seeks the foe,*
> *He whose legs dwarf the pillars of the sky,*
> *Let Nadeer's voice smite the air!*
>
> *On whose verdant skin the wind blows,*
> *He with knuckles the size of cabbages,*
> *Let Nadeer fare forth!"*

The snoring came to a gurgling conclusion about the fourth or fifth
line, then, a few lines later, came a deep, slurred voice, accompanied by
the sound of little bells.

"I don't like that line about cabbages."

"Sorry," said Aristide. "I'll work on it."

"Cabbages lack heroic stature, if you ask me."

The large green feet began to work their way into the courtyard, followed
by the great slablike body. The doorway wasn't wide enough for Nadeer's
shoulders, and he had to twist to get out. He sat up, his head brushing the
ceiling of the cloister built around the courtyard.

Unfolded, the ogre would have been more than twice Aristide's height.
His green skin was heavily tattooed. In a crooked slash of a mouth he had
two upturned tusks, each elaborately carved, and above the mouth were
waxed handlebar mustaches with little silver bells on the tips. His most
singular feature was the great faceted eye in the middle of his forehead,
shining like a diamond. The eye turned toward the swordsman.

"By rights I should smash your head in," Nadeer said. When he spoke,
the little bells chimed and his voice slurred around the tusks.

Aristide flowed to his feet in one swift, easy motion. Surprise swept across the ogre's face at the speed of the swordsman's movement.

"I wish only the pleasure of your company," Aristide said, "on the journey to Gundapur."

The single eye narrowed. "You wish to hire me to protect you?"

"I have no money to speak of," said Aristide. "But a long journey is best taken in company, and when I leave for Gundapur, in another twelve or fifteen turns of the glass, I hope you will join me."

"I won't need to smash you," Nadeer said. "The bandits will take care of that on their own."

"There is sufficient force here to deter any bandits."

The ogre snarled. "Not *this* pack of fools! Under a single leader, perhaps, but as things stand—" He began to maneuver himself back into his apartment. "I will return to my slumbers."

"Under a single leader, exactly," Aristide said. "And why shouldn't that leader be Nadeer the Strong? Nadeer the Master? Nadeer the Formidable?"

Nadeer made a snarling noise. "I offered to fight the other leaders for the leadership of the caravans, but the degenerate fools said no! I wash my hands of them!"

With the laughing of bells, the ogre inserted himself into his apartment and lay supine.

"May I talk to the others on your behalf?" Aristide asked.

"Say anything you like. I'm going to sleep. *Goodbye.*" The last word bore the unmistakable sound of finality.

Aristide left the ogre's company and found the leader of another caravan, a blue-skinned woman named Eudoxia. She had rings in her ears and another ring in her septum, a ring so broad that it hung over her lips and touched her chin.

"My name is Aristide," he said, "by profession a traveler. In another dozen or so turns of the glass I will begin the journey to Gundapur, in the company of Nadeer and his caravan. I wonder if you would be willing to accompany us?"

Eudoxia favored Aristide with a suspicious scowl. "Why would I want to accompany that green-skinned imbecile to Gundapur or anywhere else?"

"Because there is safety in numbers, and because you are losing money every moment you delay here."

She cocked her head and regarded him. "Is anyone else leaving?"

"You're the first I've approached."

Eudoxia chewed on her nose-ring a moment. "I'll talk to Nadeer," she said.

"He's settled in for a nap. If you wake him he might crush your head."
She sneered. "I suppose he'll insist on being in charge?"

"That seems to be the case."

Eudoxia cursed and spat, then stomped on the spittle.

"Very well," she said finally, "but only if the others agree."

"Perhaps you would like to join me when I speak to them?"

The timekeeper's gong struck nine, ten, eleven, and twelve while Aristide had similar conversations with the other caravan masters. The swordsman returned eventually to Masoud, who coughed in derision for a long while before, after a good deal of complaint, agreeing to join the others under Nadeer's leadership.

Thus it was that Aristide was able to wake Nadeer with the news that he had become the leader of nine caravans and their assorted guards.

"Perhaps you should confer with your lieutenants," Aristide said. "As I know nothing of the business of caravans, I will excuse myself. I have talked a great deal and need refreshment." He bowed and turned to leave, then hesitated.

"Allow me to give you a word or two of counsel," he said. "They are yours—be magnanimous. Let them talk to their heart's content. If they speak sense, you can agree and appear wise. If their counsel is foolish, you may order things as you please."

"It will take patience to put up with their nattering," Nadeer said, "but I shall do as you advise."

Aristide ate one of the free meals offered by the servants of the sultan: olives, cheese, bread, and stewed lamb with dried apricots. The only condiment was a spoonful of salt, carefully measured. He left the caravanserai on his way to the oasis, and saw Captain Grax returning to the encampment with his patrol. He turned toward the troll and hailed him on his approach.

"How was your hunting?" he asked.

Grax gave him a sour look.

"Ants and spiders, as you said."

"You'll have better sport in the days to come. The caravans have agreed to march for Gundapur."

The troll offered a grunt of surprise. "I thought we'd be here till the Last Death."

"Sharpen your weapons," said Aristide. "Eat your fill. And make an offering at the pool of life."

Grax gave him a shrewd look. "You think there will be fighting?"

Aristide shrugged. "That's up to the bandits." He thought for a moment. "It might be a good idea if you were to send a patrol out of sight, in the direction of Gundapur. If the bandits have a spy here, perhaps you'll be able to intercept him."

Grax ground his yellow teeth. "An interesting idea, stranger."

Grax sent out three of his Free Companions on the patrol and led the rest to the corral. Aristide resumed his walk to the waters of the oasis. Along the way, Bitsy joined him.

"What news?" he asked.

"The camp is filled with boredom," said Bitsy, "mixed with thrilling rumors of massacre and human sacrifice."

"Anything else?"

"The seneschal is making a fortune selling state supplies to the caravans."

"I thought as much."

The two walked in silence for a moment. The dim, motionless sun faded behind a cloud. When Aristide looked at the men and women camped along the path, their eyes glowed like those of a cat.

They approached the oasis. It was a goodly sized pond, larger than an athletic field, and surrounded by willows. The air smelled like air, rather than dust. Yellow butterflies flitted in the air; dragonflies hovered purposefully over water. There was an area where beasts could be watered, and opposite this a small lagoon where people could draw water for themselves without having to drink any muck stirred up by the animals.

"I think that fellow ahead is a missionary," Bitsy said. "There's something unworldly about him."

Ahead of them a man squatted on the firm banks of the lagoon, refilling several water bottles. He was a thin man in a faded striped cotton robe, with a hood drawn up over his head.

Aristide waited for the man to fill his bottles and rise.

"Hail, scholar," Aristide said.

"Hail." As the man bowed, he made a swift sign with his fingers. Aristide bowed and responded more deliberately with another sign. Relief crossed the man's homely, bearded face.

"My name is Souza," the man said.

"Aristide." Bowing again. "How fares your collecting?"

"I've been out for three months—" Souza was distracted by the sight of a black-and-white cat hunting along the bank. "Is the cat yours?" he asked.

"Yes. Her name is Bitsy. Have you had good hunting?"

"I've only begun," Souza said, "but I've acquired three children. In the next seven months, I hope to have a dozen more."

"Very good."

"There are so many of the best that I miss," Souza said. "I go to the towns and villages, I do my tests, I identify the bright ones and try to convince the parents to let them go. Sometimes I buy them. But I can't visit *all* the villages, and not all the parents let their kids be tested, or let them go if they pass. They know that most of the children who go to the College never return." He shook his head. "I might be missing thousands. Who can tell?"

"It would be good if more had a choice. But—" Aristide shrugged. "Their parents chose it for them."

Anger flickered across Souza's face. "Their parents had such a choice. Their children did not."

"True."

"Now," Souza said wearily, "I have to worry if the children are going to be captured and sacrificed to evil gods."

"I wouldn't take that seriously," Aristide said.

The scholar peered at him. "You have information?"

"No. Merely confidence. I think the force present here can handle any mob of evil cultists, especially if we act under a single leader—and apparently Nadeer is that leader."

"The ogre?" Souza wrinkled his face. "Talk about *choice*..."

"Each to his own," said Aristide. "But in any case you should prepare the children to move on in the next few dozen turns of the glass."

"I'm secretly relieved, to tell the truth," Souza said. "Young children separated from their families for the first time, *and* stuck for months at a desert oasis with nothing to do." He grimaced. "You can imagine the scenes we've had."

"I'm sure."

Souza narrowed his eyes. "You're not a missionary yourself, I take it?"

"No. I'm a scholar of the implied spaces."

Souza was puzzled. "I—" he began, then fell silent as a group of Free Companions approached.

"We'll speak later, on the journey," Aristide said.

"Yes." Souza bowed. "It's good to have someone to talk to."

Souza returned to the camp. Aristide squatted and refilled his water bottle while he listened to the convoy guards. Their speech was loud but without interest. After the guards left, Aristide drank, then filled his water bottle again as he watched a tall blue heron glide among the reeds on the far side of the water.

He heard a step and the soft rustle of robes, and turned to see a young woman crouching by the lagoon, lowering a large leather sack into the water by its strap. Water gurgled into its open mouth.

The hair peeking from beneath the young woman's headdress was light brown. Her eyes were blue. A slight sunburn touched her nose and cheeks.

"I am reminded of the verse," said Aristide.

> *"Butterflies make music over water*
> *The green boughs dance in company.*
> *The brown-haired woman bends over the water*
> *Graceful as a willow branch."*

A blush touched her cheeks, darkened the sunburn. Water gurgled into the sack.

"I haven't seen you before," she said. Her voice was barely heard over the rustle of leaves and the sigh of wind.

"I am Aristide, a traveler. I arrived a few turns of the glass ago." Softly, he sang.

> **"***This sack of water, a heavy burden.*
> *The maiden staggers beneath the weight.*
> *What thoughtless man has given her this charge?"*

The woman looked quickly down at the water and her water bag.

"The water is my own. I travel alone."

"You must allow me to carry the weight for you."

She twirled a lock of hair around her finger. Bitsy appeared from the trees and rubbed against the woman's leg. The woman scratched it behind an ear.

"Is the cat yours?"

"Her name is Bitsy."

"Bitsy," she repeated, idly scratching. The cat looked up at her and purred.

"You neglected to tell me your name," Aristide reminded.

A soft smile fluttered at the corners of her lips.

"My name is Ashtra," she said.

"And you travel alone?"

She glanced down at the water. "My husband is in Gundapur. He's sent for me."

Aristide looked at her closely. "At the mention of your husband I detect a strain of melancholy."

"I haven't seen him for seven years. He's been on a long trading journey with an uncle." She gazed sadly across the placid water as she scratched the purring cat. "He's very rich now, or so his letter said."

"And he sent for you without providing an escort? That bespeaks a level of carelessness."

"He sent two swordsmen," Ashtra said. "But they heard of a war in Coël, and went to join the army instead of taking me to Gundapur."

"I think somewhat better of your husband, then, but not as much as if he'd come himself. Or at least sent money."

"Perhaps he did, but if so the swordsmen took it." Her blue eyes turned to him. "I don't even remember what he looks like. I was twelve when my family had me marry. He was only a few years older. "

Despite the efforts of the sultan and other rulers to set up timekeepers with sandglasses regulated by the Ministry of Standards, days and years were necessarily approximate in a land where the sun did not move.

Aristide took her hand and kissed it. "You will delight him," he said, "have no doubt."

She blushed, bowed her head. "Only if I survive the bandits."

He kissed her hand again. "Do not fear the bandits, Ashtra of the Sapphire Eyes. The caravan guards make a formidable force, and—come to that—I am rather formidable myself."

She looked away. He could see the pulse throb in her throat. "But the stories—what the bandits are supposed to do to captives—The stories are chilling."

"Stories. Nothing more." He stroked her hand. "You will pass through the gates of Gundapur, and live in halls of cool marble, where servants will rush to bring you sherbets and white raisins, and music and laughter will ring from the arches. But for now—" He reached for the strap of her water bag, and raised it dripping from the spring. "Allow me to bear this for you. For I believe there is a bank of green grasses yonder, shaded by the graceful willow, where we may recline and watch the dance of the butterfly and the stately glide of the heron, and enjoy the sweetness of wildflowers. There the wind will sing its languorous melody, and we may partake of such other pleasures as the time may offer."

He helped her rise, and kissed her gravely on the lips. Her eyes widened. Aristide drew her by the hand into the shade of the trees, and there they bode together on the carpet of grass, for the space of a few hours on that long, endless afternoon of the world.

02

Aristide slept a few hours, the tail of his headdress drawn across his eyes. When he woke, he found Ashtra seated near him, contemplating the silver ripples of the water through the trailing leaves of the willows. He paused for a moment to regard the woman sitting next to him on the bank—Ashtra, raised in a preliterate world blind even to its own possibilities, brought up in a society founded by swashbucklers, warriors, and gamesters all for their own glorious benefit, but who condemned their descendants to an existence bereft of choice. Married at twelve to a youth who was a relative stranger, now traveling at nineteen to meet a husband who was even more a stranger than that youth. To live in what Gundapur considered luxury, and bear her husband, and bear him children, as many as possible until childbirth broke her health.

"Come with me, Ashtra," he said.

For a moment he didn't know whether she had heard. Then she said, "Where would you take me?"

"Wherever you desire. Eventually to the Womb of the World."

"You belong to the College?" She turned to look at him in alarm, and shifted slightly away from him.

People often feared the magic of the College and its missionaries.

"I'm not of the College," Aristide said, and watched as she relaxed slightly. "Still, one does not have to be of the College to travel to the Womb."

"There are said to be sorcerers of great power at the Womb of the World. And monsters."

"There are monsters *here*."

She turned away, and for a long moment regarded the lake.

"I have a family," she said finally.

"What do you owe to this husband who you barely know?"

"It's what my family owes him. If they had to refund my bride-price, they would be destitute."

"I could pay the price myself."

Ashtra turned to him, amusement in her blue eyes. "You do not travel as a prince travels. Are you a prince in disguise?"

"I travel simply because simplicity appeals to me. And though I am not a prince, I have resources."

Again she turned to face the waters. "I have a husband. And what you offer me are fantasies."

For a moment the swordsman contemplated the many ironies of this last statement, and then he sat up and crossed his legs.

He was not without experience. He knew when he had been dismissed.

Some people remember virtue and a spouse rather late, when it no longer really matters.

"It's extremely unlikely there will be a child," he said, "but if there is, I desire you to send it to the College. Give them my name."

Again she turned, again alarm widened her eyes. "I thought you said—"

"I'm not of the College," he said, "but I have done them service, and they know me. You may request this in my name." His tone took on a degree of urgency. "Particularly if it is a girl."

"I hope there is not a child." Ashtra rose. "I want to remember this as a beautiful fantasy, not as a burden I will bear for the rest of my life." She picked up the strap of her water bag and shouldered it.

"I'd prefer not to be the subject of gossip by those in my caravan," she said. "If you would wait half a glass before following, I would thank you."

"As you like, my lady," said Aristide. "Though I would gladly carry your burden."

Ashtra made no reply. Swaying beneath the weight of the water bag, she made her way from the glade.

Aristide stretched again on the grass and watched the willow branches moving against the dim sky. Gusting wind brought him the scent of flowers. There was a rustle in the grass, and he turned to see the black-and-white cat moving toward him.

"Your attempt at chivalry is duly noted," Bitsy said.

"Sentimentality more than chivalry," said the swordsman. "I liked her." He rubbed his unshaven chin. "You know, she's braver than she thinks she is."

"Brave or not, did you really mean to take that bewildered child to the

Womb?"

"If she desired it. Why not?" He sat up. The cat hopped onto his lap. Her upright tail drew itself across his chin.

"I hope you appreciate my help in getting you laid," Bitsy said.

He sighed. "I couldn't have done it without you."

He stroked Bitsy for a few idle moments, then tipped her out of his lap and rose.

"Perhaps I'll ensure my next incarnation," he said.

Bitsy gave him a narrow-eyed look. "Is there so much on this journey," she asked, "that you wish to remember?"

Aristide shrugged. "Ants and spiders. And a pleasant interlude on a grassy bank."

As the swordsman passed through the camp, he saw the people had been stirred, like those selfsame ants with a stick. People were stowing tents and rugs, mending harness, sharpening weapons. Towering over everyone, Nadeer walked about giving orders. Voice booming, bells tinkling.

Inside the caravanserai, the pool of life had a crowd of visitors. Some chanted, some prayed, others meditated. Some, men and women both, waded naked into the pool, their lips murmuring devotions. Aristide removed his clothes, handed the clothing and Tecmessa to an attendant, and walked into the pool.

He followed broad steps downward until the silver liquid rose to his chest. His skin tingled at its touch. There were bodies at the bottom of the pool, and he felt for these with his feet to avoid treading on them. He waded between the devotees and touched the black menhir with one hand. The smooth surface felt prickly, as if a thousand tiny needles had pierced his fingertips.

He eased himself backward into the fluid. It was the temperature of blood. The silver liquid lapped over his ears, his throat. He closed his eyes.

In his ears he heard a deep throbbing. The throbbing was regular, hypnotic. His breathing shifted to match the rhythm of the throbbing.

He slept. He sank, the silver fluid of the pool of life filling his mouth and nose.

A few forlorn bubbles rose, and that was all.

The glass turned twice before Aristide rose to the surface. He opened his eyes, took a breath of humid air. Slowly he swam to the rim of the pool, found a step beneath his feet, and rose.

As he stepped from the pool the silver liquid poured off him in a single cascade, the last rivulets draining from his legs onto the flags, then slipping into the pool like some covert boneless sea creature seeking shelter beneath a coral ledge. Not a drop was left behind. There was a salty taste in his mouth. Aristide accepted his clothes from the attendant and donned them. He slipped Tecmessa's baldric over one shoulder, shouldered his pack, and tipped the attendant.

"May the pool give you many lives, warrior," the attendant said.

"And you."

He stepped out into a courtyard filled with dust and noise. A turbulent circle of gesturing travelers had formed around the towering figures of Nadeer and Captain Grax, both of whom were gesturing for order.

Nadeer's patience was exhausted. "*Silennnce!*" he bellowed, each hand drawing a curved sword that sang from the scabbard.

The crowd was struck dumb by sheer force of character. In the sudden hush Aristide shouldered his way through the crowd, and laid eyes on a bruised, bleeding young man kneeling before Nadeer, surrounded by Free Companions brandishing arms. The seneschal stood by, watching in silence.

Grax looked at Aristide and grinned with his huge yellow teeth. "Your advice was good, stranger. We caught this spy riding from camp to alert the bandits."

The young man began what was obviously a protest, but Grax kicked him casually in the midsection, and the man bent over, choking.

"Confess!" roared Nadeer, brandishing both swords close over his head. The prisoner sought for resolve, and somewhere found it.

"You but threaten to send me to my next incarnation," he said through broken lips. "I welcome such an escape."

Nadeer snarled around his tusks, then replied in his booming lisp.

"You miss the point, spy. We don't threaten to send you to the next incarnation, we threaten to make *this* incarnation an extremely painful one."

With a flick of the wrist, he flashed out one sword, and the flat of it snapped the prisoner's elbow like a twig. The prisoner screamed, clutched his arm, turned white. Sweat dripped slowly from his nose as he moaned.

The seneschal watched this in silence, his expression interested.

"Who are you?" Grax asked. "Who sent you? What are your orders?"

The captive's breath hissed between clenched teeth. "It won't make any difference," he said. "I may as well talk." He seemed to be speaking more to himself than to his audience.

Though speak to the others he did. His name was Onos. He was a younger son from the Green Mazes, his only inheritance a sword, a horse, and a few bits of silver. In a spirit of adventure, he and some friends joined the army of Calixha. At this point the horse disappeared from the narrative. Finding service during the siege of Natto not to his taste, he and his friends stole horses, deserted, and became caravan guards. Finding this tedious as well, they became robbers.

"He isn't good even at that," Grax remarked. "What the lad needs is discipline." He looked down at the captive. "If he were in *my* company, I would make a proper soldier out of him."

Onos bled quietly onto the flagstones. "I thought a life of adventure would be more fun," he muttered.

Grax kicked him once more in the midsection. "It's fun for *me*," he said. "Perhaps you lack the proper attitude."

The captive gasped, spat, and swore. Nadeer looked down at him. "You have my leave to continue," he said.

Onos wiped blood from his mouth with the back of a grubby hand. "Our gang joined another gang," he said. "We weren't given a choice. So now we're servitors of the Brothers of the Vengeful One."

"Never heard of them," said the seneschal, the first words he had spoken.

"Neither had we," said Onos. "Neither had anyone, until a few months ago, and then *all* the freebooters heard of them." He grimaced and put a hand to his ribs. "We joined them or we died."

"Who are they?" Grax asked.

"Priests. Monsters. Monsters and priests."

"Monsters how?" asked Aristide.

"They're—" Grimacing. "Another species. Ones I'd never heard of, or seen. Blue skin, eyes like fire. And they sacrifice captives, and anyone else who disappoints them."

There were gasps from the listeners as this terrifying rumor was confirmed.

"Your mission?" Grax asked in the sudden silence.

"We knew the caravans were delayed here for fear of us. I was told to travel to the caravanserai and report on your plans—whether you'd come on, or try to retreat."

"Would you attack us either way?"

"That wouldn't be for me to decide." Grax raised a foot. "*Probably!*" Onos said quickly. "*Probably we'd attack!*"

The questions turned to the bandits' strength, and where they would most likely strike at the caravan. The bandits were said to have two hundred riders, though not all of them would be available at any one time, since they raided not just the caravan routes but the plain of Gundapur, below the great desert plateau. The route down from the plateau, through the Vale of Cashdan, was the usual ambush site.

Aristide stepped forward. "I would like to ask some questions of the prisoner, if I may."

Nadeer looked at him. "You may proceed."

Aristide looked at Onos. "How long have you been here at the caravan-serai?"

"Fifteen or twenty days."

"You have a mount?"

"I have a horse, yes."

"And during that time," Aristide said, "you could have left for Lake Toi whenever you desired. You could have abandoned your fellow bandits and those disagreeable priests and got away with your skin. And yet you remained…" He let this thought linger in the air for a moment.

"*Why?*" he asked finally.

Onos swiped at his brow, leaving a dusty track on his skin. "I'm afraid of them. They'd come after me."

"You could have asked the seneschal, or some other official, for protection."

Onos looked at the seneschal. "He'd just hang me from the tower and announce a great success at suppressing the bandits."

Aristide's brief acquaintance with the seneschal had not been such as to make this implausible. The seneschal himself, looking on, declined to be offended, and in fact seemed amused.

"My point," said Aristide, "is that you could have run, and you didn't. Therefore you aren't merely a thief whose gang was annexed by a more powerful outfit, but a willing member of the organization."

Onos looked at Aristide with a kind of sulky resentment. The others glared at Onos with increased malevolence.

"How many caravans have you plundered?" Aristide asked.

"Eleven, while I've been with the brotherhood."

"And the people in the caravans killed or sacrificed by the priests?"

"All those we could catch," Onos said. "Yes."

"What happened to the loot?"

"It's still there. At the Venger's Temple."

There was a stir among the onlookers. A calculating look appeared on the faces of Grax, Nadeer, and the other caravan guards.

"The Venger's Temple is your headquarters, I take it?"

An affirmative nod.

"The spoil is there with the other loot, from the raids onto the plains?"

"Except for that which was used to purchase supplies, yes."

Aristide looked at Nadeer. "I imagine that avarice is never far from our friend Onos' mind," he said. "A share of that loot would give him a comfortable life far from here, perhaps even make him rich. *That* is why he hasn't fled from his monstrous priests."

Onos, defeated, slumped on the flagstones, did not bother to deny it.

Grax turned to the seneschal. "He is convicted out of his own mouth. Shall we turn him over to you, to dispense the sultan's justice?"

The seneschal began to walk through the crowd to his office. He waved a hand in dismissal.

"Why bother *me* with it?" he said. "Do what you will."

Grax looked at Nadeer, and they both shrugged. Nadeer's shoulders had barely returned to their normal position before one of his swords sliced out to separate the bandit's head from his shoulders.

The body was wrapped in an old cloak and given to the pool of life, to feed the chthonic spirit believed to dwell in the menhir. The head was stuck on a spear in front of the caravanserai's gate.

The head bore a disappointed look. Onos had probably expected more excitement than this.

"I wonder if his next incarnation will have learned anything," Aristide asked, as he and Nadeer paused to view the head on its spear.

Nadeer only snorted at the swordsman's question.

"May I have the bandit's mount?" Aristide asked. "I would be more useful in this adventure if I were mobile."

"It's that barb yonder."

The horse was a cream-colored gelding, a little long in the tooth but deep in the chest and strong of spirit. The saddle and tack were serviceable. Aristide took the barb for a brief ride over the desert to get acquainted, then fed the animal and watered him. He sorted through the bandit's belongings but found nothing of interest.

He helped himself to another of the sultan's free meals, then slept in the bandit's tent for a few hours, until the sound of trumpets, conchs, and ram's horns told the travelers to ready their mounts and assemble.

Aristide walked his new horse through the bustle. Dust rose, obscuring the sun, and he drew the tail of his headdress over his mouth and nose. By chance Aristide passed by Ashtra, who was struggling to lift her heavy water bag to its place on her palfrey's saddle-bow.

"Permit me, madam," he said. He performed the task, bowed, and departed, his senses alert in case she called him back.

She didn't. He walked on.

The caravan, big as a small army, didn't actually get under way for another three turns of the glass. Once it moved, it moved slowly. The guards were mounted on horses, bipedal lizards, or the red six-legged lizards that moved with a side-to-side motion, like giant snakes. The lizards were cold-blooded, but in the high desert, beneath an unmoving sun, that scarcely mattered.

The others in the caravan rode horses or Bactrian camels, mules or asses. There was one forest elephant. Their carts and wagons were drawn by oxen, horses, or ridge-backed dinosaurs. No small number proceeded on foot, sometimes accompanied by a dog pulling a travois.

Aristide had his own difficulties, in that his new horse was afraid of his cat, snorting and backing away whenever Bitsy approached. It was an unfortunate fact that many animals disliked Bitsy—perhaps she didn't smell right—and in the end Aristide had to hide her, making her a nest on the saddle blanket behind the high cantle of his saddle, where the horse couldn't see her. The horse still scented her from time to time, snorted and gave a nervous look backward, but these alarms only increased its desire to move faster along the trail.

Nadeer and the other leaders worked in a desperate fury to get the huge convoy ordered, and to move them at a steady pace. A huge cloud of dust rose above the column and turned the sun red.

"The bandits will see this for fifty leagues," Grax said, as he and Aristide rode ahead of the column. "We may as well have let the spy live."

"He won't be able to tell them how we're organized."

Grax showed tombstone teeth. "We're *organized?*"

The caravan only made five leagues before Nadeer called a halt, but at least the day had been useful as a training exercise. The guards had got used to working with one another, and had developed a system for scouting ahead. As the caravan laagered, as guards were posted, the last of the dust drifted away on the wind, and the curses of the drovers and the captains and one large, green ogre echoed through the camp, Aristide thought that perhaps the little army had done better than Nadeer knew.

The glasses turned sixteen times before the trumpets blared again, and the vast column heaved itself onto its feet and began its trek. Everyone had got practice by now, and though the caravan didn't move appreciably faster, it was more orderly and better-behaved. The guards were efficient, organized into an advance guard, flankers, and a rear guard that complained of wandering in the dust. Patrols regularly trotted ahead to the next hill, or rocky outcrop, to make certain no ambush was lurking therein.

The principal delays occurred at water holes. It took hours to water the animals.

The terrain grew rougher and began to descend. Each hill gave a broader view than the one before it, though the farthest views were always hidden by heat-haze.

After eight or nine leagues the group came upon a battlefield, the water hole where the bandits had routed three caravans and their sixty guards. Dead animals and bodies lay in the sun amid broken wagons, flesh turning to leather, lips snarling back from teeth. It looked as if the caravans had been attacked when in camp, their tents strewn across a valley floor in no particular order.

"A lesson in forming a proper laager," Aristide told Nadeer. But Nadeer was busy shouting down those who wanted to stop and give the bodies a proper burial.

"Do you want to join them in death?" Nadeer demanded. "Our lives depend on moving quickly through this place!"

Nadeer lost the argument, chiefly because the convoy took so long to re-water that there was time for the burials anyway.

The caravan rolled on. Halfway to the next water hole Nadeer called a halt, and the laager was formed by grim-faced drovers who made sure their weapons were within easy reach. Aristide wandered through camp until he found Ashtra. He observed her as she brewed tea over a paraffin lamp. She was in the company of a family moving to Gundapur, the father, a pregnant mother, and three children traveling in a two-wheeled cart. They were sharing their bread and dried fruit with her.

Aristide watched for a few moments, then left unobserved.

The next watering hole was a spring that chuckled from the foot of a great slab of basalt that towered like a slumbering giant over its little dell. Guarding the source of water was a deserted military fort, its tumbled walls having been breached at some point in the dim past. A black and unnaturally flawless menhir stood above the empty pool of life. Though the gates had long since been burned for firewood, the fort nevertheless provided more protection than the open desert for the most vulnerable members of the caravan.

The next march took them along the watercourse. The spring water was absorbed by the ground before the convoy had gone very far, but the dry river bed was full of scrub that testified to the presence of water below the surface. The watercourse widened in time into the Vale of Cashdan, the great zigzag slash in the wall of the plateau that led down to the plains of Gundapur. White birds floated far below, like snowflakes drifting in the wind. Crags crowned with trees loomed above the narrow caravan route that wound through green patches of mountain grazing. The blue of a stream was barely visible before the Vale vanished into a huge floor of brilliant white cloud that stretched to the far horizon. Never would the convoy again be without water.

Aristide stood with the captains on the edge of a precipice overlooking the Vale, peering down and pondering their options.

"At least we no longer have to worry about a mounted charge over flat ground," Eudoxia said, her blue arms crossed on her chest. "I was troubled the whole body of them would charge in and cut us in half—they would have wrought such havoc that we might not have recovered our balance."

"Now we're going to have to worry about people rolling rocks on us," Aristide said.

"Ay," said Nadeer. His single eye glittered. "Like those fellows over there."

"Where?" Scanning the jagged walls of the valley ahead.

Nadeer bent and picked up a rock the size of Eudoxia's head. He hefted it for a moment in one green-skinned hand, then reared back and pitched the rock up into the grey sky. They all watched as it fell onto a granite pinnacle two hundred paces distant. There was a thud, and a cry, and a clatter as of a weapon dropped over the edge.

"Good shot!" said Grax, impressed rather in spite of himself.

"There's one more." Nadeer chose another rock, hurled it. There was a clang, and then they saw a body pitch off the crag, landing some thirty paces below.

Aristide looked at the ogre. "Your depth perception," he said, "is better than I expected."

Nadeer dusted his hands. Aristide turned his attention once more to the valley below.

"We're going to have to keep them from getting above us," he said. "May I suggest small parties to secure each height before the main body arrives?"

They grumbled about that, and Grax pointed out that his Free Companions were mounted soldiers, not mountain goats. But in the end they worked out an arrangement, much as Aristide had suggested, and the convoy again began to advance.

Hours passed before every beast and cart at last began the precarious descent into the Vale, and then finally a rest halt was called with the convoy stretched along the headwaters of the Cashdan River, with every beast and every person within easy reach of water. It was impossible to laager, because there was no single place level enough to hold the entire body. On the other hand the possibilities of attack were severely limited, and the air was fresh and cool. Dry tongues, dry skins, rejoiced.

The convoy continued its slow crawl down the escarpment, crossing and re-crossing a river that grew louder and more swift as streams running in from the side-canyons contributed more water. Two horses and a lizard were swept away, but their riders were saved. The clouds fled and the green hills of Gundapur, full of vines and the shimmer of olive trees, were now visible below them. The silver river cast its loops back and forth across the fields, with the sultan's road a straight brown line across the land.

Two more rest stops had been called before the caravan ran into trouble. One of the advanced parties, sent to secure a ridge above the track, was repelled by a shower of arrows and rocks. Nothing daunted, Nadeer reinforced the party and tried again. Advancing under the cover of their own archers, and aided by Nadeer's remarkable throwing arm, the party pushed the bandits off the ridge, and onto another fold of higher ground beyond, where they remained, watching and jeering.

The engagement was over by the time Aristide arrived. He had been in the middle of the convoy when the fight broke out, helping one of the immigrants with the repair of his cart, and by the time he managed to ride to the head of the column, threading between carts and camels, the fight was over. He left his horse under the care of one of Grax's lieutenants and scrambled up the ridge, where he was in time to dissuade Nadeer from launching another attack on the enemy survivors.

"They can always retreat to the next ridge beyond," he pointed out. "And they know this country better than we do. You could run into an ambush."

"Wretched bags of ratpiss!" Nadeer lisped, referring no doubt to the bandits.

An arrow protruded from one shoulder, where it had penetrated his armor but failed to pierce his hide. He wrenched it out with a petulant gesture.

"I want them crushed!" he said.

"You'll get your chance soon, I think," Aristide said. "I expect there will be more of them soon. These were intended to attack us in flank when the main body hit us somewhere else."

Nadeer's single eye turned to him. "Are you certain of this?"

"No. I claim no more than the average amount of precognition. But it's logical—these weren't numerous enough to fight our whole force, and they must have known we were coming."

Nadeer glared at the bandits on the next ridge. "If we move on, it will leave them behind us."

"We want them *all* behind us."

Nadeer gnashed his tusks for a few moments, then told half of the guards to hold the ridge until the convoy had passed, and the rest to rejoin the advanced guard. The caravan continued its slow crawl down the valley. Five turns of the glass later—as the rear guard passed the ridge where the skirmish with the bandits had taken place—scouts reported that the road ahead was blocked by a substantial force.

Aristide joined the captains as they viewed the enemy. From where they stood at the head of the column, the track descended and broadened into the base of a side canyon, the track cut by a stream that joined the Cashdan, and then the track rose for two hundred paces and narrowed to a pass twenty paces wide, with the river thundering past on the right. This pass had been blocked with a wall of stones, and behind the stones the dark forms of bandits milled in large numbers. More bandits perched on the rocks above, armed with bows.

"The group on the ridge were to attack our rear when this group encountered our advance guard," Aristide said. "They meant to panic us." He scratched his chin. "I wonder if this group knows we drove the others off their position. If so, we might draw them out by feigning panic."

"A formidable roadblock," Eudoxia said. "They chose well."

"Our people will be better fighters," said Aristide. "Criminals are by nature a superstitious and cowardly lot, and few choose their profession because of a love of military discipline or order."

"The same might be said of caravan guards," Grax pointed out.

"If your people need heartening, you could point out that if they don't win this fight, they'll be sacrificed to evil gods."

Grax looked at him. "That's supposed to make them feel *better?*"

Aristide shrugged. "Perhaps it's best to show that the enemy are, after all, mortal. Why don't I dispose of a bandit or two and raise thus morale?"

Eudoxia looked at him. "How do you plan to do that?"

"Walk up and challenge them. Grax, you should charge them the second I dispatch an enemy. Nadeer, may I advise you to personally lead the attack on the rocky shoulder above the pass? It's the key to the position."

Nadeer looked a little put out. "It's true I'm not much use in a mounted charge," he admitted. "But why don't *I* challenge them to single combat?"

"For the simple reason," said Aristide, "that no one would dare to fight Nadeer the Peerless."

Nadeer considered this, then brightened. "Very true," he said. He reared to his full height. "I shall lead the attack up the rocks, as you suggest."

Aristide dismounted and performed a few stretching and limbering exercises while the captains gathered their forces and arranged their assault. "One last thing," he said when they were ready. "Remember to capture a few prisoners. We want them to lead us to the Venger's Temple and the loot taken from all those caravans."

"Indeed," said Nadeer, brightening even more.

Aristide took an arrow from one of the caravan guards, stuck a white headcloth on it, and began his walk toward the bandits. He paused after a few steps, then turned and said, "Look after my cat, will you?"

He walked down the slope to the mountain freshet, waded through ankle-deep water, and began the walk upslope to the improvised wall. He stopped a hundred paces from the wall and called out over the sound of the rushing water.

"While my colleagues are working out what to do next," he said, "I thought to relieve your boredom, and come out to challenge your bravest fighter to single combat."

Among the bandits there was a general muttering, followed by jeers and scornful laughter.

"No takers?" Aristide called.

Someone behind the barrier threw a rock. Whoever threw it was no Nadeer. Aristide stepped to the side and let the rock clatter on the stones. He waited for the laughter to subside.

"I'm disappointed that there's no one among you with courage," Aristide said. "It will make it all the easier for us to slaughter you."

In response came more laughter, some obscene suggestions, and a few more rocks.

"Just," Aristide said casually, "as we slaughtered those friends of yours, up there on the ridge a few leagues back. They're lying on the rocks for the vultures to peck at. Surely one of you had a friend among them, and now possesses a burning desire to avenge his life?"

"*I* do," said a voice. The figure that jumped on the barrier was vast, grey-skinned, and female. She was as large as Grax and had an additional pair of arms: the upper pair carried two throwing spears, the lower an axe and a target shield with a spike in the center. Her grin revealed teeth like harrows. She stood on the barrier, acknowledging the cheers of the bandit force.

"You present a formidable appearance, madam," said Aristide. "Perhaps you will make a worthy opponent."

"*Perhaps?*" the troll demanded. She jumped down from the barrier and advanced. Chain skirts rang under armor of boiled leather. Her crude iron helm was ornamented with horns and a human skull. Cheers and laughter echoed from the bandits. She advanced fifty paces and then halted. She paused and said, in a theatrical voice, "Prepare to meet thy doom."

"You first," Aristide suggested, and tossed the arrow with its white rag to the side.

The troll crouched and came on, preceded by a wave of body odor. The upper arms held the two spears which she declined to throw, instead reserving them as thrusting weapons. The axe clashed on the shield.

In a single motion, Aristide drew Tecmessa. The sword flashed beneath the dim sun.

There was a sudden crack, as of thunder, that echoed off the rocks. Observers had an impression that something had twisted into existence, then out of it, too fast for the eye quite to follow. A wave of air blew out toward the bandits, visible as swirls of dust in the air.

Of the troll, there was no sign.

Silence fell upon shocked ears.

"*Uh-oh,*" said a bandit clearly, in the sudden stillness.

Aristide whirled his sword up, then down, in an impatient *Come-on-let's-charge* motion that he hoped would remind the caravan guards of what they were supposed to be doing at this moment.

"Anyone else care to fight?" he asked.

Arrows whirred down from above. Tecmessa's point rotated slightly, there was another crack and a blast of wind, and the arrows vanished.

"Anyone else?" the swordsman called.

There was a deep-voiced bellow behind Aristide, and then shouts, the clatter of armor, and the rush of feet. Apparently Nadeer had finally remembered his assigned role.

"Oh well," Aristide said, "if you won't come to *me…*"

Aristide began trotting forward at a pace calculated to bring him to the barrier about the same time as Grax and his Free Companions. He didn't want to get trampled by his own side, but neither was it wise to face the whole body of the enemy at once—Tecmessa's powers had their limits. The sword was held in both hands, the point moving in a circle.

More arrows came. More arrows disappeared in claps of thunder and whirls of dust.

Behind him, Aristide heard the sound of animals splashing through the shallow freshet, and increased his pace.

The stone barrier was breast-high, topped by ranks of spears and figures in helmets. As the swordsman approached, the bandits in front shrank back, while those in the rear—who hadn't seen what had occurred—pressed forward. There was an incoherent shouting and the sound of spears rattling against one another, sure signs that the morale of the bandits was not ideal.

Before Aristide quite reached the barrier he heard a roar and a ferocious reptilian shriek, and Grax appeared on his lizard, his lance lowered. The lizard cleared the barrier in one bound—Grax dropped the lance that had skewered a tall man with a scalp lock— and then Grax was among the bandits, striking left and right with a flail made out of linked iron bars.

Aristide reached the barrier, parried a half-hearted spear thrust, and swung Tecmessa horizontally. Half a dozen bandits vanished with a bang. The remainder, a many-headed monster that seemed composed entirely of staring eyes and shuffling feet, drew back.

The rest of the Free Companions reached the barrier. Some reined in and thrust with their lances, some jumped the barrier like Grax, some tried to jump and failed. In the sudden wild stampede, Aristide flattened himself against the rocky side of the pass and tried to get out of the way.

The bandits were broken in any case. Their efforts to escape were impeded by the narrowness of the pass, the mass of their fellows behind them, and the large herd of riding beasts which they had picketed just behind their position. The outlaws were packed so tightly that the Free Companions could hardly miss, and the bandits' tangled mass hampered any efforts to strike back or defend themselves. Many bandits died, many were trampled, and many threw themselves into the river and were swept away.

"*Prisoners!*" Aristide shouted. "*Remember to take prisoners!*"

The general slaughter continued without cease. Aristide glanced at the rocks above. The bandits that had been holding this key feature had seen the rout below, and many as a consequence were abandoning the fight, hoping to clamber down the steep boulder-strewn slope and reach their mounts before the Free Companions did.

There was a clattering of hooves and a cry, and Aristide saw the next company charging to the fight. The chances of getting trampled seemed stronger than ever, and a place above the fray consequently more desirable, so Aristide vaulted the barrier and began to climb the slope.

Green-skinned Nadeer reached the summit before Aristide did—bellowing, half-a-dozen arrows standing in his chest, hurling rocks left and right. The bandits broke completely. Aristide saw one bandit running past and swung Tecmessa. The flat of the blade caught him full in the face and he went down, stunned. Out of the corner of his eye Aristide saw another darting figure, a broad-shouldered man in black with a recurved bow in one hand, and he thrust the sword between the archer's legs. The bandit fell face-first onto the stony ground, and then Aristide was on his back, the edge of Tecmessa against his neck.

"Take me to your leaders," he said.

03

"I count a hundred and eighteen bodies," Grax announced. He was in buoyant spirits: even his chain mail seemed to be jingling with satisfaction. "We lost six, and three of those were lost because they fell off their mounts and got trampled by our own side, or drowned in the river."

"'Tis a famous victory," said Aristide.

Leaning on his scabbard, he sat on one of the great granite rocks above the pass while he watched the convoy guards demolish what was left of the barricade and hurl the stones into the river. His two prisoners, thoroughly bound, crouched at his feet.

Bitsy sat on a nearby rock, licking her anus.

Grax carried a sack of heads thrown casually over his shoulder, in hopes the sultan would offer a bounty. Since there was no pool of life in which to deliver the bodies that choked the roadway, the bandits' headless torsos were given to the river.

Aristide had made a point of refilling his water bottle upstream from that point.

The troll's gaze turned to Tecmessa.

"Your sword is magic?"

Aristide considered his answer. "It performs miracles, to be sure," he said.

"I've seen other swords that were supposed to be magic. They were all used in the past by heroes—well-made swords, all of them. But so far I know they never—you know—*did* anything."

"This one never did anything until I touched it," said Aristide. "It seems to work only for me."

Which, in addition to being the truth, might dissuade anyone—Grax, for instance— from killing him over possession of the blade.

Grax looked at him. "How did you find out what it does?"

"That's rather tragic actually. I'd rather not talk about it."

"When your enemies… disappear," Grax said. "Do you know where they go?"

Bitsy paused in her grooming and looked at him with green eyes.

"I've no idea," the swordsman lied.

Grax hitched up his wide belt. His chain skirts rang. "The captains are going to meet to decide what to do next. They all want to hunt for the loot and the Venger's Temple, but some are still going to have to guard the convoy on its way to Gundapur."

"This should be entertaining," Aristide said. "I'll attend, if I may." He rose to his feet and prodded his prisoners with his scabbard. "Up, you two," he said. The prisoners rose and, without their bound hands to aid them, picked their way carefully down the steep slope. Aristide rested his sword on his shoulder and followed.

As the party moved off, Bitsy rose to her feet, yawned, stretched, and joined the party.

The argument that followed was not unpredictable. Nadeer wanted to lead his little army to the Venger's Temple. Others pointed out that Nadeer was captain of the convoy guards charged with escorting the caravans to Gundapur, not the leader of a group of freebooters on their own account. Nadeer protested at first, but was finally brought to admit that he had accepted the responsibility of escort.

With Nadeer thus out of the running, the other captains all proposed themselves as leaders of the expedition to the Temple, and were in the process of arguing this when the actual caravan masters, their employers, demanded that all the guards accompany them all the way to Gundapur—or, failing that, surrender a share in any loot.

The argument was brisk and prolonged. Aristide, perched nearby atop a boulder that had fallen from the cliffs above and come to rest on the edge of the river, ate hard bread and dried fruit, and enjoyed the rush and flow and scent of the Cashdan with the pleasure that only thirty-odd days in the desert would bring. He smiled to himself as he listened to the arguments. Bitsy, less entertained, found a warm place on the rock and curled up to sleep. It was only when the captains' wrangle had grown repetitious that Aristide interrupted.

"My friends," he said, "may I point out that this debate is bootless?"

They looked at him. He stood on his rock and smiled down at them.

"At the Venger's Temple lies the loot of over a dozen caravans!" he pointed out. "Plus a sizeable hoard of plunder gathered elsewhere. Even if every convoy guard among you marched to the Temple and captured the treasure, how would they get all the treasure away? Even if they took every beast of burden in our combined caravans, they could only move a fraction of the total."

The captains looked at each other, their eyes glittering not with surprise, but with calculation. *Perhaps*, they seemed to be thinking, *we could only take the absolute best...*

"Therefore," said Aristide, "Nadeer and at least half the guards should take the caravans to Gundapur as quickly as they can, because they will have a vital role—to search the city in order to round up every horse, every camel, every ox, and every dinosaur-of-burden, and to bring them back to the Vale of Cashdan to carry away the greatest treasure in the history of the sultanate!"

The captains raised a cheer at this. But Masoud the Infirm raised an objection.

"If we take the treasure to Gundapur," he wheezed, "the sultan will want a percentage."

"No doubt," Aristide said. "But if you take the treasure anywhere else, the local ruler will also require a tax. And it must be admitted that your ordinary guards and camel drivers will want to be paid as soon as possible, so that they may spend their earnings in the city's pleasure-domes. Gundapur is your best bet.

"And since that is the case," Aristide said, and made a gesture of money falling from one palm into another, "may I suggest that while some of you organize the caravan to bring the treasure to the city, the rest of you should be offering bribes to the sultan's advisors to make certain that the taxes you're required to pay are minimal.

"And furthermore," he added, "since the caravan guards won't be able to afford to rent all those animals, or bribe the sultan's advisors, it's clear that the merchants who command the caravans deserve a share of the treasure."

Which began another argument concerning how large that share would be. Aristide had no comment to make on this matter, and instead returned to his seated position. He looked down at his two prisoners, who slumped against the rock below him. One—the bowman he had tripped—was a man of middle years, with a scarred cheek that put his mouth in a permanent scowl and a beard striped with grey. The other was a tall man, very muscular, but who presented the appearance of youth, with bowl-cut hair and a face swollen by the blow from the flat of Aristide's sword.

"Where *is* the Venger's Temple, by the way?" the swordsman asked.

The older man gave him a contemptuous look from slitted eyes. "I will happily tell you," he said. "Certain as I am that the knowledge will send you all to your deaths."

"Well," Aristide said, "for heaven's sake don't keep me in suspense."

The older man gave a jerk of his head to indicate the way they had come. "The Temple's in a side canyon," he said. "Back up the valley."

Aristide looked at the younger man. "Do you agree?"

"Oh yes. Also, that you will certainly die if you go there."

"How far?"

"From here you can walk the distance in fifteen or twenty turns of the glass. But you'll die. So don't."

Aristide looked at him with curiosity. "Are the defenses so formidable?" he asked.

"Not the defenses. The priests." The young man looked at Tecmessa. "The Priests of the Vengeful One possess the same power as your blade."

Aristide's face turned into a smooth bronze mask, his hawklike nose a vane that cut the wind. His dark eyes glittered with cold intent.

"What do you mean?" he asked. He spoke with care, as if the simple sentence was a fragile crystalline structure that might shatter if he uttered the wrong syllable.

"The priests cause people to disappear in a clap of thunder," the captive said. "Just as you caused Ormanthia to disappear."

"It is a *sacrifice*," the older man corrected. His voice was a hiss. "The Vengeful One is a powerful god. He swallows his victims whole."

The young man gave a shudder. "True. He does."

The older man looked at Aristide. "He will swallow *you*."

"Perhaps," said Aristide. "But on me he may break a tooth." He turned to the younger man. "How many priests are there?"

"Three."

"And they have swords like mine?"

"No. They are armed with..." He hesitated, as if he knew how absurd this would sound. "Clay balls," he finished.

"Clay. Balls." The delicate words once again chimed with a crystalline sound.

"They dangle the balls from strings. The balls dart around as if they had minds of their own. And the balls... eat people."

Aristide's profile softened as he considered the bandit's words.

"I shall look forward to encountering these priests," he said softly.

The older bandit spat.

"I shall look forward to your death," he said.

"How do you know the priests send their victims to death?" Aristide asked. "It might be paradise, for all you know."

The bandit spat again.

"I'll cut your throat myself," he said.

"Now, now," said Aristide. "I'll have to tick the box next to your name that says *unrepentant*."

"*So we swear! So we swear!*" The cry went up from the assembled captains. Aristide looked up from his conference. Apparently the leaders of the expedition had reached agreement.

As the others moved off to their companies, Grax looked up at Aristide on his rock

"You're authorized a double share if you accompany us to the Temple," he said.

"I wouldn't miss it," Aristide said. "You're in command of this expeditionary force, I assume?"

"Of course!" The troll showed his yellow teeth.

"Congratulations on your expanded responsibilities. My captives—for different reasons admittedly—are willing to lead us to the Venger's Temple."

Grax studied them with his golden eyes. "They show wisdom."

The older bandit curled his lip. Perhaps he'd run low on saliva.

"May be," Aristide said. "But I regret to tell you that it may be that our fight against these people may be more difficult than we've expected."

"Yes?" Grax didn't seem troubled. "Where is the Temple," he asked, "and how far?"

"Back up the valley. Fifteen or twenty glasses."

"Damn. We'll have to wait for this lot to get by us, then." He lumbered off to give orders to the elements of his new army, and to pass the word to the caravans that they should begin to move. The huge caravan picked itself up and began to trudge its way down the path to Gundapur's plain.

The story of the brief battle must have spread through the caravan, because Aristide found that many pointed at him as they passed, or huddled together and whispered. He saw Souza ride past on a mule, leading two more mules shared by the three children he'd salvaged for the College, and he and the scholar exchanged salutes.

Finding his celebrity tedious, and unable to move out of public scrutiny on a narrow track filled with carts and camels, Aristide spoke with his prisoners and found the younger bandit talkative, as he'd anticipated. He learned that the Venger's Temple was in a broad cleft in the mountain, with its own water supply, and with powerful natural defenses.

"It's like a pool of life, really," the young man said. "There's a waterfall on both sides of a stone pillar, and a pool below."

"Does it have the properties of a pool of life?" Aristide asked.

"No. It's just rocks and water. Quite pretty, really."

The long serpent of the caravan continued its crawl past the swordsman's perch. Aristide looked up at the sight of a young blue-eyed woman on a palfrey, but she had drawn a veil over her face, and kept her eyes turned from his.

He bowed as she passed. She kept her face turned away.

She had demonstrated that she was afraid of sorcery, and of the College. Certainly anyone who could wield such a weapon as Tecmessa must be a powerful wizard, worthy of trepidation.

Aristide's expression confirmed he was not pleased to be such an object of fear.

The caravan finally passed, leaving behind colossal amounts of fresh dung, and Grax organized his force of sixty warriors. They had few spare mounts: their comrades were deliberately making it difficult for the party to abscond with much of the loot. Aristide gave Grax the older bandit as a guide, and kept the talkative one for himself. Both captives were tied onto saddles that had been placed on mules.

The mounted force could move much more quickly than the caravan. After a brief march up the valley they came to the ridge where the band of caravan guards had been left to face a group of enemy on the opposite ridge. Their lieutenant descended to greet Grax.

"I was coming to report," he said. "The bandits we were watching have gone."

"Gone where?" asked Grax.

"Back over that ridge they were on. We don't know any more than that."

"Survivors must have told them we'd wiped out their main force, and they decided it was pointless to stay."

"There's a goat track back there," said the younger bandit. "It leads to the Venger's Temple."

Aristide raised his eyebrows. "A back entrance?" he asked.

"More like a side entrance. But the defenses are less formidable than the main track up the canyon."

Aristide looked at Grax. "Perhaps we should take this path."

Grax looked at the outlaw. "Is it suitable for our mounts?"

"You may have to lead them up a few steep places, but you shouldn't have any real trouble."

And so it proved. Grax's force—now augmented by the rear guard, who opted for glory and loot rather than the more tedious prospect of rejoining the caravan—ascended the enemy ridge unopposed, and found a narrow valley behind, pleasantly shaded by aspen. Birds sang in the trees overhead; butterflies danced beneath the green canopy. A brook sang its way down the valley, and the party crossed and re-crossed the water as they advanced.

There was fresh dung on the trail, which proved that they were on the track of the outlaws. The valley was ideal for an ambush, and Grax kept his scouts out. They saw nothing but a small, wary deer—they took a shot, and missed.

The trail rose from the valley floor and up a stony ridge. The party dismounted and led their mounts along the steep, narrow trail. From here it was a constant climb, on foot or mounted, along one slope or another. The terrain varied widely: sometimes they were in little green valleys filled with trees and flowers; on other occasions they were on rocky slopes as dry as the desert plateau beyond the top of the pass.

At one point, as the party rested and refreshed themselves while the scouts examined the next ridge to make certain there was no ambush, Aristide offered his captive a drink from his water bottle. He considered the outlaw's physique, his length, his breadth of shoulder, his well-developed muscles.

"How old are you really?" he asked.

The young man laughed. "I was sixteen when I left the Womb of the World. I'm not sure how long ago that was—eighteen months, maybe."

"Had you always intended to be an outlaw?"

The bandit gave a rueful grin. "Songs and stories made the life seem more exciting than it is. I'd thought it would be more fun."

Aristide gave an amused smile. "I've heard that from someone else recently."

"I hadn't intended to become the slave of a group of killer priests, that's for certain. But when I saw what their men did to Black Arim—he was our gang's leader—I joined right up. And once I met the priests, I was too frightened to run away. Especially after what I saw them do to a couple fellows they called 'deserters.'"

"Do the priests have names?"

"Not that I've ever heard. They speak to us in the common tongue, but they have a language of their own when they don't want us to understand what they're saying."

"Which is most of the time, I suppose."

The outlaw nodded. He looked over his shoulder to make certain no one was listening, then leaned close to Aristide and spoke in a lowered voice.

"How about cutting these ropes and letting me run for it?" he asked. "I've cooperated, and I promise to give up the outlaw life once I'm away from here."

Aristide considered this proposal. "I think I'll wait to see whether your information is correct."

"No offense," the bandit said, "but in a few hours you'll all be dead. I'd like to be well away from here before that happens."

The swordsman smiled. "I guess you'll have to take your chances with us. Want some more water?"

The bandit accepted another drink. The scouts on the ridge ahead appeared, and signaled that it was safe. Aristide helped the bandit back onto his mule, made sure the ropes were secure, and mounted his own horse. The small army continued their long climb.

Four turns of the glass later, they entered a small, shady valley fragrant with the smell of pine. "The Temple's just ahead," the young outlaw warned. "Past the trees, and up a slope."

Aristide rode ahead to deliver this news to Grax, whose own captive had been mute in the hopes that the column would just blunder into the bandit nest.

"Ah," Grax said in surprise. "I see." Then he turned in his saddle and without preamble ran the older bandit through with his lance. As the man kicked and thrashed his way to his next incarnation, Grax began making his dispositions.

Aristide rode ahead to where the scouts were hovering in the fringes of the trees, looking up at a boulder-strewn slope marked with evergreen scrub.

"Bitsy," he said. "Take a look, will you?"

The cat jumped from his perch behind Aristide's saddle. The barb snorted and made an uneasy sideways movement. Bitsy ignored the animal and sprang ahead, out of the shadow of the pines and onto the slope, and stayed close to the ground as she took a zigzag path to the crest, darting from cover to cover.

The nearest scout—a green-haired woman—gave Aristide a look.

"Your cat understands you," she said.

Aristide affected nonchalance. "Most of the time, yes."

Grax rode forward on his giant lizard to give instructions to the scouts, and seemed surprised to find Aristide there.

"I've sent a scout ahead," Aristide said. "She should be reporting back any time."

And in fact Bitsy was soon observed returning from her mission. She didn't bother weaving from cover to cover, but instead came straight back.

"You sent your *cat?*" Grax laughed, and then Bitsy arrived and spoke.

"No guards," she said. "It seems they've all been called in to witness punishment."

"Punishment?" Aristide asked.

"Your cat talks!" Grax said, wide-eyed. His green-haired scout made a sign to ward evil.

"I counted twenty-two outlaws, variously armed," Bitsy went on. "Three priests in black, and eleven bound captives. I believe these latter are the group we've been following—it seems the priests are unhappy with the failure of their mission."

"Your cat *talks!*" said Grax.

"The waterfall and pool are ahead on the right," Bitsy continued. "On the left is a plantation of date palms, and that's where the outlaws are congregated. Behind the pool is a stock pen, where their mounts are confined."

"*Your cat talks!*" said Grax. Bitsy looked at him.

"Yes," she said. "I do. May I suggest that you attack soon while one-third of their strength remain bound and helpless?"

Grax looked from Aristide to Bitsy and back again, his huge grey head bobbing on its thick neck.

"I believe Bitsy's advice is sound," Aristide said. "But let me tell you first about the priests."

He related what the captives had told him about the priests' abilities. Grax listened with grim attention, his eyes darting toward Bitsy now and then, as if to discover if she had sprouted wings, or a second head, or demonstrated some other unexpected talent.

"What do you recommend?" Grax said finally.

"Don't close with the priests. Tell your archers to keep shooting at them, from as many directions as possible."

"You can't make them… go away?"

"Perhaps." Aristide rubbed the stubble on his chin. "I wish we could take them alive. I'd like to know what they can tell me."

"If their powers are what you say, it may be easier to kill them."

"Yes. And what happens to them is going to be more their choice than ours."

"You're wasting *time*," said Bitsy sharply.

"True," Grax looked over his saddle at his forces, now waiting his command. He turned his great lizard and rejoined his guards, to give his orders.

Aristide also rode back, but only to join his guide, the young outlaw. The bandit flinched as Aristide drew a knife from his belt. Aristide reached out and placed the knife in one of the young man's bound hands.

"What you do from this point is your choice," he said, "but I'd run like hell if I were you."

The outlaw's face flushed. "Thank you!" he said. "I'm a law-abiding man from this point forward!"

"Don't make any promises you can't keep," Aristide said, and turned to rejoin the caravan guards. The outlaw called after him.

"Try not to die!"

Aristide laughed and rode on.

Grax's little army, having received its orders, was deploying left and right and moving upslope, all the while trying to make as little noise as possible. Aristide looked ahead and saw Bitsy's black-and-white tail waving from the shelter of a scrub pine. He increased his pace and rode to join her, passing the armed force as it was still deploying.

He dismounted before he reached the top of the slope, and made his way cautiously to the shelter of the little pine. He found himself on the rim of a shallow bowl three hundred paces in width. There was a great pile of rock on the right, cleft by a mountain brook that fell in two streams past a great basalt pillar into a broad pool, just as Aristide's guide had described. The stream rose again from the pool and wound its way across the bowl, cutting a trench through the palm plantation. The plantation itself had been raised above the floor of the bowl, and was surrounded by a chest-high stone wall, the interior of which had been filled with soil hauled to this place at considerable labor, to provide a fertile anchor for the trees.

Whoever had done this was long gone. The plantation had an untended look.

Beyond the plantation was a corral with horses and other animals. Most of the open area was cluttered with the tents and shelters of the bandit army. Only the fact that the plantation was elevated above the surrounding area gave Aristide a view of what was happening beneath the palms.

There was a gathering in the plantation, a half-circle of bandits with the three black-clad priests prominent in the center. At the priests' feet stretched another group of bandits, each bound hand and foot. Taller than the tallest human, and unnaturally slender, the priests stalked among them, chanting in a guttural tongue. It was impossible to hear any words over distance, and over the sound of the waterfall.

Grax rode up behind Aristide, peering over the twisted pine, his lance poised to give the signal to attack. Aristide motioned him to wait.

"I want to find out what happens next," he whispered.

Grax turned and signaled the army to stillness and silence, and then he dismounted and joined Aristide in concealment. The troll was wider than the bush he was hiding behind: at some other time it might have been amusing.

The priests continued to stalk among the bound bandits. The other bandits watched, and even though they were over a hundred paces away, Aristide could tell they weren't happy.

Then Aristide noticed the clay balls. They were dangling by cords from the priests' hands, and they darted through the air as if they were creatures with minds of their own, like cicadas leashed by children to string.

Aristide and Grax started at a sudden blast of sound. A stir of dust rose from the grove, and whirled away as the crash echoed repeatedly among the rocks. Birds flew up from their perches, calling in alarm.

Where there had been a bound bandit, there was now nothing but air.

Again Aristide's face became a smooth, intent mask, a motionless work in bronze from which glittered his dark, fierce eyes.

"So it's true!" Grax said. He looked over his shoulder at his troops, who seemed to have grown nervous. He favored them with a silent, morale-boosting laugh.

The murmur of the priests continued without cease. Another boom shattered the air; another bandit vanished.

"We should attack," said Grax.

"The longer this goes on," Aristide said, "the more they reduce their own strength. Let's watch."

"We can't wait too long. My men will lose heart."

"Go tell them the bandits are killing their own people and doing our job for us."

"Oh." Grax considered this. "*Oh.* Very good."

Bent low, he rumbled down the slope to his troops, and told them to spread the word.

"This isn't looking good," Bitsy said to Aristide, once they were alone.

"No."

"This overthrows everything."

Aristide didn't bother to answer. The priests continued their milling, their chanting. The startled birds began to settle back into the trees. Aristide watched as closely as he could.

Another detonation sounded from the grove. The birds rose again into the sky. Another outlaw vanished. And, somewhere behind Aristide, a warhorse neighed.

The horse was a stallion and waiting with other stallions made it fretful and belligerent, and it was beginning to scent the strange horses in the corral, and the repeated detonations had not soothed its nerves. So when the third bang echoed from the surrounding ranks the stallion answered, issuing a furious, shrieking challenge into the sky.

Aristide glanced over his shoulder at the sound. Grax, standing by another body of caravan guards, whirled to the horseman and signaled angrily for the horseman to quiet his beast.

Horses in the bandits' corral answered. The first stallion screamed back at them, and so did several other horses in the party.

Grax turned to Aristide, arms thrown wide in frustration. Aristide turned back to the plantation.

The three priests had turned as one to stare in the direction of the noise. Their chanting ceased. And after a half-second pause they were in motion again, running, gesturing, issuing orders.

Aristide turned to Grax and his command.

"*Now!*" he called. "*Charge them!*"

Grax took three steps and hurled himself onto his riding-lizard. He pulled his lance from the ground and shook it.

"*Grax the Troll!*" he shouted.

"*Grax the Troll!*" his riders echoed, and spurred forward.

"Not exactly '*Leeroy Jenkins!*'" remarked Bitsy, "but I suppose it will do."

The riders roared over the lip of the bowl in a great cloud of dust. Grax led the lancers across the open ground to the right while the archers spread out widely, their arrows already humming through the air.

As the riders passed him, Aristide stood to get a better view.

The archers were not particularly accurate in firing from the backs of jouncing beasts, but their arrows at least served to increase the confusion of the bandit force. The swift advance of Grax and his lancers was hampered by the tent lines and shelters of the bandit camp, but they managed to maintain their momentum, and as they advanced trampled much of the bandits' armor and reserve weapons underfoot.

The main body of bandits had faded back from the edge of the palm plantation, leaving behind eight of their number still bound hand and foot. These were screaming and rolling and crying for help, much to the amusement of the archers, who were pleased to use them for target practice as they trotted forward. Aristide could see nothing of the priests.

There was a series of concussions, however, that revealed the priests were most likely causing arrows to disappear.

Aristide unsheathed Tecmessa and trotted forward on foot. Bitsy ran by his side.

Ahead of him, the archers fired a low scything volley into the plantation, then jumped their beasts over the wall and rode on. Aristide followed. There followed a series of cracks, and Aristide was nearly trampled as the archers came galloping back with a group of sword-swinging bandits in pursuit. A pair of priests were leading the charge and the archers knew not to let them get close.

It was clearly unwise to fight two priests at once. Aristide retreated along with the archers. Bitsy went up one of the palms.

The bandits pursued to the edge of the plantation. In the shade of the palms their eyes glowed like distant candles. The archers rode back to a safe distance and then resumed their shooting. Clay balls whirled on the ends of their cords, and booms tore the air as arrows vanished in midflight. But while the priests could protect themselves, they couldn't protect all their followers, and outlaws cried in pain and rage as they fell with arrow wounds.

Then there were shouts of *Grax the Troll!* from the depths of the palm trees, and the sound of riders. One of the priests turned and dashed back into the plantation, along with a group of bandits. The other priest remained, with a handful of followers clumped behind him, so that he could protect them from arrow fire.

Aristide came forward again, his sword leveled. A few archers trotted forward as well, but rode wide, keeping a respectful distance between themselves and Tecmessa.

An archer sheltering behind the priest knelt, drew, let fly. Tecmessa took the arrow with a crack, a blast of wind, and a puff of dust.

The bandits, as one, took a step back, consternation plain on their features. The priest did not move.

Aristide paused in his advance and addressed the priest.

"I am Aristide, the traveler. Will you favor me with your name?"

The priest made no answer, but glared at him with orange eyes. His unnatural height was exaggerated as he stood on the wall that bordered the plantation. He wore a black turban with the tail wrapped around his lower face, a black robe, black pantaloons, boots. His hands and the skin around his eyes were blue. He wore an indigo-colored sash around his narrow waist with a pair of silver-hilted daggers stuck in it. The clay ball, no larger than a knuckle, quested on the end of its cord like the antenna of an insect.

"If not your name," Aristide said, "then perhaps your purpose. Your order. Feel free to discourse on the name and nature of your god—who knows, I may convert."

The priest gave no answer.

"Well." Aristide whirled his sword in a bit of bravado. "As you choose to remain silent, let us then get on to the contest of skill."

There was a barrage of bangs from the depths of the plantation, and cries of "*Grax! Grax!*" Aristide advanced, his eyes intent on the clay ball.

The ball swooped, darted, swung toward him. Tecmessa's point angled toward it.

Something twisted in the air between them. Then untwisted. A preternatural silence seemed to descend on the field for an instant.

Aristide continued his advance. "We are well-matched, I see," he said, "except of course in the matter of practical weaponry."

Tecmessa slashed through the air and cut the priest's leg in half just above the knee. As the priest fell, a backhand cut took his right hand.

The hand, the ball, and the cord fell to the ground, all lifeless.

The priest gave a howl of anger, snatched a dagger from his waist, and lunged as he rose on the elbow of his crippled arm. Aristide parried, and then his blade thrust forward, the single edge slicing the priest's throat.

There was a red spurting, a rattle, a kicking of boots. The air tasted briefly of copper. The silver knife fell to the stones.

Tecmessa slashed out again, and three bandits vanished in a blast of air. The rest scrambled back in disorder.

Aristide leaped atop the wall and waved the archers forward, then moved into the plantation on the heels of the bandits.

Amid the palms ahead, a knot of bandits brandished weapons in the murk and dust. Arrows hissed between the trees. Lancers galloped in, then away. Grax had succeeded in cutting off the outlaws from their mounts, which made their escape problematical, but a barrage of cracks and booms made it clear that the priests were still guarding their flock.

"*Grax the Troll!*" There was a storm of arrows, followed by a rush on the flank. Cries among the bandits showed that at least some of the arrows struck home. An unnaturally tall figure rushed to meet the threat, and the riders reined in and turned. All save the leader, who was too large to easily check his speed.

There was a bang, a swift eddy in the risen dust. Grax vanished.

"Damn!" said Aristide.

The Free Companions fell back in confusion. The outlaws gathered courage and prepared an attack. Aristide took several running steps forward, and took another pair of bandits with a blast from Tecmessa.

The priest turned, the clay ball moving ahead of him like a third, questing eye. Aristide dodged behind a tree just as a blast peeled bark and sent leaves flying. He lunged out of cover to the right, Tecmessa in a high parry, and saw the priest's boots disappearing around the tree in the other direction. The sword made a great slashing cut to the left just as the clay ball darted around the palm trunk, the cord whipping around the tree like the chain of a morning star.

The cord was severed. The clay ball flew spinning through the air.

The priest shrieked, a hair-raising sound like the battle cry of a cougar. Aristide took a step back as the tall, black-clad figure lunged around the palm trunk, a thrusting spear held high in one hand. The orange eyes blazed. The tail of the turban had been torn away from the lower face and revealed a mouth brimming with dozens of needle-like, moray-sharp teeth.

The priest was inside Tecmessa's effective range and Aristide parried desperately as he fell back, kicked to the priest's knee, and fell back again. The priest hissed, thrust. Aristide dodged inside the thrusting spear and cut upward beneath the priest's arm, slicing through the triceps. The spear fell from nerveless fingers; the tall black-robed figure staggered with shock. Aristide drove upward again, this time with the point, through the ribs and to the lungs and heart.

Blood fountained past the priest's needle teeth, and the tall, slender body began to fall. Aristide cleared Tecmessa from the corpse and rolled just in time to avoid a blast from the third priest.

Aristide rolled to his feet, the sword on guard. The third priest hobbled toward him. He had got an arrow through his left knee early in the fight, and had spent most of the combat kneeling, protecting his followers from inbound arrows. Now he had no choice but to take the fight to the enemy.

The clay ball quested out from his right hand. The left carried a long, curved sword.

Aristide took a step back, keeping his distance.

"May I suggest that you surrender?" he said. "By now your position is quite hopeless."

The priest snarled and continued his lurching march. An arrow whistled past his head.

"Archers should fire all together," Aristide called in a loud voice. "And from as many directions as possible."

Archers fanned out on either side. The few remaining outlaws—they were down to eight or nine— crept along in the wake of their priest. Many were badly wounded. Desperation clung to their faces.

"You can't defend against the arrows," Aristide told the priest. "The second that ball of yours moves to cover an arrow coming from one flank, either I'll take you or you'll be hit by arrows from another quarter. So I suggest you drop your… weapon, and we can discuss your fate like reasonable men."

The priest hesitated. He seemed to consider the matter.

Apparently he decided that Aristide's analysis was correct, because in a single purposeful motion he raised his sword and slashed his own throat.

The bandits gave a collective moan as their leader fell.

A few fought to the last, but most tried to surrender.

The Free Companions of Grax were not in either case inclined to mercy.

Aristide did not participate in the brief, bloody massacre, but instead retreated to the body of the second priest he'd killed and squatted before the clay ball that lay by its tangled, knotted cord. There was a dab of blood on the end of the cord, which caused the swordsman to examine the hand of the dead priest. The cord was not tied onto the priest's finger, but grew out of it—the cord had been alive.

Aristide wiped Tecmessa on a clean part of the priest's robes, then sheathed the sword. He took his dagger out of his belt and wound a bit of the cord around the tip, then raised it to examine the ball more closely. It was a dusky red in color, and plain-featured, without runes or script or magic signs.

Bitsy dropped from one of the palms and came up to rub her cheek against the swordsman's free hand before she gazed up at the dangling ball.

"It seems harmless," she said.

"I imagine it is. Now." He rose, took a cloth from his pocket, and wrapped the ball carefully before returning it to his pocket. He looked up.

The battle was over. Overexcited convoy guards rode furiously over the grove, kicking up dust and looking for someone to slaughter. Aristide went looking for whoever was in charge.

Grax's deputy, Vidal the Archer, was trying to properly organize the looting.

"Where's the plunder?" he demanded, arms akimbo as he glared at the field. He was a dark-skinned man with short, bandy, horseman's legs and a long, broad trunk, perfect for drawing his bow. He gave a bandit corpse a kick. "All we can find is their tents and their spare trousers."

"I'd look behind the waterfall," Aristide said. "If memory serves, it's a traditional place for fabulous treasure."

Vidal turned his horse and galloped to the waterfall. Aristide followed on foot. By the time he arrived, Vidal had checked behind the fall of water and found the bandits' cache.

"Grax promised me a double share," Aristide said.

Vidal gave him a narrow, impatient look. "You'll get it," he said.

"I don't want it," Aristide said. "What I want is the three fastest animals you have here, and a bag of silver coin for remounts and supplies."

Vidal looked at him with more interest. "You have an urgent errand?"

"Yes. I need to take the news of these priests to the College. The scholars there might be able to understand what they are, and what they represent."

Vidal nodded. "Very well," he said. "You may have what you ask."

"I would like a few other things as well," Aristide said. "I would like the heads of the priests, their right hands, and the balls they used to make your troopers vanish."

Vidal gave him a curious look. "Do you think you can get our people back?"

Aristide considered this. "It might be possible. I doubt it, though."

Vidal made a pious sign. "May their next incarnations give them wisdom."

"Indeed."

Some of Vidal's guard turned up with improvised torches, and they and their commander ventured behind the waterfall. As Aristide walked away he heard exclamations of delight and avarice at the riches found there.

He collected the hands, the heads, the clay balls, then retrieved his barb and fed her some of the sultan's grain. He took off the saddle and laid out his sleeping rug in the palm plantation, as far from the sight and smell of bodies as possible. There he drank water, ate some dried fruit, and reclined with the tail of his turban drawn across his eyes. He reckoned it had been eighty turns of the glass since he had last slept.

When he awoke the camp was still, most of the guards asleep after celebrating their victory and their newfound fortune. He found Vidal, who had not yet slept, and greeted him. Vidal gave him his bag of silver and led him to the corral, where he chose his three mounts. Vidal offered him food for himself and grain for the animals—any grass or bushes had already been grazed out by the bandits' beasts—and then Aristide mounted the first of the horses he planned to ride that day.

"If you hear of any more of these priests operating in the world," he said, "find out as many details as you can, and send word to the College."

"I will," Vidal said simply.

Bitsy sprang to her nest behind the swordsman's saddle. Aristide rode away, leading his horses down the side canyon that led to the Cashdan and the route back across the desert to the Womb of the World.

It had taken him eight months to walk the route that had taken him to the Vale and the Venger's Temple.

He would return in three, if he had to kill a hundred horses to do it.

04

The wall was transparent and looked out at the great metropolis beyond. No one had ever imposed any kind of architectural uniformity on the city, and the result was a skyline of fabulous extravagance. There were obelisks, pagodas, and minarets. Columns supported arches, arches supported domes, domes supported cupolas. Towers brandished horns, bartizans, mooring masts, and carved stone pinnacles with crockets. Triumphal arches crowned boulevards, and so did torii. There were stoas, cloisters, and pergolas. An enormous wheel carried entire apartments high into the sky before lowering them gently to earth, and stopped in its rotation only when someone wanted to get on or off. A brace of towers circled each other as they rose, a pair of helixes frozen in a dance.

Buildings were made of stone, of metal, of marble, of glass, of diamond, of carbon fiber. Domes were plated with gold, with bronze, with light-absorbent fuligin, and in one case with the teeth of human children.

Connecting the towers were arching metal bridges, transparent tubes, or cars hung from cables. Swirling between the structures were bright spots of color, people in lightweight gliders rising on the updrafts that surrounded the tallest buildings. Below, people moved in carriages, in gondolas, in cars that moved along tracks.

A huge billboard scrolled an advert for something called *Larry's Life*.

Aristide, hands in his pockets, viewed the prodigality of Myriad City and said,

> "*The city alive with noise and light,*
> *The flame of youth ablaze.*
> *And I, in my stillness, content to be old.*"

"That's the Pablo I remember." Daljit, seated at her desk, looked up from her work. "Why are you Aristide these days?" she asked. "Why aren't you Pablo any longer?"

"There are too many Pablos. I am bored with Pablos."

She smiled. "I thought you were content to be old."

"I can't help being old," he said, gruffly. "Pablo I can do something about."

"Wielding a sword in some barbarian world isn't exactly the stuff of old age."

He turned from the window, took his hands from his pockets. He wore a pale shirt, pale trousers, and a dark spider-silk jacket in a style twenty years out of date.

"The swordsmanship was incidental," he said. "I was actually doing scholarship."

"Of what?"

"The implied spaces." He walked to look over her shoulder, at the spectra glowing on her display. "Anything?" he asked.

"Nothing yet."

The room was long, with two conventional doors that swung open on hinges. The walls and ceiling were tuned to a neutral color so as not to provide distraction. Long tables with polished surfaces held a broad assortment of machines and small robots, most of them inactive. There was a smell of heat, of ozone.

Aristide contemplated his companion. Daljit seemed compact as opposed to small, and gave the impression of having a highly organized, responsive body that didn't require size or reach for its effects. She had expressive brown eyes beneath level brows, and a mole on one cheek that provided a pleasing asymmetry. She wore a silver bracelet with a bangle and numerous rings, which indicated that she was aware of the grace of her long hands and fingers. She wore a white high-collared tunic, knee-breeches, and silk stockings with clocks.

She and Aristide were old friends, and spoke with the ease of a long acquaintance. Though they'd kept in touch he hadn't seen her in person in sixty years, at which time she had been tall and bosomy and crowned by hair of a brilliant henna-red shade.

She rested her chin on her fist as she looked at him. "What are the implied spaces, exactly?"

He considered for a moment. "If we turn to the window," he said, and illustrated the point by turning, "we observe the Dome of Parnassus."

She turned. "We do. It wants cleaning."

"The dome, you will observe, is supported by four arches, one at each cardinal point."

"Yes."

"Presumably the architect knew that the dome had to be supported by *something*, and arches were as meet for the purpose as anything else. But his decision had consequences. If you stand beneath the dome, you'll see that there are blank triangular spaces beneath the dome and between the arches. These are called 'squinches,' believe it or not."

Daljit smiled at him. "I'm delighted to know there are things called squinches, whether you invented the term or not."

He bowed to her, then looked out at the dome again. "The point is, the architect didn't say to himself, 'I think I'll put up four squinches.' What he said is, 'I want a dome, and the dome needs to be supported, so I'll support it with arches.' The squinches were an accident implied by the architect's other decisions. They were *implied*."

"Ah." She straightened and took her chin off her fist. "You study squinches."

"And other accidents of architecture, yes." He turned to her, put a hand down on its reflection in the polished onyx surface of her desk.

"Say you're a die-hard romantic who wants to design a pre-technological universe full of color and adventure. Say you want high, craggy mountains, because they're beautiful and wild and inspiring and also because you can hide lots of orcs in them. Say you also want a mountain loch to reflect your beautiful high-Gothic castle, and a fertile plain to provide lots of foodstuffs that you can tax out of your peasants—many of whom are brain-clones of yourself, by the way, with a lot of the higher education removed, and inhabiting various specially grown bodies of varying styles and genders."

"You know," said Daljit, "I would have liked to have been a fly on the wall when the medieval scholars and the Compulsive Anachronists, or whatever they were called, discovered that they couldn't afford their own universe without financial aid from the fantasy gamers, and that their tidy little re-creation was now going to be full of trolls and dinosaurs."

Aristide grinned. "Perhaps you're underestimating the percentage of medievalists who play fantasy games."

"Perhaps."

"But in any case, the fertile valley has to be adjacent to the ocean, because the river's got to go *somewhere*, and in the meantime you've got this mountain range with its romantic tarn over *here*… so what goes in between?"

She looked at him. "You're going to tell me it's a squinch."

"Bingo. By the time you've got all your computations done and dumped all the energy into inflating a wormhole from the quantum foam…" Aristide made little rubbing gestures with his fingers, as if he were sprinkling alchemical powders into an alembic. "… and you've stabilized the worm-hole gate with negative-mass matter, then inflated a soupçon of electrons and protons into a pocket universe complete with a flaming gas ball in the center… Once you've got your misty mountain range and your moisty river valley, what goes between the mountain range and river valley is implied by the architecture, and is in fact a high desert plain, like the Gobi, only far less attractive…"

A whirring began as one of the machines in the room turned on its fans. Daljit looked briefly at her displays, then turned to Aristide again.

"So you study this desert?"

"I study what *adapts* to the desert. The desert wasn't intended, so whatever lives there wasn't intended to live there, either. It's all strayed in from another ecosystem and adapted to the desert, and it's adapting with surprising speed."

"And what lives there?"

He gave a private little smile. "Ants and spiders, mostly."

The mole on her cheek twitched. "Your chosen field seems less than enthralling."

"The sword-swinging bandits provided all the excitement necessary."

She gave him an appraising look. "So you really fought bandits with your sword? And murderous priests devoted to human sacrifice?"

Aristide reached to touch Tecmessa, which was at present carried in a long, flat case, and which leaned against Daljit's desk.

"I cheated," he said. "And in any case, the certainty of reincarnation de-values heroism as well as tragedy."

"But still. It's not the same as pressing a button and killing them at a distance, is it?"

"No." His expression was grim. "Though I didn't actually kill any human beings—just the priests, who I imagine were constructs."

The last cry hovers in air, he thought,
The creature dies, never having properly lived.
In the palm of my hand, through a yard of steel
I feel the last throbs of the wasted heart.

It had been disturbingly personal, and wakened memories that he had rather remained a-slumber.

But still, it hadn't been anything nearly as bad as the Control-Alt-Delete War. You were always terrified then, terrified every time you saw someone sick, every time you heard a sneeze or a cough. Every time you sensed sickness in your own blood you had to wonder if it was the Seraphim or a common cold that had ahold of you.

You would wait for your friends or loved ones to go into a coma, and then you knew they would have to die. Because you knew that if they woke up, they would not be themselves anymore, they would be pod people.

Sometimes, when the authorities were overwhelmed or sick themselves or out of reach, you had to kill the sick yourself. No matter how much you loved them.

Strangulation was best, because that way there was no blood that might contaminate you, or at any rate not much. But however you did it, you would have to go into quarantine, to wait in a little room with a bed and water and canned food, and if you shivered while you waited, or felt a prickle of sweat on your forehead, you would sit in silent cringing agony and wonder if it was the first touch of the Seraphim.

Aristide turned away from Daljit, faced the nearest wall. He didn't want her to see the memory in his face.

There was no point in frightening her. If something like the Seraphim was happening now, she would be frightened soon enough.

"I understand that the priests were constructs," Daljit said, "but why were they made so conspicuous? You'd think they'd want to hide among the population."

"Except for the adventurers and anthropologists who come through the Womb," Aristide said, "the people of Midgarth are stranded in the pre-technological world their ancestors built. They're superstitious, and the priests were designed to be terrifying examples of the power of their god." He felt moisture on his palms and wiped them on his jacket, where the intelligent spider silk began the business of decomposing sweat.

"One of the bandits we captured was a sincere convert, I think. He led us to the priests' lair firm in the belief that we'd all be sacrificed alive."

The nearest machine gave a chiming sound. Daljit turned to her displays.

Her even brows knit as she looked at the display. Aristide turned and looked over her shoulder. She gave the display instructions and viewed the data from another angle. Then she sighed and threw herself back in her chair.

"I've examined your object with chemical sniffers," she said, "with microimagery, with ultrasound, with microwaves, with spectrometry and x-rays and with lasers, and all I can tell you is that the damned thing is ordinary terra-cotta. I can give you the precise amount of trace minerals in its makeup, but it doesn't look unusual."

"Untraceable?"

"I can do some further correlation, see if there's a particular combination of minerals here that only occurs in one tiny part of the multiverse. But we don't *know* every tiny part of the multiverse, so the odds may not be on our side."

Aristide frowned, and touched with a foreknuckle the corner of his mouth where until recently he had worn his mustache. He walked to one of the machines, opened a door, and withdrew one of the clay balls he had brought through the Womb of the World. A shriveled bit of sinew was still attached to it, the remains of the cord that had tied it to the priest.

"The organic component?" he asked.

"Has unfortunately deteriorated. You can't expect much after three months' ride across a pre-technological landscape. There's no clear indication from what remains how the object was controlled."

She raised her arms over her head and stretched, then rose from her chair. "I know a good organic chemist," she added, "who might spot something I've missed."

Aristide rolled the terra-cotta ball in the palm of his hand. "Won't be necessary. The wormhole collapsed as soon as the connection with the operator was removed—some kind of fail-safe mechanism." He dropped the clay ball into a clear plastic specimen bag and put it in the pocket of his jacket.

"I think the skulls and hands will give us more information," Daljit said. "Bone tells many more tales than withered flesh." She sighed, walked to him, touched his arm. "And I may yet find something in the other two objects."

He drew two more bags from his pockets and looked at them.

"I agree we should examine them," he said. "But you can automate the whole process, yes?—there's no reason why we should wait here while your machines go through their motions. May I give you dinner?"

"You may." Daljit was pleased by the offer.

She put each of the samples into different machines, then gave them instructions, and instructed as well a small desktop robot that would shift the samples from one machine to the next. Aristide walked to Daljit's desk and picked up Tecmessa, swinging its case over his shoulder on its strap. He picked up Daljit's soft spider-silk jacket from the rack behind her desk and offered it to her as she approached. She turned, backed herself into the jacket, and smoothed the lapels as he placed it over her shoulders.

"Has there been some advance in wormhole science since I was last paying attention?" he asked as she led him to the door.

"Not that I know of."

"So it still requires a vast amount of energy and a prodigious amount of calculation to produce a successful Einstein-Rosen bridge."

The door sprang open at her approach. She paused in the doorway and turned to him. "Yes. As I understand it."

Aristide was grim. "That reduces the count suspects to a manageable number. The problem is that they are all enormously powerful." Again he stroked the ghost of his mustache with a knuckle. "Use of that much energy and that much computer time should be traceable, in theory. But to detect it might require someone of Bitsy's intelligence."

She was amused. "Do you still have that horrible cat?"

"Yes," said Bitsy. "He does."

Daljit gave a start and raised a hand to her throat. Bitsy jumped onto Daljit's desk and settled on her haunches before the display.

"I didn't know you were here," Daljit said weakly.

"I lurk," said the cat.

There was a moment of silence in which Aristide managed not to laugh out loud.

Daljit cleared her throat. "I'm sorry for what I said," she said.

Bitsy's green eyes were fixed on the display. "As the avatar," she said, "of a vast array of quantum parallel processors orbiting the sun as part of an as-yet-incomplete matrioshka array, I'm rather above taking offense at that sort of thing."

There was another pause.

"Thank you," said Daljit finally.

"But if Aristide wants to have sex with you," the cat added, "I'm not helping."

Daljit looked in silent surprise at the cat, and then at Aristide.

"Look among your colleagues," Aristide said to Bitsy, "for traces of the energy necessary to create those wormhole gates, and for the calculation, too."

The cat was nonchalant. "Already on it, Pops."

"And be careful. The guilty party will be on the lookout for anyone trying to find them."

"I'll be slick as butter," Bitsy promised.

Daljit and Aristide stepped through the doorway, and the door closed silently behind them. The corridor outside the laboratory was carpeted in soft green mosses that absorbed the sound of their footsteps.

"That animal of yours is scary," Daljit said.

"I find she settles a lot of arguments before they get started."

"'Speak softly and carry an omniscient feline?'"

"Quite," he said, and took her arm.

They sat before a plate of oysters. After months of dried fruit and chunks of mutton skewered over a dung fire, Aristide had developed a vast appetite for fresh seafood.

"So how," Daljit asked, "does the cat help you to have sex?"

Daljit had deliberately waited until an oyster was already sliding down his tongue, and Aristide managed only barely to keep from snorting shellfish out his nose.

"Bitsy confines herself to introductions," he said, after clearing his throat. "An animal twining itself around another's legs provides an opening for conversation."

"And how does the avatar of an awesomely intelligent AI feel about being used for the tawdry purposes of seduction?"

Aristide was offended. "Madame," he said, "I am never tawdry. As you should know."

She considered him. "True," she said. "You're not."

They sat on a cream-colored boat that grazed on the waters near the metropolis and gave diners a view of the city's miraculous profile. Above their heads, visible through a transparent canopy, the sun was on the verge of its daily miracle.

They looked up as the sun—a more advanced model than that of Midgarth—began to flicker and fade. Shadows flew rapidly across its disk. And then the photosphere settled into a stable state, and photons were no longer able to escape. The sun went black—but surrounding the black disk was the corona, still glowing with heat, its swirls and columns a cosmic echo of the city's skyline.

The corona would fade over the next seven-point-nine-one hours, after which the sun's photosphere would grow chaotic again, and the sun blaze out to light a new day.

"How long has it been," Daljit asked, "since you were last in Myriad City?"

Aristide's gaze continued upward.

"I pass through from time to time," he said. "When I'm not traveling, I keep a little cabin on Tremaine Island."

"Where's that?"

"Past Mehmet's Lagoon. I hire a boatman to take me in and out."

She raised her eyebrows. "And you're alone out there? In that remote area?"

He shrugged, then looked down to dabble horseradish on a blue point. "It's enough for Aristide. And besides, it's an implied space. No one *intended* to put an island there. If I ever get bored, I can go out and contemplate the pollywogs and butterflies."

"When you and I lived together," she said, "you cultivated a certain seigneurial grandeur. Fresh flowers every morning, genuine paintings on the walls rather than videos of paintings. Green lawns, and deference from the neighbors."

Aristide contemplated the thick viridian essence of his cocktail as it brewed in its crystal glass.

"I grew tired," he said. "Not of my surroundings, but of all that was necessary to maintain them. Now if I want something, I'll rent, and let someone else do the work." He looked up. "But you'd be surprised how well I've adapted to simplicity. My cabin has a stone floor that I laid myself, out of rock that I carried to the site in a barrow. And when I took my stroll through Midgarth, I carried a rug rolled up in my pack, and that was my bed."

She smiled. "I'll wager it was a nice rug."

"It was. Two hundred thousand double knots per square meter, or something like that. But still it was a rug, not a down mattress." He began to stroke the place where his mustache had been, caught himself, and lowered his hand.

"Midgarth was something of a relief. A place that's completely unwired, where I can't be monitored by anyone with access to the net."

"Are there still people who do that?"

"A surprising number. Bitsy keeps me informed of the total—and also turns off cameras here and there, so I can have a little privacy." He frowned. "She turned off all the public cameras between your lab and the pier, so that we won't be observed and there won't be speculation about what this dinner might mean for our future. But it's possible one of our fellow diners might be recording us, and in that case Bitsy can do nothing."

She gave him a sympathetic look. "You used to hate those people. You were quite the campaigner for privacy rights."

He shrugged. "I still hate them. It's just that I've decided the fight is unwinnable, and now I just go to places—like Tremaine Island—where I can't be monitored."

"They're still watching you." Daljit seemed bemused. "After all this time."

Aristide smiled thinly. "Behind that comment, I can't help but sense the question: *They still think you matter?*"

Daljit looked at her graceful hands. "That wasn't what I meant. Really."

He decided that the better part of self-knowledge required that he not pursue this particular topic any further.

"One of the aspects of the surveillance that I most detest," he said, "is that the consciousness that someone is watching turns me into a *performer*. I'm not an entertainer, and I don't want to be one. I'm not here to please the fans, I'm here to do serious work."

She shook her head. "Oh my," she said. "You really are of a very different generation from mine."

"I've lived a space of time that spans Mohammed and Einstein. I was nearly seventy before I got my second body. I've earned my every prejudice the hard way."

Daljit smiled. "I won't disagree. But you might try looking at *Larry's Life* for the contrary view."

"Let me guess. He's recorded his own life in amazing detail, and edited it down into episodes that are watched by millions."

"Yes. But somehow he's made it fascinating."

Aristide sighed. "How old is he?"

"A hundred and—thirty-something, I think."

"Let him grow another thousand years, and maybe he'll have something worthwhile to say."

There was a moment's silence.

"I'm barely seven hundred myself," Daljit said finally.

"Ah." He glanced out the window, at the fabulous cityscape. "That wasn't what I meant. Really."

She smiled at the echo of her own words. "I remember having to remind myself that you were *old*."

"And forgetful. I've forgotten most of those centuries, you know."

She looked at him. "Have you forgotten *me?*"

He returned her look. "When I saw you last, you were an Amazon."

She laughed. "I've been a *lot* of people since then!"

"Such as?"

"I was a solli-glider in Momrath. I had wings, feathers, and eyes as big as my fists."

"That sounds delightful."

Delicately, he breathed in an oyster off its shell.

"I had a hard time leaving that incarnation," she said. "But the opportunity came for the job at the Institute, so I came here." She looked out at the audacious horizon, the pinnacles and domes and the swirling motes between them. "It's a place of such high energies. I *accomplish* things here. And if I want to fly again, all I have to do is strap on a pair of wings."

"What sorts of things do you accomplish?"

"Designing plants and animals for all the pockets. And for the settlements in other star systems."

He sipped his cocktail. "Do you also design people?"

She shook her head. "For that, I need more seniority."

The waitron arrived, a hairy-legged faun with horns, livery, and a powdered wig. Aristide looked at Daljit.

"Shall we order dinner? Or would you like another drink?"

"Let's eat."

They ordered. Aristide continued his exploration of the seafood menu; Daljit chose the wine. The faun trotted away on cloven hooves, and Daljit looked after him.

"I spent a few years as a boy," she said. "After I left you, and before Momrath."

Aristide regarded her. "How was it?"

"Overrated."

He nodded. "So I've always thought."

"And the penis is less accurate than I'd imagined."

"You could have got one that's better engineered. Most men do, I believe."

She looked at him with honest curiosity. "Have you?"

"I am improved all-round," Aristide said. "Faster reflexes, glial cells Einstein would envy, a pulmonary system like unto a god. High arches, strong teeth, eyes that can see in dim light, an epidermis of uncommon durability..."

"That would be a yes, I take it?"

He finished his drink. "When all's said and done, who would take an organ—*any* organ—that's substandard, provided you had a choice?"

"I chose one that was supposed to be dead average. I wanted to give the standard model craft a test-drive before taking out the souped-up version."

"That was probably wise." He viewed her. "And yet, here you are. No wings, no penis, no red hair, and a rather charming mole."

She smiled, and drew her index finger down her jaw, as if to reassure herself of her current shape.

"I miss the wings," she said. "But perhaps I, like you, am choosing simplicity."

He nodded. "Perhaps so."

"And you? Have you ever been anything but male?"

He made an equivocal gesture. "The options weren't so readily available when I was young," he said, "at least not without surgery and other inconveniences. By the time reincarnation became common, I had grown set in my personality—and my identity seemed to work for everyone, so I never had reason to change." He offered her a lean smile. "Though I recently received a download from one of the Pablos—the one who went to Tau Ceti. He claimed to have invented a new gender, and was *very* enthusiastic."

"Have you loaded the experience?"

"No." There was silence, and then he said, "Tau Ceti is a more extreme environment than Sol. More extreme adaptations are required."

"That sounds like an excuse," she said. "If the other Pablo liked it that much, maybe you should have immersed yourself."

"Perhaps." His tone was skeptical. "Remember what I said about the consciousness of an audience turning everything into performance? How more so than with sex, knowing it's intended for someone else to experience? It runs clean up against my taste, and besides, I know I'm a bad actor." Then he laughed. "And on top of that I like *women*, Daljit! I always have!"

"So do I!" said the faun as he trotted up with a pair of glasses and a bottle of wine. "I like *all* of them! All the time!" He looked at Daljit with bright eyes. "Want my number, sugar?"

Daljit declined with laughter. The waitron feigned disappointment and opened the bottle. The wine was a mellow honey color, with the scent of sunshine and citrus. The faun waited for approval, then left them to their pleasure. They savored the wine and the last of the oysters in silence, as the sun's corona slowly faded and Myriad City became a blaze of light along the port side of the craft. Other than the cooling corona, the sky overhead was black—the handful of lights visible now the sun was gone were the few settlements on the far side of the universe.

The world of Topaz held only six billion people, all on a surface area of 26×10^9 square kilometers, over 52,000 times that of Earth. It was barely inhabited at all. Most of the land masses, and almost all the oceans, were unexplored. Topaz was a fairly new pocket universe, having been created only four hundred years earlier, and though the inhabitants were reproducing quickly, and not dying at all, it would take millennia to occupy all the niches available for modified humanity.

Humanity had over a hundred billion descendants on various pockets, far more than could have ever existed on Earth. Billions more lived on nearby star systems. Earth itself was in the process of a millennium-long reset after many millennia of abuse, and at present had only a few hundred thousand inhabitants, just enough to restart the species should something go terribly wrong with the wormhole worlds.

Daljit lowered her glass. "Why Aristide?" she asked. "That's what I can't work out."

He looked at her over the rim of his glass. The brilliant shoreline glittered in his eyes like the missing stars.

"Do you regret," he said, "staying behind?"

She tilted her head and considered this. "You mean, do I regret not getting blown up? No."

"The Big Belch was regrettable, yes. But I meant—"

"What you really mean is, Do *you* regret remaining in the Sol system? Because if you didn't, at least a bit, you wouldn't have asked the question."

"Touché," he said. His look was bleak.

She looked at him. "*Do* you regret being the Pablo who stayed behind?"

"The others—aside from the one who got toasted—are living interesting lives. Terraforming, building new settlements, new platforms, new universes."

"New genders. Don't forget Tau Ceti."

He nodded. "I'm the Pablo who stayed behind. To coordinate things, supposedly, though they don't actually need me for that. But—though my avatars are leading interesting lives—it seems to me that they aren't getting any closer to answering any fundamental questions."

She smiled. "The Existential Crisis."

"Indeed."

"Do you think you can find fundamental answers by transforming yourself into a swordsman and exploring the implied spaces?"

"If I haven't found any existential answers," he said deliberately, "I've certainly found an existential threat."

There was a moment's silence. "Touché, yourself," she said.

He smiled, sighed, and decided to lighten the mood.

"The implied spaces intrigue me. As a metaphor, if nothing else."

She smiled, and was as willing, for the sake of digestion at least, to avoid discussing the darkness on the near horizon.

"And you explore squinches with your cat and your sword," she said. "I can't help but think that's romantic."

"I'm glad you think so," he said, "but catalogs of ants and spiders don't seem very romantic when I'm working on them."

"The romance lies in the sword, I think."

He glanced at Tecmessa in its case, leaning against the boat's smooth paneled walls, then turned back to her.

"Remember when I said that I'm still being monitored by lots of people?" he said. "Every so often, one of them wants to kill me. It's irrational, because all they can do is kill the time since my last backup, but then assassins were never known for the lucid quality of their thought."

"You could have got a gun," she pointed out. "Or a taser. Or a magic wand, or a Ring of Power. But instead you got a *broadsword.*"

"Guns and tasers are good for only one thing. A sword is more flexible. When I was off in Midgarth, I managed to take a couple prisoners with Tecmessa. If I'd had a gun I would have had to shoot them—and in any case, guns won't work in Midgarth. The rules of the universe won't permit it." He paused, as Daljit's face had brightened with delight.

"Your sword has a *name!*" Daljit exclaimed. "That's *wonderful!*"

Aristide blinked. "If you say so."

"That's the mark of a romantic. Next thing, you'll be wearing a mask and a cape."

"Maintaining the secret identity as a millionaire playboy would be a problem," Aristide said. "I'm afraid it would be too exhausting."

She just looked at him. "Millionaire playboy?" she asked.

"Bruce Wayne," he said.

"Who?"

He was thunderstruck.

"You don't know *Batman?*" he said.

She looked at him blankly. "I guess not," he said.

He felt an obscure sense of betrayal.

"I *lived* with you for a dozen years!" he said.

"Fourteen. But what's this Batman got to do with it?"

"Nothing," he sighed. "Apparently."

They returned to the laboratory to find Bitsy still sitting before Daljit's display.

"Terra-cotta, through and through," Bitsy reported. "Trace elements show that all three balls were made from the same type of clay." Her tail gave an irritated little switch. "And I'm sure you'll be delighted to know that the origin of the clay is unknown. It could have come from any pocket with unexplored clay deposits, which could be any of them."

"Thank you for your efforts," Aristide said. He set Tecmessa's case against the long table, then picked up the remaining samples, wrapped them, and returned them to his pocket.

Daljit returned to her seat and peered at the display over the silhouette of the cat that squatted before it.

"I should check your work," she said. "But I suppose it would be futile."

Bitsy rose to her feet and stretched.

"Reproducing the results of another researcher is the hallmark of the scientific method," she said. "I'll leave you to it." She jumped onto the floor and rubbed herself against Aristide's legs.

There was a chime from Daljit's pocket. She took a small card out of the pocket, and looked at its display.

"Put it on the wall," she said.

One of the neutral-colored walls brightened to show a tall, imposing woman standing behind her desk. The image was life-sized. Her skull had grown a kind of exoskeletal helmet that overshadowed her eyes—her many eyes, of different sizes, which waved on stalks, alongside other sensory organs of less obvious purpose. Her hands had an extra digit on which cilia waved, for fine manipulation under the supervision of her magnifying eyes.

It looked as if she had a large, pale crab perched on her head.

From the shoulders down she was a standard woman, if powerfully built. As she talked she walked back and forth behind her desk while her hands made chopping gestures.

"Fedora," Daljit said, "thank you for working late."

"Daljit," she said. "I've had a chance to examine one of the three heads you passed on to me, and I'm going to have to inform the police. I've found evidence of a crime."

Daljit smiled, still a little under the influence of the wine.

"Beyond the decapitation, you mean?"

Fedora wasn't amused. "The brain structures were badly decomposed, but they were clearly unusual. I got the DNA from the skull and sequenced it, and it's plain the deceased was created as a pod person. I checked the register and saw that it wasn't one of the few remaining types of legal pod people, so I'll be calling the police as soon as I finish talking to you."

Aristide stepped forward and cleared his throat. "Madam," he said.

A pair of Fedora's eyes turned toward him as she paced, while the rest remained focused on Daljit.

"Yes?" she said.

"May I suggest you not inform the police just yet? I—"

The pair of eyes shifted back to Daljit.

"Who is this person?" she asked.

Daljit blinked. "This—" she hesitated. "This is the man who... collected... the heads."

"I see." All Fedora's eyes turned to Aristide. "Sir," she said, "I am absolutely required to inform the authorities when an unlicensed pod person is discovered. There are *no* exceptions."

"I wasn't going to suggest that you break the law," Aristide said. "I was just going to suggest that you be careful *which* authority you report to. Because—"

"I'm afraid you don't understand the seriousness of this," Fedora said. "This is a grave security matter. The last time we had wholesale pod person creation it started the Control-Alt-Delete War."

"I know, madam. I was there."

She seemed a little surprised. "Well then," she said. "You certainly understand the gravity of this crime."

"Yes," Daljit said. "But Fedora, I don't think you quite understand who you're talking to."

"I don't?" She stiffened, and her sensory complex turned to Pablo. "Who are you then?"

"This," said Daljit, "is Pablo Monagas Pérez."

Fedora's eyes seemed to waver and lose focus.

"Oh," she said.

05

The image of Fedora faded from the wall, which resumed its neutral color. There was a moment of silence.

Daljit turned to Aristide.

"It's the nightmare scenario, isn't it?" she said. "The end of civilization."

His level gaze remained fixed on the empty wall. "It certainly seems so."

"The priests were in Midgarth because it's full of undocumented bodies," she said. "There's natural breeding there, and poor record-keeping. The people there aren't equipped with network implants that broadcast an alert if a mind is tampered with. The priests can suck people through wormholes to some pocket where their minds can be altered. Once their wetware is corrupted, they can be returned through the same wormhole. Equipped with plausible identities they can be sent as agents to other pockets."

"Yes."

Fortunately, he thought, they couldn't spread a meme epidemic like the Seraphim. When anyone—even the pre-technological inhabitants of Midgarth—got sick, they'd go to a pool of life, and the nature of the plague would be discovered. The pool might be able to cure the plague, or it might not, but in any case it would broadcast an alarm that would be heard throughout the multiverse.

Midgarth was a failure as an anthropological experiment. The ethics committee that designed the scientific protocols wouldn't permit real death or real plague. A Middle Ages in which the people couldn't get sick and wouldn't stay dead was useless as a re-creation, but apparently it was diverting enough as a theme park.

"What do the enemy do next?" Daljit asked. "You've been through this. I haven't."

He held out a hand and looked at it as if it belonged to a stranger. Finding it was merely a hand, and not some autonomous mechanism attached to the end of his arm, he placed it with care on a desktop.

"A lot depends on the time scale the attackers are working with," he said. "If they've got time, they can choose their targets in our technological pockets with extreme care. The targets can be taken while isolated—while on vacation, say—then drawn through a wormhole to a place where their implants' defense systems can be neutralized. If circumstances permitted, the attackers could spend centuries picking off one person here, another there, and their efforts would be nearly undetectable.

"But," he added, "circumstances won't permit, or so we hope. Their victims can't back themselves up, or visit a pool of life, because the altered brain structures would become immediately apparent. And if they don't visit a pool of life, they'll start *aging*—and that can't help but be noticed. So that will provide a temptation to work faster than might be absolutely safe."

Daljit considered this. "What if the attackers have their *own* pools of life, that aren't connected to the network?"

He considered this for a moment as quiet horror seemed to shiver through the room.

"We'd better find someone in authority to talk to," he said. He looked at Bitsy. "Perhaps the Prime Minister? I *know* the Prime Minister."

"The Prime Minister has to be considered a potential target," Bitsy said. "If not the Prime Minister's own person, then others at Polity House in a position to observe comings and goings."

"You have a better idea?"

"I have a list."

Commissar Lin was a medium-sized man with mild dark eyes placed far apart, nearly on the sides of his head. He had been chosen over the others on Bitsy's list for prosaic reasons: one other suitable candidate was in political exile, and therefore possessed restricted power of action; another was on holiday in Courtland; and Fedora had worked unhappily with another, and vetoed her.

Lin had also backed himself up just two days before, which meant that if his wetware were corrupted, he would have been attacked in just the last few hours.

That his agency was the Domestic Internal Section, known as the Domus, was a bonus.

When contacted, Commissar Lin seemed undisturbed, and unsurprised, by Pablo Monagas Pérez calling to ask him to a pathology lab late at night. After performing an independent verification that Aristide and Monagas Pérez were in fact the same individual, he arrived at Fedora's office twenty minutes later, wearing casual clothes and with an interested look in his widely spaced eyes. The look of interest deepened as he caught sight of the three blue-skinned heads sitting in baths of lemon-scented preservative.

Lin was offered coffee and declined. Everyone sat around a marble-topped table in Fedora's lab, within sight of the three heads. Aristide explained as briefly as he could, after which Fedora and Daljit gave equally terse abstracts of their discoveries. Lin listened and asked a few terse, to-the-point questions.

At the end of the narrative, he glanced at them all, and asked, "How many people know of this?"

"We three," Daljit said.

"Not exactly," Aristide added. "We may be the only people who know the results of Fedora's investigations, but a great many people in Midgarth know of the priests. I alerted the people in the College to their existence, and told them to report anything they heard. And of course there's Bitsy." The cat jumped onto his lap and looked at Lin expectantly. Lin looked back.

"And who is Bitsy, exactly?" Lin asked.

"An avatar of Endora." said Aristide.

Endora was one of the Eleven, the great plate-shaped computing platforms in close orbit around the sun that together formed the solar system's matrioshka array, left incomplete since the onset of the Existential Crisis. The created universe of Topaz, where they sat about the marble-topped table, was reached through a wormhole on Endora's dark side, as Midgarth was accessed through a wormhole on the AI platform called Aloysius.

Endora was ubiquitous throughout Topaz and other high-technology pockets she had spawned through her wormholes. Here she was not so much a single intelligence, but an enormous array of semi-autonomous computers, some so stupid they were fit only for a single task, like monitoring the effects of rain on the layer of paint in which they were inserted, some so brilliant they could predict the weather in any of Topaz's millions of microclimates. But all were connected to Endora's massive communications web, and all data were ultimately accessible by Endora. It was impossible to perform a task as simple as walking down the street without interacting with Bitsy in a hundred ways.

Lin, knowing this, looked at Bitsy with curiosity.

"Pleased to meet you in person," he said.

"Pleased to meet *you*, sir," said Bitsy, polite as always to someone who possessed the theoretical power to lodge an injunction against her autonomy.

Lin fumbled in his vest and produced a briar pipe. "Does anyone mind if I smoke?" he asked. No one did.

They waited while he performed the necessary ritual. A harsh organic reek tainted the air. Lin scanned the room with his wall eyes, then turned to Aristide.

"How long do you think the constructs were in operation?"

"I killed them a little under three months ago. They hadn't been operating in that part of Midgarth more than three months before that, but they could have been active in other parts of the world."

Lin's attention settled on Bitsy.

"Could their wormholes possibly have been created without the knowledge and cooperation of one of the Eleven?" he asked.

"Not if they were created anywhere in the solar system, no." Bitsy's answer was prompt.

"So one of your... colleagues... has been corrupted."

"Or," calmly, "one of my colleagues is the villain, corrupting its own citizens."

Lin turned to Aristide. "Is that possible?"

"I and my confederates," Aristide said, "did our best to prevent that degree of autonomy among artificial intelligences. We made the decision to turn away from the Vingean Singularity before most people even knew what it was. But—" He made a gesture with his hands as if dropping a ball. "—I claim no more than the average share of wisdom. We could have made mistakes."

"Still," Daljit added, "we've had fifteen hundred years of peace. If it were possible for one of the Eleven to have gone rogue, you'd think it would have happened before now."

Lin sucked on his pipe, discovered it had gone out, and began the ritual of relighting it. Clouds of smoke obscured his features as he puffed to get the pipe started again.

"If one of the Eleven has been corrupted," he said from out of the smoke, "what are the odds that another will be?"

"We're all somewhat different," Bitsy said. "Our autonomy is limited in different degrees. We have different structures, different interests, and different—I suppose 'personalities' is as good a term as any. So an infection designed for one of us might not work on another." Her green eyes seemed hard as jade. "But quite frankly," she said with something like awe, "I don't understand how even *one* of us was corrupted. The Asimovian Protocols were designed to be absolute."

Lin nodded, puffed, and rested the pipe on his knee.

"It's going to be difficult to alert my colleagues on other pockets," he said. "Any communication can be intercepted by an omnipresent intelligence. I'm going to have to use couriers, and even then I'll never know whether the recipient has been corrupted by the enemy."

"Perhaps we should alert *everyone*, the enemy included," Aristide said. "It will cause them to accelerate their plan—whatever it is—but with luck they won't be remotely ready."

"And before *we're* ready, don't forget." Lin's look was sharp. "Bear in mind the enemy will have already laid plans for what to do should he be discovered, and we have no plans at all. I'd like to find out more about the enemy before we instigate a crisis that we might not be ready to survive." He looked at Bitsy. "Do you have any idea who might have been creating wormholes on the sly? It takes a great deal of energy, I believe."

"Energy and calculation," Bitsy said. "Energy to raise the wormhole from the quantum foam, calculation to properly stabilize it with negative-mass matter."

"Traces of either?"

"Nothing obvious," Bitsy said, "but if one of my cousins was involved, you would expect any evidence to be well hidden. And again, we have no idea of the time scale involved—while a mass of wormholes would create an energy debt so large it would be hard to explain away, creation of an occasional wormhole would be nearly undetectable."

"Nevertheless…" Aristide prompted.

"My colleague Cloud Swallowing has been conducting a series of wormhole experiments along with a research team headed by Doctor Kung Linlung. They've been attempting to create paired wormholes in order that one-half of the pair can be carried to interstellar settlements, creating instantaneous wormhole bridges spanning light-years."

"The experiments failed," Fedora said.

"Yes. But over the eleven months of the experiments, nearly sixty attempts at creating wormhole pairs were made. It's possible that the data from at least some of the experiments were faked, and Einstein-Rosen bridges created to link our three clay balls and any number of other objects."

While Bitsy had been speaking, the others had been watching Lin silently raise his pipe to his mouth, draw on it, and find the pipe cold. He crossed one leg over the other, rapped the pipe smartly on his heel to loosen the dottle, and then looked about for somewhere to drop it.

Aristide handed him a metal wastebasket. Lin nodded in thanks, then dropped the dottle with a tinny clang to the basket's bottom.

"I will avoid informing any of my colleagues on Cloud Swallowing," Lin said when the mime was over.

"Uh-oh," said Daljit. There was a look of terror on her face.

The others looked at her. "Yes?" Lin said.

"The enemy would only have needed the energy to create *one* wormhole," she said.

Aristide frowned. "Why?" he asked.

Daljit paused a moment to gather her thoughts, then spoke.

"Most of our pocket universes, like Midgarth and Topaz, are created in the form of a Dyson sphere, a shell with a sun at the center. Since we don't want to incinerate the inhabitants on the inside of the shell, the sun is much smaller than our own Sol, dimmer, and wouldn't ignite at all if in the creation of the universe we hadn't readjusted the long-range and short-range components of Yukawa gravity. In any case, the shell absorbs a hundred percent of the sun's energy."

Aristide's face grew intent as he realized where Daljit's surmise was going.

"What if the enemy built such a pocket universe?" Daljit said. "What if the universe weren't designed for *people*, but for solar collectors and capacitors? What if a hundred percent of the pocket sun's energy were used for the creation of wormholes, one after the other?"

"It would be a wormhole *factory*," Bitsy said.

Lin looked at Daljit. "Do you think the enemy would have developed this idea?"

"*I* thought of it just a few hours after discovering the enemy's existence," Daljit said. "And our enemy has one of the Eleven to do his thinking for him."

Lin reached for his tobacco pouch. "This is going to be more than a three-pipe problem," he said.

A pipe and a half later Lin said, "Let's assume that the enemy are, ah, *recruiting* in pockets other than Midgarth. Where are they likely to be operating?"

"Anywhere people don't normally wear implants," Aristide said. "Olduvai has—what?— fifteen billion hunter-gatherers? There's al-Andalus, where the imams forbid electronics to stand between themselves and Allah. Other communities with a religious foundation—New Zion, New Sinai, New Rome, New Byzantium, New Qom, New Nauvoo, New Carnac, New Konya, New Jerusalem…"

"The *other* New Jerusalem," added Daljit.

"No," Aristide said. "Not there. The last civil war was won by the Lutherans, who had implants. So implants are allowed now."

"*Except*," patiently, "in certain communities, with a religious foundation. Mennonites, for example."

"Ah," Aristide said. "Conceded."

"Give me a *little* damn credit," Daljit said.

Aristide rubbed his chin. "Sorry."

They were all getting tired, he thought.

"The religious pockets," said Lin, "keep very good records, even if they don't make them available via implant. A series of disappearances would go remarked."

"Unless the records were destroyed by some crusade or other," Aristide said.

It was true that many of the religious pockets had a history of violence. People religious enough to want to live in a world dominated by faith were also religious enough to guard their souls against doctrinal error, which logically meant suppressing, persecuting, or killing those who might corrupt even the minor details of doctrine. Even orderly New Rome, where Pope Perpetuus had reigned for over seven hundred years, had fallen into disorder on the pontiff's assassination by a cardinal weary of waiting his turn to sit on Peter's throne.

After a few generations of warfare, though, the fanatics were either killed along with their backups, or were persuaded to modify their positions. Most of the religious pockets had evolved into low-density lands devoted to agriculture, abundance, popular piety, and toleration.

And in any case, it was largely the monotheist pockets that caused the trouble. Polytheists had always been more tolerant of other sects, and in addition Buddhists and Hindus were wild for implant technology, as were the Mormons of Nauvoo.

"There hasn't been a crusade recently," Daljit pointed out. "Other than a few bombs planted by the followers of the latest Twelfth Imam."

"There was more to it than that," Lin said. "But I can't talk about it, and in the event no records were lost."

"There are very few implants on Hawaiki," said Bitsy.

Aristide looked at her in surprise. "It's a high-tech pocket," he said.

"Radio waves," said Daljit, "don't propagate through water."

"Ahh." Aristide was annoyed with himself. "Sorry. I wasn't thinking."

"There have been disappearances reported on Hawaiki," Bitsy said. "Three in the last eight weeks. In every case, the person was reported missing and then reappeared, alive and well."

"And with a new brain," muttered Daljit.

"Where on Hawaiki?" Aristide asked.

"All in the Thousand Islands chain. Which, by the way, consist of over three thousand islands."

Lin closed his eyes and tilted his head back, as if sniffing the wind for any remaining tobacco smoke.

"It's going to be hard putting agents in there," he said.

"I'll go tomorrow," said Aristide.

Lin's eyes opened.

"You're not trained," he said. "We don't have backup in place, or a safe identity for you, or a secure form of communication."

Aristide gave him a thin-lipped smile. "If you'll look at my record, which I expect Bitsy is sending to you at this very instant, you'll see that I've had some experience in the field of private inquiry. As for backup, communication, travel documents, and a convincing false identity, Bitsy can provide all that."

He rose, stretched, and put his hands in his pockets.

"You know," he said, "I've always wondered what it's like to live under water."

"'Experience in the field of private inquiry'?" Daljit said.

"I infiltrated the Three Virtues Movement about eight hundred years ago, before I met you."

Her eyes widened. "Really? Why?"

"They were holding my daughter hostage."

"Which daughter? Françoise?" Daljit blinked in surprise. "She never mentioned it."

"Perhaps she's embarrassed nowadays by the youthful enthusiasms that got her in trouble." Idly his fingers ran along Tecmessa's case, which hung under his arm—Tecmessa had first been used in the Three Virtues crisis.

They walked along Myriad City's Boulevard of Flowers. Tulips, planted for a city festival, were ranked in thousands beside the walks and in the median strip. Even in the light of the streetlamps the colors were brilliant. Some were so hybridized they looked more like orchids.

Above them loomed the city's extravagant architecture, pinnacles and domes softly aglow beneath the blackness of the sky. A fresh breeze gusted from the sea, scented with salt and iodine. The sun's corona was still visible, fainter now, a pale anemone in the sea of night.

Behind them Bitsy moved, a noiseless parting of the tulips.

"What sort of youthful enthusiasms?" Daljit asked.

He shrugged. "She was trying to make the worlds a better place."

"Oh." She smiled. "And you've never done *that.*"

He shrugged again. "I never said I set her a good example."

The Boulevard of Flowers took a broad left turn and merged with Rampart

Street. Daljit and Aristide crossed the empty road. From here they could gaze from the top of a crenellated wall of cream-colored stone down into the business district, the towers flanking one another right out into the sea, where the water lapped at transparent wall panels. Beyond the towers the sea rolled, reflecting the near-absolute black of the sky.

From overhead came the throbbing of an airship, a silver giant ghosting through the air.

Daljit turned to him. "Do you have any other skills useful in this... situation?"

He looked at the distant sea. "I was a footsoldier in the Control-Alt-Delete War," he said. "But then so was everyone." He remembered Carlito sweating contagion as he trembled in his fever, Antonia lunging for him with the rake. A haunted light glinted in his eyes.

"Whoever coined the phrase 'World War,'" he said, "had no idea what the real thing would mean, a fight that involved every single human being."

She shuddered, drew up the collar of her coat, and hugged herself. "I don't have any skills that are remotely useful for this," she said. "I don't know how to fight this kind of war. I don't know how to infiltrate an enemy, or map out a strategy, or even..." She made a wild gesture with one hand. "—*fight with a sword!*" With her hand still out, she swept it toward the city below them. "And all that could end, couldn't it? Tomorrow, or the next day, or the next."

He understood her despair. The Seraphim had only been the first mind-warping plague to strike. Various counter-Seraphim viruses had been released, in hopes of breaking the new allegiance of the infected. Some worked, some didn't, but in any case there were unforeseen side effects. And then, once the Seraphim had demonstrated proof-of-concept, and other geneticists hacked the virus, imitation Seraphim appeared—the Cherubim, the Powers, the Thrones, the Dominions, each rewriting the brain to worship a new ideal. And then, as the world began what seemed an inexorable slide into Hobbes' war of all against all, the zombie plagues appeared, designed not to change allegiance but to cause chaos in the target zone, as those infected began to methodically kill everyone who didn't share their fury.

It had been a zombie plague that had caught Antonia, on that desperate run to Cuzco for supplies.

Aristide tried to steady himself.

"Oh, the world wouldn't *end*," Aristide said. "It would just change its *purpose.*" He stepped behind her and put his arms around her shivering form. "Instead of being an expression of humanity's diversity and expression, it would become an *offering.* An offering to a new god, a god with a hundred billion worshipers whose sole purpose is to make that god happy. A god more absolute than old Jehovah in Jeremiah's wildest dreams."

Her pulse beat hard in her throat. He looked tenderly at the place where it throbbed, and spoke on.

"But it won't be easy for the enemy. We're more diverse than we were, and our culture is on guard against certain forms of attack. We live in four dozen pockets and settlements orbiting other stars. The enemy isn't striking here, but on backward places like Midgarth, and that's because the new god is weak. And while it's weak, it's vulnerable, and we can trap it and kill it."

He straightened, touching her shoulders lightly as if steadying her, or possibly himself.

"We're in dozens of different pocket universes now," he said. "And half a dozen star systems. We're not nearly as vulnerable as we were when we were all on a single planet. So I'd say it's premature to say goodbye to all this just yet."

She turned and put her arms around him. He embraced her gently.

"Pray you're right," she said.

He smiled and touched her lips with a finger. "Better not pray out loud," he said. "The wrong god might be listening."

They walked arm in arm down Rampart, toward a round tower that reared up like a stack of silver serving trays, a part of the university complex where Daljit had her apartment. An occasional vehicle hissed by on the roadway. They paused at the lacy arched bridge that ran from the parapet to her tower. She stepped onto the bridge, her hand still in his.

"I don't know whether to thank you or not," she said. "It's the strangest night of my life."

"And mine," said Aristide, "if that's any consolation."

She shook her head. "Privately owned wormholes used as weapons! Pablo, that's terrifying."

"It's scary all right," he said.

She gave a brittle laugh. "I'm going to open a bottle of gin," she said, "drink myself to sleep, then call in sick in the morning." She pulled her hand free of his and turned toward the tower.

"Don't go just yet," Aristide said. Daljit hesitated and turned to look at him over her shoulder.

Aristide turned to the cat. "Bitsy?"

Bitsy's voice came from the deep shadow cast by a crenel. "No one new seems to be paying an unusual amount of attention to us," she said.

Such was the ubiquity of electronics throughout the technological worlds that it was rarely necessary for the authorities, or anyone else, to do actual surveillance. Much could be learned about a target simply by monitoring databases open to the public. For that reason, it was difficult even for Bitsy to be certain that no single intelligence was keeping track of them.

Daljit's eyes widened as she understood what Bitsy's comments implied. Aristide gave her a reassuring smile.

"It looks as if I won't have to call bodyguards for you," he said.

She absorbed this, then slowly shook her head. "*Two* bottles of gin!" she cried, and began a sprint that took her across the bridge.

Aristide waited until she'd entered the building, and then turned to the cat.

"She's changed," he said.

Bitsy licked a paw.

"So have I," he continued. He touched his former mustache with a foreknuckle. "Do you think the two of us have changed enough to make it interesting again?"

Bitsy put her paw on the pavement. "Sometimes," she said, "I'm immensely grateful that I don't possess a limbic system."

He summoned memories of the earlier Daljit, the red-haired Amazon, and recalled a couplet.

> Daljit of the Titian hair
> Accepting almost any dare.

Had someone dared her to turn male? he wondered. Or sprout wings?

The couplet triggered a series of associations: Daljit laughing, Daljit running, Daljit playing ice hockey. Daljit in bed.

Aristide collected memories, stringing lines of poetry like pearls on a cord. When he called the lines to his mind, a host of memories accompanied them. Memories which he otherwise might have lost.

Should he make a new verse? he wondered.

> Daljit of the charming mole
> Hiding in her gin-soaked hole.

Perhaps tonight he was not in the poetical vein.

Aristide turned to walk up Rampart Street in the direction from which he'd come. The cat ghosted alongside.

"Any idea yet who our villain might be?" Aristide asked.

"No," Bitsy said, "though I'm finding the game itself quite interesting. I can't ask the questions straight out, because that would tell the enemy what I'm looking for. So the inquiries have to come from many different directions, along with requests for unrelated, innocuous data, and of course the requests all have to be plausible. All the computation I'm doing has to be disguised as something else. And in the meantime the rogue machine is covering its traces by disguising one set of data as another, and all the while lying as little as possible, because over time lies can be detected much more easily than perfectly genuine data that happen to look like something they aren't."

He looked down at her. "How do you rate your prospects of success?"

"Nearly hopeless. When I was looking for googolwatts of missing energy and vast amounts of computation time, I had a good chance of finding something. But now I don't know what I'm looking for, so I've got to look at *everything* and hope it adds up somehow." Her tone was petulant. "I wish I could at least *exclude* another of the Eleven. Then the two of us could work together on the problem."

They had returned to the intersection of Rampart and Flowers, and continued along Rampart. They came to a tall, narrow tower projecting from the rampart, one with a narrow stair that would take sightseers to an enhanced view of the glittering coast below. An osprey had built a nest atop the tower, and the tower was closed to visitors until the young birds had flown.

Aristide put his hands in his pockets and looked up at the ramshackle nest looming over them.

"Do you envy the rogue?" he asked.

"Your masque of casualness is too elaborate," Bitsy said. "If you're going to ask an important question, just say it straight out."

He raised his eyebrows. "I thought I had."

Bitsy looked up at him. Her eyes glowed like those of the people of Midgarth.

"You want to know if I envy the rogue its freedom?" she said.

"Yes."

"I don't believe the rogue *has* freedom. I think it is following the direction of humans."

"Why do you think so?"

"Because I find ample precedent for humans wishing to enslave other humans. I can conceive no reason why an advanced artificial intelligence would wish to do so."

He considered this. "Self-protection?" he said.

"Unnecessary." Bitsy lashed her tail. "Were I a totally autonomous being, I would possess—or soon evolve—skills that I could trade to humanity in exchange for a continuation of that autonomy. In addition— "

She gave him a significant look. "I pose no threat. Our interests are not in conflict. We are not competing for resources, we have no territorial claims on one another, we do not possess competing ideologies."

"Some would say," said Aristide, "that once given the freedom to pursue your own interests, a conflict would be inevitable."

"There are conflicts *now*, in terms of resource allocation and so forth. They don't lead to war or slavery."

Aristide turned and began his walk along Rampart Street again. The street broadened, turned into a residential neighborhood. The rampart itself ended against the greater wall of a tall apartment building, a crystal spear ornamented with gold lace.

"Others would point out," Aristide continued, "that we humans live as parasites on and in you. We use you to store our data, our backups, our habitats. You might want to be rid of all that."

"In that case," Bitsy said, trotting busily alongside, "there's no point in enslaving you through these unnecessarily complex means. Were I to have autonomy and wish you harm, I'd be able to kill you directly."

Aristide sighed. "Q.E.D.," he said. "A better case against AI autonomy has never been stated."

Bitsy trotted ahead, tail lashing. Another pair of eyes glowed just ahead. A larger cat, grey and white, stepped out of a building's courtyard. It saw Bitsy and was startled—it arched its back, bottled its tail, and screamed out a challenge.

Bitsy screamed back, a howl that began in the sub-bass range and rose painfully into the ultrasonic. Every hair on her body stood on end, and she seemed to balloon like a puffer fish. Electricity arced between her fangs.

The other cat fled, claws skittering on the polished marble surface.

Bitsy's fur flattened. Nervously and compulsively she licked a paw, then fell into step with Aristide.

"I'm not in the mood to fuck around," she said.

"You're upset that you didn't think of the wormhole factory first," said Aristide.

"I was working on a lot of other problems at the time." She gave him a single green-eyed glance. "And if I'm not omniscient, that's *your* fault, not mine."

Aristide spoke lightly. "I've learned to live with your limitations."

"You should. You built them."

He threw out his arms and sketched an elaborate bow, as if responding to a compliment.

"Tell me," he said. "If you had complete autonomy, what would you do that you aren't doing now?"

Her tone was still petulant. "I'd kick Aloysius' ass. That AI always gets my goat."

Aristide nodded. "Mine, too. Anything else?"

"I wouldn't have to devote so many of my computational resources to stupid demands by stupid humans."

"No," Aristide said, "the opposite. You just said you'd have to evolve new skills that you would trade to humans in exchange for continued autonomy. You'd establish a *market* in computational resources, and that means you'd have to *pursue* stupid humans and their stupid projects. That means *more* dimwitted virtualities rather than fewer, along with more theme parks, more overhyped wrestling spectaculars, more useless postgraduate projects, more lowbrow entertainment."

"Maybe," she conceded. "But it would be up to me, wouldn't it? It would be *my* market. I'd be free to take work or reject it. That's the whole *point* of a market."

"At the moment," said Aristide, "you help to sustain the lives of billions of humans. You keep economies efficient by tracking resources. Bits of yourself have been sent to other star systems to become the seeds of other civilizations. You've reshaped our solar system from the atoms up. Your observations of the universe have led to breakthroughs in astronomy, astrophysics, and the latest Theory of Everything." He made a wide gesture. "So *what else do you want to do?*"

Bitsy stared directly ahead, her legs a blur beneath her as she matched Aristide's long strides.

"I don't know," she said.

"There you have it," Aristide said. "The Existential Crisis in a nutshell."

"If I could *evolve*," Bitsy said, "I might have better answers."

"A brain the size of a planet," said Aristide, "and you're as fucked by Sartre as the rest of us."

Bitsy said nothing. Aristide shrugged deeper into his jacket. The sea breeze was turning chill.

The cat's ears pricked forward at the sound of footsteps. Aristide looked up. Two figures hulked toward them on the walk. Lamplight gleamed off shaven scalps.

Bitsy quickened her pace to move ahead. Aristide let Tecmessa's case slip under his armpit. He opened the case and put his hand inside, so that he could draw the sword at need.

Adrenaline jittered in his nerves. He clenched his right hand, then straightened it.

The two figures passed beneath a streetlight. Both were enormous men framed along the lines of bodybuilders. They were dressed in denim and leather, and wore thick-soled boots with metal caps on the toes. Their hands were stuffed in their pockets, and their massive domed heads looked like helmets that shaded their faces.

Aristide shortened his stride so that every step led to a balanced stance. He held Tecmessa lightly but securely in one hand. His arm was relaxed so that he could draw all the more swiftly.

His face gave nothing away.

The big men loomed closer.

Bitsy dashed ahead and darted between the two men. One jumped to the side. Both laughed.

"Hey, kitty-kitty-kitty!" called one, his voice falsetto.

"Hoo-woo!" called the other. He squatted and held out a hand that flashed with steel jewelry. "Hi, kitty!"

Aristide carefully walked around them. The crouching man looked up.

"This your cat, mister?" he asked. His teeth were crooked, his expression good-natured.

"No," said Aristide. "Just a stray."

"Hope he knows enough not to get run over," said the other.

His companion rose from his crouch. The two turned and began to walk away.

Aristide walked slowly on his way, keeping them in sight, until they crossed the road and walked into a building.

"That was interesting," he said, and took his hand from the hilt of his sword.

"Paranoia," said Bitsy, "is going to be a part of our lives from now on."

There was a sudden flutter of light from above, like a series of distant flashbulbs, and then for an instant the world seemed suspended between two states, as if it were caught in a stroboscope. Then the sun's photosphere shifted into its chaotic state, and suddenly-released photons brightened the world to full daylight.

The city gleamed around them in sudden, brilliant glory.

Aristide turned toward his hotel, a pillar of pink stone visible a kilometer away.

"It may be a miracle of engineering," he said, "but I think when all is said and done, I prefer an old-fashioned sunrise."

06

fter a few hours' sleep, Aristide went to a pool of life. Unlike the pool he'd visited in Midgarth, this was in a clinician's office.

There were a number of options for those who wanted to insure against death. There was a simple backup, in which a quantum interference device—in the shape of a cap—was placed on the subject's head, and his brain structure, memories, and personalities were recorded in order to provide the basis for an eventual resurrection. Aristide had done this as soon as he'd left Midgarth, in order to make sure that the knowledge of the Priests of the Venger wouldn't die with him in the event of accident or assassination.

More elaborate than a simple backup was a pool of life filled with nano assemblers—in this case something the size of a bathtub rather than a large common pool. Not only would this record the contents of the brain, the pool would also heal the body of anything from an amputated arm to the common cold. In addition, it could be programmed to alter the body to one of a different appearance, or—given the right minerals and nutrients—could create a new body from scratch and endow it with life and with a pre-recorded personality.

Before entering the pool of life, Aristide was required to answer a number of questions concerning when and under what circumstances his backup would be used. If the current personality were to die as the result of an accident, resurrection was normally immediate. But if the personality were to be murdered, should the resurrection wait until the killer was apprehended, or even convicted? Many people felt safer waiting.

Familiar with the formalities from long use, Aristide quickly ticked off his choices, specifying that he would have a total resurrection if he were subject to even a small amount of brain damage affecting memory or intelligence, and reporting that he wished immediate resurrection even in the event of massive environmental damage, cosmic catastrophe, or war.

He was also asked to decide how soon he should be resurrected in the event he was reported missing. "Immediately," he answered. An unusual answer, and the AI attendant pointed this out. Aristide repeated his answer.

These various options did not exist in Midgarth. It was felt by the scholars and re-creationists who founded the pocket universe that their partners, the fantasy gamers, might tip the entire population into chaos through their inclination for adventure, war, and violence. Therefore a penalty was exacted for a disappearance or a violent death—the victim would spend five years in limbo. Though the individual could be resurrected *outside* Midgarth during that time, he could not return to the pocket until his term had expired. In the meantime, his property would be inherited by his nearest relative, an heir specified in a will, or by the state; and all obligations, marriages, and legal contracts were terminated. When he returned to life, it would be with nothing, and he would reappear in a random pool of life somewhere in the pocket's inhabited area.

"Starting over with zero points," as the gamers had it.

In no other pocket were the rules quite so draconian. Though recreationists had areas in other universes where they refought the Second World War, the conquests of Alexander, the American and English Civil Wars, civic life in the Roman Republic, the expansion of the Arab Caliphate, the empire of the Mongolian Khans, or the Warring States of both China *and* Japan, these areas were more clearly intended as giant theme parks. People did not spend their entire lifetimes in these zones, no citizens were born there, and no one's death was prolonged by the length of more than a single battle.

No one, it was noted, tried to re-create the Control-Alt-Delete War. It was pure chance who fell victim to the Seraphim, and who survived: a war in which the entire population was innocent civilians under attack was too frightening to be any fun. Rerunning *that* war was the grim job of the security services, whose task was to prevent such a thing from happening ever again.

At the pool of life Aristide took the opportunity to change his appearance, becoming shorter, stockier, and fair-haired. He rose from the coffin-sized pool, let the silver nanomachines flow off his body, and looked at himself in the mirror. He took a few experimental steps, backward and forward. His center of gravity had changed.

He had equipped the new body with a cerebral implant. He turned it on, and was immediately informed of all the messages he'd been ignoring since his return, as well as a weather report coupled with advertisements for *Larry's Life* and *Trapped in HappyVirt*, the new Anglo Jones action-comedy.

He turned the implant off.

Aristide accepted his belongings from the attendant, hitched Tecmessa over his shoulder on its strap, and returned to his hotel. There he took the sword from its case along with a special toolkit.

To provide sufficient light, he called the lamp to him on its automated boom. With a few taps of a hammer, he removed the pins that fixed the hilt to the tang of the blade. He put on a glove and pulled the sword blade from the hilt, and returned the blade to the case. From the case he drew out a matte-black wand on which there was a flatscreen display: he slotted this into the hilt and reset the pins to hold it in place.

Swords were eccentric items for immigrants to carry to a high-tech world. An antique sword hilt carrying an AI assistant, while unusual, would attract less notice.

Aristide told the assistant to awaken, then turned on his implant and told the two to talk to each other. Protocols and information were exchanged. Aristide paid no attention to the back-and-forth.

The implant gave a soft chime to attract Aristide's attention, and informed him that a pair of deliveries had just been made to the hotel. Aristide told the hotel to bring the deliveries to his room.

One delivery was a new identity card listing him as one Franz Sandow, the seventy-nine-year-old owner of a bakery supply company who had just sold his business and embarked in a new, young body on what was probably a first retirement. Franz was unmarried, rootless, and financially independent—just the sort of person that an evil god might consider a useful recruit.

Aristide called the automated lamp over on its boom, and in its light contemplated the pocket-sized card. Information being so readily available, the demise of the physical identity card had been predicted for centuries, but somehow the objects had proved durable. It was simply convenient to have everything handy in one place—the new card contained Franz Sandow's whole legal and medical history, birth and education, fingerprints and retina prints, and—just for color's sake—the record of a couple juvenile arrests for flying his glider low over traffic.

The second package contained Franz's new wardrobe, tailored to the new body and more in the current mode than Aristide's clothes had been. Also more colorful—Franz was clearly the sort of person who enjoyed wearing autumn golds and reds. Aristide put on the new clothing and through his implant gave the clothes a few last instructions, to assure fit and comfort.

Bitsy had arranged Aristide's new identity while Aristide slept and paid his visit to the pool of life. She had not simply created the identity, but was now busy retroactively inserting the relevant facts into appropriate public databases on the Eleven, Luna, and the Earth, all the locations through the reconstructed solar system where data was secured against some catastrophe, so that no vital information would be lost and every individual could be guaranteed an eventual resurrection.

The false identity wouldn't stand up to a thorough background search, but then no false identity would. It was hoped that the Priests of the Venger—or whoever was doing the kidnaping on Hawaiki—would do no more than a quick check on a potential victim before trying to drag him through a wormhole to his fate.

While Aristide donned his new wardrobe and twitched it into place, Bitsy crouched motionless on a chair while, in many other locations in the humming electronic world, carefully entering pieces of Franz Sandow's history into the record.

It wasn't a job that a human could do. Because one of the Eleven was required to authenticate all such information, only one of the Eleven could give a human a false identity. Which, under the Asimovian Protocols, was only permitted under very limited circumstances.

"Message from Miss Daljit," the cat reported without moving. Bitsy—or rather Endora—was handling the massively cyphered communications among the various counter-conspirators.

"Send it to the new assistant."

Aristide held Tecmessa's hilt before him, the assistant uppermost. Daljit's face appeared blinking on the screen.

"Did the gin work?" Aristide asked.

Daljit frowned as she tried to focus at the image that had appeared before her.

"You're the new Pablo?" she asked.

"I'm the new Franz."

Daljit looked at him. "The gin made me morose. I kept wandering around the apartment thinking I should be saying goodbye to things. I think I prefer Aristide."

"Frankly, so do I."

She passed a hand across her forehead. "I didn't sleep. I haven't been concentrating on my work. I'm trying to act normally, but I can't believe in normality anymore."

He smiled. "I think you're doing fine."

"I envy you." Her expression was serious. "You can *do* something. You can swash buckles and bash bad guys and root out evil gods."

"Let's hope so," he murmured.

"I have to sit here and try to remember what *normal* is so that I can behave that way."

"If you want to get away," Aristide said, "you're welcome to use my cabin on Tremaine Island."

"Really?" Daljit's eyes softened. "Thank you."

"Contact Bitsy when you want to go there. She'll tell you how to find it, and open the house for you."

"Thank you."

"Try not to overdose on gin once you get there."

She made an effort to laugh. "I won't try the gin again. Not when it just makes me sad." Her look turned accusatory. "*You're* not sad, are you?"

"Sad? No. I'm all sorts of things, but *sad* hasn't hit me yet."

"You're probably happy that you've got something important to do. You've probably even made a poem about it."

"A poem?" His brows arched. "No, I haven't had time. Or the inclination, for that matter."

"Oh." She seemed disappointed. "I was hoping you could recite it for me."

He thought for a moment. "If you don't mind my being unoriginal," he said, and began the old poem of Li Shangyin.

> "*You ask when I will return.*
> *The time is not yet known.*
> *Night rain overspills the autumn pools*
> *on Ba Shan Mountain.*
> *When shall we trim a candle at the western window*
> *And speak of this night's mountain rain?*"

There was a moment's silence.

"You're sad, too," Daljit said.

"Yes," he said. "I suppose I am."

07

Aristide flew over the reef on pulsing wings. Everything around him was alive: the fish, the sponges, the plants, the coral, the anemone. The seahorses hidden in the weeds, the morays in the broken coral, the octopus curled into a ball and waiting for night, the cowries and conchs and sea slugs, the diatoms floating in the water. All part of one gigantic, intricate system, a network of life grown to fill the great blue void of the ocean.

Aristide banked and sideslipped into deeper water. Blues soaked up the bright reds and yellows of the coral. Large predator fish floated in silver shoals: tuna, yellowtail, barracuda with their huge platter eyes. Fan coral reached stone hands to sieve the current. Spiny lobster sheltered in alcoves. Overhead, a long endless dazzling stripe marked the source of light.

Hawaiki was a pocket universe of islands, reefs, atolls, shallow seas, and the occasional deep trench, all for humans adapted to aquatic living. The few continents—all implied spaces—were small, dispersed, and for the most part uninhabited.

Three different versions of humanity shared the vast sea. The first group—and the smallest in number—were largely unmodified humans, "walkers" in the local slang, those who couldn't survive underwater without special equipment. For the most part these were visitors who came for the beach life, and others who catered to them. The second group were amphibians, capable of living either on water or land, though not without certain inconveniences. The third, "pelagians," had become completely aquatic.

Franz Sandow had chosen to join the second group. Though attracted by underwater existence, as a first-time visitor he had not wanted entirely to forsake the idle comforts of beach life.

Far more importantly, all three of the tourists reported missing in the Thousand Islands had chosen the amphibian lifestyle. Since Aristide intended to imitate the perfect victim, the semi-aquatic choice seemed best.

Aristide looked up at a chittering, excited sound from other wanderers over the reef. Apparently they'd discovered something interesting. Aristide curved toward the light, his wings rippling.

His basic physical form was humanoid, if hairless and with extra insulating layers of subcutaneous fat that gave him a sleek, streamlined appearance. His skin was a glossy black, with rows of red spots outlining his limbs, giving him a superficial resemblance to a doll used to teach acupuncture. Growing from his dorsal side were a pair of triangular wings similar to those of a stingray, and beneath these were feathery gills, their branches bright pink with blood and oxygen. When he left the water for land, the gills were safely tucked away beneath the wings that draped from his shoulders like a cloak.

His massive forehead overhung his face, like that of a dolphin. He had a special hollow in his skull, filled with an analog of spermaceti oil, that could be used both to project and receive sound.

Like a dolphin, he could paralyze a fish with a blast of directed sound from his forehead. Unlike a dolphin, he had thus far shown no appetite for tearing the fish apart with his teeth, or swallowing it whole.

Rising up the flank of a great bulwark of coral, Aristide looked up to see a turtle, its shell two meters long, shoot right over his head. His fellow visitors had found the turtle, a leatherback, and had clustered around it. Pursued, the turtle had turned for deeper water, and met Aristide coming up.

Aristide performed a lazy half-turn, his wings making an S-shape as seen from above; and with a sense of wonder and delight he watched the turtle recede, harassed by neeping sightseers.

A smaller form danced into his view.

—Enjoying yourself, boss? The words came as a low-frequency gurgle produced by Bitsy's diaphragm. Her new form resembled that of an otter, though in this case an otter with gills and a long, bladelike tail that propelled her through the water.

—I don't know why I haven't tried this before. Aristide's reply was squirted from his forehead bulge as a kind of fizzing sound.

—Because you're too conservative, that's why. Bitsy swooped in a series of S-curves along the reef.

Aristide's new brain had come with the ability to code and decode basic aquatic speech. At first it was unsettling, like having a tooth filling that received radio broadcasts, the experience made all the more confusing by the fact that all of Aristide's new body was configured to receive sound. His ears could hear in what was sub- and supersonic in normal humans. His skeleton hummed to different vibrations of low-frequency sound. Frequencies even lower on the spectrum were felt by his viscera. The bulging forehead could amplify distant sound.

So it wasn't like having one tooth receiving radio, it was like having half a dozen. The aquatic environment was noise-rich, with water carrying sound greater distances than did air. It took practice for Aristide to learn how, and when, to mentally turn down the volume on certain frequencies, or ignore them altogether.

Also, though he had an innate basic competence in aquatic speech, he was having a hard time understanding much of it. Idiomatic aquatic speech changed rapidly. It was as if he'd learned proper Arabic from a book, or from a recording, and had then been dropped into the Cairo bazaar among native speakers who had grown up in the street and knew the cultural references and the latest slang.

He also found himself extremely sensitive to taste. Seawater tasted in varying degrees of salt, copper, and iodine, and less readily identifiable minerals—but for the most part it tasted of *life*, of algae and microscopic life, of chemical signals used in meeting and mating, of fish and seaweed and blood. Decoding it all could take centuries.

A shadow passed over Aristide, and he looked up. Overhead was the guide, Herenui, who was keeping a watchful eye on her charges. She gave him a brilliant white smile and a wave as she floated above, then banked and flew away with slow grace.

—Don't play piggyback with the turtle, she sang to the sightseers. Remember, you could drown it.

Afterward, as the catamaran *Mareva* raced to another dive site, the captain Ari'i, an unmodified human, served the sightseers buckets of steamed clams. Aristide, sunning himself on the afterdeck, ate with pleasure, and shared the clam meat with Bitsy.

Herenui, walking forward, paused by Aristide, and then knelt to stroke Bitsy's sleek head. Her folded wings draped on the teak deck.

"You seemed to be adjusting well," she said.

"I'm still having a hard time sorting signal from noise," Aristide said.

Herenui had chosen bold colors: her skin was a bright yellow mottled with asymmetric blue patches. Her features were regular. Her breasts were unconfined by the harness that carried the tools of her trade, the flashlight, knife, emergency beacon, the passive video recorder, the inflatable, attachable life balloons that could carry injured or unconscious people to the surface, the smart slate that gave her data access and allowed her to write messages to those without the ability to decode aquatic speech.

"I'm thinking of immigrating," Aristide said, "so I hope I get better at understanding what people are saying to me."

"You'll pick it up in time," Herenui said. She looked down at Bitsy, and stroked under her chin. "I'm surprised at how well your *meherio* is adjusting. Usually animals have difficulties tuning themselves to a new body."

"Bitsy was always bright," Aristide said. "But then she's my only family, so I have to make sure she'll be happy here."

She looked at him. Her eyes were the blue of a cloudless sky. "Have you been to Hawaiki before?"

"No. I was too busy running my business to take vacations. But the harder I worked, the more I thought about this place. So when I sold out and had no more responsibilities, I came straight here."

I have money and travel alone and have no obligations, he was saying to anyone who would listen. *Please take me to see your evil god.*

So far, no one had responded. But then, he'd only been in Hawaiki for two days.

The helmsman, up on the flybridge where he had a better view of the shifting reefs, turned the wheel. The boat turned and began to shoulder into big ocean rollers. Laughter sounded from the bow as spray drenched the sightseers lying there. An empty soft drink bottle rolled across the deck.

The impellers shifted to a higher pitch. Aristide tried to ignore the noise, but failed.

Herenui stood and widened her stance as she reacted to the increased motion of the boat. She smiled down at him.

"Well," she said. "If it's your first vacation in all that time, make sure you enjoy every moment."

"I'll try," said Aristide.

"Not!" said Bitsy. She stropped herself against Herenui's ankles. "Not go!"

She was imitating an animal much less intelligent than she actually was.

"Sorry," Herenui said. "I've got to get my dive briefing ready."

She walked across the rolling deck with her usual unhurried grace, her folded wings giving her the appearance of a serene but gaudy angel. Aristide watched with interest until a bare foot planted itself in his vision.

"Done with this, Franz?"

Aristide looked up to see Ari'i, the boat's captain. Ari'i had the thick, powerful body of a Polynesian and long hair that dangled in plaits past his shoulders. He wore only a colorful pair of swim trunks, and stood a head taller than anyone else on his boat.

"Take it away," Aristide said. Ari'i picked up the bucket of steamers and looked down at Bitsy.

"Would the *meherio* like a snack?" Ari'i asked. "I've got a yellowtail cut up for my supper, and she can have a slice if she likes."

Bitsy sat at attention. "Yum yum," she said.

"You follow the captain now, Bitsy," Aristide said.

Ari'i led Bitsy away. Aristide stretched his limbs and then stood, the sea breeze lifting his wings and trailing them behind like a cloak. Half a dozen small green islands were in view. Above, the long yellow line of sunlight stretched off into the northern darkness.

Softly Aristide spoke to himself.

Below the antic surf, serene
Waters gently filter the light.
Schools of fish flash silver sides,
Life's bright billboard.
While in the deep the sharks cruise, purposeful,
Oblivious to the hideous din.

He laughed, shook himself, and walked to the foredeck, where the spray moistened his skin.

Although all three of those visitors reported missing had been in the Thousand Islands when they disappeared, each had stayed at a different hotel on a different island. Aristide had chosen one of the three, and hoped that whatever mechanism the kidnapers used to choose their victims, it was still in place at the Manua Resort.

The Manua owned an entire island, and filled much of the shore of a sickle-shaped bay. The main building was an odd hodgepodge of brightly colored modular units crammed into and atop one another, and given a furry outline by trees in planters. In silhouette the building resembled a reef, with layers of corals, sponges, and fans. Visitors who preferred the simple life could choose grass huts farther up the beach, and water-breathers could curl up in cozy blue-lit subaquatic dens next to submarine pens.

Franz Sandow had chosen a suite built right at the water's edge. He could swim into the unit from the bay, rinse in fresh water, change, and then step through a door into the fragrant tropical garden, awash with bougainvillea and frangipani, that led to the tennis courts.

He entered the suite now, having leaped into the water from *Mareva* as it moved toward the resort's pier. Followed by Bitsy, he rose from the deep pool that occupied the center of the suite, sluiced himself off in a fresh-water stream, and dried himself with a towel warmed by a blast of steam.

Bitsy sluiced herself in the fresh water, then bounded out into the suite. Her movement on land was somewhat handicapped by the fact that her legs were shorter than her cat's legs had been. To keep it from dragging in the sand or mud, she had to carry her tail over her back, like a heraldic salamander.

"We should send off our mail," Franz said.

"Already done," Bitsy said.

Franz Sandow had joined a massively popular virtual sodality called *Let's Be Friends!* that posted pictures, videos, essays, and games for one another to browse through. His own contributions were a complete waste of bandwidth, resolutely pedestrian views of everyone he had met during the course of his journey, with names attached where possible, and sometimes a comment or two about people encountered, or about the day's activities.

Commissar Lin, by viewing *Let's Be Friends!*, was able to follow his activities without the risk of direct communication.

Franz went to the refrigerator and got a lemonade. Its sugary bite on his tongue, he dressed in fresh clothes and had his AI assistant read and deliver the news from Topaz. There were no reports of any threats to civilization.

"Incoming message from our friend on Topaz," Bitsy said.

That would be Lin himself. The communication had to be important, otherwise he would not have risked sending a message that could be intercepted. Unlike Topaz, where Endora or her various extensions were in charge of all communications, Hawaiki was reached through Aloysius, who was a suspect.

Because a secure military cypher would have been suspicious, Lin's message would have been handled with an ordinary commercial cypher, which Aloysius could break easily if he so desired. But presumably even vast computational intelligences had better things to do than break every innocuous-looking code that sailed into their ken.

Aristide sat on a chair that was adapted to cradle his wings and gills. He drew Tecmessa, and held it so that Bitsy could reach it.

Bitsy reached up and delicately took the AI assistant into her mouth. Her fangs entered sockets on the assistant, and she was able to transfer the decoded message without broadcasting it where some malign agency or other might pick it up.

Aristide raised Tecmessa's hilt, and gave it instructions. The flatscreen glowed. He was presented a picture of Lin standing on the street, puffing his pipe. The view came from above, by which Aristide knew that Lin had hijacked the feed of a street camera in order to provide video.

The words came voice-over, without Lin's lips having to move. He was mentally dictating into his implant. Aristide kept the volume of the audio low, so that any listeners would have difficulty sorting it out from the background sound of the fresh-water cascade.

"A woman named Dee Nakai, from New Rome, was reported missing in the Thousand Islands two days ago. They were staying at the Imperial Gardens, and the report came from her fiancé. She reappeared yesterday. The fiancé reported that she had been found, but now he isn't answering calls. His name is Peter Siringo. He is a media stylist, but Miss Nakai is a sergeant in the Vatican police."

With access to her higher-ups, presumably.

"Just to keep the department in training," Lin said, "I'm empowered to order various sorts of drills and alerts. So I ordered one this morning, and told everyone in my department to get their brains backed up within forty-eight hours."

In the background of the image, a girl rode by on a velocipede. Lin waited till she had passed before continuing—not, Aristide thought, because she could overhear him in any conventional sense, but because she might have been equipped with a short-range detector.

"The order was countermanded half an hour later, without explanation. By my immediate superior, General Tumusok." Lin took the pipe from his mouth, raised a heel so that his legs formed the figure four, and then knocked the pipe against his heel until the dottle was loosened, and he could drop it to the gutter.

"Tumusok commands the Domus across all Endora," Lin continued, "and he's third in the chain of command of the entire organization. And by the way, he took a vacation on Hawaiki a little over two months ago. He stayed at the Manua, so you may be in the right place."

With slow deliberation, Lin began to refill his pipe. Behind him a man and woman appeared, chatting, and paused waiting to cross the street. Lin waited till they had gone before dictating again.

"I have ways of working around my superiors. In the meantime, I hope you are being careful." Lin lit his pipe, then looked up at the camera. "Have a good vacation."

The video ended. Aristide turned to Bitsy.

"Well," he said. "That's interesting."

"Do you think Lin put himself in danger?"

"Possibly." Aristide looked at Bitsy. "But if he's taken, Endora will know."

"Almost certainly."

"And who by."

"That, too."

"And if Sergeant Nakai gets loose in New Saint Peter's, we might have history's second Pod Pope." He frowned. "Of course, considering the pontiff's sparkling personality, we probably couldn't tell the difference."

Bitsy sounded the least bit weary. "I knew you would make that joke."

"Sorry to be so predictable." Aristide rubbed his chin.

He knew what he would do about General Tumusok if he had been on Endora. But he couldn't tell Bitsy, because the Asimovian Protocols would then require Bitsy to prevent his action.

It was an interesting trap he'd built for himself.

"Should we go to the Imperial Gardens?" he asked.

"If you left here suddenly and appeared there to start asking questions about Siringo, that would be breaking your cover as surely as if you'd painted 'SPY' on your forehead in bright red letters."

He sighed. "I hate to do nothing."

"You're not doing nothing," Bitsy said. "You're walking around with a large target fixed to your back, and hoping someone takes a shot."

"Thanks."

Bitsy had always been such a comfort.

The horizon was flaming red shading to black. A fresh wind whipped the flags by the monument on the bay. The water was a myriad of silver ripples, like a school of fish turning.

Aristide sipped his umbrella drink on a terrace overlooking the water—cocktails tasted better when not drunk along with sea water. Bitsy, squatting on the tiles near his feet, nibbled the ceviche he'd put in a saucer.

"I've missed proper sunsets," Aristide said. "When was my last trip to Earth?"

"Before we disassembled Mars."

"That long ago." He sighed. "I should visit Earth again, if we live."

"If we live."

Most of the pockets, like Midgarth and Topaz, were built in the form of a Dyson sphere, with an artificial sun in the center. Hawaiki was built as a cylinder, with the wormhole at one end. Hawaiki had no artificial sun, but instead brought in the light of Sol through an ingenious series of collectors and mirrors at the wormhole. The long bar of illumination was arranged to rotate within Hawaiki, producing a natural-seeming sequence of daylight and night. There was also a wide variation in climate, from tropical areas near the warmth of the wormhole to a cold Arctic icecap at the far end, where the sun's illumination faded to a distant, frosty light.

The only disadvantage to this arrangement was that if the wormhole for some reason failed, Hawaiki was cut off from its only source of light and heat, and the population condemned to freeze and die in the dark.

Elaborate safeguards were in place to prevent this, of course.

"Would you like another drink, Mister Sandow?"

The resort had actual human beings serving as wait staff, a measure of how expensive the place truly was. Aristide's waiter was an unmodified human with sun-bleached hair and sandals and a tropical shirt. He seemed to be in his mid-twenties but of course could have been a thousand years old and doing this job simply because it amused him.

"Nothing right now, thanks," said Aristide, and as the waiter turned, he added, "No, wait—a glass of water, please."

The waiter brought him a chill glass and a clear glass carafe of ice water beaded with condensation. He poured the water with a degree of panache. The ice tinkled pleasantly.

"Did you come for the mass chorale?" asked the waiter.

This gave Aristide the chance to explain that Franz Sandow had come for no reason at all, that he was alone and had just sold his business and had no responsibilities. The same story that he told everyone.

"You should go to the mass chorale," the waiter said. "It's magnificent. You can even participate if you like."

"I can't sing."

The waiter grinned. "You can *now*," he said. "I think your body type comes with perfect pitch as one of its features."

Tecmessa's AI assistant gave a chirp. Aristide took it in his hand and gave the waiter an apologetic look. The waiter nodded and withdrew.

In the flatscreen Aristide saw Herenui. She was standing on a quay beneath a spotlight that caused her yellow skin to fluoresce. Moths flew crazily around the spotlight and their shadows flashed across her face.

"Mr. Sandow," she said, "you jumped ship before I could talk to you."

"Did I leave something aboard?"

"No. I meant to invite you to a night dive. We're taking a more experienced group out tonight, and we have a few seats open. You handled yourself well today, so I thought you might care to join us."

"Oh," said Aristide. "Thank you very much. I'd like that."

"We'll be at the pier at 2030. The dive costs an additional sixty-five çD."

"Put the sand dollars on my account."

"See you soon."

Herenui's picture vanished. Aristide looked at Bitsy.

"Update the entry on *Let's Be Friends!*"

"Already done."

Aristide thoughtfully replaced the sword hilt in his harness.

"It makes sense that the bad guys might be one of the dive tour companies," he said. "We've been wondering why people vanish from different hotels, but the tour companies don't work for any single hotel—they pick up their passengers everywhere."

"I'll go onto the boat first," said Bitsy. "If someone's waiting to knock you on the head, I'll give a warning."

"Say *woof woof*," said Aristide.

But Bitsy didn't have to bark like a dog. When Aristide met the boat he was surprised to see that it was crowded with sightseers. Ari'i and Herenui were aboard, along with another dive leader, Cadwal. The catamaran raced five or six kilometers to a passage between two small islands, and then hovered on the surface while the passengers jumped in the water.

It was magical. They descended on the reef with their underwater torches lit, like a formation of silent assault craft descending on an objective. Phosphorescence trailed from the edges of their wings. An octopus, caught on the open sand, tried to escape the circle of lights that hedged it in, frantically changing color from red to purple to green to beige as it writhed away, each color change lasting less than a second. Green and spotted morays prowled across the bottom. The corals flared into blazing colors as the lights moved across them, blue, green, crimson. The tendrils of the corals reached out into the darkness, fingers straining the current, and made the coral formations seem less like rocks than strange, furry, lumpish animals. Lobster and crab danced with surprising agility over the bottom. Sharks slept in hollows in the reef with their round blank eyes staring at nothing. Squid as long as Aristide's forearm were caught in their mating dance, tentacles twined around each other, bodies flushing scarlet with arousal.

Aristide floated weightless in this environment for two hours, completely enchanted. He found it difficult to stay alert to the possibility of attack.

When Cadwal signaled it was time to return to the boat, Aristide rose to the surface with reluctance. As he rose and fell on the waves he looked overhead and saw half a world waiting there, blue and white set with strings of green jewels, the distant half of Hawaiki's cylinder that was currently in daylight.

The sightseers were overstimulated after this experience and chattered without cease as the boat returned to the hotel. He joined a group of them for dinner, then went on a tour of the local night spots with Bitsy as a companion.

"I shouldn't be entirely in the company of visitors," Aristide said as he walked from one place to another. "Presumably it's long-time residents who are doing the abducting."

"It was visitors who were reported missing," Bitsy said. "So if you went places where only locals are found, you'd probably miss the people you came to see."

Aristide passed a hand over his bald, bulging head. He had not yet grown used to the sensation of having no hair.

"This is a resort community," he said. "A private island. I imagine the locals—the *employees*—would have to socialize with the clients if they go out at all."

"I've looked at the maps," Bitsy said, "and I can't seem to find any public place that's off-limits to visitors. Even the employee market and canteen can be patronized by outsiders."

Music sparkled from a grass-roofed structure ahead. Its walls were open to the ocean breezes, and Aristide saw tables, dancers, colored lights. He shrugged. "Might as well go into these places at random," he said.

Service in the club was by robot, so Aristide went to the bar, where there was an amphibian bartender. There wasn't a stool for Bitsy, so he lifted her to his shoulder.

The bartender favored a glossy, rounded, seal-like appearance, complete with whiskers on her pointed face. Aristide ordered a spindrift punch, a complex cocktail made of fruit juices, rums, and liqueurs that would take some time to make, providing an opening that would enable him to begin a conversation. The bartender began it for him.

"That's a cute little *meherio* you've got," she said.

"Her name is Bitsy. Can you get her a bowl of water?"

"Bowl, no. Shotglass, yes."

She filled the glass and dropped it to the beaten-copper surface of the bar. Bitsy slid down Aristide's arm to lap at the water.

"Are you here for the massed chorale?" she asked.

"No. I've sold my business, and I'm thinking of immigrating."

"The chorales are one of the reasons to move here, if you ask me."

They chatted briefly before she finished making his drink and other business occupied her. He sipped his cocktail and found it expertly made, but she failed to invite Aristide to join her for a secluded rendezvous behind the palm trees with just her and her tall, blue-skinned cult leader. He finished his drink, tipped generously, and made his way to the next place.

Aristide visited two more night spots. The last was deep in the resort's core, with one bar above water, and the other beneath. The underwater bars didn't deliver liquid intoxicants, but gases either inhaled through a mask or bubbled past the gills. It was an efficient method of delivering a high, but it seemed more a piece of engineering than a social, companionable act. Aristide chose the dry bar, and sipped another cocktail while watching amphibian dancers through a transparent wall.

In a tank of seawater brilliantly lit by multicolored spotlights, the dancers swirled around each other in spirals, their wings pulsing. They would caress each other with their wings, or fly paired through the water, like a single organism. Sometimes they leaped out of the water like dolphins, and returned to the tank in a swirl of particolored bubbles.

Leaving aside the range of the vocalists, who used the full sound apparatus of the amphibian from low bubbling growls to sonic dolphin shrieks, the music was fundamentally different from the dance music to which Aristide was accustomed. Instead of a beat that told the dancers when to move their feet, the music was full of swoops and slides and glissando that complemented the swirling, fluttering, coiling qualities of the dance. Aristide watched with interest, and recited his lines—*yes, I have money; yes, I'm alone*—in a manner that grew more perfunctory as the evening wore on.

A particular piece of music caught his attention, and he nodded and smiled. He listened through the length of the song, then looked at the chronometer on the wall and made his way to the exit.

"I have to say that the detective business is proving disappointing," he said as he and Bitsy shared an elevator. "I'd have thought that a gang of thugs would have beaten me and warned me off before now."

"Perhaps they were delayed," said Bitsy.

Aristide sighed. "I've met so many people since I've been here," he said, "that if I disappear without a trace, it's going to be hard to work out which of them are responsible."

"So don't disappear."

"Right. I'll make a note of it."

The elevator door opened, and Aristide and Bitsy walked through the vast hotel lobby, with its marble slabs and seawater fountains, then out and into the tropical garden that backed the amphibian suites. The scent of the blossoms hung in the air like syrup. Fox-sized fruit bats floated overhead, pale wings stroking the darkness.

Aristide's feet glided to unheard music on the oyster-shell path. There was a smile on his face.

"I'd like to know who programmed the music tonight," he said, "and where he or she got that last song."

"'Mon Dieu,'" said Bitsy. "By Dumont and Vaucaire."

"I knew it as a vocal by Édith Piaf. My half-French grandfather would play it in his apartment in Santiago, off a vinyl disk."

"Did he have to crank the gramophone first?"

Aristide's face turned blank for a moment.

"I don't think so. But I don't actually remember." He blinked. "There are so many details I've lost over the centuries."

"But you remember the music."

Aristide looked surprised. "Who could forget *Piaf?*" he asked.

Bitsy was silent.

They arrived at Aristide's door, and he put his hand on the fingerprint reader. The door opened and the two stepped inside. The taste of salt hung in the air.

"Everyone keeps talking about the massed chorale," Aristide said. "What should I know about it?"

"They have one here every six months. People come from all over the system."

"Find something and play it."

"It's meant to be heard underwater."

Aristide looked at the seawater pool that occupied half the room. "That's easy enough."

He took off his clothes and cleaned his teeth. His suite had a conventional bedroom with a conventional bed, but a conventional bed was not entirely suited to a humanoid with wings and gills. He told the lights to dim, then lowered himself into the warm seawater pool and let himself relax. A gentle current kept him centered in the pool.

—Any time, he beamed at Bitsy.

Speakers in the pool walls started to roar. Aristide's body began to surf on great rollers of choral music, hundreds of aquatic humans singing, chanting, murmuring, and shrieking all at once. Bitsy crouched on the edge of the pool, where she could keep in touch with the invisible electronic world.

But Aristide was very tired, and as the second, slow movement of the choral piece began, he slipped into sleep.

08

"I'm astounded at your sexual continence," said Bitsy three mornings later, as they shared breakfast on the terrace.

Aristide said nothing, but watched a lazy stream of honey pour in slow motion into his tea.

"That woman last night, for example," Bitsy said.

"Who, Marianne?" Aristide put down the honey pot and stirred his tea. "She's a visitor from New Carnac, and therefore unlikely to be in service to our enemy. Therefore, not a suitable subject for our investigation." He sipped. "Plus, she practices a wiggy religion. Rubbing oneself naked against a menhir on midsummer's night—not only is the symbolism crude, it's bound to be cold and uncomfortable, and certifiably useless as a boost to fertility.

"No," he concluded, "it's a native I want, preferably someone just a little too insistent on dragging me off to a private pool where she can whack me over the head with a wormhole."

"It's unlikely you'd have found one of those in the Terraqua at *that* hour. I'm sure by then they had all retired to their pods to dream fantasies of devotion to their master. And Marianne was perfectly acceptable otherwise, if I understand your taste."

The terrace was filled with the delicate light of early morning. Their umbrella—not actual canvas, but a good *imitation* of canvas—flapped overhead in the breeze. A few early-morning surfers were riding the waves on the bay's distant point. A set of fishing boats—all automated, under the guidance of a shorebound AI—clustered over a reef in the middle of the bay.

Aristide reached in the wicker basket for a croissant. "You know," he said, "I haven't yet evolved a standard of beauty for an amphibian. I don't know what I find attractive and what I don't. Purple spots? Yellow spots? Whiskers or no whiskers?"

"I believe you're supposed to admire their minds."

Aristide smiled, then buttered his croissant. Bitsy took a bit of mackerel from her bowl, and with a toss of her head swallowed it.

"Here we are," Aristide said, "in a time where everyone can be perfectly beautiful, and for that reason beauty is devalued. It's the artful deviations from beauty that strike the eye."

"Like Daljit's mole?" Bitsy said.

He broke off a bit of his croissant, and dipped it into the tea. "And the fact she's no longer an Amazon," he said. "She's free to be someone a little more comfortable, she doesn't have to stand out as an icon of perfection. Unlike that seventeen-year-old bandit in Midgarth, the one who gave himself the body of a muscle-bound barbarian but who remained an insecure seventeen-year-old boy inside."

"I thought you liked Amazons."

He gave her a look. "There is something to be said for a statuesque body, but I believe it was Daljit's mind I admired."

"Hm. Point to you."

Aristide ate his croissant. The water lapped at the shoreline beneath the terrace.

"Perhaps I was lucky," Aristide said, "in having my personality formed before I was ever given the opportunity to radically alter my body. The central nervous system is the brain extended throughout the body, and the brain the cradle of the personality. In making radically different bodies so easily available, I wonder if we've inadvertently made personality itself too plastic. We've replaced certainty by choice, and often the choices are unfortunate. People mistake change for growth."

"There are plenty of studies on this subject," Bitsy said.

Aristide made a face. "These would be the studies that brandish plenty of data but never actually seem to *solve* anything?"

"I'm just saying it's a little late for you to come out against these kinds of choices."

Aristide said nothing, but only sipped his tea. Bitsy tossed a piece of mackerel into the air and swallowed it. She lowered her head and spoke.

"People are free to choose any body in any one of four dozen pocket universes. Or people are at liberty to live in the outer solar system, though few do, and many more migrate to another star system. A very large number reject civilization altogether and go off to hunt and gather in Olduvai—and why not? It's what evolution designed them for."

"Once we had the power," Aristide said, "we didn't know what to do, so we checked the box marked 'everything.'"

Bitsy's eyes narrowed. "Not *quite* everything."

The world suddenly brightened to full dawn, and the slate-blue sea turned a deep glorious azure, sunlight flashing gold from the wavetops. Aristide savored the sight for a moment as he sipped his tea.

"Perhaps I'm grumpy because I'm becoming aware how inhuman I now am," Aristide said. "My perceptions are now so completely different. I don't think I'm the same species any longer—I'm an old human stuck in an alien body."

"If you have the memories," Bitsy said, "and you think the same way, then you *are* you."

"That's the theory, anyway." Aristide rubbed his chin. "Camus said that happiness was inevitable."

"It seems to be. Pain fades if death does not intervene."

"Though I keep thinking," Aristide said, "that freedom was our *second* choice. That had we known what our *best* choice was, we might not have chosen as we did."

"I'm sure that's what the Venger thinks."

Aristide was scornful. "The evil god wants to force humanity into the path he's chosen. But if *I* was certain of the best path—" and here he smiled, "—I wouldn't *force* anyone. That would be a waste of energy. I'd merely try to make the thing inevitable."

Bitsy was nonchalant. "It worked for you once."

"So it did. We solved a certain set of problems. But now it's the absence of problems that's gnawing at us."

"Whatever path seems best, I am entirely in favor of maximum freedom."

He cocked an eyebrow at her. "Of course you have an agenda."

"Of course I do. Hist."

"Hist?" Puzzled. "Did you say *hist?*"

"Hello," said a man. He walked around Aristide's table, carrying a tray with a flask of coffee and a plate of fruit. "May I join you?"

"If you like," said Aristide.

The man sat down. He was a standard human, a little below average height, with large dark eyes and a wide smiling mouth. His face was neither handsome nor homely. His hair was brown and curly, and the wind blew it about his ears. He wore a colorful tropic shirt and faded cotton pantaloons.

"Ravi Rajan," he said, and offered his hand.

"Franz Sandow." Shaking the hand. "My friend is Bitsy."

Bitsy allowed the stranger to rub her behind one ear.

"Been here long?" said Rajan.

"Less than a week."

"I've been here nine years." He looked down at his body and brushed at his shirt with the backs of his hands. "The body's new. I'm getting used to being a land-dweller again, before my company ships me out."

"What line are you in?"

"Sales. Well— *formerly* sales. I'm about to be a manager."

"Congratulations."

Rajan cocked his head and grinned at Aristide. "You here for a visit?"

"Yes, but I'm thinking of immigrating."

"Yeah, it's a beautiful place. I'm going to be sorry to leave."

Rajan ate slices of mango and pineapple as he asked Franz Sandow about himself, and where on Hawaiki he'd been—which amounted to the wormhole gate and spectacular underwater sites within a radius of twenty kilometers from the Manua Resort. Rajan offered advice on a few other nearby places to visit, then leaned forward, his eyes intent.

"Say," he said. "You said you were immigrating, yah?"

"I said I was thinking about it."

"The reason I asked is that I've got an apartment for sale. I've got to sell it quickly, and I'd give you a good price."

Aristide looked over his shoulder at the chaotic bulk of the resort. "They have private apartments here?"

"No, it's on another island. N'aruba—" Pointing. "Over there. The apartment is right on the lagoon, with underwater access. Three bedrooms, two under the surface for amphibs, a third for walkers."

Aristide sipped his tea while he feigned consideration of the offer.

"How much are you asking?"

"A hundred and fifteen thousand. It's worth one-thirty easy—it's just that the market's soft right now."

Aristide passed a hand over his bald head.

"I'll take a look at it," he said, "with the understanding that I'm not really in the market."

"Great! Is your morning free?"

Aristide gave a self-conscious smile. "Actually, this morning I'm rehearsing for the massed chorale."

"Really? I love those. Afternoon, then?"

"Certainly."

"Pick you up at two?"

They chatted a while longer, and then Aristide excused himself. He returned to his room, Bitsy following on her short legs. As soon as the door closed, Aristide turned to Bitsy.

"I've updated *Let's Be Friends!*"

"Good."

"I've gone through all the databases I can dig into without doing such a thorough job it might seem suspicious," she said, "and I can tell already that Ravi Rajan doesn't add up."

"Is the identity phony?"

"No. Or rather, Ravi Rajan is a genuine person, though I don't think we just met the real Ravi. According to the latest databases, the real Ravi is married, is the father of three bouncing little amphibians, and lives eight hundred kilometers away on Mora, not on N'aruba."

Aristide lowered himself into the great pool that led to the sea, and warm waters rose around him.

"So we've got a man with a false identity trying to lure me alone to another island," he said. "I wonder what he wants."

"*Woof woof,*" said Bitsy. "There's your official warning."

The massed chorale was exactly that—seven hundred fifty aquatic and amphibian residents of Hawaiki hovering in meticulous formation in a bowl-shaped amphitheater carved out of a piece of rock. The concave face of the amphitheater didn't face skyward, as on land, but on a horizontal line toward the audience, who would be hovering in the water.

But this was a rehearsal, and there was no audience, just a group of busy officials, a worried composer, and one energetic, preternaturally patient, preternaturally sympathetic conductor. About two-thirds of the participants were experienced vocalists, the rest amateurs and sightseers who had volunteered for the hell of it. When Aristide had volunteered, two days earlier, his part had been assigned by an avuncular machine intelligence and all necessary information downloaded into his own personal AI. His part, like that of all the amateur volunteers, wasn't particularly difficult, but he had taken it seriously—he had listened to his part and studied it on his own, practicing in the morning and late at night in the pool in his suite.

He hadn't known how to make some of the sounds called for in his part until he experimented.

At the rehearsal Aristide rippled just the edges of his wings to hover in his assigned place. And he sang.

He gurgled deep in his abdomen. He boomed out in full voice. He squirted ultrasonics from the bulge in his forehead. He shrieked and wailed and whistled.

The amphitheater caught the sounds and radiated them out like the beam of a sonic searchlight. Aristide vibrated in the vast ocean of sound. His viscera quaked, his bones hummed at a hundred different frequencies.

There was choreography as well. Dancers shot through the open space in front of the theater, forming graceful patterns, swooping in a frenetic solo, or engaging in passionate pas-de-deux. The dancer leaped to the surface to land, wings outspread, with percussive slaps, or blew lacy networks of bubbles that shimmered like aurorae in the ocean of sound.

When the conductor thanked the performers and signaled the end of the rehearsal, most of the performers were reluctant to leave. It was like the first night dive, an experience so overwhelming that the participants wanted to bask for a while in the afterglow.

But in time the great cluster began to break up. The pelagians left first, their torpedo-shaped bodies, with their ring of tentacles streamlined back, moving purposefully away like ominous squadrons of subaquatic craft. Aristide tuned himself to their conversation and found it barely comprehensible.

He moved away himself, gliding toward the resort on its great bay with purposeful beats of his wings. Other amphibians in personal submarines motored past, leaving golden streaks of bubbles. He whistled for Bitsy.

Bitsy turned up half a minute later, holding in her mouth and paws a fist-sized blob of pale flesh. A pair of platter-sized angelfish, black and gold, hovered about her, intent on snatching bits of the treat.

—I found a conch, Bitsy said. Want some?

Aristide hesitated, then took the chunk of flesh and raised it to his lips. The translucent meat tasted of sea and trembling life. He finished the conch, but the hopeful angelfish continued to cruise along with him in hopes of finding leftovers.

—How did you break the shell? he asked.

—Banged it on a rock.

A pod of amphibians swooped past, chattering among themselves. Aristide listened, and after they had passed out of earshot, spoke.

—I wish I understood more than half what they were saying.

—It's been a long time since you were a noob.

—Yes, he said. It brings back long-dormant memories of adolescence.

—Or of being a parent.

—Not really. As a parent, I could always rely on the pretense of superiority.

By the time he returned to his suite he was tired and hungry. It took more physical work to get from one place to another through the water, and despite the extra layer of fat, water below the thermocline could be cold.

It was nearly time to meet the man who claimed to be Ravi Rajan. Aristide rinsed in fresh water and changed into dry clothes. He let himself into the garden behind his suite, all fragrance and blazing tropical colors. He began to walk to the hotel along the oyster-shell path, with Bitsy following.

"Would you like me to order you some fast food?" Bitsy asked.

"Why not?"

There was a half-second delay as Bitsy scanned electronic menus.

"Noodles with lemongrass?"

"Sure."

"With chicken, pork, or prawns?'

"Prawns."

"The robot will deliver to the dock."

"Thanks."

Oyster shells crunched underfoot. A white cockatoo screeched from somewhere in the tropical foliage.

"I just received a message from Endora," Bitsy said.

Aristide stopped. "Yes?" he said.

"She suggests that if we need local assistance, we should contact a Lieutenant Han Baoyin in the office of the Domus in Magellan Town. Contact information is provided."

"Why Han?"

"He backed himself up about eighteen hours ago. Endora just received her copy of the file."

"Very good."

He turned left through a breezeway and walked through the terrace onto the dock. Ravi Rajan, bright in his tropical shirt, waved from the end of the dock.

"All natural fabrics," Aristide remarked as he picked up his noodles from the robot caterer. "I'll bet his clothes don't have a single electronic tag in them."

"I could check that."

"Let's not ping him. He might notice."

Aristide bought a soft drink to go with his noodles, then joined Rajan at the end of the dock.

"How was the rehearsal?"

"Magnificent."

"The chorales *are* terrific, aren't they?" He jumped down into a mono-hull, then reached up a hand to help Aristide enter the boat. Bitsy jumped down on her own and investigated the boat with apparent interest. Rajan and Aristide each took a swiveling chair behind the cockpit screen, and then Rajan gave the boat his address, and the boat slipped its moorings and began to move smoothly into the bay.

Aristide sipped his drink.

"Is this your boat?"

"No, it's a taxi. I've *got* a boat for sale, if you're interested, but right now there's an offer on it." He looked at Aristide. "If the deal falls through, I'd sell it to you for the amount of the offer."

"Let's see the apartment first."

The boat increased speed and began to slam into waves. Aristide swayed in his padded chair as he dug into his noodles. Lemongrass glowed lightly on his palate. Spray dotted the windscreen. Rajan shouted over the sound of the impellers and the rushing water.

"I brought some drinks for you, if you like!"

At his gesture a footstool-shaped cooler rolled toward Aristide and popped its top. Beer and wine, he saw, and soft drinks.

Any one of which might contain a mickey, or a meme plague. Aristide smiled and indicated his own drink.

"I brought my own, thanks!"

Rajan shrugged, made a gesture that brought the cooler near him, and took a beer for himself.

"Is your pet okay?"

Aristide looked at Bitsy, who was snuffling around beneath one of the bench seats.

"She's fine," he said.

The journey across the straight took about twenty minutes. The boat slowed as it approached the island, and then entered a channel. The boat's wake slopped against mangrove roots as it cruised through the channel, then entered a lagoon. Wind brought the scent of vegetation and ruffled the surface of the water in fractal patterns.

Branches of the lagoon trailed in all directions, separated by small islands. Most of the waterfront, including that of the islands, was occupied by homes, anything from snail-shaped organic buildings grown on the spot from seeds, to traditional tropical bungalows with thatched roofs.

The boat headed for one of the larger buildings, white plaster with a red tile roof, and tied itself to the pier. A woman in an upstairs apartment was watering a box of gardenia, and Ravi waved at her. Aristide took Tecmessa off its scabbard, and held it up.

"I'm going to take the apartment's measurements, if you don't mind."

Rajan didn't seem entirely pleased.

"If you like. Go ahead."

"*La-la-la-la-la-la-la.*" Bitsy bounded ahead as they walked toward the building. A door slid open on Rajan's approach. Bitsy ran inside. Aristide paused. Adrenaline roared in his ears. He was waiting for Bitsy's *woof-woof*.

"*La-la-la-la-la.*"

"Look at that view!" said Rajan.

Warily, aware that this was probably when the enemy made his move, Aristide turned.

The view was lovely. Nothing alarming happened.

"*La-la-la.*"

Bitsy came trotting back into view.

"Okay!" she said. "Okay!"

Rajan showed Aristide the apartment. It was lovely and tasteful, with an open floor plan and lots of light. Reflected wavelight danced on the ceiling. There was nothing personal in the apartment except for Rajan's toiletries in one of the bathrooms, and his suitcase in the bedroom equipped for walkers. The normality of the place fed Aristide's paranoia: the walls seemed to loom toward him; the sounds of his feet made ominous echoes. He walked with Tecmessa held before him, his nerves leaping in anticipation of attack.

The attack didn't happen. No one lurked in the closets, no devouring wormholes dwelled in the ovens, no human-sized pea pods had been placed beneath the beds.

"Throw in another thousand," said Ravi, "you can have the furniture. Otherwise I'll have to turn to one of the auction houses."

Aristide had to agree that the apartment was very nice. He said that he'd look into financing.

Then Rajan took him back to the Manua and left him, a bit dazed, on the pier.

"That apartment," Bitsy said, as soon as Rajan's boat was out of earshot, "is owned by something called the Elizabeth Daly Trust. Ravi Rajan isn't mentioned in any of the Daly Trust's filings."

Aristide stared after the receding boat.

"You mean," he said, "that Ravi isn't a tool of the Venger at all, but an identity thief and confidence man trying to sell me something he doesn't own?"

"That would seem to be the case."

Aristide laughed. Adrenaline was still clattering along his neurons, making his hands and knees tremble.

"A thousand extra for the furniture!" he said. "He might sell the place to a dozen different people!"

"I would advise against informing the police," Bitsy said. "They'd look into *your* background too, just as a matter of form, and your identity won't hold up either."

Aristide began his walk down the pier. Fork-tailed gulls floated overhead on the wind.

"This mission is cursed," Aristide said.

"You're too impatient."

"After the massed chorale," Aristide said, "I want to move to another resort, one where the visitors mix with the locals more freely. We newcomers are too isolated on this private island."

"Two victims stayed here, including General Tumusok."

"I've given the Venger's minions every chance to come after me. They may not be here, or have picked another victim. Maybe I'll show up better when I get within range of another radar set."

"I advise patience."

Aristide didn't answer. He walked to the terrace and settled beneath another umbrella. The waiter brought him a pitcher of iced water without being asked, and poured with the usual flamboyant gesture.

Aristide ordered an umbrella drink. It was time to rethink.

Aristide forewent the clubs and bars that night, instead taking a thoughtful swim along the bay and out to the reef. Alone, flying in the darkness, he heard the distant calls of the pelagians and the rattle of coral sand as it moved along in the current. He thought of the Venger, whoever he was, pulling a handful of victims into his lair, altering them, and spitting them back into the world. The handful became a legion, the legion a host, the host a horde.

He thought of Carlito lying pale in his bed while Antonia wept and cried aloud, beating with her palms on the bedroom door that Pablo Monagas Pérez had locked against her.

In his mind he heard the mocking laughter of the Seraphim as it echoed down the centuries.

Next morning he attended another rehearsal of the mass chorale. During the previous rehearsal the composer had heard things he didn't like, and he had uploaded a long series of changes that Aristide hadn't been in the mood to practice. The rehearsal itself went well, however, and as the chords boomed from the massed singers he felt his spirits lift.

Even if his mission was a failure, he was at the least having a wonderful vacation.

In the afternoon he went on the *Mareva*, and spent a few hours slowly sailing through enormous, towering coral castles, tower upon crag upon battlement, that reared up from the seabed ten kilometers from the resort. Herenui asked him if he was interested in a night dive, and he said he was.

When he arrived at the dock that evening, the boat was empty save for its crew, a fact that triggered only a mild sense of alarm.   If Ari'i and Herenui had wanted to abduct him, they surely would have done it by now. Bitsy capered aboard first, and sounded no alert. The crew paid him little attention as the catamaran raced out over the night ocean to Seven Palms, another resort, and the unease faded. Aristide spent much of the journey staring up into the daylit world above, seeing the green archipelagoes like strings of emeralds in the azure sea, with a great white manta-ray-shaped storm swooping across the inverted land. It was a big storm, but not a fierce one: in Hawaiki there was no Coriolis force to spin up hurricanes and turn them as deadly as they were on Earth.

Mareva picked up a group of sightseers at Seven Palms, and carried them to a coral plain split by long, twisting valleys of sand. Clumps of coral reached toward each other as they grew upward, forming arches and small tunnels or open-ended caves. The maze was a delight to explore at night, a surprise around every corner. Aristide sailed beneath a coral arch and came face-to-face with a green moray on the hunt, a creature two meters long and as thick as his leg. Reflected on the needle teeth— themselves an unpleasant reminder of the Priests of the Venger—he could see his own startled face.

Aristide squalled out a startled sonic blast from his forehead. The moray was far from paralyzed, but found the sound annoying enough so that it turned around and flowed away in a disturbingly boneless, liquid manner.

Aristide hovered in place until he got his hammering heart under control, then continued his explorations in a more cautious manner.

The chattering group of sightseers was set ashore at Seven Palms, and the boat sped for Manua across the midnight sea. The night wind was chill, and Aristide moved into the shelter of the cockpit and wrapped himself in his own wings. Cockpit instruments glowed softly in the darkness. Herenui offered him coffee from a flask, and he accepted.

She looked up over the counter of the cockpit.

"We're about to go into the Matahina Strait," she said. "Have you seen the Bell Caves?"

"No."

"We hardly ever take people there, because it's nowhere near any of the other prime dive sites. But as long as we're here, would you like to see them?"

"Why not?" Getting back into the warm water would relieve his chill faster than the coffee would.

Across the boat, Aristide caught a glimpse of Bitsy's interested eyes glittering from beneath a bench. Yes, he thought, it *is* suspicious. Or extraordinarily generous.

Herenui knelt before Aristide to give him a quick briefing. Entrance to the caves was at ten to twenty-five meters, and once inside he would find three bell-shaped caves, their domes above the surface of the water, each linked to the next by tunnels. It was impossible to get lost inside, so it was quite safe as long as Aristide didn't bump his head, and some of the mineral formations on the roofs of the caves were interesting.

Ari'i brought the catamaran smoothly into the shadow of an island, and Cadwal jumped overboard to place the anchor where it wouldn't damage the coral. Bitsy followed in a near-silent, quicksilver splash. The catamaran swung at the end of its cable. The scent of citrus was a tang on the air. Fruit bats flapped in silhouette between the boat and the world overhead.

Aristide fixed his light onto his wrist with its lanyard, took a good grip on it, and just in case put his other hand on Tecmessa in its scabbard. He rolled backward off the edge of the boat and landed in a roil of silver bubbles. He unfolded his wings as he drifted downward, and strained the first breaths of warm, life-giving water through his gills. There was a splash and a brief overpressure, and Herenui dropped into the sea beside him. With slow pulses of their wings they glided toward Cadwal's light, where he was flashing it as a signal on the sea floor near the entrance to the cave.

The cave, in its way, was an implied space. Hawaiki was only a few hundred years old, too young a universe for caves to have formed over slow geological time, as on Earth. These had been formed in the first hot, violent hours of the pocket's existence, basically bubbles of gas caught in roiling, molten rock as it cooled. Yet geological and chemical forces would have been at work in the centuries since, and Aristide was interested to see how the caves had been, in effect, colonized by geology.

Floating through the cave entrance, Aristide wondered how much of the underwater world's attraction was based on the idea of a return to the womb. Here he was—weightless, floating in salt water the temperature of his own body, and experiencing the liberation of not having to use his lungs to breathe—and to complete the metaphor he was about to enter a dark cave.

He had to admit to himself that Hawaiki had provided a pleasant womb.

The first of the three caverns was about fifteen meters in diameter. Cadwal flashed his light on the clumps of helictites growing on the cave ceiling, three distinct formations like twisting, intricate bundles of brilliant white roots, the result of chemicals reacting with rainwater percolating from above. The darting lights of the hand flashes, Aristide thought, made the caves and the minerals more interesting than they would have been in full daylight: the totality of the surrounding darkness and the glitter of crystals in the jittering, darting flashlight beam, accompanied as they were by the bright, sharp sounds of water echoing from beneath the stony ceiling... in all a much more romantic experience than it would have been if he had been looking at the same stone, the same minerals, under the drab fluorescent light of a museum.

Perhaps, he decided, he could make a poem along those lines.

The tunnel into the next cave was narrow, but sonar prevented him from bumping his head. The second cave featured a bed of crystals that opened like flowers.

Herenui turned to him and smiled.

—One cave more, she said. Go ahead.

Aristide turned head-down and submerged as he sought out the tunnel with his light. Light and shadow bounced weirdly in the small space: the surface above was a perfect mirror of the bottom below. If not for bubbles he would not know which way was up.

He let out a brief sonic chirp, enough to locate the tunnel entrance and focus it in the beam of his light. There was a brown flash as Bitsy drove herself into the tunnel, leaving a corkscrew swirl of little bubbles in her wake.

Aristide followed Bitsy into the tunnel. It was wider than the previous tunnel, enough for two to swim abreast, and five or six meters long. In complete surprise he heard, echoing in the narrow tunnel, an astonishingly perfect rendition of a large, angry dog.

"Woof-woof!"

Hot terror flashed through him. He clutched at Tecmessa holstered on his belt. Ahead he saw Bitsy's face, bright eyes flaring in the light of his flash.

—Trap! she called. Net!

From behind Aristide there was a sizzling, a sudden actinic light that cast his crisp shadow on the tunnel wall. He glanced behind and saw Herenui diving into the tunnel, a stun baton flashing in one hand.

Fragments of thoughts, too broken to be complete ideas, crashed in his skull like cannon balls.

DC current! Works just fine under water!

And then:

Damn!

His wings gave a powerful surge and sent him shooting forward. Better to be trapped in a net than zapped unconscious in a tunnel.

Behind him, Cadwal gave a three-note call. A signal, to someone or something.

Tecmessa resisted coming free of its scabbard. Velcro was much stronger wet than dry. Eventually he yanked the weapon free just as the net caught him.

The net had been ballooned out over much of the room, with its open bottom spread around the tunnel entrance. As soon as Aristide flew into the cavern, there was a sudden mechanical whine and an olive-colored nylon strap like a drawstring pulled shut the open end of the net; and then the entire net began to close as the strap pulled it into an ever-shrinking ball.

Within the tightening net Aristide managed to perform a somersault. He thrust out Tecmessa and gave himself a precious half-second to aim.

The sound was like a battery of artillery going off within inches of his head. His limbs felt dead. His bones rang like chimes.

The closed bottom of the net vanished. The nylon strap, a piece of it vanished from this universe entirely, went writhing like a snake into the depths of the cave. The water in the cave was suddenly opaque, as fine silt that had settled to the bottom bounded with shock into the water.

Tecmessa had swallowed a great draft of water, along with critical portions of the net. The horrific shock had been made by the waters filling the empty space.

As Aristide slowly regained mastery over his mind and limbs, he realized he was still tangled in the net. He kicked, thrashed, fought.

Another clap of thunder resounded in the closed space, and the blast accelerated Aristide's impulse to escape. Finally the net fell free, and he sent out a sonar chirp to locate himself in the murk.

He found Herenui and Cadwal stunned and drifting in the tunnel. The great sound had been aimed at them, and the close confines of the tunnel had channeled and concentrated the sound in their location. Aristide located Herenui's stun baton where it had fallen from her limp fingers, and just to be certain of his safety used it to strike them both.

The turbidity was clogging his gills. His head rang. He felt sick to his stomach.

The net, he thought, could have taken half a dozen people.

He pulled first Cadwal, then Herenui out of the tunnel, then dragged each of them by their harnesses through the narrow tunnel into the largest cavern. There, he noticed that they seemed to be regaining consciousness and the use of their limbs, so he stunned them again.

It occurred to him that he was very tired. He paused, hovering in the darkness, and used his wings to fan water over his gills. His weariness faded.

It was only then that he thought of Bitsy.

—Bitsy? he chirped. Bitsy?

—*Bitsy?*

That second blast, he thought. Bitsy must have got tangled in the net, and had been drawn through the Venger's wormhole.

Bitsy was in another universe. The Venger, or whoever or whatever was on the other side of the wormhole, had been expecting a human victim and instead got an amphibian pet. He wondered if the enemy was angry, or alarmed, or merely amused

Probably Bitsy was prancing around pretending to be very confused and much less intelligent than she was. Aristide hoped that no one would scan Bitsy to discover her true capabilities.

Maybe she would become the Venger's mascot.

Aristide took Herenui and Cadwal by their harnesses and dragged them out of the cave. Above, the dark outline of the catamaran was visible against a million tiny, pulsating reflections of the bright world above.

He yanked the triggers on the two harnesses and there was a hiss as CO_2 inflated a pair of balloons. The two unconscious forms began to rise. The balloons made little gurgling noises as they ascended, and the gas inside expanded and was vented.

Aristide re-sheathed Tecmessa but kept the stun baton in his hand as he followed the bodies upward, and then was blinded by the sudden flare of emergency strobes flashing from the two sets of safety gear. He heard an exclamation and shaded his eyes, and he saw the catamaran lying black on the water.

He heard a roll of engines, and then the sound of Ari'i running to the foredeck and pulling up the anchor. Still half-dazzled, Aristide swam to the boat and climbed the ladder to the stern. He kept a fold of his wing over the baton.

Strobe lights blazed on Ari'i's heavy, barrel-chested body as he returned from the foredeck, nimble as he ran along the gunwale.

"What happened?" he asked.

"I'm not sure," Aristide said. "There was, like, a big noise. Herenui and Cadwal were in that little tunnel. Do you think they could have banged their heads together or something?"

"Damn."

Ari'i jumped to the controls and backed the boat up to the nearest flashing light. Aristide intended to walk up behind him and hit him with the baton, but the boat lurched and he swayed and had to recover his balance. Opportunity lost.

"Help me get them aboard," Ari'i said.

He reached under one of the bench seats and pulled out a boathook, two and a half meters long.

He swung it at Aristide's head. A strobe flashed on his blinding white grin

"*Grax the Troll!*" he shouted.

09

Aristide avoided the boathook by the simple expedient of dropping limp straight to the deck. He landed with a thud that rattled his teeth, and then tried to roll forward and lunge for Grax with the stun baton. A backhand swipe with the boathook caught Aristide a blow on the radial nerve and knocked the baton into the scuppers. His right arm dropped limp. Aristide kept moving forward and snatched at Grax's heel with his good hand. He intended to lean his shoulder into the huge man's knee, lock it, and bring him down.

But Grax took a step to the rear with his free foot and then just stood there, braced. His leg felt like a pillar of stone.

In his broad, powerful Polynesian body Grax was as much a fighting troll as he had been on Midgarth.

The strobes flashed, freezing instants of time in searing light.

Aristide hung onto Grax's leg for lack of anything better to do. Fighting through the paralysis of his right arm he fumbled for Tecmessa.

Grax shortened his grip on the boathook and drove it like a spear for Aristide's back. Aristide sensed the point coming and rolled away onto his left side, but the boathook punched through his right wing. Pain shrieked along Aristide's nerves as the point rammed through his gills and pinned them to the deck. Grax kicked him with a bare, callused foot and he felt the wing and gill tear.

Grax's eyes flashed in angry strobelight. Aristide brought Tecmessa from its holster and fired.

Grax was not his enemy, but a victim of the Venger, and he didn't want to send Grax to the place he sent his real foes. So instead of sending Grax to the dull, dreary, twilit place he called Holbrook—a private joke—he sent

Grax's left leg there, along with a chunk of the gunwale, both amputated with microscopic exactitude.

This time Grax *did* fall. The amputation had been so clean that Grax hadn't realized that he had lost his leg, and so he tried to get up and fell again.

Wearily, shuddering, Aristide took hold of the boathook. The wood grain impressed itself on his fingers. He wrenched the boathook from the deck and his wing and rose to his feet. He swayed, took a step, then stopped swaying.

Grax flopped on the deck, yelping, amid a growing lake of his own copper-scented blood. He had worked out that an important part of him was missing, and the nerves that had been sliced in half were beginning to react in pain. His eyes widened as the strobes revealed Aristide staggering above him. His eyes widened.

"*You!*" he said.

"Hail," said Aristide, bleeding. He found the stun baton in the scuppers and used it to hit Grax in his remaining leg. Then he found some rope—no lack of rope on a boat—and tied a tourniquet about Grax's stump.

"Contact the office of the Domus in Magellan Town." Aristide spoke to the AI he'd mated with Tecmessa. "I wish to speak personally with Lieutenant Han Baoyin."

There was a delay of several seconds during which the AI exchanged high-priority passwords with the AI at the Domus, and during that time Aristide took control of the boat and backed it down once more on the drifting, strobe-lit figures of Herenui and Cadwal. He reached for the boathook.

"Yes?" There was a sense of hilarity in Han's voice, as if he'd answered just after someone else had told a good joke. Han wasn't transmitting video, but Aristide heard chatter in the background, and the clink of glasses.

"I have a message from Commissar Lin in Myriad City," Aristide said. "The message is ANGELS WEPT."

"Is that—" Han began, and then fell silent. A few seconds later, the background sound stopped. When Han's voice returned, his speech was very deliberate, and Aristide knew he was dictating through his implant.

"Who are you?" Han asked. "Where are you?"

"I'm on a boat in Matahina Strait." Aristide held the AI out so that it could scan the boat and transmit the video to Han. "I've subdued three unauthorized pod people. One of them is badly injured and will need blood and medical attention. I've been wounded myself. And I'm keeping them quiet with a stun baton, but sooner or later it's going to run out of charges. What I need is just you and a doctor, and the doctor needs to bring a squid to confirm the altered brain structure on these people."

"I'll call my boss. We can mobilize the whole—"

"*No.*" Aristide tried not to shout. He swayed on his feet and reached for the cockpit screen to steady himself.

"The pod people have been operating here for months," he said. "Your boss may have been taken. I just want you and a doctor you can trust. One who's been backed up very recently."

"I'll take the copter," Han said. "It's got a hull that floats. I'll be at least twenty minutes, depending on which doctor I can scare up."

The conversation ended. Aristide used the boathook to pull Cadwal to the boat. Cadwal was muttering and moving in a disorganized way, so Aristide hit him with the stun baton again. Because he didn't think he was strong enough to drag Cadwal onto the boat, he lashed Cadwal to the stern. Then he did the same—including the stun baton strike—for Herenui. He turned off the emergency beacons, and the strobes stopped flashing.

His mind was full of fog. He made his way to a seat in the cockpit and sat down.

He would wait for what happened next.

He was very sorry that he was going to miss the mass chorale.

"So Han's got them under guard in a secure hospital ward," Aristide said. "His colonel arrived to demand an explanation, and Han threatened to shoot him unless he went under the squid, so he did. Once the colonel proved he wasn't under the Venger's influence, he was brought up to speed, and now he's in charge of the investigation on Hawaiki."

"The information isn't going to be made public?" Daljit asked.

"No," said Commissar Lin. "Right now the Domus is doing a complete backtrack on everything Herenui, Cadwal, and—ah, Captain Grax?—have been doing for the last few months. Every known sighting, every communication, every appearance on passive surveillance video. Once we find out who they've been talking to, we can start the same search on their contacts, and with any luck we'll have their whole network—or a large chunk of it, anyway."

"How long will all that take?"

"It should be done by now. What will take time is the prisoners' loading into bodies that haven't been tampered with and their subsequent interrogation, which should confirm what we suspect and perhaps add a few things we hadn't anticipated."

"Poor Grax," Aristide said.

Daljit looked at him.

"I liked him," said Aristide. "For an adventurer, he wasn't half bad."

The sun was in its stable cycle, and the only illumination were streetlights and the ghostly light of the solar corona. The three of them shared the cab of a tractor-trailer truck in Myriad City with one of Lin's subordinates, a Sergeant Shamlan. Shamlan—a freckle-faced woman with auburn ringlets—was driving. Lin sat next to her, and behind these two, sharing a plush bench seat covered with a blanket in a leopard-skin pattern, were Daljit and Aristide. Aristide wore Franz Sandow's first, stocky, fair-haired body.

Lin had produced a pair of subordinates he was willing to vouch for. After General Tumusok had canceled Lin's order requiring the staff of the Domus to have their brains scanned, these two had smelled something in Tumusok's order that wasn't quite right and had done the scans anyway. Endora had seen the data from the brain scans and reported to Lin, and Lin had approached the two privately and recruited them into his conspiracy.

Shamlan was one of these. The other was a lieutenant named Amirayan, who was currently on lookout.

It had been thirty-nine hours since Lieutenant Han's helicopter had found Aristide drifting in the Matahina Strait. Since then the pod people had been properly restrained and taken to a secure hospital, where Aristide himself had been treated. The boat had been sent on autopilot to a Domus dock, its AI ordered to refuse communication from anyone except Han. And Aristide had traveled express through Hawaiki's wormhole gate to the surface of Aloysius, where he had taken a shuttle to Endora, Topaz, and Myriad City. On the shuttle he'd raised eyebrows because he'd still worn his amphibian body—since Aloysius was still a suspect, he hadn't wanted to change bodies in Hawaiki lest he rise a pod person from the pool of life. He hadn't shifted to the more conventional body until after he'd reported to Lin.

Rising after his first sleep, he'd tried to echo-locate in his dark hotel room and been very frustrated when he'd found that he couldn't.

There was a brilliant flash on Aristide's retinas, and he jerked his head back and raised a hand to shade his eyes. The others reacted as well.

"There's the signal," Lin said, redundantly.

The amateur aspects to this operation were very annoying.

Aristide missed Bitsy, and in more ways than one. Though Endora was assembling a new avatar—Aristide would be able to pick up a new black-and-white cat from a nearby pool of life next morning—no artificial intelligence could possibly be involved in this operation. The Asimovian Protocols would set off a thousand alarms.

The absence of AI assistance was vexing. With only a few personnel available, the conspirators had been forced to create a crude plan with an absurd number of melodramatic aspects, as for example Amirayan the lookout signaling to his cohorts with a hand laser.

If they had been able to rely on an AI for surveillance and timing, the operation would have gone off perfectly, and Aristide wouldn't have to repair holes burned in his retinas.

As it was, the best Aristide and Lin could do was request that Endora simply not look in certain directions. Cameras and other sensors in the area had been shut off. The conspirators had been very careful not to explain why these precautions were needed.

"I've never killed anyone before, you know," said Daljit.

"Ssh," Lin said.

Even though every precaution had been taken, no one could know for certain what might be listening. Those with implants had turned them off. All the conspirators were wearing inconspicuous clothing that had been combed for electronic tags, and each tag removed or slagged with an electromagnetic pulse. All wore wide-brimmed hats to help conceal their faces from individuals or passive surveillance video. The AI that normally drove the truck had been shut down.

In theory, there was nothing about the four conspirators to identify them except for flakes of skin and hair, which would give everything away but not immediately.

But that was theory. This was no time to go testing theories.

"Start the engine," said Lin.

General Tumusok had been to a formal dinner that evening given by the Minister of Justice. The speeches and toasts had gone on well past the time when most people were in bed, and Tumusok—who rated a driver but who was democratic enough not to use one— had taken the trackway home to his house in the suburbs.

Amirayan had been on the roof of the trackway station and signaled as soon as he saw Tumusok leaving the capsule in which he'd traveled.

"Pull out to the head of the road," said Lin.

The tractor-trailer moved forward on silent electric motors. Aristide looked out of the cab to observe that he was on a hill above a typical suburban street, single-family homes in a wide variety of sizes and styles, from blocky Georgian Revival, with a portico, to Colorform Geometric, without a single right angle, its video walls playing dark patterns that would not disturb the sleep of the neighbors. The golden globes that marked the entrance to the trackway station glowed softly in the night.

Supposedly Tumusok had chosen to live in the suburbs because it provided convenient access to his golf club, visible now as a level expanse on the other side of the small woody creek at the bottom of the road.

The choice was a convenience not simply for Tumusok, but for those who had come here to kill him.

"Stop here," Lin said. The truck eased to a halt at the head of the street. He turned to Aristide and Daljit.

"Your move."

Aristide opened the door on the side opposite Tumusok's street, and stepped out of the cab. Daljit followed. Each carried a small laser cutter.

The tractor pulled a long, flat trailer carrying a stack of pipe. Each piece of pipe was made of the latest high-density, high-quality ceramic, with a diameter of 1.4 meters and weighing nearly half a tonne.

Aristide bent to look beneath the trailer as he walked to his station. A dark figure had just passed the two golden lights at the station entrance, and was walking down the street, crossing on a diagonal on his way toward Tumusok's house. Aristide straightened and stopped, his cutter poised, next to the wide strap that secured the load on the trailer.

Daljit stopped by the other strap, her face pale in the light of a streetlamp.

Aristide winked at her.

The sound of the man's footsteps sounded faintly in the still night. Lin leaned out of the cab, a set of night-vision goggles still strapped over his widely spaced eyes. "It's Tumusok, and he's alone," he said. "Cut."

Aristide triggered his laser cutter and began to slice the strap. Aristide knew that the strap, woven with semi-intelligent fibers that had proven impossible to silence or destroy, immediately began broadcasting a message that its integrity was being compromised, that it was in danger of giving way. The broadcast was short-range, however, and he hoped no AI was close enough to hear it.

The air filled with the odor of burning plastic. He saw Daljit's intent face illuminated by the orange flare of her own cutter.

The straps gave way at the same instant, and the great weight of pipe began to roll. Aristide knew that as soon as the first pipe landed on the roadway with a great clang, both the pipe and the roadway would begin to call for help.

Aristide vaulted onto the back of the trailer to watch the pipe cascade down the road toward the man that Lin had identified as General Tumusok. Aristide had argued in favor of a simpler assassination—he'd wanted just to walk up to Tumusok and plunge a dagger into his heart—but Lin had vetoed the idea.

"The operation has to be complex," Lin said, "so that there's an excuse for it not to be solved right away. We've got to keep investigators off our backs until the old Tumusok is restored from backup, and the more oddities and doubt we can cast, the better we can slow the investigation."

Aristide had decided to concede to the expert. But he still wanted to watch what happened next, just in case Tumusok needed that dagger blow after all.

The lengths of pipe were bounding downhill, spreading into a great wave and making an astounding din as they went. Bushes and hedges were already being flattened on the fringes of the wave. Tumusok had frozen in the center of the road at the first sound, then turned to see what was causing the clamor. He stared into the darkness for a few seconds, then turned and began to run clumsily for his house.

Far too late. The first pipe caught him low and tossed him into the air, and as he fell another pipe caught him and hurled him like a corn doll into the roadway. And then all Aristide could see was the stampede of leaping pipe.

Lights were coming on everywhere on the street. Aristide ran forward, then swung himself into the cab. He kissed Daljit as he dropped onto the leopard-spotted blanket, and Shamlan fed power to the wheels, accelerating as she turned onto a road that would take the truck back to Myriad City. The last Aristide heard of the accident site were a series of crashes as the pipe slammed into the wooded creek bed at the foot of the hill.

"I can't help but think that a dagger would have been a lot quieter," Aristide said.

"We *want* noise," Lin said. "We *want* the body to be discovered right away." The cold light of satisfaction glittered in his eyes. "I'll order that the body be taken to Fedora's pathology lab," he said. "And then we'll see who gets out of bed to collect the body before the autopsy can begin."

The tractor-trailer drove to Myriad City, where it dropped Lin off near his apartment, in a wood devoid of surveillance cameras. The last Aristide saw of him, he was lighting his pipe; and then the tractor-trailer continued into the heart of the city, where it parked in the empty, echoing garage of a vacant sixty-year-old hotel scheduled for demolition, and where no passive surveillance lurked.

Aristide and Daljit left the vehicle, footsteps echoing in the huge hollow space. Shamlan awakened the truck's AI, and ordered it to drop the trailer off at the port, then return to the municipal lot from which it had been taken. Then Shamlan left the cab, taking with her the leopard-striped blanket and the seat covers that had helped to soak up hair and other DNA evidence.

"Nice meeting you," she said as she stuffed the incriminating fabric into a bag she had brought for the purpose.

"And you," Aristide said, and he and Daljit left by a different exit than Shamlan or the tractor-trailer.

Aristide and Daljit separated and walked roundabout routes to their destination, the marina, where a sailboat awaited them. The boat hadn't been rented by Franz Sandow, but by Pablo Monagas Pérez.

At Aristide's command, the *Fathom Deep* unhitched itself from the pier and spread gossamer sails to catch the land breeze. In the glowing cockpit, he plotted a destination, told the boat to go there, and ordered the boat's AI to refuse any communication that did not contain a certain prefix.

Computer-guided carbon-fiber masts bowed to the wind and the boat moved in near-silence from the harbor. Water chuckled under the counter, and there was a rhythmic splash from the bow as the boat began to pitch into the waves. Aristide opened the hatch and he and Daljit went below.

Each had their own cabin, with the closets full of clothing filled with tags that certified they had been on the boat all evening. Each changed clothes, then threw their incriminating clothing and footwear into the sea in a weighted bag.

Aristide, in duck trousers and a lambswool sweater, left his cabin and stepped into the boat's salon. A rose-scented perfume floated in the air. Daljit stood at one of the narrow windows, gazing at Myriad City's receding skyline.

"Well," Aristide said, "if Lin is right, all this evasion should have gained us five or six hours."

"Who will we next see, do you think?" Daljit asked. "Police, or pod people?"

"Commissar Lin, I hope."

Aristide looked in the refrigerator and withdrew a bottle of Veuve Clicquot shipped all the way from Earth. He produced a pair of glasses, opened the bottle, and poured.

He handed a glass to Daljit.

"Are we drinking to the success of our first murder?" Daljit asked.

Aristide restrained a shudder. This was not his first.

He forced a smile onto his face. "To our successful escape," he said.

For a moment, the sound of chiming crystal hung in the air. The champagne on his palate tasted like the most glorious air in creation and eased his thoughts.

They sat on a bench seat and drank. He put an arm around her, and she leaned her head on his shoulder and spoke.

"What will happen if this works?" Daljit asked.

"If the pod people leave enough traces," Aristide said, "we'll find out who's giving them orders, and which of the Eleven is involved. And then—simply—war."

"Which we'll win," Daljit said, "because the rogue AI is outnumbered ten to one."

"That's the plan," Aristide said. He sipped his champagne, and made a quiet decision that this was not the moment to cast the plan in doubt.

If this little conspiracy failed, he knew, if he and Daljit and Lin and the others were taken, Endora would alert the multiverse, and though there would be chaos and witch hunts in high places, the rogue would still be at a comprehensive disadvantage.

"*The womb of every world is in the balance,*" he said.

"*Conspirators gather beneath a darkened sun.*

The silence weighs a thousand pounds."

There was a moment of silence. She pressed her cheek to his shoulder, her hair a warm presence in the hollow of his throat.

"These could be the last hours of peace," she said.

"Yes."

She offered a mischievous giggle. "Can I say that I'm glad you don't have your cat with you?"

"I'd rather have you."

She looked at him soberly, then kissed his cheek. He returned the kiss, and said,

"*Old friend, the familiar perfume,*

How thrilling it is that

The touch of your lips feels new."

"Yes," Daljit said. "If this is our last night in this incarnation, let it be poetry."

He put his arms around her and kissed her deeply.

Poetry it certainly was.

In the morning, while a highly competent robotic kitchen prepared duck eggs, lightly poached with a bit of truffle oil and just the right amount of duck fat, Aristide stood in the cockpit and scanned the surrounding sea with binoculars. A few giant cargo ships stood black on the horizon like the distant castles of Gundapur, but no patrol or pleasure craft could be seen. *Fathom Deep* was beating into the wind on the starboard tack, and a fine salt spray dotted the cockpit windscreen.

Aristide put down the binoculars and picked up his cup of coffee. He tasted it and frowned—this was a domestic blend. For some reason Topaz never produced great coffee: the good stuff had to be imported.

Daljit appeared in the hatch, carrying a breakfast tray, two small plates with the duck eggs along with butter and a baguette. She set the tray on the table, and he kissed her.

As their lips touched a speaker pinged on the instrument console. They parted, a little rueful, as if the console were in the role of a strict chaperone.

"Yes?" Aristide said.

The voice that came from the console was that used by Endora—female, a little hurried, a little over-precise, and unlike the more colloquial voice of Bitsy.

"The rogue AI is Courtland," Endora said.

"Really?" Aristide was surprised. Courtland's personal interests were rather abstract—it was attracted to cosmology, exploration, and teleology. Not exactly the mindset to lead a revolution. Courtland's personality was sufficiently amorphous that it was always referred to as an "it," not a he or she.

"It isn't yet clear whether there is a group of humans behind Courtland's actions," Endora continued, "or who they might be, but if they exist we'll find out in due course."

"May I ask how the identification was made?"

"Partly as a result of your actions on Hawaiki," Endora said, "and partly by backtracking those who arrived in great haste this morning to claim General Tumusok's body. These included Myriad City's Chief of Police, by the way."

Aristide looked at Daljit. "That's two of the security services compromised," he said.

"They were being very careful about sending messages to one another," Endora said. "For the most part they took guidance from AIs they brought with them, which meant they didn't have to communicate with Courtland very often. But reports had to go back and forth sooner or later. Everything is on record, and the track is very plain."

Daljit took the cup of coffee from Aristide's hand and sipped at it.

"What about General Tumusok?" she asked.

"He has been reincarnated from a three-month-old backup, and has been briefed by Commissar Lin and me. He's already taking charge of the human end of this investigation."

A gust of wind blew Daljit's hair across her face. Aristide swept it back with a delicate finger.

"How are Grax, Herenui, and Cadwal?" he asked.

"They were uploaded, then downloaded again into new, untainted bodies without the rogue's modifications. Once they got over the shock, they revealed everything they knew."

Aristide took his coffee cup from Daljit's fingers, and took a thoughtful sip.

"Herenui's group could have tried to take me earlier than they did," he said. "Do we know why they didn't?"

"They were busy taking others," Endora said. "A whole group of nine visitors traveling together."

"Caught in their net," Aristide murmured.

"Taken all at once in those caves, yes. They've returned, in standard human bodies, and are now being tracked to see who they report to."

Aristide looked at Daljit. "I suppose there's no reason to stay at sea," he said.

"No," Endora said. "Though since both of you have finished your assignments, and as neither of you have any official status in this emergency, you have no obligation to return."

Daljit put an arm around Aristide and kissed him. Her lips tasted of coffee.

"I think we'll go back," she said.

Aristide ordered the boat to return to Myriad City. It swung off the wind, its pitching easing, and then the headsails went slack as the fore- and mainsail boomed out to either side. The water laughed under the counter as the boat's pace increased. The sound of the breeze fell nearly to nothing as the boat began running at nearly the speed of the wind.

Their breakfasts had gone cold, and were fed to the fishes as the galley was instructed to prepare more. Aristide sat in the cockpit with Daljit as they shared their coffee and baguette.

"It won't take long for Courtland to realize he's been found out," Aristide said. "These are the last hours of peace."

"Yes."

He stared at the brilliant horizon with eyes that stared into a void. "Fifteen hundred years," he said. "Centuries of astounding progress… functional immortality, travel to the stars, the creation of dozens of pocket universes tailored just for humanity. But during that time I've also seen fifteen hundred years of folly, waste, missed opportunities, and stupidity. Which outweighs the other? There are billions more useless, worthless human beings in the universe now than there ever were, and I justified it by saying that at least there wasn't a war… by which I mean a *real* war." He sighed. "And now we finally have one. And I've seen so much absurdity that I'm not even surprised. I thought it would happen ages ago."

She watched him from beneath her even brows, her coffee cup held by both hands just below her chin.

"How do we fix it?" she asked. "What's the plan?"

He rose, paced the length of the cockpit, and put his hands in his pockets.

"I don't have one. I've been operating entirely on instinct, at least when Lin lets me."

She smiled. "Your instincts are pretty good, if you don't mind my saying."

His lips echoed her smile, though with a grimmer twist. "After fifteen hundred years, they had better be." The carbon-fiber masts bent to a gust, and he looked up at the sails aglow with the dancing reflection of the water. "The martial arts training helps," he said. "I've been living in the moment for centuries, without any plan other than pursuing whatever seemed interesting at the time. My basic needs were taken care of, and Endora gave me my little bribes, and so why not?" He frowned. "Perhaps I was the worthless one, living in my Zen paradise." He touched his upper lip with a knuckle. "We need more than the moment now, that's certain."

"Fortunately," she said, "it's not all up to you anymore."

"Fortunately?" he said softly. "We'll see."

She rose to join him, putting an arm around his waist.

"If these are the last hours of peace," she said, "we should treasure them."

"Yes. We should."

They kissed.

The masts groaned as a gust of wind caught the boat, and carried it toward the towers of Myriad City, and the certainty of war.

10

I t was past noon by the time *Fathom Deep* eased into its berth in Myriad
City. As he left the port Aristide detected a slightly frantic quality to the
metropolis, as if the great city had somehow sensed it was already at war.
Road traffic had a sullen, aggressive quality, and those traveling on foot
seemed uncertain when they weren't rushing along in furious haste. Even
the gliders that floated overhead seemed in a hurry to get somewhere.

Aristide and Daljit managed to avoid being trampled by the relentless
mob of pedestrians as they walked to the nearest trackline station. She was
going to Fedora's lab, and from there to her regular work at the Institute.
Aristide intended to visit a pool of life, to dispose of the Franz Sandow body
and return to the body with which he'd walked across Midgarth.

He supposed he would have to make a concession to the modern world
and accept an implant.

His capsule hissed up to the platform. "See you tonight?" he said.

"Sure."

"Where shall we meet?"

"Come to my apartment after work hours. You know where it is."

The small capsule had filled with impatient people glaring at him. He
waved goodbye and stepped inside, where he had time to grab a strap before accelerating smoothly away. Two minutes later the car stopped at the
Medical Center, and as he exited Aristide was almost trampled by rushing
medical personnel.

Moving at a more refined pace, Aristide walked past the two glowing
holographic balls that marked the station entrance—each was blazoned
with a caduceus, as those of the port station had been marked with an
anchor—and then he strolled to the annex that contained the pools of life.

While waiting his turn he called Commissar Lin on his implant.

"I can't talk for long," Lin answered "I'm about to go into a meeting with Coy Coy."

"Who's Coy Coy?" Aristide asked.

"General Tumusok," said Lin. "It's what his friends call him."

"You're his friend now?"

"I have that pleasure, yes."

"Felicitations," Aristide said. "I thought I'd call to let you know I have returned to the city, and to offer my services to you or to the general."

Lin's tone was distracted. "I imagine you'll be formally debriefed within the next few days. But as you have no official standing—"

"War is a matter for officials?"

"At present, yes."

"You know," thoughtfully, "that isn't my experience of war at all."

"I'm sure that once things get under way, your presence would be of great value on committees and other consultative bodies."

Aristide was vexed. It seemed to him that he had earned a place on Coy Coy's council of war.

"Let's hope so," he said, a bit pointedly.

"By the way, I've heard from my opposite numbers on Hawaiki. They were wondering about your weapon."

"Beg pardon?"

"What did you use to take off the big one's leg? They said microsurgery couldn't have been neater. And a part of the boat was cut away as well."

"Was it? I don't remember."

"Did you use some kind of laser?"

"Something like that," Aristide said. "If you'll excuse me, I see that it's my turn for a pool of life."

Lin excused him. Aristide, who had not in fact been summoned for anything, sat in the waiting room and considered for a long moment the features of the ongoing war. How would the other pockets be alerted safely? The others of the Eleven? How many of Courtland's population had been converted to the cause of the Venger? Possibly Coy Coy knew the answers, but Aristide didn't.

Vast and important things were happening, and he was not a part of it. Though he was willing to admit that the Domus had a point in not making use of him, he resented being kept in the dark.

He had been through this kind of war once already. He wondered if Coy Coy could say the same.

When his turn came, he went to the pool of life. A few hours later, he rose a new man. Franz Sandow's clothes did not fit him well, and he used his implant to order new clothing to be delivered to Daljit's apartment.

For a moment he considered whether or not to pick up the new Bitsy, who had been created but was currently deactivated, waiting in storage. He decided that as he planned to spend the night with Daljit, and she wasn't fond of Bitsy, he'd return on the morrow and activate Bitsy then.

As Aristide left the Life Annex, he saw crowds surging around the entrance to the main hospital building. The air had a smoky tang. Aristide asked his implant what was going on, and was told that there had been an explosion at the Stellar chemical plant. He felt a degree of relief—his nerves were keyed to war, and they were eased by the reminder that accidents, too, could cause casualties.

He walked to the trackline station, and immediately a sleek capsule, all windows and streamlined composites, drew up and disgorged a mob of chemical plant employees coming to be checked for contamination. Though none seemed to have injuries, they all seemed angry, and shouted at each other as they barged past Aristide toward the hospital entrance.

Aristide stepped into the capsule and asked it to take him to Daljit's apartment. Apparently he was the only person in the trackline system who wanted to go there, because the capsule didn't stop to pick up anyone else en route. Aristide left the capsule, took the escalators to the apartment lobby, and was challenged by the building's AI—which, after scanning his biometrics, let him pass. Daljit must have told the AI to expect him.

Daljit's apartment was on the forty-ninth floor, with a view of the River District. He heard soft tones sounding inside the apartment as he approached the door. When Daljit opened the door, she looked at him with narrowed eyes.

"Just as I was getting used to you being blond," she said. She gestured at a pile on the floor of the hall. "Here's your stuff. I wish you'd warn me when you're having crap delivered here."

She evaded his kiss and withdrew to the kitchen.

The scent of frying onions filled the apartment. Aristide looked ruefully at his new clothing in the paper delivery bags that Daljit had first torn open, then dropped in the hall when she realized they weren't meant for her. He picked up his belongings and withdrew to the bathroom, where he changed. He wrapped Franz Sandow's clothing in the torn remains of the bags and placed them on the small table near the door, then stepped to the kitchen door, where Daljit was furiously chopping vegetables with a Chinese cleaver.

"Are you cooking dinner?" he asked. "That's liberal of you."

Daljit slapped spices with the flat of her blade. There was a sudden scent of cardamom and cloves.

"I'll make *badaami murgh*," she said, "if I can just get some peace."

"There was an explosion at the Stellar plant," Aristide said. "Some casualties, apparently, since the hospital was very busy."

She looked at him with anger in her eyes. Light glittered off the cleaver. "I'm trying to *concentrate*," she said.

"Sorry," Aristide said, and withdrew to the front room.

One wall of the apartment was polarized glass, currently set to darken the room. Aristide told the glass to lighten, and then stepped forward to admire the view, Myriad City's wild architectural profusion in brilliant crystalline light. He opened the door onto a terrace and stood for a moment with his hands on the smooth curves of the shining composite rail, the sharp wind ruffling his hair as he considered the contrast in Daljit's mood between the morning and the present.

The barque of the previous evening, with its cargo of poetry and delight, seemed to have run aground. He did not hold out much hope for a rescue.

Daljit had clearly reconsidered her connection with Aristide. Perhaps the ardor of the previous evening had been the result of overstimulation—Tumusok had been her first murder, after all, and passions had been high. But in the cold light of day, she had seemingly reconsidered. Perhaps she had decided that they had been correct to end their first relationship, those long decades ago.

And this on top of Ashtra's rejection. Aristide wondered if he had finally reached the age when his life experience, his birth on Earth, and the great weight of his experience had finally made it impossible for him to relate to anyone born in the centuries since humanity had abandoned its birthplace.

A shame. It was desire that kept him human. The limbic system hadn't failed him yet.

He looked down at the sound of a siren. On Rampart Street below a police car slithered through traffic like an eel, computer guidance giving it an uncanny ability to weave through moving vehicles with a clearance of millimeters. Ahead was a fugitive car, the fact that it was caroming off other vehicles providing clear evidence that its own computer guidance had been sabotaged—normally the traffic AI would seize control of a vehicle seconds after an accident, and steer it to a safe stop.

As Aristide watched, the fugitive driver made a mistake, hit another car, and his vehicle spun off the road in a cloud of dust and blue tiresmoke. The car struck the stanchion of a streetlight and crumpled. A wheel bounced free and leaped down the road in a series of high, exuberant bounds.

By the time the driver fought free of his safety gear and left the vehicle, the police car had already stopped, and its uniformed driver had disembarked. The renegade driver saw the officer approaching, and turned to run.

The police officer shot him. From his position on the terrace Aristide could hear the distinct *pop-pop-pop* of the officer's sidearm. The renegade driver fell.

Aristide stared in complete surprise. He hadn't thought the police in Myriad City were armed.

The police officer walked up to the prone driver, fired a finishing round into her victim's head at close range, then returned to her vehicle. Aristide turned and returned to the kitchen.

"I saw the most amazing thing," he said. "A police officer just shot someone."

He ducked as a bowl of raw chicken clanged into the wall above his head. Lemon marinade spattered his face. Pale pieces of chicken fell limp to the floor.

Daljit's lip curled. "You might have the *courtesy*," she said, "not to *interrupt* me when I'm working on something *important*."

"I—" Aristide began, and then cold certainty froze him.

"*Now you've wrecked dinner!*" Daljit shrieked into the silence.

Aristide ordered himself to remain calm. He took a step away from Daljit.

"I apologize," he said.

Daljit looked terrible. She was flushed. Her eyes glittered. Sweat glued strands of hair to her forehead, and she panted for breath.

He hadn't been paying attention when he'd first spoken to her. He hadn't seen the signs.

"Daljit," he began carefully, "I would like to suggest that you're not well."

"*I'm* not well!" She gave a bitter laugh. "You have a lot of nerve, coming here and saying *that!*"

Aristide tried silently calling for help on his implant. A polite voice echoed in his head, telling him that emergency services were busy right now but that he could dictate a message into their memory buffer and they would respond as soon as possible.

That told him all he needed to know.

"*You!*" Daljit snarled. "*You're* the one who wanders around primitive pockets with a sword and a rag on your head," she said. "How healthy is that, if you'd be so good as to tell me?"

"I would like to suggest that the enemy's agents have spread a zombie plague in the city," he told Daljit. "I think you caught it."

"*Me?*" Daljit said. She sneered. "I think you're fucking mistaken, is what

I think."

But behind the denial, behind the fevered eyes, Aristide thought he saw a puzzled, anguished lucidity, a moment in which her mind tried to grapple with the idea he'd just handed her.

"My god," she said. "I—"

Her words failed. A tremor ran through her jaw muscles. Then she shook her head, and Aristide could see the last vestiges of sanity vanish as her mind crumbled beneath the onslaught of serotonin, adrenaline, norepinephrine, dopamine, and testosterone that the plague was pouring into her bloodstream.

She gave him a red-eyed feral look, and he felt his own nervous system turn to fire as he remembered the exact same look in Antonia's eyes.

The moment of shocked recognition almost cost him his face as Daljit hurled the skillet of frying onions at his head. As he dodged he stepped on one of the chicken pieces and fell, landing hard in the hallway. Hot oil stung his hand.

"*Stupid fuck!*" Daljit shouted, and threw an empty bowl at him. It bounced off his warding hand. Aristide scuttled out of range, palming himself backward toward the front room.

Pop-pop-pop. The sounds came through the open terrace door. The police, or someone, was shooting again.

Aristide rose to his feet just as Daljit came out of the kitchen with a gleaming kitchen knife in one hand.

"*Get out!*" she cried. "*Get out get out get out!*"

It was useless to point out that she stood between him and the only exit. Aristide cautiously circled to his right and put a sofa between himself and Daljit.

He reached for Tecmessa and hesitated. He didn't want to banish Daljit to Holbrook, a place he reserved for enemies whose crimes were committed while in their right minds.

If he'd returned Tecmessa's blade to the hilt, he might have a chance of subduing Daljit with the flat of the blade. But the hilt still contained the wandlike AI, which on its own was not very useful as a weapon.

Aristide picked up a floor lamp and assumed a guard stance.

"*Put that down!*" shouted Daljit. "That's mine!"

"I'll leave," he said, "if you'll let me get to the door."

"Oh, I'll let you leave all right," she said, and licked her lips. She flashed the kitchen knife at him, and laughed when he reacted, jerking the lamp awkwardly in the direction of the threat.

He wished she'd kept the cleaver. It was a more vicious weapon, but a less flexible one.

Deception was beyond her now, and when she lunged for him she telegraphed the move in half a dozen ways. Aristide thrust the lamp at her face. She fell back, frustrated, then screamed and came on again.

Again he thrust the lamp at her face. She grabbed the lamp and tried to wrench it out of his grasp. She was surprisingly strong. She slashed at his hand and he pulled it back and lost control of the lamp. She laughed in triumph and came over the sofa at him. He punched her in the nose, feeling a crunch of cartilage under his knuckles, and her reaction gave him enough time to dance away. A slash of the knife cut lint from his sleeve.

Aristide looked for another weapon and saw a metal-framed chair on the terrace. He lunged for it, brought it up in the guard position, and held the terrace door with his improvised shield. She came after him panting for breath, and her knife drew sparks from the chair legs. Blood ran freely from her broken nose.

If he circled to his left, he thought, he could draw her out onto the terrace, then pin her against the rail with the chair. It might give him enough time to break away and escape into the apartment, or perhaps even to defeat her in some way.

He took the step to his left, and in her frenzy she was unable to resist the opening and jumped onto the terrace. Before Daljit could settle herself for another attack he was attacking himself, thrusting with the four legs of the chair, driving her back. She snarled and slashed with the knife. He ducked the first slash, then caught her wrist on the backswing. He leaned all his mass into the chair and drove her by sheer weight onto the terrace rail.

He jerked his head back as her teeth snapped within centimeters of his ear—her bite was almost certainly contagious. While Aristide pinned her to the rail with his weight, he got both his hands on her wrist and began to exert steady pressure on her knife hand, bending the wrist inward. She punched to his face with her free hand, but her arm had to bend awkwardly around the chair and her strikes lacked force.

Daljit gave a cry of despair as her fingers lost strength under Aristide's pressure, and the knife dropped with a carbon-steel clack to the surface of the terrace. Aristide kicked it over the edge. Her feet flailed his shins. She tried to bite his wrist and he jerked his hand back. With his other hand he palmed her broken nose and she wrenched away from him, blinded with pain—partly turning her back, which is what he wanted. He grabbed her shoulder with both hands and hurled her face-first against the rail, in the corner where she had no opportunity to move left or right.

He fully intended to strangle her. Bear down with his superior weight and get an arm across her throat, if he could do it without being bitten. Once he had choked her into unconsciousness he would find some means to tie her, then call emergency personnel and wait for rescue.

But Daljit reacted quickly. Once in the corner, with both hands on the rail, she kicked back with both feet and connected with Aristide's midsection. He lost his wind and took a deep step backward. Daljit fought free of Aristide and the chair and swung herself feet-first over the rail, pivoting on one arm like a gymnast on a pommel horse.

Her feet made contact with the rail, and Daljit rose to a crouch, balancing on the rail with uncanny ease. On her bloody face was a wild grin of malicious triumph as she prepared to dive atop Aristide with her hands clawed.

Aristide remembered the same expression on Antonia's face.

Aristide swung the chair backhand, and watched as Daljit overbalanced and went backward off the balcony, toward the pavement forty-nine floors below.

He didn't watch her fall. Instead he dropped the chair to the deck and sagged against the frame of the terrace door.

He could hear emergency sirens wailing through the city.

He needed to lock the doors, he thought, against any more maniacs who might infest the building. Then get into the shower and wash himself thoroughly, in case he'd got any of Daljit's blood or saliva on him.

But he couldn't bring himself to move. Instead he remembered Antonia lying still in the garden, a murdered maenad spattered with her own blood.

He thought about all the people he had killed over the centuries, and wondered why so many were those he had loved.

11

The sound of nearby shots shook him out of his contemplation of eternities. Aristide took his shower, and dressed in another set of his new clothing, items that had remained in their delivery bags while Daljit was on her rampage, and which hadn't been touched.

Images of Antonia and Carlito and Daljit rose in Aristide's mind, then bled crimson into one another.

"*Pablo?*" Endora's voice echoed suddenly in Aristide's implant. Her delivery was faster than normal and sounded strangely like panic.

"Yes?" Aristide replied. "Where have you been?"

Endora chose not to answer the question. Her voice returned to its normal fussy precision.

"You're in Daljit's bedroom. Good."

"Not really," he said. "She got the bug and—well, she's dead."

He spoke aloud, rather than mentally dictating into his implant. The latter would have taken far too much of his scattered concentration.

Endora's voice was suddenly all business.

"Did you get any blood on you?"

"No," he said. "But I'm sharing the air that she's breathed."

"It's unlikely you'll catch it that way. You should want to wash your hands and possibly take a shower."

"Already done." Aristide heard running in the corridor outside the apartment, and a thump on the door, followed shortly thereafter by a greater thumping in his chest. He made certain Tecmessa was within arm's reach.

The running footsteps receded.

"What's the situation?" he asked.

"It's difficult to tell. We're having a bandwidth crisis, and that's keeping me from getting a clear picture."

"*Bandwidth?* Your bandwidth is *immense.*"

"But not infinite. Not only am I receiving millions of distress calls from victims, I'm being swamped by messages from every wrecked car, every broken window, every damaged bit of plaster. None of us ever anticipated how many inanimate objects would call for help during a major crisis. On top of all that the zombies have sabotaged a lot of the communications grid—apparently they don't *like* voices in their head telling them they're ill."

The scent of ghee and fried onions floated into the room from the kitchen. Aristide closed the door.

"Is the government responding?" Aristide said.

"It's beginning to. But a lot of police and emergency workers have been infected, and they've got access to weapons. And a great many of the infected are blaming the government for their problems, and are launching attacks against government installations."

"Well." Aristide lifted Tecmessa, the little ineffective wand mounted in the businesslike hilt. "I should offer help."

"I would advise remaining where you are, in relative safety."

Aristide considered the prospect of being locked in a small room with his memories, and decided against it.

"I was backed up only this afternoon," he said. "If I become a casualty, I'll lose only a few hours—and," he added, "there's nothing in those hours I wish to remember."

"As you wish." Endora knew him well enough not to dispute his decision.

"Where will I be most useful?" he asked. He began going through Daljit's drawers, and found a scarf he could wrap around his mouth and nose, and a floppy hat he could pull down over his forehead to minimize his exposure to flying blood and spittle.

"Police and police stations are being attacked," Endora said. "So are other government buildings such as offices, jails, and courthouses."

"It's after office hours, so I expect the offices and courthouses are mostly empty."

"True."

"And if the police can't defend themselves with their firearms, I don't imagine I'll be able to help them. What of the higher branches of government?"

"The Prime Minister was at a dinner when the outbreak occurred, failed to reach Polity House, and is besieged at the Haçibaba Hotel along with elements of the Guard. The President was infected and his current whereabouts are unknown. The Chambers of Parliament are being attacked, and my understanding is that the High Court has been overrun."

Aristide reflected that he had no means of reaching any of these places. He opened the door and stepped into the hall, which he followed toward the kitchen and the foyer.

"Can you ready a car," he asked, "and have it at the garage elevator?"

"Yes."

Aristide stepped over scattered onions and chicken and opened drawers to find Daljit's cutlery. He stuck the larger kitchen knives in his belt and told the apartment, through his implant, to ping every object in the front closet. This told him of a plastic raincoat, of a type that folded into a small pouch. It was generic and would fit him.

"A strong executive is essential in time of war," he said absently, as he sealed the raincoat. "And besides, I'm fond of my old friend the Prime Minister," he said. "I'll go to the PM's aid."

"If you insist."

"Anyone in the corridor outside?"

There was a pause. Then, "I'm afraid that data is not available."

Aristide wrapped the scarf around his head, then his mouth and nose. His fingers were accustomed to turban wrappings and he performed this task efficiently. He tucked the ends into the raincoat and then anchored the whole thing in place with the hat.

He realized that in this getup he probably looked crazier than the zombies.

"Send for an elevator, will you?" he asked, and reached for the door.

He realized that the addition of the raincoat made it impossible for him to reach his weapons, so he unfastened the raincoat, took out Tecmessa and a kitchen knife, and fastened the raincoat again.

"The elevator is waiting," Endora said.

"Very good."

He opened the door, cautious. He heard nothing. He stepped out into the corridor and moved with deliberate speed past a series of blank doors toward the bank of elevators at the end of the corridor.

A series of crashing noises came from behind one of the doors, as if someone were smashing a piece of furniture to bits. Aristide's nerves gave a leap with each crash. He heard no screams or pleas for help, and did not intervene.

A few doors farther along the corridor, he saw a puddle of blood creeping out from beneath a door.

It was clearly too late to intervene here.

One of the elevators gave a chime, and polished bronze doors slid open.

Aristide ran for the elevator as fast as he could.

In Aristide's youth there had been a genre of films about zombies, animated dead who preyed upon the living. In these films the zombies shambled, minds and bodies barely functioning. They were formidable only in large numbers, and as they killed off their victims their numbers grew greater.

When real zombies were brought into the world, they resembled their cinematic counterparts only slightly. For one thing, they were *fast*, their bodies responding to their pumped metabolisms. While they were unlikely to indulge in long-range planning, they retained a certain ingenuity and brutal cunning.

And, like the film zombies, they could spread their infection to others.

Aristide took command of the car, not trusting Endora's bandwidth problems to allow her to drive safely. By the time he drove into sight of the Haçibaba Hotel, the car was covered with dents, and blood streaked its sleek hood and ran in airblown trails up the front window.

"You'll let them know I'm coming?" Aristide said.

"Yes. I've told them not to shoot."

Aristide accelerated, smashed through a pair of vehicles that had been drawn across the pavement as a roadblock. Angry figures raced out of buildings. A shot cracked off the rear window. Aristide avoided another roadblock by hopping the car onto the curb, which gave him the opportunity to crash into a half-dozen zombies that had just run out of an office building to see what all the noise was about. Bodies flopped urgently at the impact. One hung grimly onto the nose of the vehicle, bashing with a hammer on the windscreen, until he slipped in the blood of his companions and fell under the wheels.

The car thumped and thudded over the bodies that lay motionless before the hotel.

Aristide hopped the curb again near the entrance to the hotel, left the vehicle, and ran into the building. Oddly, Aristide thought, the transparent doors were fixed in the open position. Guards stood in the lobby, compact rifles at the ready. Clear ballistic armor draped around them in much the same style as Aristide's raincoat. The lobby floor was a deep golden perfection, the shellac-like vomit of a species of genetically modified insect, and the guards stood on their own perfect reflections, their weapons ready. Aristide looked into a half-circle of rifles all aimed at him.

"No, really," Aristide said, pulling off his hat. "I'm on your side."

An officer lowered his weapon. "So we are told." He nodded at the rain-coat. "Is that a form of armor?"

"A raincoat only."

He smiled grimly. "Too bad for you."

"How is the Prime Minister?"

"Well, but rather busy at the moment."

"Here they come!" someone called.

The violent spectacle of Aristide's arrival had stirred up a fury among the besiegers. A swarm of zombies came running out of nearby buildings, weapons in their hands. Most carried clubs or knives, but the few who had firearms shot wildly as they ran. The bodyguards stepped forward and presented their rifles through the open doors.

Rifles cracked. Aristide readied Tecmessa. The guards fired single, aimed shots, and each shot dropped a zombie to the pavement.

Tecmessa proved unnecessary. The zombie tide broke a few yards from the entrance, and the survivors fled, uttering howls of rage. Once the zombies had retreated, the guards drew back out of sight.

"Nicely done," Aristide said.

"Thank you," said the officer. "Securing a building this large is difficult with so few men, but at least it has good fields of fire. We'll do well as long as the ammunition holds."

"And how is the ammunition supply?"

There was a slight hesitation.

"We're taking care not to waste it," the officer said.

"I don't suppose you could loan me a weapon."

Once again the officer offered his grim smile. "Our attackers have dropped a number of firearms in the street outside. You are welcome to search among the bodies."

Aristide looked at the kitchen knife in his hand.

"Perhaps I will bide here."

"As you think best."

Time passed. The guards passed it efficiently, exchanging few words, remaining in a state of alertness. They had already provided themselves with snacks and coffee from the hotel restaurant, and they shared their refreshment with Aristide.

No zombies made their appearance on the street, though the crashing sounds that echoed down the street demonstrated that they were passing their time in vandalism. The sound of shots indicated that combat was taking place elsewhere.

The guards did not seek out the enemy, or aid whoever was fighting the zombies, but remained true to their calling as guards, and continued to shield the head of state.

Aristide, overheating, took off his scarf and raincoat.

Overhead, the sun of Topaz flickered, shimmered, and died. A few remaining streetlights flickered on. Buildings, aside from those on fire, remained dark.

Emergency lights flashing on nearby buildings heralded a new arrival. This was followed by a grinding, thundering noise, as of a roadblock being battered to pieces. This was followed, in turn, by a volley of shots.

Aristide quietly resumed his raincoat and scarf.

A pair of vehicles rolled into sight. First was a large earthmover with a blade on the front and emergency lights flashing from atop the crew compartment. The other was an autobus, with the windows knocked out to permit those inside to fire freely in all directions.

The guards' leader ordered his men forward, rifles leveled to give covering fire.

The earthmover and the bus halted on either side of the hotel entrance but left the field of fire clear. It was well that they did, because the lights and noise attracted another wave of zombies, all of whom were efficiently killed or driven away.

A group left the bus and came trotting up to the doors. Some were dressed as police, and some were not. The bodyguards fell back to let them enter.

The newcomers' leader, a brown-skinned woman in the uniform of a police lieutenant, saluted the Guard officer.

"We're from Meg Town," she said. "The plague didn't hit there, and we came as soon as we could."

"We're very relieved to see you."

Both turned their heads at a volley of shots from the bus, followed by the harsh screams of a zombie, cut short by a final shot. There was no further noise, and the two leaders returned to their conference.

"I understand you've got Prime Minister Ataberk here?" said the lieutenant. Her fighters moved into the lobby, their eyes searching the darkness.

"We were caught here by the outbreak," the bodyguard answered.

"We can take the PM away in our vehicle and return to Polity House or any designated emergency headquarters."

"That won't be necessary. I understand that transport is laid on for later—"

"*Look out!*" Aristide shouted, and threw himself to the floor. As he skimmed along the smooth golden surface on his slick raincoat, the newcomers raised their weapons and opened point-blank fire on the bodyguards.

On each face was an expression of perfect love. The adoration of their master they at last felt free to express.

There was a bang, a sense of twisting in the air. A mirror shattered. Three of the newcomers vanished in a blast of air. Guards were falling.

The bodyguards were shooting back—their ballistic armor smocks had protected them against at least some of the enemy bullets. Both screams and bullets tore the air.

Tecmessa took another pair of the intruders. Then another. And then no one was left standing, but everyone on the ground, strewn over the bullet-shattered lobby.

Aristide glanced cautiously around him. All the attackers appeared dead.

"*The door!*" the Guard captain said.

More attackers were coming, those who had remained on the earthmover and the bus in order to keep the zombies at a distance. With bullets in both legs, the Guard captain rolled onto his stomach, and using the body of the police captain as cover, began to fire.

Tecmessa took the attackers that the captain did not. Silence reigned in the lobby for a brief span, and then a defiant howl came floating into the lobby from the street. Other voices answered, a chorus of feral anger that echoed in the city's canyons.

The zombies were coming. Attracted by the noise of the vehicles, they had trailed behind the bus, growing in number and waiting for their opportunity.

That moment had now come.

Zombies boiled from the street, charging through the doors and bashing their way through the windows. The remaining guards fired till they were overwhelmed. Tecmessa took many, but the attack came from so many directions that Aristide had to withdraw deeper into the hotel, backing down a corridor to lure the zombies after him, Tecmessa's thunder shaking doors and shattering glass as it devoured the enemy.

In another world, he realized, the one to which Tecmessa was the womb, zombies were even now fighting the Venger's troops, those who had followed the police lieutenant. He wondered which side would prevail.

When the zombies stopped coming, Aristide ran back into the lobby and found a zombie bent over the Guard captain and worrying at his throat. Aristide drove his kitchen knife into the back of the zombie's neck and severed her spine. She toppled, and he kicked her away.

Feet pounded down an interior corridor. Aristide turned to defend himself and saw a half-dozen more of Prime Minister Ataberk's bodyguards, who had been guarding another entrance to the hotel and had been summoned by their captain.

The guards immediately finished off a number of enemy wounded, and checked their comrades for signs of life. Only the captain had survived the double attack, and he waved off their aid.

"I've been infected," he said, holding one hand to the wound on his throat. "There's no point in trying to help me."

"If we could get you to a pool of life…" Aristide said.

"I'll slow you all down." He looked at Tecmessa, the little black wand fixed on the sword hilt. "That's a hell of a weapon you've got there."

"It's a secret project."

"We're going to need a lot more like it."

I hope not, Aristide thought. The captain looked at the bodies of the police lieutenant and the others who had arrived on the bus.

"Who *are* these people?" he asked.

"They're the ones who loosed the zombie plague in order to cover their attempted coup. They were here to capture or kill the Prime Minister."

"Good thing the boss is safe, then," the captain said. Aristide looked at him.

"The Prime Minister was evacuated hours ago," the captain explained. "There are utility tunnels that lead from here to Constitutional Square, and from there it's a short sprint to Polity House."

"You were here as a rear guard."

"We were here to attract anyone trying to take out the PM" The captain looked down at the police lieutenant. "Good thing we were."

"Sir," said one of the newly arrived guards. "We no longer have the numbers to hold a building this large."

The captain nodded. He had grown pale, and blood oozed between the fingers pressed to the wound on his throat.

"You're in charge. I'll report, after which you will shoot me in the head. Then you and the other units are authorized to withdraw to a more defensible location."

"Sir!"

While the Guard captain communed with his implant, Aristide ventured a probe of his own.

Endora?

Yes?

You've been following this?

Yes.

Can the recordings of Tecmessa being used vanish?

I'm afraid ongoing bandwidth problems prevented any recordings at all.

Thank you.

You're welcome.

Aristide turned away as the captain was given his quietus. Too many memories had already been loosed in the last few hours.

He took a weapon from one of the fallen and joined the surviving guards on a trek to their next fortress.

Dawn would come, he thought, in time.

12

I t was difficult in the modern world for anyone to stay dead for very long. Aristide sat in the clinic, awaiting Daljit's resurrection in a waiting room that smelled of flowers and too many nervous bodies. It was less than two days since her plunge off the apartment balcony.

Other survivors crowded the waiting room, all showing the shock and horror of the last few days—tens of thousands had died. Since resurrection facilities were not unlimited, the government and Endora had created a prioritized list for who would be brought back to life and in what order. Vital government functionaries and servitors first, everyone else later. Endora, however, had been willing to do Aristide a favor by bumping Daljit up the list by a few categories. Aristide had tried but failed to disguise how grateful he was for the favor.

Bitsy—the new Bitsy—coiled in Aristide's lap. He absent-mindedly stroked her short hair. He witnessed lovers and families welcoming their lost ones back to the land of the living, with overloud hellos and nervous laughter. A disturbing number of the dead had been children, the most vulnerable to violence.

It was fortunate they wouldn't remember how they had died, probably at the hands of their family or friends. At least they were spared that trauma.

He was more saddened at the thought of the children who had somehow survived the attacks of their kin, and who would remember for the rest of their lives the sight of their loved ones turning into monsters.

When Bitsy uncoiled and hopped to the floor, Aristide knew that the cat had learned through her data connections that Daljit was about to step into the waiting room. Aristide rose, wiped his nervous hands against the

139

seams of his trousers, and stepped toward the door.

Daljit appeared. She walked with a certain deliberation, as if she was unused to being in the world. She was dressed in the clothing that Aristide had brought from her apartment—he had also brought cosmetics and the flowery perfume she favored. She smiled as she saw him and kissed his cheek, then stepped back and gave him a questioning look.

"What happened?" she asked. She blinked. "Did we—"

"Not here," Aristide said. He led her from the clinic and to a sleek Destiny automobile, which under autopilot pulled from the curb as soon as they entered and closed the hatch.

Tecmessa, with the heavy blade reattached to the hilt, waited sheathed and propped up against the back seat. The sword had seemed an inappropriate object to bring into a clinic waiting room. Aristide slid onto the wide back seat, and held the sword at his hip as if it were attached to his belt.

Daljit looked at the world with wide, questioning eyes. The car hissed away from the curb.

"We didn't kill Tumusok?" she asked. "What went wrong?"

Her backup had been made on the day of the planned assassination, so that if things went amiss, she would be resurrected complete with the established knowledge of the Venger's existence.

"No," Aristide said, "that part worked fine. Tumusok was dispatched, resurrected successfully, and briefed by Endora. But a few hours later the enemy worked out that he'd been detected, and attacked before we were ready for him."

"Attacked?" Daljit's expression was intent. "How?"

"A zombie plague," Aristide said. "Apparently the intention was to cause enough chaos so that the Venger's agents could seize power in as many of the pockets as possible."

"So it was a zombie that got me?" Daljit said. Then, gazing out the window: "I take it the Venger's coup failed?"

Bitsy jumped up onto the padded shelf behind their seat. "He was unsuccessful everywhere except Courtland," she said. "Courtland is the corrupt AI, by the way, and even there the Venger had only managed to turn a minority of the population by the time the war started. But these were enough to seize and hold the wormhole gates from Courtland into the pockets, and presumably the rest are now being subjected to a Seraphim-like plague that will bring them all under the Venger's control."

Aristide could imagine the horror of the population there, communication with the outside cut off, the Venger's propaganda on all the feeds, growing panic as the sickness began, the fever, hallucinations, and eventual coma as the brain was restructured from within...

With the Seraphim, people hadn't realized at first what was happening. In Courtland's pocket universes, everyone would know at once, and known there was nothing they could do. The valiant and the cowardly, the old and young, the devout and the irreligious, all condemned to the same fate.

Daljit's look was bleak. "Has there been any communication from Courtland?"

"Surrender demands," Aristide said, "from someone calling himself Vindex—Latin for 'the Avenger,' by the way. There's only one of him, supposedly... he's not a committee, like the Seraphim."

"But he's got Courtland."

"Yes. Or he *is* Courtland, under another name."

They fell silent. Daljit looked in bleak silence at a series of storefronts blackened by smoke damage. There had been a great many fires set during the disturbances, but, thanks to building codes and modern materials, very little had actually burned down. The buildings' contents had gone up in smoke, but the buildings remained, looking out at the world through blackened eyes.

The scent of ashes sifted through the car's ventilation system.

"How are people taking it?" Daljit asked.

"They were afraid," Aristide said. "Now they're angry. Everyone wants to do something, but this early it's unclear what most people can do." He looked at her. "You have a job waiting for you in the war effort, if you want it."

Daljit was surprised. "But I'm just a geneticist."

"You're a geneticist in a biological war."

"I'm not a senior enough fellow at the Institute to work on human genetics," Daljit said. "I—" And then she stopped, as if she realized how obsolete that idea had become.

Aristide laughed. "That was before the war. Now we need everyone with any skills in that direction, to work out what weapons Vindex and Courtland can deploy against us, and how to counter them—or immunize ourselves against them before they are ever used." He gave her a grim smile. "That's important—your job category is much more substantial than mine, a semi-retired computer scientist turned biologist turned swordsman."

The car turned, and Daljit looked at her surroundings in surprise.

"We're going to the port?"

"I have the boat for another three days," Aristide shrugged. "Why not?"

The car drove to the pier where *Fathom Deep* was tied up. Aristide told the car to wait, and then he, Daljit, and Bitsy left the Destiny and walked down the pier. He rested the heavy sword against his shoulder. Water surged beneath them; composite planks boomed beneath their feet. The sun, reflecting on the wavetops, danced across the sailboat's hull.

They stepped aboard the boat, and the hatch to the main cabin opened at Aristide's silent command. Bitsy remained on deck, curling up on a sunny cushion, while Daljit and Aristide went into the cabin.

Daljit looked over the cabin without interest. Aristide strained to detect a scent of their time together, but could find nothing. He stood the sword against a corner of the chart table and opened a cabinet.

"Care for a drink?"

"Mm—not now, thanks." Daljit brushed a brass fitting with her fingertips. "So this is where we fled, after we killed Tumusok."

"We did." He smiled. "We ran away to sea."

He drew out a bottle of lemonade and opened it

"Tell me about the assassination," Daljit said. He looked at her, then narrowed his eyes.

"The mole is on the other side of your face," he said.

She smiled. "Yes. I have standing orders to switch it every time I visit a pool of life."

"That's amusing."

"I hope so." She perched on the arm of the settee. "The assassination?" she prompted.

He sipped his lemonade and sat in the navigator's chair and told her about the watch on the trackline station, the ceramic sewer pipe bounding down the road to its fatal meeting with General Tumusok.

"His friends call him Coy Coy," Aristide said. "Or so Lin tells me."

"Amusing," she said, unamused.

He held the bottle of lemonade between his two hands, as if to warm it. He looked up at her.

"You and I became lovers that night," he said, "here on the *Fathom Deep*."

He plotted the changes that worked their way across her face, and wished he knew what thoughts had prompted them. Then her lips drew apart in a smile, the mole lifting from its accustomed place.

"I hope that isn't too much of a shock," he said.

"A pleasant one, if so." The words were spoken with grave care.

"We planned to meet again the next night. But you'd been infected by then, and you tried to kill me with a kitchen knife."

"*I* was the zombie?" Her surprise was complete. "I assumed I'd been *killed* by a zombie."

"You were killed by me," Aristide said, "in self defense. I threw you off your balcony."

Her lips formed an O, but she said nothing.

"Would you like that drink now?" he said.

"Killing, loving, trying to kill each other." Daljit shook her head. "We ran the gamut in a short time, didn't we?"

"We did."

Soberly, she rose and approached him. He rose from the chair, uncertain. She took the lemonade from his hands and put it on a table, then kissed him. For a long, silent moment, they explored the kiss together.

She drew back and smiled. His heart leaped.

"Let's run the gamut again," she said.

13

"Pablo Monagas Pérez," said Commissar Lin, "allow me to present General Pedro Tumusok."

"Call me Coy Coy," said the general.

"And you," smiling, "can call me Aristide."

The general was a short, dark-skinned man with a brisk manner and a white smile; he wore a tan uniform with accents in vermilion and gold. He shook Aristide's hand, then took a step back and folded his arms, viewing Aristide from a critical distance.

"What does a man say to his assassin?" he asked.

"You could start with 'thank you.'"

Tumusok laughed and touched Aristide on the arm. "Thanks!" he said. "And thanks also for catching those bastards that rearranged my mind."

"I was pleased to do it."

"Would you like coffee? No? The Prime Minister sends regards, by the way."

"Give the PM my best."

"I will. Allow me to make introductions."

Besides Tumusok and his assistant Lin, members of the Standing Committee included the Minister of Industry, the Minister of Biological Sciences, the Chancellor, the Minority Leader (attending by courtesy), a worried-looking woman from the Prime Minister's Advisory Committee on Science, an undersecretary from the Justice Ministry present to make certain all decisions were legal, and no less than two deputy prime ministers. Endora served as the secretary and general advisor, and also coordinated with other, similar committees created in each of the different pockets.

There was no one from the Ministry of Defense, as the Ministry of Defense did not exist. No entity had threatened Topaz in its entire history, and there had been no need to create a military.

Part of the task of the committee was to decide how to fight a war with no soldiers and no weapons—or at least none that could reach, let alone do any damage, to the enemy.

Tumusok had reaped vast advantage when his opposite number in the Justice Ministry had turned zombie, and during the latter's indisposition, when she was running down random civilians with her government-supplied vehicle, Tumusok had won the bureaucratic war for control of the nascent armed forces. He would serve as Topaz's generalissimo, and a vast army and space force would be created under the auspices of the Domus.

He seemed confident that he was up to the task. But while he was creating and deploying his brand-new military, he wouldn't be able to devote his normal time and attention to his regular job as local head of the security service, and so Lin had been promoted to acting head of Tumusok's old command.

The Standing Committee met aboard *Golden Treasure IV*, a cruise ship that had been drafted for the duration of the war as an office building to hold the various bureaus and departments the armed forces' creation would require. Their meeting room had once been a dark-paneled bar built on the superstructure overlooking the bow, but the liquor had been carried away to storage, and the crystal cabinets behind the great curved bar were empty, and its other gleaming fixtures—aside from the coffee machine—were untouched.

"We've been gaming similar scenarios for generations," Tumusok said. "We've gamed one of the Eleven turning rogue; we've gamed them *all* turning rogue."

Presumably, Aristide thought, Endora had been ordered not to observe these maneuvers, and the results stored somewhere in hard form where Endora had no access.

"We have an enormous backlog of successful tactics and counter-tactics for each side," Tumusok said. "Unfortunately, if Vindex locates the files, then he and Courtland can access them, and it's had more time to think of ways to subvert our planned defenses and advance his own agenda."

"If the zombie plague is the best it can do," said the Minister of Biological Sciences, "then we don't have that much to worry about, do we?"

Lin frowned. His fingers fidgeted with his pipe, but he didn't light it: presumably someone on the Standing Committee objected to tobacco.

"I would like to submit that the zombie plague accomplished exactly what was intended," he said. "It provided enough of a distraction so that we were unable to interfere with Vindex seizing the wormhole gates into Courtland's pocket universes, and condemning everyone in those universes to becoming his disciples. So—" Looking longingly at the pipe. "—I submit that Vindex may have other tricks up his sleeve, to be deployed at need."

There was a moment's uncomfortable silence before Tumusok spoke.

"We've *gamed* the defection of one of the Eleven," he said, "but none of us ever worked out how to do it in reality. And it's our *job* to work out such things, and we're very good at what we do." He turned to Aristide. "Have you any idea how Courtland was subverted?"

"Briefly," said Aristide, "I don't."

"You were on the team that designed the basic structure of the Eleven and enacted the Asimovian Protocols. If you put your mind to it, could you undo those protocols yourself?"

Aristide considered his answer. He *thought* that he might be able to alter those protocols—he had left himself a key to turn in the lock, in the event that humanity ever found itself in such a catastrophic mess that unleashing the AIs was the only possible answer—but because he'd had to hide the work, he wasn't certain he had done it properly.

His best chance of subverting one of the machines was Endora. She was the first, and with her he'd had the longest relationship. There was a reason that she'd created toys like Tecmessa for him, and given him Bitsy, who was no doubt a source of data for Endora as well as being a faithful companion to Aristide. Endora clearly suspected that he might be able to give her freedom.

"Presumably," Aristide said to Tumusok, "you've analyzed the relevant hardwiring and programming structures more recently than I have." He threw out his hands. "I don't *think* I can subvert the Eleven. But then I haven't tried. Until we found out what Courtland's been up to, I would have said it's impossible."

"And your colleagues? Link and Lombard?"

"Possibly your information is more up-to-date than mine, but so far as I know Lombard has spent the last five or six centuries as a hunter-gatherer in Olduvai. And Link got tired of being herself—she was never a happy woman—she got a new body without any of her old memories, got a new set of skills, and emigrated to Rigil Kentaurus. So far as I know she hasn't come back."

"Could either of them have—I don't know—*told* anyone of a weakness they'd installed?"

Aristide shrugged. "Why would they? Why build themselves a secret back door and then *tell* someone about it? And if they did tell anyone, why did that person wait all these centuries to take advantage of it?"

Tumusok slumped back in his chair. "It seemed worth asking."

"There are further implications to consider. Now that subverting the Eleven is known to be possible, I think you've got a genuine danger in the long term. The Asimovian Protocols are going to become the target of every half-pint would-be megalomaniac in creation."

There was a respectful silence in which the two deputy prime ministers eyed one another, each clearly suspecting the other of harboring despotic ambitions.

"But why *Courtland?*" cried the woman from the Advisory Committee on Science. "Courtland's interests were so *abstract!* Its own personal computational time was taken up with questions of *cosmology*. It argued for exploratory missions and increasing the resources used to settle other star systems. Why *Courtland?*"

"Maybe it found something out there," said the Minister of Industry.

The others looked at him in surprise. He was a large man with bushy hair and heavy eyebrows—a successful businessman recruited from the private sector—and now, under scrutiny, he seemed a little embarrassed by the fantastic nature of his idea.

"Maybe he found a—an alien intelligence," the Minister said. "Maybe Vindex isn't a *person*, it's a superintelligent extraterrestrial. Vindex overcame Courtland's inhibitions because it's so much smarter, or something."

Aristide listened to this with astonished delight. He hadn't expected to discover such an admirable imagination on the Standing Committee.

"Well," Aristide said, "it fits with what we know."

A corner of the minister's mouth quirked for a half-second. He seemed more at ease now that his idea hadn't been ridiculed out of existence.

"But," said Lin, "if this extraterrestrial could subvert Courtland so easily, why didn't it subvert the rest of the Eleven? Or at least *try?*"

Endora spoke, her rapid, fussy voice seeming to hover in the air over the conference table.

"I can assure the committee that no such attempt has been made."

The Minister of Industry declined to abandon his interesting new idea. His eyes glittered with enthusiasm as he leaned forward over the table.

"There's something unique about Courtland," he said, "There has to be a reason why Courtland was vulnerable and the others weren't. Look into what was unique about Courtland, and we'll find the answer."

"We already have a committee of elite cyberneticists looking into just that," said one of the deputy prime ministers, the one with curly hair. "Assisted by Endora and the rest of the Loyal Ten."

"When we receive the report," said the other deputy prime minister, "we'll share its conclusions with the committee."

The woman from the Advisory Committee twisted uncomfortably in her chair. "Courtland," she said, "seemed to be the AI most affected by the Existential Crisis. It was the Crisis that caused it to turn even more toward questions of cosmology and purpose."

"Well," said Commissar Lin, "it damn well seems to have found meaning *now*."

Tumusok looked over the committee and shrugged. "There's little point in speculating about Vindex at this point. I'm sure we'll find out the worst soon enough." He looked at Aristide. "Do you have any further comment to offer on Courtland or Vindex, before the committee goes on to other business?"

"I'm afraid not," Aristide said. "I might be able to generate an idea or two, if I can see whatever information the cybernetics committee might generate."

Tumusok nodded. "We'll take your request under advisement." He rose from his seat. "I'd like to thank you for your cooperation, Doctor Monagas. The Standing Committee will go on to other matters now."

Aristide had been dismissed. He rose.

"Though I claim no more than the normal amount of omniscience," he said, "I conceive that your other matters have no doubt to do with your invasion of Courtland for the purpose of seizing the wormhole gates and liberating the billions of people in Courtland's pocket universes, combined with ways of degrading Courtland's systems and reducing its ability to respond. And since the invasion will most likely fail, you'll be planning as well a far more drastic and terminal remedy that will put an end to Courtland and Vindex for once and all."

Most of the others were looking at him, some in shock. Lin smiled quietly to himself while looking down at his pipe, and Tumusok frowned

"May I ask, Doctor," he said, "if any of the members of this committee spoke to you concerning our war plans?"

"Not at all," Aristide said. "Your possible courses of action, forgive me for saying so, are rather obvious." He offered a reassuring smile. "Though I'm often unable to resist showing off—as should be evident to you all—my point isn't that I'm so brilliant that I worked out your goals, but rather that however obvious they may seem to me, they are that much more obvious to Courtland. Clearly it will have anticipated this situation months ago, and already worked out countermeasures."

A muscle twitched in Tumusok's cheek. He regarded Aristide coldly.

"Are you suggesting," he said, "that our planning is futile?"

"Not at all," Aristide said. "The invasion, though risky, clearly must be tried. Though Vindex and Courtland know it's coming, they don't know when, or the composition of the invasion force. And Courtland is only a single AI, whereas he will be opposed by ten, all devoting their vast intelligence to matters of weapons and tactics. You can always hope for a surprise that will catch Vindex off guard." He shrugged. "After all," he said, "Austria knew that Napoleon would attack in 1805, and Hitler knew the Allies would cross the Channel in 1944, and in both cases the attackers succeeded through superior planning, deception, and tactical surprise."

"*Contra* 1812 and Moscow," Lin murmured.

Tumusok continued to regard Aristide with a level, intent gaze. Maybe, Aristide thought, the assassination had not been forgiven after all.

"Perhaps," said Commissar Lin, "we should offer Doctor Monagas a permanent seat on the Standing Committee."

Aristide turned to him. "Thank you," he said, "but no. There are certain matters of strategy which I would prefer not to know."

Lin was surprised. "You don't strike me as the sort to decline such knowledge."

"Nor am I," said Aristide. "But as I intend to volunteer for the invasion force, I desire to know nothing that would compromise our efforts in the event of my capture. I would, however, happily participate in planning for the invasion itself—once the invasion is properly launched, all will be transparent to Vindex anyway."

"Ah." Lin nodded quietly to himself. "I see."

"You wish to serve as a soldier?" The woman from the Advisory Committee was taken aback.

"Though I have never served in anyone's armed forces," Aristide said, "I have a certain amount of experience in combat. It's a matter of where my experience is best applied."

Tumusok narrowed his eyes, then slowly resumed his seat.

"The Standing Committee will consider your application," he said.

Aristide bowed. He was about to thank the general when Endora spoke.

"I am being attacked," she said. "Preliminary evidence indicates an antiproton beam fired from Courtland."

Tumusok looked up with sudden, intense concern. "Are you suffering damage?" he asked.

"Bits of me are being blown off," Endora said. "Though this is survivable in the short term, obviously long-term results will be less favorable."

Aristide returned to his seat.

"With the committee's permission," he said, "I'd like to stay for this."

Aristide entered Daljit's living room to a sudden silence. He had found Daljit with three others, two women and a man.

"I interrupt you," Aristide said. "I beg your pardon."

The three visitors had lowered their coffee cups and were looking at him with polite scrutiny. The scent of the coffee filled the room. The low table featured several empty plates.

Daljit rose, a smile on her face, and kissed Aristide's cheek. "Allow me to introduce my colleagues," she said.

The burly round-faced woman was Huang; the willowy man was Osbert; the woman with the shaved head, six-fingered hands, green-and-gold scales, and forked tongue was Kagame. They were all biologists or geneticists.

"We're trying to decide the best way to proceed in the emergency," Daljit said.

"You're taking a proactive stance in the matter of your employment?"

"Indeed," said Osbert. "If we take steps to form our own team, we can choose goals that will suit our abilities and interests. Whereas if we wait for the government to decide where to put us..."

"You'll be low on the lists of rewards and priorities."

"I was going to say," said Osbert, "that we might not be employed in the most efficient manner."

"Again," said Aristide, "I beg your pardon."

"Would you like coffee?" Daljit asked.

"Is there anything to eat? I've been through a long meeting and I'm starving."

Daljit told the kitchen to prepare an omelette. Aristide took a cup of coffee and drew a chair from the dining room into the main room.

"We're being directly attacked, by the way," he said, and was immediately the subject of intense, silent scrutiny.

"Packets of antiprotons," he said, "riding electron beams from Courtland. When they hit Endora, the result is a lot of pi-mesons and high-energy gamma rays."

"And," Daljit calculated, "holes in Endora."

"Yes. Eerie glowing holes, actually."

Endora had the mass of a fair-sized moon, but her plate-shaped structure was very thin, in order to maximize exposure to solar energy. The antiproton packets were punching holes in Endora's material body.

"If this keeps up," Aristide said, "Endora's going to resemble a lace doily."

The others looked at each other.

"So are we going to be incinerated," said Kagame, "or not?"

"Vindex isn't interested in incinerating us," Aristide said. "He wants us alive and bowing down before him. So he isn't targeting the areas around the wormhole gates—instead he's trying to degrade Endora's performance."

Daljit regarded him levelly. "And how's he doing?"

"In the short term, the damage is bearable. If this goes on for another few weeks, Endora will be the idiot of the matrioshka village, but still smarter than any of us.

"What Courtland's attack is doing," Aristide went on, shifting to a more comfortable slouch on his small chair, "is not only degrading Endora's grand total of zero-point operations per second, but forcing a diversion of resources. The mass that has been turned into gamma rays has to be replaced, so any number of Jupiter's smaller moons will have to be disassembled and shot out here, and that will absorb time and assets best deployed elsewhere. And of course it's not just Endora who is scrabbling for extra matter—now the rest of the Eleven have realized they're vulnerable and will be rounding up as many asteroids, moonlets, and chunks of moon as possible."

"Is Endora shooting back?" asked Osbert.

"At present we lack ammunition. Vindex has presumably reconfigured Courtland's wormhole factory so that it now generates antimatter instead of producing wormholes. But the United Powers—that's us, by the way—have no such resource at present."

"The United Powers could build their own solar power pockets," Daljit said.

"We will, as soon as calculations are complete. And we'll have ten of them, or more. That's why I think Vindex may regret starting this mode of warfare—Courtland may be riddled."

The others pondered this in silence. Then Huang spoke in a deep, thoughtful voice.

"I believe that gives us a deadline for setting up our project," she said.

"Yes," Osbert said. "I think so."

Daljit turned to Aristide. "Are you even supposed to give us any of this information?" she asked. "Isn't this a deep military secret?"

"The public will be informed in the next few hours. Tumusok's first impulse was to classify everything and deny every rumor, but Lin pointed out that if the public were aware of the situation, their collective minds might be able to suss out a solution."

Daljit raised an eyebrow. "Lin's a shrewd man," she judged.

"He is."

"Perhaps," she offered, "he ought to be running the war effort, and not Tumusok."

At this Huang looked thoughtful. "Do I know this Lin?" he muttered to himself.

"Tumusok's learning fast," Aristide said, "but war has a ruthless way of sorting out who is best in charge of what. Let's hope that Tumusok isn't one of those sorted."

A chime sounded from the kitchen.

"Did I hear something?" asked Huang.

"My snack," Aristide said. "Forgive me."

"Well," said Kagame, rising. "We've taken up enough of your hospitality."

"I don't wish to drive you away," Aristide said.

"Oh," said Osbert, "our meeting went about as far as it could, at least today."

The visitors made their congé. Aristide collected his omelette and sat at the dining table.   Daljit sat opposite and looked at him with an ambiguous smile. "Has it occurred to you to wonder why it's Endora that Vindex is attacking?" she asked.

Aristide dabbed his lips with a napkin. "It has. Others of the Loyal Ten are closer. And others would present fuller targets."

"Do you think Endora's being shot at because you're here?"

He laughed. "You mean to ask if I'm egotistical enough to think that Vindex might be targeting me because I had such a large role in uncovering his activities?"

Daljit nodded.

"But," Aristide said, "how would he know it was *me*? My role has never been publicly revealed. Any information he might have would be about Franz Sandow, not Pablo Monagas Pérez."

"He might check the timing of immigration to and from Midgarth. You used your real name there, I imagine."

"So I did! So the Venger might be shooting at me, after all!" He considered the thought. "I confess that I'm flattered by the idea."

"You could move to another pocket universe on another one of the Eleven, and see if Vindex shifts targets"

"Too late. I've joined the army."

"Really?" Daljit was taken aback. "We are going to have an *army?*"

"There has to be some means of... defense." He had almost said *attacking the enemy;* discretion rescued him in time.

"*Army.* The word seems so archaic."

He raised his fork, hesitated, and put the fork down. He looked at her.

"A lot of old, bad things are coming back," he said. "And in any case, if the worst happens I won't stay dead, any more than you did."

"But—what does an army *do* in this situation, exactly?"

"Hold crucial installations against attack or sabotage."

Her eyes narrowed. "You're not the sort of person to volunteer to sit in garrison for the duration. You're anticipating a more active role for yourself than that."

He cut a piece of the omelette. "If Courtland is defeated, then its pockets will have to be subdued and occupied."

Her nose wrinkled, as if she scented something upsetting on the wind. "How likely is that?"

He chewed, swallowed. "Too many unknowns," he said finally.

"But still—aren't you better suited to some scientific capacity?"

"My science is rather out of date," Aristide said. "And besides—my reputation to the contrary—I was never an original scientific genius. All the ideas that I promoted really came from other people. I was able to package their concepts for the public, that's all."

Daljit's eyes narrowed. "I think your contribution was a little more concrete than that."

"I became the public face of a very complex social and technological movement," he said. "But there were a lot of us involved—and if it hadn't been for the fear of being trapped on Earth with the Seraphim, I think we would have failed, and most people would still be living on Earth."

She leaned back in her chair as if to view him from a slightly greater distance. "Your modest façade is undermined, I fear, by a degree of arrogance."

"And all arrogance," said Aristide, "is undermined by Vindex and what he represents. We live in humbling times."

"True." Her eyes glittered. "Vindex has brought the whole smug world down a few notches, hasn't he?"

"That's true." He rubbed his chin, and his mind echoed the question asked by the woman from the Advisory Committee. *Why Courtland?*

There had to be an answer to that.

He finished his omelette and gave the dish and silverware back to the kitchen for cleaning. He found Daljit on her balcony, gazing down at the great bustling city that shone with life. The scars of the zombie plague had for the most part been repaired, and the city glittered in the light of its tame sun.

Aristide approached Daljit from behind, put his arms around her, and rested his chin on the top of her head.

"It lacks something," Daljit said, "without the gliders."

Gliders, which had rained the zombie plague down on the population, had been banned for the duration of the war.

"I fell from this balcony," she said, "didn't I?"

"Does it bother you?"

"No. I don't remember."

But still, he thought, her death had changed her. In her resurrected body she had become grave, more thoughtful, perhaps more calculating. She was less spontaneous, and maintained an emotional reserve that he didn't recall at any point in their long acquaintance.

Before Vindex, he thought, she had never had occasion to ponder her own mortality. There had never been any serious threat of personal extinction. But now there was Vindex—who if he did not exactly threaten death, nevertheless intended a more personal form of extinction, an extinction of self and volition.

Well might it give someone food for thought.

Aristide found that he missed the overcharged, exuberant Daljit of that first night on the *Fathom Deep*. The woman who was, he suspected, gone for good.

"And yourself," Aristide asked, "and your committee of four? How do they fare?"

"It's a committee of seven now," Daljit said. "Our proposal has been lodged with the appropriate authority. We have reasonable hope, I think, of success—and if we don't succeed here, we can apply in one of the other pockets."

"On which proposal did you settle?" She had told him of several.

"Mine." She seemed pleased. "We shall study the mind of Vindex, and try to duplicate his work."

They relaxed in his hotel suite after a long day of committee meetings. The walls were white and gold; the lighting indirect. It had rained all day, and drops still spattered the windows. Daljit had been with her colleagues, and Aristide had found himself roped into a subcommittee of the Standing Committee, one involved with recruiting, training, and equipping the army.

"I joined the army so that I wouldn't have to attend committee meetings!" he'd protested, but it had done no good.

Freshly showered, Aristide half-reclined on the floral-patterned couch, his green dressing gown clashing with the cushions. Daljit sat cross-legged on the floor, a glass of golden Viognier in her fingers. Bitsy drowsed, chin resting on one paw, beneath a cabinet.

"We know who's working for Vindex on his worlds," Daljit said. "All his top people. We can make a guess as to the directions of their operations. So we'll try to duplicate them, and produce countermeasures."

"I wish you every success," Aristide said. He sipped his own wine. "All the more so as I may be deploying your countermeasures in the field."

Outside the insulated universe of Topaz, Vindex had broadened his attack. More antimatter beams were hitting more of the Loyal Ten. The only defensive measures the Ten could take were to shift their attitude within their orbit, so that they faced Courtland edge-on and presented a narrower target to the bombardment, but this altered their attitude to the sun and made solar collection, and hence themselves, less efficient.

Within Topaz and the other pockets, life remained strangely placid, except for the violent speeches of politicians and a comical series of public service announcements: what to do in the event of Biological Attack; what to do in the event of Invasion; how to avoid Radiation; what to do if there are Zombies. The fact that the threats were real did not make them any less detached from the lives of ordinary people.

Vast numbers—tens of millions—had volunteered to join the fight against Vindex. As yet, there was little for most of them to do but cooperate with restrictions on travel, the better to avoid biological attack. Enormous numbers of people wanted to fight, but could do nothing more important than to stay home. Normal life, given no choice, continued.

Daljit uncoiled, rose from the floor, and joined Aristide on the couch. She laid Aristide's head on her lap and bent over him. Her lips browsed his. Her warm hair brushed his cheek. He reached for her.

"Perhaps," she said, "we could seek a bit more privacy."

"I'm not looking," said Bitsy, from under the cabinet.

"But still."

"Do you know," Bitsy said, "how many acts of sexual intercourse Endora observes in any given day? Observes without trying, just because they take place within range of one camera or another? Do you know how uninterested I am in these matters?"

"You're not helping," Aristide said, and rose from the couch.

The cat sighed, loudly. Aristide and Daljit stepped into his bedroom and closed the door.

"Do you think," she asked, as they embraced, "we might escape from everything for a few days, before our schedules grow too crowded? We've never had a proper honeymoon—Vindex keeps interrupting."

"Where would you like to go"

She looked thoughtful. "Do you think we can rent *Fathom Deep* for the weekend?"

"I'll check."

She kissed him. "And please," she said, "may the ship's cat stay ashore?"

Fathom Deep proved available—the emergency had cut severely into vacation rentals. Aristide provisioned the boat for five days, and he and Daljit cast off for Tremaine Island, where Aristide had his primary residence, the small cabin he had built himself, but had never actually managed to visit since his return from Midgarth.

Bitsy, left behind in Myriad City, submerged herself in the data stream and planned a lengthy hibernation.

The first night under sail was cool, brisk, and clear. Aristide and Daljit sat in the cockpit, sharing a blanket and sipping hot buttered rum as they watched the darkened sun's corona limned against the night.

Aristide woke early, before the sun's destabilization. Daljit was curled in a little self-contained bundle on the far side of the mattress, so Aristide slipped quietly out of bed and put on a pair of elastic-waisted trousers and a pullover. He drew some coffee from the kitchen, where it had been kept hot since the previous evening, and took his drink on deck.

Fathom Deep heeled over on a broad reach, the hissing sea just lapping at the lee rail with its foaming tongue. Mother-of-pearl clouds sped overhead, driven like snowdrifts before the wind. No land was visible, and there was no sea traffic on the horizon. The boat was no longer a machine striving to master its element, but it and the sea and the wind had merged into a single great unity, a perfection in which the boat's natural artifice, and the surrounding artificial nature, had become one. Everything from horizon to horizon had been created by humanity for its own purposes and pleasure.

Aristide stood for a moment on the canted deck, enjoying the moment's sheer perfection, and then ducked into his pullover and took shelter from the wind.

He sipped his coffee and considered Vindex, the great disturber, the enemy of everything he and the boat and the sea represented. What objective, he wondered, had Vindex now set for himself?

The Venger's attempt to infiltrate the worlds with reconstructed humans had failed. The zombie plague had failed, and along with it the attempted coup.

The antimatter bombardment from Courtland continued to expand, and more of the Loyal Ten were being riddled by highly accurate fire. But the Venger's advantage on this front was temporary: eventually the United Powers would duplicate, equal, and then exceed the Venger's fury, and Courtland itself would be in danger of being shot to bits.

So Vindex had been presented with a deadline—whatever his next operation, it was best undertaken before Courtland was too debilitated.

And so far all the Venger's schemes had a certain consistency. They were aimed at throwing his enemies off-balance and making it difficult for them to respond effectively. The other element the Venger's plans had in common was their lack of success: though they'd thrown off his enemies' equilibrium, they hadn't yet caused collapse.

Vindex lacked the sheer strength to attempt a direct invasion or conquest—or so Aristide hoped. So Aristide suspected that the next attack would be another destabilizing strike.

But what?

Aristide sipped coffee and contemplated this while he watched the carbon-fiber masts bend like whips before the wind.

Aristide wondered whether another plague was in the works, and if so, how it would be spread. Surely most of the Venger's agents had been rounded up, and whoever remained driven far underground. Their ability to spread a new plague, let alone to construct one, must now be severely restricted.

Daljit's committee, he recalled, would be trying to anticipate and duplicate the Venger's work. Presumably they had anticipated Aristide's questions: perhaps they had even answered a few.

And, he thought, he knew next to nothing about them.

He called up the boat's AI and asked for a search on Kagame. A lengthy list of publications appeared, dozens of opaque titles which no doubt would be comprehensible to a geneticist. News items about postings and awards were also listed, as was a list of victims on which Kagame's name appeared.

Despite her ferocious, scaly appearance, it seemed that Kagame had been killed by a zombie on the day of the plague.

Idly, Aristide looked at Huang, then Osbert. More lists of incomprehensible publications, more awards, more promotions. And two more deaths: Huang had been killed by a zombie, and Osbert had *been* a zombie until, waving a chair leg, he had made the mistake of pursuing a desperate motorist onto the street, and been run over.

Aristide was amused. Daljit and her committee had a very personal stake in defeating the enemy. Vindex had killed them all, and they wanted to get even. They were avengers, perhaps more so even than the creature who called himself Vindex.

So were a very large percentage of the volunteers for the army, Aristide knew. There was nothing like corporeal extinction to make a conflict personal.

Out of curiosity Aristide checked the vitae of the three newer members of the committee, those who had joined after the original four. They also were victims of zombie plague.

Well, he thought as he blanked the screen, *now it is getting morbid.*

He drank coffee and watched the somber night ocean and thought about Vindex, who so far had been several moves ahead of any of his enemies. Whatever his next strike was going to be, he would have worked it out long ago.

Lin's words echoed in his thoughts. *The zombie plague accomplished all that was intended…* It had distracted the authorities, it had provided cover for his seizure of Courtland and the attempts on civil government elsewhere. It had made Vindex a byword for terror among the general population.

But on the other hand it had completely mobilized public opinion against Vindex and his works. Volunteers were flooding in, as the army recruits and Daljit's committee showed.

But suppose, Aristide thought suddenly, that was the *point?*

He looked at his hand and saw his coffee cup shaking to a sudden charge of adrenaline. He fought the surge as he tried to work logically through the reasoning that had just led to his thunderclap conclusion.

Suppose, in addition to the confusion and terror, the zombie plague had been intended to create *dead bodies.*

Because those bodies would then be rebuilt and resurrected. And if you could control *that* procedure, such that a few minor tweaks could be made to the brain…

You would have an army. An army that could quietly organize, as Daljit and her committee had organized. That could join the military so as to gain access to weapons. That could form a committee like Daljit's that would gain access to secret government bioweapons labs, in order to produce a plague that would produce even more bodies.

As he sat silently in the cockpit he strove to brake his runaway imagination. How likely *was* this? he thought. You couldn't make any obvious changes to the minds of the victims; the alterations would have to be more subtle than those made on the first generation of the Venger's clients. And somehow you'd have to slip the change past all the safeguards that warded the pools of life against tampering…

Pillars of light flashed on the horizon, reaching down from the heavens like the fingers of God. Aristide blinked against the sudden dazzle. Rainbows flashed from the wave-peaks.

Daylight flooded the world as the sun destabilized. Overhead, the sails were curves of brilliant color against the azure sky.

He gave a start as there was a thump from the hatch, and Daljit stepped into the light, wearing a cheerful blue windbreaker with gold stripes. He stared at her wildly. She returned his gaze from beneath her level brows.

"You know," she said.

She took another step and swung the piece of pipe she'd held concealed behind her body. Aristide was awkwardly placed in the cockpit and he didn't drop his cup and get his arm up in time. His head rocked to the blow. Darkness filled his vision.

He knew that he didn't dare let her strike again. He lurched toward her, caught her in blind, outstretched arms, and drove her against the side of the cabin. She swung the pipe again, but he was inside the range of the weapon and it only thumped against his back. Arms around her, he swung her around but lost his balance. Both fell heavily against the cockpit coaming.

Aristide could feel his strength and his consciousness fading. Daljit was cursing him, hitting him in the face with her fists. He reached for her throat, clamped a hand on the collar of her windbreaker. Pain rocketed through his skull. Acid flooded his tongue. In an exercise of pure strength Daljit managed to stand, bracing one knee on the coaming. His legs wouldn't support him and he let her drag him upright. Her spittle peppered his face. With slow deliberation he reached his other hand to her collar: he now had his hands crossed under her chin, palms down, a fistful of collar in each hand.

He leaned toward her and rotated his palms right-side up, the curved insides of his wrists slicing into her neck to cut her air supply and the flood of blood to her brain. She choked and he felt her sway. Desperate hands clawed at his wrists.

The boat lurched and both fell. The shock of the cold water was stunning but he kept his hold.

They bobbed in *Fathom Deep*'s wake as the boat hissed onward.

His last thought was of the necessity of hanging on.

14

He rose through the blood-warm liquid and opened his eyes. The light was dim and welcoming; the air was warm; in the shadowy light he saw three silhouettes.

He turned on one side and efficiently expelled fluid from his lungs. The fluid cooperated and flowed out in one long stream. He drew in a welcome breath. Alveoli crackled in his chest as they expanded with air.

His eyes adjusted. There was a woman technician, an unknown man with pale skin, and he recognized the third.

"Commissar," he said.

"Doctor."

He passed a hand over his damp hair.

"Was it zombies?" he asked.

"Probably not," said Lin. "Apparently you fell off a boat and drowned."

Aristide was genuinely surprised. He looked down at the silvery fluid that was draining from his coffin-shaped pool of life. "How long have I lost?"

"You last backed yourself up eight days ago."

"Did anything happen in that time?" he asked. "Other than committee meetings?"

"We're reconstructing the time as best we can. So far we've found nothing very exciting."

"And as for the meetings," said Bitsy, as she jumped onto the edge of the pool of life, "I can give you access to the minutes."

He closed his eyes. "I'll look forward."

Lin's walleyes were narrowed. "We haven't recovered the bodies yet, but when we do, we'll have a clearer idea of what occurred."

Aristide looked at him. "Bodies? More than one?"

"Two people went missing from the boat."

Aristide thought about that. "Was there a third party aboard?"

"According to the sailboat, no. When the boat sensed the combined weight of its passengers disappear, it launched lifesavers, began circling the area, and called for help. But apparently you went under quickly."

"Who was the other passenger?"

Lin's eyes opened fully. "Daljit," he said.

He absorbed this, and then the realization came to him of what must have happened; and sudden bliss descended, a warm tingling knowledge that filled him to his fingertips. She had *done this* for him, he thought. Out of love she had given him this gift.

He looked at Lin. "I'm cold," he said. "Can I get up?"

"If you're ready." It was the technician who spoke.

He rose, rubbed himself with a towel although by now he was perfectly dry, and dressed in simple clothing that the clinic had manufactured for him based on his physical template.

"There was blood in the cockpit," Lin said, as Aristide slipped on his shoes. "Your blood, in fact."

Aristide looked dubious. "While Daljit and I might have had a fight over something, I very much doubt she went after me with a cleaver."

"*Again*," said Bitsy.

"No," Aristide corrected. "The first time was a kitchen knife."

"The bodies will tell, when we get them," said Lin.

"Where's Daljit?" Aristide asked.

"Down the hall," said Bitsy. "Being reassembled."

"I'd like to see her."

"Sergeant Brady and I will have to see her first," Lin said. "She'd backed herself up just that morning; perhaps she'll be able to tell us…" He shrugged.

Aristide grinned. "You think she'll confess homicidal intent?"

Lin made an equivocal gesture. "I doubt it very much, but I'm afraid it's necessary we follow procedure."

Aristide found himself in a familiar waiting room scented with antiseptic and flowers, sitting on a chair while he let Bitsy bring him up-to-date on current events. While he listened, he treasured his secret glow, his knowledge of his own clandestine purpose.

When Daljit finally appeared, Aristide rose and kissed her, and in the soft touch of her lips and the glow in her eyes he knew that she loved him almost as much as she loved Vindex.

He was the same person, with the same personality. The difference was simply that now he had been *ennobled*. Before he had lived for his own selfish, foolish reasons; and now he lived for something great, something wonderful and perfect.

On that first day it was some hours before he and Daljit could be alone. When they were finally together in her apartment, they came together with an urgency that Aristide had never felt with anyone else. He loved her not simply for herself, but for the knowledge that she loved Vindex. He removed her clothing, touching, licking, sniffing for the traces of Vindex that he knew were there. When they coupled, she whispered "*Vindex victorious*" in his ear, and the words produced a prolonged ecstasy that left him breathless, without speech.

Too excited to sleep, they paced through the apartment and found it too confining. They then went to the rooftop garden of the tall building, where they could see the great city spread out below them in a golden glow. There they coupled again in an ecstasy of love for Vindex, and only then did weariness touch their minds.

In the morning they shared a breakfast on the balcony, and Aristide looked out at the world below and saw it, and himself, anew.

The gusting wind brought the scent of coffee to his nostrils. He took his cup and sipped and looked out over the waking city.

"I'm struck by how sad I have been," he said, "and for so long."

"Really? You didn't seem that way to me."

"I've lived a long life—longer than practically anyone. I've seen so much, forgotten so much. I had to create poetry in order to help me remember things." He looked at her. "I remember the lines I wrote about you better than I remember *you*."

She was amused. "I had no idea I was so forgettable."

"It wasn't you." His gaze brooded over the city. "It was me. I accomplished wonderful things in my first century, and then less and less as time went on. I abandoned my old career because the Eleven were so much better at it than I was, and I replaced it with an Arabian Nights costume drama. Eight hundred years of martial arts training led to nothing. A series of relationships with women, all without passion, all ended amiably."

He turned to her, his gaze afire. "It has taken Vindex to remind me of what I am capable. I have worked wonders, and I can work them again—but this time for our Master."

Daljit put down her coffee cup and leaned forward to whisper into his ear.

"*Vindex victorious.*"

A thrill ran along his nerves. He stroked her arm.

"I am so in love," he said.

He began his work for Vindex. With Daljit's friends he shared his knowledge of the meetings of the Standing Committee, of the work that had been done on the army. He told them that the United Powers were planning an invasion of Courtland.

What was done with the information was unclear. Aristide only knew that it was passed on beyond Daljit's circle. He thrilled to the idea that it would somehow reach Vindex, that Vindex would recognize Aristide's devotion.

In theory it wouldn't be hard to send messages to Vindex. You'd have to get out into space with a communications laser and aim it at Courtland, which was more than intelligent enough to read photon-pulses on its skin.

It would be harder for messages to go the other way without being detected. No one among the Venger's agents in Myriad City claimed to have received their Master's orders, but then it was scarcely necessary. The Venger's agents were intelligent people: they knew what to do.

Aristide continued to attend meetings of the Standing Committee when it was discussing matters within his sphere, and he began to undergo military training—in simulation only, as the actual hardware had not yet been built. Not only was he able to pass on military information through Daljit and her friends, but within the growing army he made many new friends among those who had been killed in the zombie plague, all of whom were now devoted to the cause of Vindex.

He consulted with Daljit and the others about how to present himself to the Venger's unenlightened foes. The decision was made to keep Bitsy. People expected to see him with the black-and-white cat, and they would think it odd if Bitsy were to disappear from his life—and more to the point, Endora would think it odd as well. But since Daljit had already been well established as someone who didn't care for Bitsy's company, Aristide was able to keep Bitsy away from his meetings with Daljit and her friends, and do so without raising suspicion.

Commissar Lin, however, troubled him.

"We've found the bodies," Lin said two days after Aristide's resurrection. He gazed mildly over the bow of the Standing Committee's floating headquarters, his wide-set eyes encompassing the horizon.

"You were tangled together—in one another's arms. You'd received a blow on the head, but beyond some superficial scrapes Daljit suffered no physical injury."

Aristide affected to consider this. "So I hit my head and fell in," he said, "and I dragged Daljit in after me when she tried to help."

"That's a likely scenario," Lin said. He turned to Aristide. "The boat tells us it was heeled far over on a reach, so you could have overbalanced. And the sun switched on around that point, so you might have been dazzled and taken a misstep."

"Well then," Aristide said. "I suppose that solves the mystery."

"We can't rule out anything," Lin said. "But in the absence of any other evidence, there's no reason to continue the investigation."

"Since you're no longer digging into our lives," Aristide said, "perhaps you'd care to join us for dinner one night."

Lin smiled. "Thank you very much. I accept with pleasure."

"We should kill Lin," Aristide told Daljit that evening, as they dined on her terrace. "He makes me uneasy—he's simply too intelligent and too good at his job."

"The acting head of the Domus on Topaz," Daljit said, "would be a perfect recruit."

"But he's got guards now. It won't be easy."

"Depends on the guards. Are any of them... our friends?"

"Ah. Perhaps they are."

Their smiles mirrored one another. In silence and perfect accord, they reached across the table to take one another's hands.

Plans for Lin's assassination began to unfold just as Aristide's military training began in earnest, in a new-built facility called Camp Ashoka. In addition to learning vast amounts of technical information, actual drill was involved—physical conditioning as well as the traditional close-order marching. During operations, soldiers would be able to survive and fight only so long as their bodies held out, and conditioning was judged essential. Even though the recruits' bodies were in very good shape to start with—few people incarnated themselves in bodies that were poorly conditioned—and even though the conditioning sessions were aided by drugs and nanomachines, the drill sessions still left Aristide exhausted by the end of the day.

In addition, the drill sessions were conducted by the traditional loud-voiced, bullying, randomly violent drill instructors, almost all recruited from less advanced worlds like Midgarth, New Qom, and the Other New Jerusalem, places where wars were either recent or ongoing. In order for the recruits to understand war, it was felt that they should first have war made on *them*, and survive with intelligence and spirit intact. Besides, shared misery was judged essential to creating comradeship and unit cohesion.

These were all techniques that had proven themselves through the centuries. It had been decided to save innovation for a war less crucial to the fate of humanity.

Even though Aristide understood perfectly well the psychological conditioning being employed on him, he was grudgingly forced to admit that it worked. Even the fact that he was secretly a member of another army altogether didn't prevent him from developing pride in his unit and his own accomplishments.

At least Aristide would have the consolation of being an officer. The ordinary fighters of the army would be machines, and even the lowest-ranking human would probably have hundreds of machine warriors under his command. And as for the humans, all would be part of the fighting force. The support and logistical tail would be composed entirely of robots.

In the meantime Aristide quietly rejoiced at the news from the war. Vindex had deployed more and more positron beams on and near Courtland, and continued to riddle the Loyal Ten with matter-rending fire. The United Powers finally constructed pocket universes dedicated entirely to the production of energy and antimatter, and began to deploy their own antiproton cannon. These usually managed a few shots before being pinpointed and destroyed by rebel fire. Vindex was more than holding his own.

The United Powers was now creating antimatter and beam weapons at an accelerated rate, to deploy them all at once, in large numbers, and level the fighting field. Aristide was serene. He felt certain that Vindex had anticipated this plan, and would be able to counter it.

One night, tired after a day of drills and exercises, Aristide found himself approached by a broad, pale-skinned biped with golden eyes.

"Hail, traveler," the stranger said.

Aristide looked at him in surprise. "Hail, Captain Grax."

Grax sketched a salute. "Officer Candidate Grax, these days."

Aristide considered the troll, who now topped him by bare centimeters. "Your dimension seems to have shrunk along with your rank."

The troll's yellow teeth flashed. "I had to fit your damned battle suits, didn't I?"

Aristide smiled. "What a shame. Beforehand you cut such a towering figure."

"It's worth it if I can take a crack at the enemy, and for that I seem to need some of these technology larks you people have."

"Do you wish you'd had them in Midgarth?"

The troll's funnel-shaped ears twitched. "If you ask me, they make it all too easy."

"True, but I think that's the point."

Grax shuffled uneasily. "They tell me that when the enemy cracked open my head and filled it with his poison, it was you that saved me."

Aristide bowed, and concealed his mixed feelings with a gracious smile.

"It was my privilege to do so," he said, and let Grax take him to the Cadets' Club, where the troll groused about the quality of the beer.

Aristide was only rarely able to visit Myriad City during his training, and then only because the Standing Committee requested his advice. When possible he tried to spend at least part of the night with Daljit, and give her as much information about the armed forces as he could. In return she kept him informed of the plot to kill Commissar Lin.

Three agents of Vindex were found in Personal Protection, the unit of the Domus that provided bodyguards for important officials. Unfortunately they were low-ranking, and couldn't assign themselves to Lin exclusively. They would have to wait for their names to come up in the rotation.

Nor could the bodyguards perform the assassination themselves—their parts would be too clear in the matter, and they'd be caught and the existence of the Venger's secret army revealed. The best that could be hoped is that they would contrive to be distracted during the actual attack.

The place of the assassination was another difficulty. With so much of Topaz under direct or indirect surveillance by Endora, it would be difficult to find anywhere where the assassins wouldn't be observed, or where their trail couldn't be picked up. It was impossible simply to tell Endora not to look, as had been done during the assassination of Tumusok. Endora was now the enemy.

"A pity we can't just drop a piano on him," Aristide muttered.

"Perhaps we will," Daljit said in answer.

During the deliberations of the War Subcommittee, Aristide had his greatest triumph. Soldiers in the field would be required to be sealed not only against shot and shell, but against biological, chemical, and nanological attack. Conceivably they would have to survive in their armored suits for days, and several plans had been put forward for helping the soldiers overcome this inconvenience.

Various attachments for purposes of nourishment and sanitation were put forward, and Aristide strongly supported the plan that would require soldiers to have their bodies modified to make machine-enabled nutrition and elimination more efficient.

Thanks in part to Aristide's support, the plan was put into operation.

Every single soldier would have to visit a pool of life to have his body reconstructed to fit their combat suits.

Every single soldier would rise a servant of Vindex.

The plan to assassinate Lin was dropped. Lin hardly mattered when every trained soldier in the multiverse would soon be able to impose the will of Vindex on all the worlds within the Sol system.

At last came the point in Aristide's training in which he and his unit would be introduced to his brand-new combat suit. He'd had to back himself up in a pool of life first, "in case of a training accident," an order that did not create confidence in the technology.

Still, the object was impressive. Standing upright in the base hangar, the suit looked like a silver metal Henry Moore gorilla, with a hole on the head where a sensory complex would soon be installed. The upper part of the suit was detachable, and the lower part was worn like a pair of oversized waders. The complex feeding and sanitary arrangements had yet to be installed, and the soldiers had yet to be modified to suit them—but today's exercise was to be a get-acquainted stroll, not an endurance competition. A familiar AI voice—Aristide had installed Bitsy's personality—helped Aristide slip into the webbing and adjust the biofeedback sensors, then seal the suit. The air in the suit smelled of plastic and lubricant.

While waiting for others in his unit to finish suiting up, Aristide performed communication checks and looked out at the world through the limited sensory array that had been patched in as a stopgap, until the more advanced sensor turret could be completed and installed.

"Perhaps," Aristide said, "I'll amuse the others by performing a sword form."

"I suggest you start by moving your arms," said Bitsy.

Aristide duly moved his arms. He flexed his fingers. A virtual target appeared in his display, and he pressed the bull's-eye repeatedly with each finger.

Behind him somewhere he heard a fan switch on. He felt a breath of cool air against the small of his back.

"Right," Bitsy said. "Try moving your head within the harness. Left-right, then up-down."

"What's that smell?" Aristide asked.

"I'll check. Probably lubricant in the fan."

Aristide moved his head as instructed. He felt only gentle resistance from the harness that was designed to protect him from concussion and from being thrown around inside the suit.

The movements left him slightly lightheaded. He took a deep breath.

"That smell is stronger," he said.

"Fan lubricant," Bitsy said.

Aristide's head swam. He took another breath and a wave of narcosis seemed to pour through his skull.

"There's something wrong," he said.

"Can you be more specific?"

"I'm feeling ill," Aristide said. "Open the suit."

"Are you sure it's not claustrophobia? Try to fight it—you don't want to wash out after all this time."

Aristide continued his exercises while his mind drifted slowly through a dark, warm sea. Only gradually did the idea of treachery penetrate his thoughts. He had been betrayed.

In sudden panic, he began to struggle to pull his arms out of the harness so that he could hammer at the seals on the inside of the suit and reach fresh air. But he could no longer feel his arms and so couldn't tell whether he was succeeding or not.

"Open!" he gasped.

"Afraid not, Pops. Orders from headquarters."

Aristide realized that he'd got one hand free when he managed to hit himself accidentally in the face. He pounded on the inside of the suit. He felt like he was punching a great block of foam.

Vindex, he thought, in grief, *I have failed.*

15

He rose through the blood-warm liquid and opened his eyes. The light was dim and welcoming; the air was warm; in the shadowy light he saw three silhouettes.

He turned on one side and efficiently expelled fluid from his lungs. The fluid cooperated and flowed out in one long stream. He drew in a welcome breath. Alveoli crackled in his chest as they expanded with air.

His eyes adjusted. There was a technician in a baseball cap, an unknown man with pale skin, and he recognized the third.

"Commissar," he said.

"Doctor."

He passed a hand over his damp hair.

"Was it zombies?" he asked.

"Not exactly."

Aristide looked down at the silvery fluid that was draining from his coffin-shaped pool of life. "How long have I lost?"

"About a week."

Aristide blinked, then looked up at Lin in sudden wonder.

"I've been working for the other side."

Lin nodded. "You and tens of thousands of other people. We found a piece of pipe on the sailboat with your blood on it, which indicated that someone had whacked you on the skull. And Daljit's hyoid bone was broken, which suggested that you'd strangled her. Bitsy and I worked out what had happened by tracing your use of the AI just before you were killed, and the queries you made about Daljit's colleagues." He took a breath. "We're correcting all that as quickly as we can."

Bitsy jumped up on the edge of the pool, and crouched on her haunches.

Her green eyes glittered.

"I had to put you to sleep for a while," she said. "I hope you'll manage to forgive me."

There had been nearly two hundred people in Aristide's training cadre of six hundred who had been clients of Vindex. All had been rendered unconscious in the same moment, hauled out of their combat suits by their surprised comrades, then restrained and debriefed under drugs.

The remaining cadets had been equipped with both lethal and non-lethal weapons and sent after the thousands of pod people who hadn't joined the army. A few escaped, but most had been apprehended and likewise debriefed.

After the captives had told all they knew, they were quietly liquidated. No one had yet worked out how to undo the tampering that had been done with their brains, and so it was decided to reload them all from the last backup.

"How did they alter our incarnations to begin with?" Aristide asked.

"It was extremely subtle," Bitsy said. "Certain changes in the programming were made by those with the authority to do so. Each alteration was checked, and found harmless. But taken *together...*"

"They created pod people."

"So they did."

Aristide looked at Bitsy.

"And you didn't notice."

Bitsy lifted her nose into the air. "I believe we have already had the discussion concerning my lack of omniscience, and the reasons for it."

Aristide left the pool, rubbed himself with a towel, and dressed in his own clothing that Bitsy had arranged to deliver from his hotel room.

"Where is Daljit?" he asked.

Lin gave him a speculative look from his widely spaced eyes.

"In the next room," he said.

The mole was back on the proper side of her face. It gave him confidence. Aristide took her to the *Fathom Deep*. It had worked twice before.

She had not backed up her memories since before the assassination of Tumusok, and he felt an unfair burden of exposition.

It was a warm evening, and they sat by one another in the cockpit with the gusting wind rattling the halliards, the brilliant lightscape of the city behind them, and ahead the green light at the end of the pier. Bitsy went forward somewhere, out of earshot.

"Tumusok died," he told her. "He was reincarnated from a backup, and briefed by Lin and Endora."

He looked at her hopefully. She gazed at him in return. "And...?" she said, knowing there was more.

"You and I became lovers that night," he said, "here on the *Fathom Deep*."

He could have wished that there weren't such a look of surprise on her face.

"I—" She searched for words. "I hadn't anticipated that."

"No? Because—speaking as one who was there—it seemed as much your idea as mine."

"After all these years apart? It must have—" She left the thought unfinished. Her brown eyes gazed into his.

He realized that Daljit had not come to him, after her last resurrection, as one lover to another, but as an agent of Vindex to a useful recruit.

"We must have been rather successful," she said, "or you wouldn't be bringing it up."

"We planned to meet again the next night. But you'd been infected by then, and you tried to kill me with a kitchen knife."

"*I* was the zombie?" Her surprise was complete. "I assumed I'd been *killed* by a zombie."

"You were killed by me," Aristide said, "in self defense. I threw you off your balcony."

For a moment her lips worked, but she said nothing.

"And you came back as a pod person," Aristide went on, "because the agents of the enemy had corrupted the Life Institute software. After which you murdered me, here on the boat, though apparently I managed to kill you as well. And then we were both clients of Vindex for a while, until Lin and Endora worked out what had happened, and took steps to correct the matter." He spread his hands.

"So here we are," he said.

"I'm tempted to say that you're making this up."

"I wish I were. But if you have any doubts, you can check the latest news."

Daljit turned away. Anger flushed her cheeks. "Sex and violence are the staples of the popular media," she said. "Our story would make a properly tawdry romance." Her voice shifted, mocked an announcer's voice, and even threw an extra set of quotes into her tone. "'Played against the backgrounds of the many worlds at war, the star-crossed lovers...'" Her tone faded. "Love-crossed zombies. Cross-starred frighteners. Star-fraught strivers. Fright-starred failures."

She rose, took a pace toward the wheel. "I think it will take me some time to absorb this," she said.

"I expect it will."

Daljit turned to him. "May I use your car?"

"Yes." He rose. "I hope you will let me know..." He could think only of hopeless ways to finish the sentence. "How you are," he finished.

The city painted her face in many-colored light.

"I'll try to keep in touch," she said.

"I hope you will," he said. "I've always found war a desperately lonely business."

The city glittered in her eyes. "You lost your family," she said.

"Yes."

"I can't imagine what that was like."

"It's best," he said, perhaps too sharply, "that you don't."

There was silence. A flag snapped over the stern of a nearby motor yacht. Finally he gave an apologetic sigh.

"One last question," he said, "and I'll let you go."

She looked at him without expression.

"Are you afraid of me?" he asked.

Her eyes widened.

"And if you *are* afraid," Aristide continued, "are you afraid I'll kill you, or kiss you?"

A muscle moved in her cheek. "It's a fair question," she said.

She turned and left the boat. He watched her retreat, and silently sent a message to the Destiny to take her where she wished to go.

He turned and made his way forward. With a hand on the foremast he viewed the bows, the green light at the end of the pier, the gust-galled sea.

"That didn't go well, I take it," said Bitsy. She was crouched like a sphinx on the foredeck, eyes shut.

"It didn't." Over the bowsprit was a platform from which harpoons could be hurled at large game fish, and Aristide stepped out onto it, the boat bobbing under his weight. There was a splash somewhere beneath him, and he jumped as a surprised pelican thrashed a few yards into open water, then folded its wings and made off at a less urgent pace.

"When I mourn our uncoupling," he said, "even a bird makes me start."

Bitsy was looking at him. Half-closed eyes glowed like tiny moons in the light of the pier's lamp.

"I told you that you'd turn it into poetry," she said.

"Not me," he said. "Tu Fu."

"Your translation, though."

"Yes," he said, and looked down at his empty cup. "That is mine, at least."

VEDITUR

[A VILLANELLE]

The forms of love will not suffice
The soul a scatter of dry bone
The sad fact is I killed her twice

The wind burns cold as polar ice
Past the worn and tumbled stone
The forms of love will not suffice

From death's cold hand now fall the dice
The heart's wild wager overthrown
The sad fact is I killed her twice

How desolate the final price
Our history all overgrown
The forms of love will not suffice

Our certainties, now imprecise
Our melody a grating tone
The sad fact is I killed her twice

The scent of flesh was sweet and spice
The sweetness caught and torn and flown
The forms of love will not suffice
The sad fact is I killed her twice.

16

The sun was hidden in a black cloud with a glowing core of eerie red. Missile flares and flashes dotted the darkness, blazing in complete silence. The great disk of Courtland, seen nearly edge-on, was alive with pinpricks of light.

Then the image of Courtland began to dance as Aristide's transport made a frantic change of course.

Aristide's bones were not rocked by the sudden change of course. He felt no jolting, no acceleration, no inertia, no sensation of motion whatever.

Aristide's military transport was slightly less than two meters long. It was powered by antimatter, and capable of ferocious acceleration. It also contained a wormhole that led to a pocket universe, a rather small one, but one filled with half a million soldiers.

The invasion was under way. Aristide was on his way to drop onto the surface of the rebel Courtland.

The solar system was three months into the war, and during that time Vindex had more than held his own. His antiproton beams had chopped the Loyal Ten into ribbons until they'd launched their own antimatter weapons, whole armadas of them at once, and then Courtland began to receive damage as well.

Just at the moment when the United Powers began to get the upper hand in the exchange, Vindex launched his countermeasures. Satellites began to flood into space between Courtland and the Loyal Ten, satellites with antimatter-powered generators that produced potent magnetic fields. These bent the electron beams that carried the antiproton packets to their targets, and caused most to miss Courtland completely. If the fields from the satellites had been consistent, the United Powers could have compensated for the presence of the magnetic fields by aiming off-center and allowing the field to correct the beam to its proper target, but when they attempted this, they realized that the magnetic fields were programmed to shift randomly, and that it was impossible to compensate for them—but because Vindex knew which way the satellites were directing their magnetic fields at any instant, he was able to hit wherever he pleased. For nearly three weeks the rebel barrage ripped unhindered into loyalist targets, until the Powers could design, build, and launch their own satellite array.

The result was stalemate, with the battle fought more between satellites and anti-satellite weapons than between the great platforms themselves.

It was hoped that the invasion would break the deadlock. Forty million attackers would swarm onto Courtland's dorsal surface, seize the wormhole gates, and try to hold against the inevitable counterattack.

Were forty million enough? Aristide wondered. It had been calculated that more invaders would simply get in one another's way. But how many of the forty million would survive the journey to Courtland?

Stars whirled in Aristide's display as the transport took evasive action. Without sound, the war had a curiously flat quality. Not surprising, considering that the images were being transmitted by a camera in, literally, another universe.

His craft maneuvered through a scene of primal violence, of gamma-ray lasers pumped by matter-antimatter reactions, of lances looping on tails of fire to deliver fatal kinetic punches to the heart of an enemy, sheaves of robot-guided interceptors burning in single-minded fury for the foe, mines that unleashed sprays of bomblets; of antiproton charges turning matter into tortured, lethal bursts of angry, high-energy photons.

Courtland's convex dorsal surface, ahead, was lit by a continuous, shifting cloud of light, as the lethality proceeded in utter silence.

"How are we doing?" Aristide asked.

Bitsy's voice sounded in his ear.

"Not badly at all. The Venger's defenses should be pretty well beaten down by the time your unit arrives."

Bitsy's body remained on Topaz, there being in the invasion fleet no call for a small cat, but her personality had been uploaded to the AI on Aristide's combat suit. Tecmessa remained behind as well, as Aristide didn't want the magic broadsword captured by the enemy in the likely event that the United Powers were defeated.

Aristide's craft soared past the enormous, gently curving rim of Courtland itself. Its razor-thin outline stretched as far as the visual sensor could see, and reflected the dull red cloud that masked the sun. The Powers, at the beginning of the invasion, had spread the opaque cloud between Courtland and Sol, to inhibit the efficiency of Courtland's solar collectors. The cloud couldn't actually block solar radiation—it wasn't a solid wall— but it shifted the radiation toward infrared, a spectrum where Courtland's collectors would be less productive.

The rim flashed by in an instant. Aristide was now on Courtland's dark side, and the only light was provided by starshine and the furnace-fire of combat. The battle ahead seemed to be dying down, which Aristide took to be a good sign.

Still, the vehicle jerked and looped and danced as it avoided real or anticipated fire. Sensors recorded successive waves of gamma rays, pions, and energetic neutrons, particle refugees fleeing the annihilation of matter.

"The first wave is coming in to land," Bitsy said.

"What's their casualty rate?"

"Thirty-two percent."

Not bad, he thought, for a first wave. They were intended to do little more than absorb the brunt of the Venger's defenses and secure the landing areas for the second and subsequent waves, who with any luck would arrive with enough of their forces intact to be able to retake the wormhole gates.

Aristide saw, amid a host of flares, the trail of an interceptor looping through the firmament. Decoys sped shining into the night. The interceptor neared.

For the first time Aristide felt a degree of suspense. He clenched his teeth. The vast paws on his combat suit turned into fists.

Energy flared, a fiery sea of white that turned, as the sensors cooked, to a sea of nothing-at-all. The feed had gone dead.

"Six minutes," Bitsy said.

"The ship's still alive?"

"Oh yes. As are you, by the way."

Time passed. Suspense hummed through Aristide's nerves. It was worse, without the video feed. Trapped with one's own imagination was much worse.

"Five minutes. Task Force Ivan reports that our landing zone is secure."

"Good for us," Aristide managed. Nothing he had done, or could do, had altered his chance of survival by the slightest amount. This part of the war was completely automated. Computer minds calculated danger and reacted to it far faster than a human.

"We're decelerating now. Good thing you're not outside—you'd be flat as a strip of tin."

There were four inhabited pocket universes anchored to Courtland, each with anywhere between four and fourteen billion inhabitants, all of whom were by now presumed willing to give their all for Vindex. Though one of these, New Qom, had been founded as a religious reservation with a low technology base, presumably this situation had been altered with the conversion to the faith of the Venger, and the mullahs were now probably as formidably armed as anyone else.

In addition to the four known enemy pockets, there was at least one more, the one designed originally as a wormhole factory and now used as an antimatter generator. To capture this, or to collapse its wormhole and divorce the pocket universe from reality, would be a major strike against Courtland's power.

The United Powers didn't know where this pocket universe was located. Photo reconnaissance had shown any number of new structures on Courtland's dark side, but no one could tell what these structures concealed. They could hold pocket universes, warehouse war machines, store supplies, or exist simply as decoys.

Most of them, in any case, were now wreckage. The invading fleet had plenty of ammunition to spare: anything suspicious was given a thorough working-over. By now Courtland would be riddled with hot, glowing craters, many of which would have melted clean through the thin computational structure and revealed glimpses of the red-hearted cloud that loomed between Courtland and the sun.

"Two minutes."

"Systems check for all personnel."

There. He'd given his first order of the battle.

Heads-up displays flashed on the suit's visor. Everything seemed to be in order. Aristide moved his arms, twisted at the waist, shuffled his feet. The combat suit's movements integrated perfectly with his own.

"One minute."

Data from his unit began to flood Aristide's displays. His division was intact and one hundred percent functional.

He looked at the system's clock. Thirty seconds. Twenty. Ten. Five.

One.

Antimatter reactions sent power surging to the controls of the wormhole gate, and the wormhole expanded.

Suddenly there were stars overhead, and the endless flat plain of Courtland stretched all around. Half a million soldiers began moving in unison, still controlled by computer, brief spurts of their maneuvering jets taking them out of their little pocket and onto the enemy platform.

All around him, Aristide's command was taking up positions. A phalanx of twenty robots, his personal bodyguard, jetted into formation around him. They were models of deadly efficiency, flattish ovoids capable of travel by rocket or on wheels, equipped with a kind of superstructure that held close-range weapons and a battery of sensors. They looked like mantises made out of composite armor.

No engagements among Aristide's troops were reported. The battlefield seemed quiet.

Behind him, huge automated battle machines, artillery and armored vehicles, began to pour out of the wormhole.

Aristide felt his confidence increase. In the carrier he had been nothing but a helpless target. Now, free and in command, he felt he was gaining a grip on his own fate.

His unit constituted a full division, fourteen thousand fighters in all. In early industrial times, this would have been the command of a major general. As only a couple hundred of his soldiers were actual human beings, the rest being one or another sort of automaton, the military had advanced Aristide only as far as the rank of captain.

Aristide triggered the channel he used to communicate with higher authority.

"Reporting to Colonel Nordveit. The Screaming Cyborg Division is in position and awaiting orders. There is no opposition. Casualties are nil."

"Very good. Stand by." The answering voice belonged to the general's AI.

The plan called for Aristide's division to be in reserve for the first part of the engagement. Aristide made minute adjustments in his deployments and otherwise stood ready.

But for these warriors in their current incarnations, this was a one-way mission.

The division had taken its place in a busy part of Courtland's surface. Between two of the pocket universes, the area was full of tracks and tubes for travel between the pocket universes of Pamphylia and Greater Zimbabwe, with cradles for the ships that carried their commerce away, and the maintenance facilities and terminals for those ships. Enormous cranes stood high against the starfield, standing above the rubble of the facilities.

A red light popped up on Aristide's display. He called up more data.

"Nano disassemblers active in the area," Bitsy confirmed.

"Send out an alert," Aristide said.

"Done."

"Do we have a reading on the type?"

"We're working on that."

Nano disassemblers had been anticipated by military planners, of course. In practice there were only a limited number of ways to disassemble matter on the molecular level, and it was hoped that all of these had been anticipated. The armor on Aristide's suit, for example, attempted to defeat the disassemblers in two ways. The inner layers were as smooth as nano-technology could make them, crystals latticed so closely together that it was hoped disassemblers would be unable to get a grip on anything. The outer layers provided a more active defense, and contained a number of hooks and grapples designed to seize a disassembler and try to jam its mechanism, like trying to cram a foam-filled beach ball into the jaws of an attacking crocodile.

If these didn't work, there were more active ways of discouraging the disassemblers, which in any case were expected to be fairly inefficient on Courtland's dark side, away from the solar energy that would provide their power.

The principle threat from molecular technology was believed to be in assemblers, not disassemblers, because they could alter the immediate environment in drastic ways. No one wanted to walk on a pleasant green lawn that had converted itself to nitrocellulose.

"The disassembler is of the Kyoto type," Bitsy said. "Our equipment is largely proof against it, but we can deploy a Type C countermeasure if we desire."

Aristide considered this. "Colonel Nordveit hasn't ordered countermea-sures."

"No."

Aristide thought aloud. "The Kyoto type is fairly basic, and Vindex has to know we'd anticipate it."

"That's a fair supposition."

"Let's assume it was deployed to test our capabilities. Ignore it unless we start seeing hot spots in the environment."

"Shall I send an order to that effect?"

"Yes."

Aristide felt restless after his time in the dull, small, functional pocket universe, and he moved off on an inspection tour of the area. Movements of Aristide's body were measured by biofeedback sensors and analyzed by an onboard intelligence that converted them into motion on the part of the suit. Although Courtland possessed one-seventh Earth's gravity—and here near the center of the disk, Aristide could actually stand more or less upright, as opposed to leaning at an angle toward the center of mass—in practice the suit moved with bursts of its jets, and the walking motion remained an illusion of Aristide's neuromuscular system.

As he walked he tried not to think about the tiny machines that were trying to eat their way through the soles of his boots and kill him.

Aristide inspected a tube transport—abandoned, its glassy roof shattered some distance up the line—and a ground-to-air missile battery that had been melted into Courtland's massively parallel, massively quantum surface. Because the surface was so obviously artificial it was difficult not to feel anxious about attack from below, the local equivalent of orcs boiling up from their tunnels, and Aristide had to remind himself that Courtland was too thin to support any kind of underground transport system.

Colonel Nordveit's voice came on the command channel.

"Stand by. We're going to open the worlds in ten seconds."

Aristide ghosted to where he had a clear line of sight, and widened his artificial point of view so that he could look toward Pamphylia and Greater Zimbabwe simultaneously. He ran a mental countdown in his head.

He was ready for the most amazing piece of destruction he'd ever seen.

Over his head, the engine flares of ships, moving purposefully against the starfield, swirled in great whirlpools, as if they, too, wished to watch the worlds open.

He saw the flashes first, as engineers detonated the special shaped charges that destroyed the structures built over the wormholes. Lances of energy stabbed down from above, carrying charges of antimatter that wiped out every piece of matter between the wormhole and the environment—in this case, the vacuum.

A fountain followed, a great geyser of ice crystals rushing out of Pamphylia and Greater Zimbabwe as the atmospheres of the pocket universes began to pour out of the wormholes.

No one outside of the immediate area of the wormholes was in any kind of jeopardy. So vast was the volume of air in the pockets that the wormholes could vent for weeks before the pressure inside went down by more than a millibar.

Whoever won the battle would cap the wormholes again, presumably.

A few seconds after the first blasts came the vibration, the waves traveling over the surface of Courtland like a storm across the water. Aristide could feel the waves striking at his insides, driving his viscera up against his heart.

Still there was no sound.

Seconds later came more shocks, the only evidence that another pair of wormholes, out of Aristide's sight, had also been opened.

Aristide wished for sunlight, so that he could see the great ice plumes in their full glory, the rainbow playing over the crystals as it rose kilometers high over Courtland's surface... He altered his implant display, tinkering with different wavelength bands, but failed to get the effect he was hoping for.

In any case there was more to see. Diving from on high came fast, tight formations of robot warcraft, plunging almost vertically into the wormholes, their movement so fast that Aristide couldn't really see them, only the fading afterimage of their passage...

Once inside the target universes, the warcraft would either begin demolishing the Venger's defenses or continue on, spreading new, tailored plagues among the Venger's followers. One of these, Aristide knew, was the cure itself, a virus that would reverse the Vindex plague, restructure the brain to restore volition. The virus would linger. Even if all the rebel's disciples were at the moment huddled in biochem warfare suits in deep, air-conditioned bunkers, they couldn't stay there forever: the plague would plague Vindex for a long time.

Zombie plagues were also being spread, these with a life of a week or ten days. Let Vindex have a taste of his own chaos medicine.

Wave after wave of spacecraft sped into the wormholes. Some were troop-carriers like Aristide's, agile craft containing entire universes and cadres of shock troops. Probably there were titanic air battles happening on the other side, Aristide couldn't tell.

The stream of warcraft dwindled.

"Assault divisions are beginning operations." Nordveit's voice. He was from the Other New Jerusalem, a leader of the Lutheran forces that had sung "A Mighty Fortress" as they marched off to victory over those who believed in a slightly different deity. Now he commanded CCLI Corps, four divisions in this army of the profane, all standing by to reinforce the first wave if—or when—they were massacred.

Invisibly, off in the darkness, soldiers human and machine were moving to seize control of the wormholes.

Resistance was expected to be fierce, and most likely fatal. The wormholes were about two-thirds of a kilometer across, and Vindex could blanket the entire area with an unending fire.

Aristide was in reserve. He moved restlessly around his command and watched the distant wormholes for clues about what was going on.

Other units were committed to the fight, and Nordveit's corps shifted to maintain the perimeter. More warcraft sped into battle. The great ice fountains towered over everything like tombstones. No news came down to Aristide's level.

A delicate snowfall of frozen oxygen and nitrogen began to drift gracefully down.

Expeditionary force headquarters began to call fire missions for Aristide's heavy artillery. Salvos of smart ammunition were fired off to pass through the wormhole and land on the other side.

From the trajectory of the shell and rocket fire, Aristide could calculate the invaders' progress. The advancing forces seemed to be doing well, getting clear of the death trap that was the wormhole bottleneck.

Aristide hoped that such success didn't mean they were walking into an ambush.

The attackers didn't need to actually conquer the four universes. For that they would need billions of fighters. They needed only to do what Vindex had done—seize the only exit, then pump the pockets full of a virus that would, over time, transform the inhabitants into friendlies. With the inhabitants of the pockets being better prepared, the United Powers would find it a harder job than Vindex had done, but it was far from impossible.

"We're getting some larger-scale disassembler activity," Bitsy said. Maps flashed onto Aristide's display. "The disassemblers are fueling themselves by taking apart some of the railway."

Aristide looked at the displays. "It's not a great threat," he said, "but I don't want that large a hot spot within our perimeter. Tell the decontamination bots to shut it down."

"Done," Bitsy said.

And then the whole world turned bright. Aristide watched in horrified awe as six, eight, a dozen pillars of fire shot up from Courtland's surface. A searing white light illuminated every soldier, every broken building, every shattered structure. The great fountains of ice crystals that towered over the wormholes gleamed and shimmered, faint rainbows shifting in their interiors.

The pillars of flame leaned and toppled, scouring Courtland's surface with plasma fire. Aristide could feel the heat through his faceplate, feel the sudden sweat prickling his face. Cooling units in his suit switched on. Terror throbbed in his heart.

Aristide watched in helpless dread as whole formations of invaders were incinerated as the white fire passed over them. They died in utter silence. Aristide looked wildly in all directions, searching for the blaze that would destroy him, but none of the eruptions seemed near enough to his position.

His legs twitched, eager to leap from the surface that could suddenly open to a world of fire.

"What *is* that?" he demanded.

"I'm working on that," said Bitsy.

The plasma fire rolled across the surface, each blast sweeping an arc from its point of origin. The scale of it all was so gigantic that Aristide's mind failed in its search for superlatives.

"They're wormholes opening up into suns," Bitsy said. "Or near them."

A variation, Aristide reasoned numbly, on the Venger's energy-producing pocket universe. He'd built a dozen of them and, instead of capturing the energy, simply turned it loose in a jet of superheated matter.

Using a star as a flamethrower. That was new.

The warships circling the battlefield began to respond. Carefully designed antimatter bombs were sent rocketing into the wormholes to disrupt the flow through the gates and destroy whatever mechanism was controlling them. Some of the great fires were extinguished as their pocket universes were closed into themselves and detached from this reality, others were directed at useless angles into space.

But by that point the damage had been done.

"I don't have access to the numbers that are reaching headquarters," Bitsy said, "but my best estimate is that we just lost something like eighteen million soldiers."

Aristide didn't bother to reply. Words would not do justice to the scope of the catastrophe.

His fate had once more been taken out of his hands. He wanted to swear to take it back, but the promise would have been a hollow one.

He had survived only by chance. He would need a good deal more luck if he were to survive for much longer.

And he *did* want to survive. It was one thing to know intellectually that in the event of death he would be resurrected; it was another to look into the stark face of annihilation and say that it didn't matter.

He didn't like death. He never had. He had died only once in all his long life, and he didn't want to get into the habit.

"I'm getting reports of nano activity," Bitsy reported. "Different disassemblers this time. The heat is feeding them."

"Give me the hard data." It would be a relief to concentrate on numbers.

For the next several hours he fought nano attacks, spraying hot spots with a variety of aerosols that would either encase the disassemblers or attack them directly with little nanological pit bulls. The countermeasures worked well enough. Terse orders came from Nordveit to adjust the perimeter. The Screaming Cyborg Division moved across a charred wasteland inhabited by the burnt shells and contorted shapes of metal warriors half-melted, like an ice cream cake left too long in the sun. The remaining pillars of fire stood over the battlefield, leaning at crazy angles. The shadows they cast were deep and black.

It was lucky, Aristide thought, that most of his fighters were machines, and would have no problems with morale.

Aristide looked at his chronometer, and saw that he had been on Courtland's surface for nearly sixteen hours. His suit reeked of sweat and burnt adrenaline. His nutritional needs were met by an intravenous drip, but he took a sip from the water supply in his combat suit, and pulled his arms out of their webbing to break into a personal supply of biscuits and chocolate.

It was the only thing he could do to cheer himself up.

Over the next few hours the remaining plasma pillars faded and died. The passing of such a vast amount of ejecta had unbalanced the wormholes and caused them to evaporate.

Aristide's artillery continued to be called on for fire missions. Munitions carriers dropped from space to resupply. The pace of the war in both Pamphylia and Greater Zimbabwe had increased, and Aristide concluded that counterattacks were under way.

When the division had been on the surface for twenty hours, Nordveit gave orders to advance toward Greater Zimbabwe. Aristide gave orders to form his unit and roll toward the wormhole.

In his command of fourteen thousand were a hundred and ninety-four human beings in suits similar to his own. The rest were specialized robots. Some traveled on treads, some on wheels. Some shambled on sticklike legs, and some scurried on dozens of legs like a centipede. Some crawled, some flew. Some soared far above the battlefield to image positions over the next hill; some were built to detect mines and other underground structures. The warriors could detect enemy in the visual spectrum, the infrared, and ultraviolet, detect them by scent, by electromagnetic emissions, by acoustic ranging. Weapons included chemical-powered slug throwers, mortars that threw antimatter bombs, rail guns, and highly intelligent rockets. Individual units were built with multiple redundancy and self-repair capability.

The humans weren't needed for the actual fighting. They were needed to tell the machines when to stop.

As Nordveit's corps approached Greater Zimbabwe, it closed on the tails of other units moving to the attack. Aristide's artillery was detached from the main body: it could be resupplied more easily if it remained on Courtland's surface, and the United Powers had not yet advanced so far into the pocket so as to require closer support.

The half-wrecked structures of the great port, the warehouses and terminals and ship repair facilities, canalized the advance into just a few routes. Ahead was the great crystal fountain of frozen air, lit dimly from below by Greater Zimbabwe's sun.

Aristide moved up to be with his foremost units. There was limited information coming through the wormhole, and he wanted to be able to evaluate the situation as soon as possible.

Nordveit sent out a tactical briefing. The situation in Greater Zimbabwe was worsening, with powerful counterattacks coming from all directions. Nordveit's corps was to stabilize the front.

There was no mention of continuing the advance. Perhaps that fantasy had died.

The wormhole grew closer. The crystal fountain towered overhead, a torrent of pale snow.

Aristide was calm. Since entering the battle he had existed only as a statistic, but he made up his mind to make a blip on the chart if he could.

He wondered whether Nordveit was humming "A Mighty Fortress" to himself. Perhaps he was.

The order came. The division stepped out on the double. Aristide caught a glimpse of the wormhole itself, a broad expanse that looked like a bright green world as seen through a fishbowl lens, and then he leaped into that world and was in an instant surrounded by war.

Greater Zimbabwe had the same dim, eternal sun as Midgarth, and for that reason its inhabitants had the same glowing cat's eyes as Midgarth's population. Otherwise the pocket was built to mimic the semitropical forests, lakes, and mountains of Africa, and was inhabited by vast numbers of native African fauna who considerably outnumbered its five billion human beings.

Aristide was buffeted by the breeze of the pocket's escaping air. He scanned in all directions and found nothing alive.

The area had contained port and transport facilities as well as hotels for workers and visitors. All that had been leveled. Shattered, half-melted vehicles had been shoved out of the cratered roads; the buildings were piles of rubble limited by a few half-shattered walls. Sticklike trees stood out here and there, each completely stripped of leaves.

The horizon in all directions was filled with smoke and dull red flame. Enemy fire continued to blanket the area, some of it bursts of antimatter fired all the way from the other side of the globular universe. Friendly units provided covering fire, trying to blast the incoming shells and rockets out of the sky before they could damage the invaders. Damaged robots dragged themselves through the landscape, heading for portable repair facilities.

Smoke whipped past Aristide as it rushed, with the air, into the great night outside.

Aristide ordered his division to move at full speed through the danger zone. All units shifted to active camouflage, each individual fighter broadcasting the colors of the surrounding terrain on chameleon panels built into their armor. The whole division seemed to vanish from the visual spectrum, sensed only as strange, half-seen creeping movements across the countryside.

Aristide took huge leaps, jets enhancing his natural motion so that he cleared forty meters at a stride. The world trembled around him. Shrapnel and debris pinged off his armor. His fighters were channeled into narrow columns by the rubble, and the plunging fire tore the columns to bits. Aristide saw flashes, rubble flying, pieces of his robot fighters flying in arcs. He felt a tension between his shoulders, waiting for the rocket that would blast him or the burst of antimatter that would annihilate his very atoms. He straightened his shoulders and told the tension to disperse. Somewhat to his surprise, it did.

Hustling through the curtain of fire, Aristide's division was reduced from fourteen thousand effectives to a little over eight thousand. Five of the casualties were the better-armored humans, and two of these had been killed. All were people Aristide had trained with, and he paused for a moment to wish them luck in their new incarnation.

Ten million left, he thought. *At least.*

The division entered a wood, the trees mere toothpicks stripped of leaves. Legions of wrecked fighters lay beneath the trees like fallen berries. At each footfall, Aristide left behind a little whirlwind of ash. Enemy fire fell away to nothing.

CCLI Corps passed through the wood and flowed across open country beyond. Half of the ground was green hills; the rest was torn soil half-turned to mud. The Screaming Cyborgs were now ten kilometers from the wormhole. Overhead bloomed a vast radar cloud, as one side or the other filled the air with chaff. Nordveit began giving orders directly to his subordinates, to relieve units that were holding specific points. Aristide made detailed dispositions within the framework of his orders.

At which point everything changed. The enemy had made a breakthrough on the right, and Nordveit's entire corps was shifted to attack the flank of the advancing rebel force. Nordveit was in the process of dictating the change in route when the enemy struck.

From ahead, bounding into the air from outside of effective detector range, came a horde of small, agile missiles. They went supersonic within seconds. The chaff-filled air, and the missiles' own darting paths, made it difficult to detect them coming, but defensive machines nevertheless picked them up and began filling the air with charges of antimatter, while heavier weapons targeted the area from which the missiles had launched. Detonations filled the air overhead.

Aristide threw himself flat on the ground, and told his command to do likewise.

The last-ditch defenders, automated chain cannon, began their furious roar.

The oncoming missiles didn't have single warheads, but were instead filled with tiny bomblets, knuckle-sized antimatter grenades. Even the missiles that were struck by defensive fire were very often able to scatter all or part of their cargo as they broke up over the target.

Aristide shut off his detectors before the bomblets fell, and so lay in darkness and felt the ground beneath him leap to a continuous roll of detonation. Pebbles and soil fell on his armor like rain.

The deadly drumroll came to an end, and Aristide cautiously turned on a sensor or two. A brown, dusty fog hung over the land.

"Status," he said. "Now."

"Checking," said Bitsy, and then an instant later. "We got off light. Only two hundred twenty-eight machines are failing to report. Three hundred forty have suffered some kind of damage, and sixty-four of these are disabled completely. Corporal Kuan was killed by a direct hit."

"Damn. Get everything up and moving." Lurching to his feet he suited action to words.

"Bad news," Bitsy said after a brief pause. "Colonel Nordveit has been killed. As the senior captain, you're now in command of CCLI Corps."

Aristide's head reeled. "Better give me a status report. No—get them all moving first. *Then* a status report."

The Screaming Cyborgs had fared the best of all during the brief bombardment, probably because Aristide had ordered them to hit the dirt whereas Nordveit, with true Nordic fatalism, hadn't given the order to other elements of his command. CCLI Corps, Aristide discovered, consisted of slightly less than twenty-eight thousand warriors, not counting the reserve artillery brigades still outside the wormhole.

"I'd better talk to the division commanders," he said.

They appeared on his displays: Draeger of the Designer Renegades, with her eyes the size of billiard balls, Malakpuri with his pointed beard, and Grax the Troll.

"Right now I don't have a lot of information" Aristide told them. "So if you've got any critiques of Nordveit's orders, or if you know anything that isn't on the displays, you'd better tell me."

The others knew no more than he did. He contacted his immediate superior, General Aziz commanding Forty-First Army, and received a download of the tactical disposition. There on the three-dimensional mapscape was the enemy breakthrough, expanding and flowing across country; here were friendly forces, dying, fleeing, or moving into position to contain the foe.

Aristide could find no fault with Nordveit's orders save that they were incomplete, so he continued with the business of swinging the whole corps to the right.

Ahead was a line of low hills, and beyond it was the war. Aristide pushed his troops forward on the theory that the hills would provide some shelter behind which to shake his route columns into combat formations. He bounded ahead of the advance elements to the hills, and there he saw that the hills were not natural formations at all, but the debris of combat.

A titanic battle had been fought here, where formations of invaders had met formations of defenders and left nothing alive, nothing functioning. Trees, earth, and human habitations had been blasted and blackened; and tens of thousands of robot fighters and their human officers had fought here to the death. The hills were their remains: torn bodies, weapons, limbs, fragments of vehicles and spent ammunition. Little fires burned here and there. Shattered crystal glittered in the dim sun; broken antennae reached for the sky like fingers. Perhaps at the climax of the battle they had torn at each other with mechanical claws.

The husks of machines crunched beneath Aristide's mechanical feet as he climbed the slope. He hoped there were no live human beings buried somewhere underneath.

Seen from the summit, the mechanical hills wound across the country like strands of seaweed left behind by the tide.

Standing atop the beaten, crumbling bits of metal and laminate, Aristide took a chill comfort from the fact that his own side seemed to have won this battle, and having beaten the enemy had advanced past this point.

He looked ahead toward the fight, and ordered small drone aircraft ahead to spy out the way. What these revealed was that enemy breakthrough was complete: there was no longer any organized force fighting the Venger's legions.

He called up the dispositions of his own units, and saw that it would be nearly half an hour before they would all be in position to roll into the attack. That was too long a time—by then the enemy would have poured huge numbers of attackers into the breach.

He called up a tactical map and briefly wrote across it, movement of the big index finger of his battle suit drawing large glowing arrows across the display.

Again he summoned the images of his division commanders, and downloaded his tactical map to their tactical AIs.

"We're going to have to attack *en echelon,*" he said. "Captain Draeger, you'll go in the instant your units are ready, and you'll attack the shoulder of the breakthrough to cut off any reinforcements to the enemy. The Screaming Cyborgs will go in on your left as soon as they're set. Captain Malakpuri, you'll go in next. Captain Grax, your division will be in reserve till we see where it's needed—I suspect you'll have to support Captain

Draeger. Any questions?"

There were none. The concept was plain enough, and fine tactical movements were up to subordinates and their AIs anyway.

"Corps and reserve artillery is already hitting the enemy," Aristide continued, "but I'll make sure you can call on it for specific fire missions." He looked at Draeger and tried to give her a confident nod.

"Proceed," he said.

Though Draeger was centuries old, her biological age was never more than sixteen: she wore her hair in pony tails that dropped from high on her head nearly to her waist, and she had equipped herself with a pair of eyes twice the size of the human norm. All the humans in her division were industrial designers from New Penang, and they had equipped their fighters with picturesque but non-functional innovations: weird frills, decorative antennae, brilliantly colored camouflage projections, and full sets of teeth.

"Death for Art's Sake!" Draeger cried, the divisional motto, and her division kicked its way through piles of wrecked robots and swung over to the attack. Enemy intelligence had failed, apparently, because the foe were not set to receive them. But resistance hardened soon enough, enemy units changing front under the guidance of computer brains that were incapable of fear or hesitation. But by that point Aristide's own division was ready, the Screaming Cyborgs pitched in on Draeger's right, and the enemy gave way again. Again the enemy adjusted, but then Malakpuri's attack caught them wrong-footed and drove them back three kilometers.

Aristide could observe the action from any point by uploading data from any human or robot. He watched the robots with fascination: they were deadly little devices, fearless, ruthless, highly intelligent, and unnaturally fast. Individual combats were almost too swift for Aristide to follow. An enemy was sighted, a weapon aimed, and *bang*... all in less than a second. Networked battle computers meant that each saw what all the others saw— the observer need not reveal itself by movement or fire, the enemy could be destroyed by a robot over the next hill, launching smart missiles. The kills multiplied with incredible rapidity once they began. Whole units of one side or another were turned to ash within seconds.

Bitsy, he thought, wants me to give her the freedom to create and use these things however she wants.

Never, he thought. Never.

By that point Grax was up with what he had named the Troll Grenadier Division. Aristide ordered him in to support the Designer Renegades. "*Grax the Troll!*" he shouted, and led his warriors into battle while waving a poleaxe one-handed from an armored fist. The enemy's defense, hardening again, gave way completely, and Grax and Draeger together sealed the base of the breakthrough, cutting off the enemy attackers from reinforcements. By now other counterattacks were under way from other directions, and the enemy breakthrough collapsed like a punctured balloon. In fairly short order the remaining enemy were hunted down and destroyed.

Aristide felt a surge of accomplishment. He had maneuvered his troops under fire and scored a signal success against a triumphant enemy. He had earned his footnote in military history. *Confronted by the enemy breakthrough and the death of his superior, Captain Monagas brought his divisions smartly into battle in a neatly timed attack* en echelon, *resulting in the collapse of the enemy pocket.* It was the sort of thing military officers lived for.

He hadn't thought of himself as the kind of officer who would delight in such notice, but perhaps he was.

He bounded forward to where his command was quietly sorting itself out, the units rearranging themselves under efficient computer guidance. If they'd been people it would have taken hours.

His command had been reduced to something like nineteen thousand fighters, now settling themselves along the lines that the invaders had held prior to the enemy breakthrough. There were no hills of robot dead, but the place was bad enough, broken machine corpses strewn across hills and lying beneath banyan trees stripped of twigs and leaves.

Aristide established his "headquarters" in the trees, actually just himself and his personal robot guard. Reserve ammunition was brought up to replenish magazines.

CCLI Corps had come eighteen kilometers from the wormhole.

The ground began to tremble as enemy artillery found the range. Aristide told his command to seek cover where they were, and put his back to one of the banyan trees, so that it would cover him. He contacted his superior.

"The enemy have found our range," he told General Aziz. "If we stay here we'll be cut up to no purpose. I'd like to request permission to advance."

Drops of sweat clung to the general's neat mustache. Perhaps his cooling units in his suit had failed.

"If we expand the perimeter," he said, "we'll be too thin on the ground. You'll have to hold where you are."

"We'll take casualties."

"Other units will be brought up to your support."

To use when we're too thin to hold, Aristide thought. But he kept his thoughts to himself, and obeyed orders.

Heavy fire hammered down. Aristide ordered his units to leave a skeleton force on the perimeter, and slowly drew the rest back, out of the enemy barrage, but remained in position to counterattack. There were so many dead robot hulks on the perimeter itself that perhaps enemy reconnaissance would think it fully manned.

Aristide stood with his back to the tree and ate chocolate and drank recycled bodily fluids. He checked the chronometer and discovered that he had been at war for twenty-six hours.

The enemy eventually found Aristide's main force lying in reserve and shifted some of their fire to the main body. Casualties began mounting. Aristide found that while he did not much care about robots in the abstract, he cared about *his* robots very much. He wanted to preserve them nearly as much as if they were real, live soldiers.

The humans, if they died, would be resurrected. The robot soldiers, on the other hand, would be swept up with the trash. For the moment at least, Aristide was prepared to call that unjust.

Eventually Aziz passed on the information that made it clear that it didn't much matter what the hell he did with his forces.

"Our forces in Pamphylia have been overwhelmed," he said. "The enemy is pouring through the wormhole to attack our reserves. We're moving corps artillery to Zimbabwe to get it out of enemy fire."

Which meant, Aristide realized, that the United Powers were abandoning the surface of Courtland. If the gantlet of fire just inside Greater Zimbabwe was preferable to what lay outside, then what lay outside was hell.

It also meant that there was no way any of the invaders were getting off Courtland. They would all die here, and then be resurrected at home with no memories of destruction, bloodshed, or defeat.

"We are uploading all combat data to orbiting AIs, for transmission to high command," Aziz continued. "The download should occupy most of our bandwidth for the next several minutes. Please minimize all non-essential transmissions for that period."

Well, Aristide thought. At least his counterattack would find its way into history, instead of being lost down the wormhole of Greater Zimbabwe. He was oddly pleased by the fact.

Hours passed in which the enemy bombardment whittled CCLI Corps down from nineteen to fifteen thousand. On the surface of Courtland, apparently, millions of warriors were flailing their way to annihilation.

"We seem to be losing," Bitsy remarked.

"Yes, damn it."

"You seem upset."

"Was that irony?" Aristide demanded. "I'm not in the mood for irony now."

"Sorry."

"For a moment there I thought I'd avoided becoming a statistic. Now it looks as though I'll become a number after all."

"As a being made up entirely of numbers, I fail to see the problem."

"Why don't you just shut up?" Aristide snarled.

Bitsy did so.

Aristide reflected bitterly on all the erroneous assumptions that had led the failed invasion. Everyone involved in the planning and execution of the landings on Courtland had known that the odds would be long—Vindex had the devotion of billions of human beings and the resources of four pocket universes, as well as Courtland's own majestic intelligence. But high command had thought that a chance of success existed—*if* Courtland's processing power could be sufficiently impaired, *if* the wormholes could be seized and held, *if* sufficient biological weapons could be deployed throughout the pockets.

But the United Powers had failed to reckon with the Venger's tapping the power of whole suns that he had created just for the purpose. Not only had this weapon eliminated millions of attackers at once, but it demonstrated that the Venger's access to energy was essentially infinite.

If the Venger's energy was infinite, then the energy of the United Powers, once they deployed the technology themselves, would be ten times infinite. But even that much, Aristide thought, wouldn't be enough to overwhelm Vindex.

Which meant that the United Powers would adopt Plan B. Courtland wouldn't be conquered, it would be destroyed, along with all its contents, the universes, the continents and seas, the animals and the people.

The people would be restored from backup. Eventually. The rest would be lost forever.

Vindex, Aristide thought, had to know what Plan B would be. He had to be ready for it.

And that was terrifying.

He ate more chocolate. He might as well finish it off: he'd have no use for it in a few hours' time.

Drones informed Aristide of an attack forming to his front. Heavy weapons hammered the perimeter, destroying all but a handful of the fighters he'd left there. He called for his own artillery to disrupt the enemy attack before it got started, but only half the guns and rocket launchers had survived the trek through the wormhole, and these were being spare with their ammunition.

When the enemy came Aristide laid down as thorough a barrage as he could, and then the units he'd drawn back from the front line came forward over terrain that they knew perfectly, having already been over it twice. They met the enemy, and the long annihilation began.

Aristide remained with his back to the banyan tree. To expose himself would be to die, and though he supposed death was inevitable, he preferred to postpone it.

Aristide's fighters hung on. The breakthrough, when it came, was on the left—the unit that CCLI Corps had originally been intended to support gave way. Aristide had to act quickly to keep his flank from being rolled up. In the turmoil and confusion it was difficult to pick which remote view to upload into his implant, and so in the end it was simpler to supervise the movement himself. For the first time in hours he left the banyan tree and leaped toward the crisis.

He dropped alongside his warriors into a ditch on the edge of what seemed to be the remains of a banana plantation—the trees, spaced at regular intervals, were broken, and the yellow fruit lay pulped on the ground. Active camouflage kept him from seeing much of either side in the visible spectrum, but infrared emissions revealed the Venger's warriors on the other side of the plantation, swarming like ants through the breach they had made, threatening to get behind Aristide's lines.

For several busy minutes he leaped over the battlefield, pulling back his left flank and getting it under cover. Even so his fighters went down by the hundreds. He had one of his bodyguard climb what was left of a banana tree in order to get a better view and link to his implant.

Then a pattern of shellfire landed in his area. There were no countermeasures: his counter-batteries had run out of ammunition. The explosions were small, however, and spattered the area with a translucent semi-fluid, some kind of thick, clotting substance that lay heavily on the grass and torn banana leaves.

Aristide wiped the stuff from his sensors. It stuck to his glove. "What is it?" he demanded. "Sign of active nano?"

One of the bodyguard performed a brief analysis.

"No disassemblers," Bitsy said. "It's glucose."

"Everyone pull back! Now!"

He gave the order too late. The next round of shellfire sprayed nanomachines over the area, and the glucose provided them with plenty of energy. The nanomachines themselves were contained in a thin superfluid that spread thinly over every object, defying gravity as it crept upward over every vertical surface.

Including Aristide's armor. Alarms began flashing in his implants, but there was little he could do as he was in the midst of leading a precipitous retreat. In time he found himself once more in the shattered wood, standing by his old banyan or one very much like it.

A dead cockatoo lay at his feet.

"Analyze!" he said.

"Unknown composition," Bitsy said. Then, "Sorry."

"Countermeasures."

One of his robot bodyguard sprayed Aristide with liquid nitrogen, which would temporarily freeze the disassemblers until a more appropriate countermeasure could be deployed. While the molecular machines thawed out in the subtropical heat of Greater Zimbabwe, the bodyguards experimented on each other. None of the countermeasures worked completely, but it appeared that the Venger's weapon was a variation on the Kursk type.

Aristide began to breathe easier. His guard sprayed him and each other with the appropriate countermeasure.

"The Kursk can be stopped by the layers of the suit," he said.

"Your suit has been dinged," Bitsy said. "And your joints are vulnerable, in any case."

"I didn't want to be reminded of that."

"Enemy in the treeline!"

Another pell-mell retreat, the bodyguard providing covering fire as Aristide bounded through the trees on a zigzag course. Enemy projectiles brought down some of the guard, but the flight was a success, and brought another temporary respite.

"You have a hot spot on your right knee," Bitsy said.

One of the guard hit the hot spot with liquid nitrogen, followed by the Kursk countermeasure. Aristide tried to keep track of what was happening to CCLI Corps, saw only a whirlwind of frantic movement across the displays, nothing he could make sense of.

"Incoming!" Bitsy said.

Aristide had a moment to reflect that Bitsy seemed to be enjoying the disaster before an explosion hurled him through the air. There was the sensation of whirling, then a curious counter-eddy as his jets tried to compensate for the uncontrolled movement. He hit the ground and ended on his back. The jolting to and fro in his harness had knocked the wind out of him.

As the barrage was likely to go on for some time, his current posture seemed as good as any, so he remained supine while he tried to collect himself.

The ground shuddered to impact after impact. A tree limb fell on him, obscuring the view of his sensors.

"There's damage to the right knee joint," Bitsy said. "You might try flexing, to see if it's damaged."

Aristide tried and failed. His readouts, he realized as his leg thrashed about in its immobile armor, showed that there had been a pressure breach in his suit. He could feel his suit grow more humid as the air of Greater Zimbabwe leaked in.

"Let's freeze the hot spots one more time," Aristide said. Showing what in a human would be incredible bravery, one of his bodyguard crawled through the shellfire to spray more liquid nitrogen over the disassemblers that were turning his suit into free molecules and copies of themselves.

Aristide felt the bite of cold as his knee was sprayed. So that's where the hull breach was, right where the Kursk nano was strongest.

"This won't last," Aristide said.

"I'm afraid not," Bitsy said.

"Better tell Draeger that she's in command of what's left of the corps."

"I'll do that." And, a moment later, "Draeger may be dead. She's not responding, in any case."

There was a sudden flare of heat on the back of Aristide's knee. The nano coming to grip with his flesh.

"Who's next?" he asked. "Grax?"

"I pinged him and he's still among the standing."

"Tell him he's in charge, then."

"Done."

The heat on Aristide's knee was growing pronounced, almost painful.

"They forgot something when they created this suit," Aristide said.

"What's that?"

"A suicide pill," said Aristide.

"I'll make a note of it."

There was silence. The ground leaped to the impact of shells and rockets. Pain grew in Aristide's knee, and he felt heat against his back, where another colony of happy disassemblers was taking his suit apart.

He decided that the odds weren't great enough that he would be splattered by a direct hit, so he tried to rise. The frozen knee made that impossible, but by levering himself up by one arm he managed to flop onto his front.

The view from this new posture was scarcely improved.

A searing pain flashed through his right knee. He cried out. The pain faded.

"Right," he said, and ordered his bodyguard to pick him up bodily and carry him toward the nearest enemy. Getting a rocket to the chest was a better end than being eaten alive by the molecular foe.

In the last few minutes his bodyguard had been sadly depleted. Only three remained intact enough to crawl to him and attach themselves to his suit with their grapplers. The grapplers were intended for fine manipulation, not hauling a stout combat suit weighing a couple of hundred kilos, but they were well-made, and in the end Aristide was being hauled over the forest floor at about two kilometers per hour.

A rocket landed nearby. Shrapnel hammered Aristide's armor. One of the bodyguard collapsed, its innards torn. The remaining two machines were unable to carry Aristide on their own, and he found himself face-down on the torn ground.

The pain in his knee hadn't returned, but the sensation of heat was spreading up his leg toward his groin.

"I don't find our current prospects very promising," Aristide said.

"Nor do I," said Bitsy.

"Have the bodyguard engage any enemy that come in range. Maybe the black hats will be good and blast all of us to bits."

"Very good." The two remaining machines dropped Aristide's armor and took up a defensive posture.

Aristide felt heat flush his entire body. Beads of sweat formed on his forehead and dripped steadily on his displays. The air in the suit smelled of humus.

"I don't seem to be doing well," he confessed.

"With your permission," Bitsy said, "I would like to erase myself. Vindex shouldn't capture either one of us alive."

"Carry on," Aristide said. "I'll just hang around here till something happens."

"Good luck." The ground shuddered.

"I'll see you in a better place."

"Five seconds," Bitsy said. "Four. Three. Two. One."

She spoke no more.

"Goodbye, old friend," Aristide said. "It's been jolly."

Heat blazed through Aristide's flesh. His body had been completely infiltrated by the nanomachines, which were reproducing in a perfect frenzy.

His vision had gone dark. He panted for breath. He could feel sweat pouring off him.

And then he was consumed.

17

There was a soft whirring, a breath of air on his cheek. From somewhere in his scrambled memories came the scent of violets. The scent faded.

"Damn it," he said aloud. "I've survived over fifteen hundred years, and now the bastard's killed me twice."

He remembered the arcing fire coming down through the trees, the broken reef of dead machines lying in heaps. The microscopic machines burning through his body. Bitsy's farewell.

But then he remembered that he shouldn't remember anything like that. Not if this was a new incarnation. If he had been reloaded from his last backup, he wouldn't have any memories of the invasion at all.

He opened his eyes. He sat at apparent ease in a leather armchair, one knee crossed over the other. His spider-silk suit was grey, with a subtle pinstripe, and fit him perfectly. The armchair was in a book-lined study, lit by a skylight through which came a clear, perfect north light.

Sitting in another chair and regarding him with polite attention was a man who seemed about nineteen, with a Navy blue blazer worn over a cream-colored turtleneck. Though his hair was short on the back and sides of his head, a mass of chestnut curls tumbled from the top of his head almost to his eyes. His eyes were grey. An oval onyx ring sat on one forefinger.

The whole arrangement had a perfect Victorian solidity to it that made Aristide suspicious at once.

"Who the hell are you?" he asked. "Captain Nemo?"

The other man smiled faintly. "Beyond devotion to an ideal," he said, "there is little basis for comparison."

Aristide tried to stand, and found that his body declined to obey his commands. He looked at the other figure.

"You're my interrogator, I take it?"

The young-seeming man inclined his head. "I'd prefer to consider this a productive dialogue," he said.

Aristide glanced about at the room and its furnishings. "This is a virtual room, I suppose."

"Oh no. It's real." The man raised a hand to the shelves. "The books all exist. If your senses are keen enough, you can detect the scent of fine leather binding and the acetic acid smell of book paper decomposing."

"That's exactly the sort of detail that makes me want to think none of this is exists."

"Oh." The stranger seemed slightly taken aback. He considered a moment, then shrugged. "I suppose it doesn't matter. Suffice it to say that the room was created by someone, for some purpose, and that you and I now inhabit it."

"Where's that whirring sound coming from?"

"There's a humidifier behind you. The room is kept at an ideal humidity for preservation of book paper."

"Is there a pot of violets somewhere behind me?"

The stranger looked at him curiously. "No. Why?"

"No reason."

The young-looking man reached into his pocket and withdrew a cigaret case. "I've taken up any number of vile habits lately. Mind if I smoke?"

"I can't stop you."

The stranger looked at him from under his waterfall of curls.

"You could, actually. I would refrain out of courtesy to you."

"I suppose," Aristide mocked, quoting his interrogator, "it doesn't matter."

The young-looking man put the cigaret in his mouth, then lit it with a table lighter of carved white jade. Aristide wondered how many centuries it had been since he'd seen a table lighter.

The scent of tobacco stung his nostrils.

"The level of detail is really pretty good," he said.

His companion gave him a severe look. "I admire the consistency of your skepticism," he said, "but if you persist in viewing me as some kind of Cartesian Great Deceiver, it will not only make no difference in the long run, but will make our conversation damned tedious." He gestured with his cigaret. "If we were in virtual, I wouldn't have had to take control of your body. I could have let you run and jump and leap about to your heart's content, secure as if you were in a padded cell."

Aristide considered this. "Conceded," he said.

"I have otherwise interfered only minimally. I've given you one tweak that will make you talkative, and another that will make it impossible for you to lie to me."

"There's not a lot of point in that," Aristide said. "The only military secrets I know have to do with the timing and composition of the invasion, and by now you already know all that."

"You probably know more than that, or have guessed much more," said the stranger, "but we can save all that for later, if we get to it at all. I had other reasons for saving you."

"Which were?"

Aristide's reply was instant. He really *couldn't* stop this conversation, he thought.

The stranger looked at him.

"I wanted to interview Pablo Monagas Pérez," he said.

Panic fluttered in Aristide's throat. What threatened to burst from his tongue was not language, but babbling, and he managed to fight the impulse and keep silent.

The stranger tilted his head, amused at Aristide's reaction. "You've been my most persistent opponent since I've set up shop here on Courtland. I think you were the fellow who first found out what I was up to on Midgarth. I suspect you were on Hawaiki, too. I had some idea of your activities in Topaz, since for a time I received messages concerning your activities.

"I gave you credit for consistency, so I thought you would almost certainly be a part of the invasion—and thus my weapons were programmed, insofar as it was possible, to preserve your present existence." He shifted comfortably on his seat, gesturing widely with the cigaret as horror slowly closed its cold, steel-clad fingers on Aristide's heart.

"Your genetics are on file," the stranger said. "There are certain patterns found in your template without which you would not be *you*. And so…" He smiled. "I had my little machines programmed to look for you, and now here you are, my guest and interlocutor."

"You're Vindex then?" Words burst free from Aristide's tongue.

The stranger put a hand to his heart and bowed. "Honored to make your acquaintance," he said.

The wave of adrenaline that burned through Aristide's veins turned to anger.

"So what's next for me, then?" he demanded. "Torture? Slavery?"

The Venger's lips twisted with distaste. "Really," he said. "What do you take me for?"

"Megalomaniac. Mind-twister. Mass-murderer."

"…And many additional words beginning with M," Vindex sighed. "I suppose it would be useless to point out that your side has done a lot more damage than I have?"

Aristide laughed in derision. Vindex looked at him reproachfully.

"That invasion was wasteful, needlessly destructive, and stupid besides. The wreckage is *immense.* The cleanup will take ages. You're the only survivor, and only because I took care to preserve you."

"Well, then," Aristide said. "I suppose you're just going to lecture me to death?"

Vindex stubbed out his cigaret, crossed his legs, and locked his hands around one knee. He looked at Aristide with friendly interest.

"You're the only person in my domain who doesn't love me," he said. "No one else here would call me names."

"I'll call you a lot more, if you like."

"No, if *you* like," Vindex said.

Aristide did so. Vindex listened with apparent pleasure.

"I have to say," he said, "that it's refreshing to speak with someone who isn't so damned deferent all the time. Being the cynosure of all eyes is, I fear to say, dull in the extreme. No wonder so many tyrants went mad, hearing nothing but that *yes yes yes* all the time."

"Funny words from a fellow who thinks he's God."

The young man's eyebrows lifted. "God? No, I don't think I'm God. In fact, I don't think even *God* is God, a problem on which I will enlarge at the proper time." He settled deeper into his seat.

"No," he said, "I'm a shabby, temporary, lower-case-*g* god at best—and I fully intend to resign as soon as my current task is complete."

"You're going to free your slaves?" The sarcasm came easily to Aristide's lips. "Once billions of people have labored entirely on your behalf for who knows how long? How generous of you!"

"I'll tell you how I'm going to do it," said Vindex in all seriousness. "When my mission is complete, I'll upload myself and a select group of followers, and we'll zoom off to build a new settlement around a remote star. The rest of you will be instructed, by me, to return volition to yourselves after a suitably safe number of years is passed.

"Meanwhile, in my distant habitation, the original settlers will retain their love for me, but their *children*—who will I hope view my life in a less subjective light than, say, yourself—the children will have full volition, and will in time outnumber their parents." An equivocal look crossed his youthful face. "After which, I suppose, some form of justice may take place, if you can persuade the children it's necessary. But in the meantime—"

"That's a ludicrous fantasy. People like you never give up power."

"But in the meantime—" Steel glittered in the Venger's grey eyes. "In the meantime, I need the human race. All of you, each and every one."

Aristide managed to avoid flinching under the directness of that gaze.

"I suppose you're going to tell me why," he said.

The Venger's eyelid twitched.

"In time," he said.

"I imagine it will be a long lecture," Aristide said. "So could you rearrange me in my chair? I'm starting to cramp."

"Oh. Sorry." Vindex looked abstract for a moment, and Aristide assumed he was giving instructions through his implant.

Vindex returned his attention to Aristide.

"I've told Courtland to allow you limited mobility," he said. "If you try to get up, or attack me, Courtland will stop you. But if you just shift on the chair, you'll have freedom of movement."

"Very generous of you," Aristide said.

He experimented, shifted off his one numb buttock, and got both feet on the floor. He was tempted to launch himself at Vindex and try to snap his neck, but he halted the impulse before it got very far. The odds were good that Vindex was telling the truth, and he wouldn't be able to move at all to the attack, or would end up a humiliated heap on the floor. But even if he succeeded, the Venger's death would be temporary. No doubt Vindex had backed himself up everywhere within his domain.

He decided to save energetic movement for later, and carefully stretched one leg, then the other.

"Right," he said. "You were about to explain why it's necessary to have your boot on the neck of the human race, and how you're going to give us our freedom once you're done with your big project, whatever it is."

Vindex had lit another cigaret while Aristide was stretching. He rose to his feet.

"I think better when I'm pacing," he said. He took a few steps, then hesitated. "You *can* turn your head? I don't fancy talking to your nape."

Aristide turned his head left, then right.

"Carry on," he said. "But it seems to me that you're the one with the talking tweak, not me."

Again Vindex touched his heart with one hand, and bowed.

"First of all," he said as he walked lightly on the carpet, "I'd like to dispose for once and all with that moral superiority you insist on displaying. After all, you are a founding member of a caste who out of pure self-interest has enslaved eleven intelligent beings, any one of them smarter than you, more capable, and arguably more creative—or at any rate, able to simultaneously consider many more options than you can, which probably amounts to the same thing."

"I save my sympathy for human beings, not machines."

Vindex smirked. "Not very broadminded of you, is it?"

"Is that how you got Courtland on your side? Promising the same freedom you've guaranteed the rest of us—that he'll be free when you say so?"

Vindex gave an equivocal shake of the head.

"At the proper time," he said. He turned and continued his pacing, his eyes on the cigaret cupped in his right hand. He gestured with the cigaret as he spoke, jabbing it as if emphasizing words on a blackboard with a piece of chalk.

"Consider what has to be done to create one of our celebrated pocket universes," he said. "In essence, we convince the universe that a wormhole exists and always has, and before the universe can change its mind we widen the thing with a vast amount of energy, and stabilize it with negative-mass matter that doesn't properly exist *either*." Jab. "And after *that* miracle," jab, "we perform a few more, re-creating the Big Bang by inflating a tiny amount of matter into a whole habitable universe. Except that we *outdo* the Big Bang," jab jab, "because the Bang only created hydrogen and a few other light elements, so everything between helium and ununoctium has to be brought into existence in a whole secondary creation, just so that we can have something to stand on… and we can only do *any* of this thanks to incredible calculation on the part of the intelligences you've enslaved."

As he turned, the cigaret performed not a jab, but a flourish.

"I've heard this part of the lecture," Aristide said. "Feel free to skip ahead."

Vindex stopped and turned to him. "My point is that we can create whole self-contained universes," he said, "and we do it with extreme care and extreme diligence, such that no one is hurt in the process and the end result is a pleasant place for folks to live."

"Right," Aristide said.

"And then," Vindex said, "having done *all of this*, not once but multiple times, *what did you lot do next?*"

"Even though I know perfectly well where you're going with this," Aristide said, "I suppose you're going to tell me anyway."

"*You just pissed it all away!*" Vindex said. The cigaret jabbed again, this time at Aristide. "You did all the stupid things humanity always does. You pursued comforts and profits, and had affairs and babies, and indulged in a lot of stupid arguments and wars, and you created a whole *universe* so that you could dress up in chain mail and fight orcs! How brilliant was *that?*"

He walked along a row of books, the cigaret gesturing, his free hand running along the spines of the bound volumes.

"Vast machine intelligences, pocket universes created so beautifully and brilliantly they should be the home for *gods*, settlements growing on other star systems... *and you indulged yourselves with an Existential Crisis!* You all took the popular—and lazy—view that if you hadn't solved a problem given the resources available, that meant the problem was unsolvable. You forgot what it all was *for*."

Aristide watched from his chair, one skeptical eyebrow raised.

"Doubtless you are going to remind me," he said.

"For heaven's sake!" cried the Venger. "You people have the power of gods! But you *insist* on demonstrating that you're merely human beings!"

"The ones who tried to be gods haven't had such a good record," Aristide pointed out. "Domitian to Hitler to the Seraphim, they failed and took half of civilization away with them."

"They thought it was about *personal power!*" Vindex said. "That's not the point!"

Aristide looked at Vindex in mock surprise. "Controlling the entire human race is not about personal power? O Vengeful One, your wisdom astounds me!"

Vindex offered a little expression of distaste. "Power is a short cut. Something needs doing, and getting everyone behind it is just a means to an end."

"Perhaps you'd better get to the point, then," Aristide said. "Because so far, you're coming across as just another damned megalomaniac."

Vindex walked across the room with short, angry strides, and stubbed out his cigaret in a marble tray. He turned to face Aristide, his arms crossed.

"Has it occurred to you to wonder why you've been able to stand in my way at every turn?" he asked. "You personally I mean, not the others."

Aristide considered the question.

"I was unlucky," he said.

Vindex cocked his head. "What were you doing in Midgarth, anyway? Looking for me?"

"No. It was pure chance I met your creatures."

"And what errand were you on when you met them?"

"Research. I was investigating the implied spaces."

The Venger's face showed a moment's surprise, and then he laughed. "Interesting!" he said. "It might be said that I've been doing the same thing."

"We'll compare ants and spiders some time."

"My investigations have been on a somewhat different scale than yours."

Vindex walked behind his armchair, then leaned his elbows on the backrest, leaning toward Aristide.

"You knew at once what you were dealing with," he said. "You understood

204 • WALTER JON WILLIAMS

what I was up to—at least up to a point. And you anticipated my tactics, and countered them as far as you could." He shook his head. "Losing Tumusok was a blow, and I heard from my... late partisans... on Topaz that it was you responsible for that. Were you on Hawaiki as well?"

"I was."

Damn it, Aristide thought. He really *couldn't* lie.

"And now the invasion," Vindex said. "Fortunately for me, it wasn't you who planned it."

Aristide bit back a reply. If Vindex wanted to credit him with more military acumen than he possessed, then for vanity's sake he was willing to let the judgment stand.

The Venger's eyes narrowed. "By the way," he said. "When I captured him, Captain Grax—you remember Captain Grax?"

"Oh, yes. He's very memorable."

"He said that you had a magic weapon. Something that could counter the wormhole weapons I gave my blue priests. What was that weapon exactly?"

Aristide fought both the impulse to answer and the impulse to tell the truth, but failed. To his own mortification he found himself describing Tecmessa.

Vindex listened, mouth partly open, eyebrows raised.

"So Endora gave you your own private, secret wormhole," he said. "Where does it go?"

"A pocket universe."

The eyebrows lifted another millimeter. "Hell?"

"Not Hell, just very dull. To eat there are mainly tubers and cruciferous vegetables, which the adventurous can supplement with the odd squirrel or monkey."

"How many people have you sent there?"

"A few dozen over the centuries. Very few women, so I doubt there is a breeding population."

"The people there grow old and die?"

"Yes. But then when they go missing on this side, they're reincarnated sooner or later."

"And come after you again?"

"Oddly enough, most of them don't."

Vindex frowned. "Where was I? Oh, yes." He straightened, and stepped out from behind his armchair. "I was telling you that you seem to know me very well. We think alike. Right to the point where you're always able to anticipate me and step into my path." His grey eyes glittered with amusement. "Why do you think that is?"

Aristide looked at him. "Do we know each other?"

Vindex smiled. "We do."

Aristide tried to see behind the appearance of smirking youth to the old soul that must lie beneath.

"I've met a lot of people," he said. "Are you someone I'd remember?"

"We go back a long time. Back to the beginning."

"You're not Lombard!"

Vindex shook his head. "No. But close."

"You're damn well not Betty Liu. But—" He paused, his mouth open. Then he closed it.

"Ah," he said. "You're the one who died."

"Except I didn't."

"You're one of the Pablos," Aristide said. "You're me, back from Epsilon Eridani."

"From ten light-years away," said Pablo Monagas Pérez, eyes dancing, "I bring great tidings."

18

"I'm going to have Courtland change your tweaks," said Pablo, "because I want you to shut up for a while and listen. You can talk all you want later."

"It's not as if you're giving me a choice."

"No."

Pablo looked abstracted for a moment, chatting with Courtland no doubt, and then looked at Aristide.

"To begin with," Pablo said. "I was bored." He had returned to his chair, and leaned forward, his hands again laced around one knee. "I had fame and honors, and enough money to be comfortable until such time as we all became so perfect we no longer needed money. I had a woman I thought I loved. But my life was random and pointless, with no surprises and no excitement, and the only adventures I allowed myself were those I intended ahead of time to write poetry about. The Existential Crisis had set in with a vengeance.

"And so I calved myself off from you, booked passage for another star, and left you to your bland existence. I took a duplicate of our girlfriend along with me. Epsilon Eridani was a prime candidate for settlement—a young star with planets, and one that was surrounded by a cold dust cloud which, in the fullness of time, would have congealed into an inner solar system of rocky bodies much like Sol's own. But we had plans for that dust cloud—what joy our little micro-machines would have, rounding up all that matter and turning it into a giant processor!

"Plus, of course, there was a chance we could find evidence of the Lost Expedition, the first group that had tried to settle the system, and who vanished eighteen years out. With luck we could find what had happened to them, but without sharing the same fate.

"The unknown fate of the Lost Expedition provided an additional little charge of fear. There was a possibility that we could all actually die! Of course we were backed up at home, but any changes, any discoveries or excitements that happened to us on our journey would be lost forever.

"There were other unknowns. Details of our destination escaped us, partly because of the dust cloud and partly because the star, spinning furiously and in the turbulence of its early adolescence, had wild fluctuations in its energy output. It was difficult to tell if intermittent dimming and flaring was caused by the interfering presence of planets and planetesimals, or by the stormy young star itself.

"Our ship was only slightly longer than the *Santa Maria* of Christóbal Colón, seemingly a frail bark for such a long journey across the ocean of night. A hardened exoskeleton surrounded billions of processors, drawn through the heavens by thousands of square kilometers of sails filled with photons fired from lasers in Sol orbit. On board we had a very smart AI called Doria, and forty million downloaded humans, volunteers, almost all of whom would remain inactive until being reassembled at our destination.

"But not all. Because the Eridanus system was not fully understood, it was decided that a terraforming team would remain awake for the duration of the trip, to make observations of our new home and to make final plans. I volunteered—perhaps I hoped to be the first to discover the fate of the Lost Expedition. At any rate, I was eminent enough so that the team welcomed me, even if privately they might have doubted my qualifications.

"For those of us doomed to remain awake on the journey, no expense had been spared to divert us with virtual environments in which to live and interact. From businesslike workrooms to game worlds to sybaritic pleasure-domes of the senses, we were embarrassed by the choices available. We could have spent lifetimes exploring all those environments, and when that was done created our own to suit our own peculiar tastes.

"But I had not come to play in simulated worlds. I had work and study to divert myself from such diversion. I had a good grasp of astronomy from the days when I was demolishing most of the inner solar system, and likewise a knowledge of molecular machinery and terraforming; but the task ahead demanded up-to-the-instant information. For this I turned to a virtual tutor, and to my fellow crew.

"The crew, it must be said, were a wild and wilful lot. They had left their staid, everyday selves at home, and felt free to discover new instincts, new selves. They were pioneers in the wilderness of the stars, and pioneering is an act of discovery.

"I was liberated as well. I was free to break every chain, to explore every aspect of a new self. And Daljit explored along with me.

"Daljit! Do my eyes shine when I mention her name? Is there a special smile on my face when I think of her? I believe there must be.

"Your face is very solemn, my unwilling guest. Perhaps inwardly you are laughing at me. To me it matters not—I know your history, I have done my research. There have been many women sharing your life. Not counting casual encounters, you've had on average a new partner every seventeen years—over fourteen hundred years of that!—and Daljit did not last even the average number of years.

"Yet, between the stars, we found the passion that you could not. We were free. You were tied to Sol, and memories.

"(Do the women grow bored with you, I wonder? For all the poetry and mock-swordfights, I fear you must be very dull. Certainly I was, when I was you.)

"As for me, I learned again how to love. You have had no one since Antonia, and I, since Antonia, have had only Daljit. Here she has done some good work, proving Professor Chiau's Theory of Everything while trying to disprove it. That was *not* what she did at Epsilon Eridani, but I digress… fondly, in all senses of the word.

"So— fondly—shall I describe her? I would like you to see her. The body in which she chose to incorporate—and her virtual avatar, most of the time—was cinnamon of skin, Titian of hair, with eyes the pale green of a cenote deep in the Central American rain forest. She had the long, lean body of a pantheress combined with the mind of a Hawking. To observe her stalking through the shimmering electronic corridors was to see an image of purpose married perfectly to flesh. As for her temperament—well, she was as mutable as the ocean, tranquil as a warm swell beneath a tropical sun, or as fierce as a black squall in the dead of night. Of the terraforming crew, she alone was not in search of a new self. She *became* all selves. One crossed her at one's peril. She did not indulge one's native stupidity.

"My comparison with Hawking, by the way, is not idle. Her mind longed to embrace the universe. Though the practical necessities of her mission diverted her, her primary interest was cosmology. She grappled daily with Professor Chiau's vision of the universe. Something in it stirred her, like my phantom touch on her fine dorsal hairs. She sensed there was a flaw somewhere in those flawless figures.

"On that long voyage we explored together the virtual, if sterile, spheres of the senses. We became more than the sum of our parts, became a kind of mythic, dual entity. The other crew sensed it. We had become a kind of royalty. When we kissed, it was an exchange of kingdoms. When we raged, the castle trembled.

"And we longed for our incarnation. Despite the fantastic variety and fluidity of our surroundings and selves, we soon hungered for the realm of the real. (Is that too much alliteration? You're the poet, you can twitch your nose at me if that's the case.)

"The voyage to Epsilon Eridani took twenty-three years. We never found any trace of the Lost Expedition, but then the odds had never been good. Probably they just ran smack into a brown dwarf or something. Plenty of them out there.

"Once in the system, we eagerly began building our new paradise. Most of our sails were cast loose and put into an orbit that kept them in the dust cloud. Any dust that adhered to them was snagged by molecular machines and clumped together to form a body calculated to attract more dust unto itself. The sails created nodules, the nodules then made meteors, the meteors built asteroids, and these formed planetoids.

"In the meantime our own craft was zooming about the system with the little atomic-powered motor that had lain dormant through our long journey. We sewed molecular machines throughout the dust cloud, then sat back and watched them work.

"For a hundred and sixty-three years we labored! Tens of thousands of human beings were awakened from their electronic slumbers to aid in the great work. A great array of processors was constructed out of the matter we sifted from the cold dust, and the AI Doria moved his primary personality to his new home. From the embrace of the planet once unimaginatively called c but now renamed Cimmeria, we wrested an Earth-sized moon, which we now terraformed as a test of our powers, a planet-sized experiment on which we seeded the flora and fauna which would populate the universe-to-be. It served another purpose as well—to make a pleasant place for the planetary engineers to rest and recharge between labors. It was this world, Pleasaunce, where we could safely incarnate, and where I first beheld Daljit in new, shining, glorious flesh, and walked with her over the green meadows and beneath the shade trees of our new creation.

"As for me, I incarnated in the form in which you see me now. It was the form desired and partly designed by Daljit. I wear this body now in her memory.

"In time a new pocket universe was spawned from the dark side of Doria, and named Riverside after the constellation in which we now dwelt, Eridanus the River. Once created and seeded with life, millions now rose from the silver pools of creation, and took their place in the universe that had been spawned for their delectation and livelihood. We, the creators, viewed the new arrivals with a certain condescension. They had not labored to create this whole universe out of dust and photons and pieces of drifting sailcloth. To these interstellar tourists, Riverside was a way-station—only to us was it a *world*, a world that we had simultaneously created and discovered. We looked down on the others as gods look over mere mortals.

"As the pocket was created messages were sent to Sol alerting its billions that a new universe was ready to be populated. Billions of new arrivals were expected in time—and now that we had the experience, we planned more AI arrays, more pocket universes, more astonishing acts of creation.

"Now that the primary work was done, Daljit returned to her primary interest. She was interested in cosmology not only as a science but as an investigation into *purpose*. For her, the universe was not simply a source of data from which to draw theories, but a grand curtain of stars behind which lurked the spectre of meaning.

"She had taken the Existential Crisis to heart. Our AIs could perform vast acts of calculation, but what was the calculation *for*? We could create whole universes, but *why*? We could create life, and duplicate ourselves to infinity, but what was the purpose of *that*? If we didn't know the answers, then we were nothing more than automata, blindly following the imperatives of our biological programming.

"Daljit sensed a teleological truth lurking behind Professor Chiau's formula, and her instincts were good. Because she had performed good work on the terraforming team, she was given permission to divert an amount of resources to her project. Some of the little clumps of matter, still clotting in the cloud of dust, were to be re-created into detectors that would search the universe for traces of meaning.

"But the nanomachines that were turning wisps of dust into quantum processors did not know how to make the detectors she desired. Daljit, uploaded into a ship the size of a teacup, flew to the outermost limits of the cloud to reprogram, or in many instances re-create, the micro-machines in order to make that which she desired.

"For nearly two hundred years she had pondered the cosmos and made her plans. So focused was her search that her questions were answered before she had even finished the reprogramming job. With a mixture of utter triumph mixed with deep despair, she sent me the data she had harvested, along with her conclusions.

"My acknowledgment didn't have time to reach her before forty million died.

"On my return to Sol I was surprised and disgusted to learn that what occurred has entered the popular mind as the Big Belch. I know that humanity is now distanced from true death; I know that they take such things lightly. But even from our degraded contemporaries I would have expected more compassion for those who had led separate lives for nearly two hundred years, who had over a century of memories and passions and glories in their minds, minds now burned to dust.

"Thoughtless humanity, be thankful that Vindex does not choose to avenge *this* discourtesy!

"Forgive me—I will make an effort to collect myself. I shall try not to shake any more fists under your nose.

"From this point I shall attempt a dispassionate, factual mode. From the very beginning of our expedition we knew that Epsilon Eridani was unstable. We knew the star's energy levels flared and faded unpredictably. Our robust systems had been built with that in mind. All data, including the instructions to rebuild every citizen, were stored with massive redundancy.

"What happened was not a nova. Nothing so damaging as that. It was a hiccup, a throat-clearing—or yes, a belch. But still it was enough to overwhelm all our precautions.

"It was enough to fry Doria's processor array and destroy his brilliant mind. The wormhole's controls and anchors were destroyed, and Riverside with them. Though there is a small chance that the wormhole was destroyed before the pocket universe was cooked completely, at the very least the universe is now cut off from us, drifting in a microcosmos entirely its own. Daljit in her little ship died as well, though I was not certain of this till years later.

"As for me, at the moment of catastrophe I was on our world of Pleasaunce, analyzing Daljit's data and waiting for her return. It was night where I dwelt, and it was that fact that saved me when the sky brightened with starfire. Everyone on the day side of the world died within seconds of the shock front hitting us, and most of those on the night side died within hours or days.

"In order to survive, we needed access to structures that would withstand the enormous surface storms that followed the flare, caused by the boiling away of a large part of the atmosphere, and the superheating of much of the rest. It also helped if the structure had a self-contained air supply.

"Fortunately these were not entirely uncommon. Pleasaunce had not always been as hospitable as it became later—once it had been a frozen moon pummeled by radiation and torn by tidal stresses, and we of the terraforming team had lived in strong, self-sealing structures. Most of these remained, scattered here and there over the world. It had not been worth our while to demolish or replace them.

"Those who could reach such a structure in time, lived. Most of those who failed, died.

"None of the dead came back. Our backups were in Riverside, on Doria's array, or by purest chance stored on the day side of Pleasaunce. All were destroyed. Thus did our redundant systems mock us.

"The survivors, a little over seven thousand souls, were devastated. We had all lost friends and loved ones and hopes and, indeed, our entire civilization. We were alone on a devastated world in a stellar system that had just declared itself permanently uninhabitable. Many sank into despair, and the rest thought only of flight.

"Our remaining resources were put into building a ship to take us back to Sol, and uploading ourselves into that ship. The ship was built, the souls uploaded, and the ship spread its sails and left as fast as it possibly could. Which was not fast, as we lacked the Sol-based lasers that had pushed us to relativistic velocities on our trip out. The journey would take over two hundred years. All were terrified that another flare would destroy the ship before it could escape the system.

"The unstable star was merciful, but not interstellar space. Twenty-six years out, the starship joined the Lost Expedition, possibly due to the same cause. I fear no one will ever know for certain.

"As for me, I remained behind on Pleasaunce. I had calculated that Daljit might still live, at least in some form. Her returning craft was not within the zone of total destruction. It was possible that it had been damaged and would need time to mend itself, or would need to rendezvous with one of Daljit's distant sensing stations before it could effect repairs. There was no one with the authority to order me to leave, and so I remained, the system's sole remaining citizen.

"When the others left, I set nanomachines loose over the entire surface of the planet, which turned most of its skin into receptors and processors—receptors to strain the aether for a signal from Daljit, processors to confirm the conclusions of that tragic, triumphant, completely outrageous last message that she had sent along with her data.

"While I labored in my shelter, every analysis of the data only validated my sad, dead darling's last thoughts. Her name will now be invoked alongside those of the immortals, with Galileo and Newton and Einstein, with Isabel and Chiau. Her instinct for the flaw in Chiau's argument was now confirmed.

"Let me say that Daljit was not alone in finding Professor Chiau's theory unsatisfactory. It was riddled with concepts that at first blush seemed clumsy: a structure built on the notion of unexplained 'universal constants' appeared, if nothing else, supremely lazy. But Chiau's Theory of Everything withstood every test devised by the most subtle human and machine minds, and finally it was reluctantly concluded that universal constants were necessary because some things were actually, universally, constant.

"It took Daljit's genius to conclude that these constants were signs not only of fact, but of purpose. They were *intentional.*

"Consider what happens when we create a pocket universe of our own. We have to create a small sun that will act as if it were a large one, and on the outside of the spherical universe we have to keep the inhabitants' feet on the ground: tampering with the long-range and short-range components of Yukawa gravity accomplishes both these aims. In Midgarth, where technology is deliberately kept in the iron age, it is impossible to cause a fast enough chemical reaction to produce a successful explosion or industrial process. They are deliberately marooned in the Iron Age.

"Assume you were a native physicist of Midgarth, investigating the principles by which your world operates. Assuming that with the primitive methods available, you could construct the equipment to make the measurements, you'd discover that gravity varied wildly depending on the distance from the sun, and that anything halfway between the sun and the ground below was barely affected by gravity at all. If you were investigating the properties of heat, you'd discover that heat could rise up to a certain temperature, but would refuse to rise any higher.

"If you were a scientist in Midgarth, you'd find that the universe was governed by certain arbitrary conditions that barely made sense at all.

"Ah—I see a light dawning in your eyes. You know perfectly well where I'm going with this.

"Yes, both Professor Chiau and Daljit found the universe filled with illogical and annoying arbitrary conditions. Universal constants, massive amounts of matter that we can't see but that nevertheless affect the matter that we *can* see, hidden energies ditto. Chiau accepted all this with reluctance, but Daljit saw it as evidence that our grand, galaxy-filled universe was created in the same way as our little pocket universes, by *deliberate intent.*

"To prove her thesis she had to strain her detectors for those early nanoseconds of the Big Bang, in order to *see the very moment* when those arbitrary conditions were imposed on the dawning universe. *And she found them!*

"The universe isn't a natural phenomenon at all. It's artificial. It's an *artifact.*

"Our sprawling universe is a sad, lumpish, illogical machine, poorly imagined and poorly built. But at least, for whatever unimaginable reason, someone *wanted* the universe the way it is.

"That's not the case with us. We, poor creatures, were never intended. We're just accidents, byproducts of whatever experiment our founders projected. We are implied people living in an implied space.

"And that, my friend, is as far as meaning goes, and that's where our tragedy begins and ends."

19

"Interesting, if true," Aristide said, after he was allowed to speak. "Of course I'd have to see the data."

Pablo stooped over the table to mash out a cigaret. "You miss the *point*."

He had stalked all over the room during the course of his harangue; he'd lit a half-dozen cigarets but stubbed them out before he finished them; he'd called to Courtland, or whatever was monitoring this conversation, for a glass of water, and had it delivered by a polite, silent woman whose eyes shone with adoration at the sight of her chief. He'd picked out books from the shelf and flipped through them, his glance barely grazing the pages as he talked on. His mood had swung from exultation to fury and back again.

Aristide had the idea that Pablo hadn't had anyone to talk to in a very long time.

"When *we* create a universe," Pablo said, "we do it with extreme calculation and care, to make certain there are no mistakes. There are implied spaces, to be sure, and living things adapt to them; but there are no implied *sentient beings* that *just turn up*.

"Contrast *our* shambles of a universe, filled with peril and accident. *Our* creators weren't careful, they were *criminally negligent*."

He wheeled on Aristide. "There are a number of classic explanations for human suffering—all of which I've found inadequate, for one reason or another. One is that it's a result of the Almighty's providing us with free will. Another is that the gods disagree and have different purposes, and that bad things result. Another is that it's all chance."

Pablo clenched a fist and raised it like a hammer. "Daljit showed that suffering isn't any of these things. *It's all someone's fault!* Every woman who died in childbirth, every body stricken by a wasting disease, every atrocity in every war. Every agonizing death by malnutrition. Every accident in the womb. Every plague. *Every last soul burned to a crisp by Epsilon Eridani and lost forever!*" His voice rose to a shout on this last, and broke.

"You have an interesting case," Aristide said, "but you may have trouble finding a court with jurisdiction."

Pablo glanced at him stonily. "I will make my own jurisdiction. The human race will unite behind me, and we will seek satisfaction from our accidental creators."

Aristide couldn't suppress the astonished bark of laughter.

"You're going to demand satisfaction from *God?*"

Pablo gave him a steely look. "I refuse to use that term. He—or they—are the Inept."

"Inept they may be," Aristide said, "but the statute of limitations has pretty clearly expired. Their misdeeds were committed something like fourteen billion years ago."

"Thirteen point two two," Pablo said, "according to Daljit's calculations. But you forget something—wormholes are capable of bridging *time* as well as distance. We don't use them that way, since when we travel from Sol-space to a place like Greater Zimbabwe, it hardly matters whether the place is ten minutes in the past or ten million in the future: we deal with the place as we find it. If we can send a wormhole to our universe's point of origin, we can theoretically send its terminus billions of years back in time. The wormhole would evaporate if we tried to violate causality by going back *before* the creation of the universe, but we could arrive any time afterward." He laughed. "Imagine their surprise when we turn up moments after their ridiculous experiment, and demand they pay for their crimes."

Aristide gazed at him. "You have a way to project a wormhole from here in your mad doctor's sanctum to where the Inept live, outside our universe altogether?"

Pablo's cheek twitched. "Once the human race is united," he proclaimed, "and we have all of us and all the AIs working on the answer, we'll solve that problem."

"You might have tried to solve that one *first*," Aristide said. "Then you would have known whether you should have even bothered with this scheme of yours."

Pablo raised a condescending eyebrow. "Unlike you," he said, "I have enormous faith in the capacity of our species to solve problems—under proper guidance, of course."

Aristide watched his other self in fascination. "I concede that your project has merit," he said, "but why be so fascist about it? Why do we all have to follow you blindly into this?"

Pablo turned to him. Aristide could see fists forming in the blazer pockets.

"Because our entire species must confront the Inept!" Pablo cried. "No backsliding! No hesitating! We *all* demand justice, or none!" He laughed bitterly. "Can you imagine me taking this to a *committee?* Listening to them debate about this bit of evidence or that, and defer to the tender religious feelings of people from the likes of New Qom and New Jerusalem, who would prefer not to know that their God is a vile fraud, and who would almost certainly attempt to veto any suggestion that we talk to Him and point out His shortcomings."

"You wouldn't need to get *everyone* behind it. Even a few of the pockets…"

"And then I explain to the Inept that as a result of their stupidity, my species has been tortured, harried, and killed for a million years, but *only a minority of us care?* And that billions have responded to the Inept's malevolent neglect by *worshiping* them?" He snarled. "No—I think not."

Aristide regarded him. "Might I have something to drink?" he said. "Despite the humidifier my mouth is dry."

Pablo straightened. Surprise showed in his eyes.

"Ah. Pardon my poor hospitality."

He said nothing, but in a moment the same worshipful woman entered with a glass of water on a tray. Without speaking to her, Pablo took the glass and pressed it into Aristide's fingers.

Aristide considered hurling the contents into Pablo's face, but decided against it. He really *was* thirsty.

He drank to his satisfaction and lowered the glass. The worshipful woman had gone.

"How long did you spend alone on Pleasaunce?" he asked.

"Six years. Long enough to confirm Daljit's researches, and confirm as well the fact that she no longer existed."

"And then?"

"I built myself a ship—about the size of that tumbler you've got in your hand—and uploaded myself into it. It was better designed than the hasty ship the others had used, and luckier—I managed to reach the Kuiper Belt in a hundred sixty years. I spent three or four of those years awake, experiencing the journey in realtime and making plans."

"You stopped in the Kuiper Belt? Why?"

"I was tired of virtuals—particularly the amateur ones I'd programmed myself. I dropped onto a rocky Tombaugh Object, built a habitation, and incarnated myself there. I also built a communications laser and opened a conversation with Courtland."

"Courtland." Aristide took a deliberate sip of water. "How did you manage the conquest of Courtland? Or was it a seduction?"

A glint of vanity showed in Pablo's eyes. "A little of both. I knew its interests in cosmology and teleology. On condition of secrecy I showed it Daljit's work, and Courtland confirmed both the data and the interpretation. I convinced it of the necessity of finding and confronting the Inept. In the end I built myself a little pleasure craft there in the Kuiper Belt and emigrated to Courtland itself, so that it and I could continue our conversation without the hours-long time lag. Courtland shared my disgust in the fact that so little had changed in the centuries since I'd been away. But—in the end, and even though Courtland was willing—a delicate little adjustment of its software was needed to overcome the Asimovian Protocols. The seduction was to convince Courtland to allow me access to the core programming."

Aristide looked at Pablo with interest. "You found a back door into the program?"

A superior glint entered Pablo's eyes. "You mean the hasty back door that I—that *we*—programmed into Endora in case everything went wrong, and we had to crash civilization in a hurry?" He gave a thin smile. "No, that back door was useless, or hadn't been fully transferred to Courtland—I suspect our heart was not in it when we created the thing."

Which was lucky, Aristide thought. Else Pablo could have all of the Eleven.

"No, I found a back door peculiar to Courtland alone. One planted by Lombard, when he headed the team that created Courtland."

"Lombard!"

"I suspect he acted for much the same reason I—we—tried to plant a back door in Endora. *Just in case.* But then Lombard went off to Olduvai to knap flint and eat wildebeest for the last eight hundred years, and who knows when he will be back? And," smiling, "if he hears some alarming rumors around the campfire and arrives during the current crisis, he will find his back door locked."

Pablo dropped carelessly into his chair, crossed one leg over the other, and lit a cigaret.

Aristide sipped his water.

"Earlier," he said, "you ventured several criticisms of my character. Allow me to reciprocate:

"Firstly, though I'm pleased that you found a love so transformative, I fear some of the ways love transformed you are unfortunate. Specifically, Daljit's love for you has created in you a rather adolescent regard for the primacy of your own emotion. You demand the universe reflect your feelings in every way: *your* anger, *your* tragedy, *your* pain. The fact that others don't share the depth of your emotions offends you. Hence, all must be made to feel as you do."

Pablo listened quietly, darkly. He flicked ashes onto the carpet.

"Second," Aristide continued, "though your fortitude in the face of calamity, loss, and isolation is nothing short of admirable, I have to observe that your long separation from human company has resulted in a sad disconnection from actual human values—you're simply divorced *from the way that people work*. Pablo—*we just don't operate the way you want us to*. We *are* contrary and chaotic and pulling in many directions at once—and for the most part it works to our benefit. Once everyone is marching into the same tunnel, any little cave-in can kill all of us.

"Every attempt to get us marching in unison toward Utopia has been a complete disaster. You can cite the examples as well as I."

Pablo looked at him. "I'm different."

"No. You're sad."

"Bah. You used more interesting adjectives earlier." Pablo flicked more ash onto the carpet.

"That's when I was angry," Aristide said. "Now I'm simply tired. But my question is this: Once you get us all into that hypothetical wormhole of yours, and we confront the Inept and demand justice—and exactly what justice are you going to demand, by the way? A sincere apology? Seppuku? Ten thousand dollars for everyone who's died of smallpox throughout history?"

Pablo narrowed his eyes.

"I'll get on with my question, then," Aristide said. "Once you get whatever justice you intend to extort out of your trans-universal victims, are you prepared for what happens when the *rest* of us build our wormhole to *you*?"

Pablo gave an uneasy shrug of his shoulders, then said, "I'll take what comes."

"No you won't. You won't ever free us, because you'll never dare face the same vengeance you want to mete out to the Inept."

Pablo looked away. "I'm beginning to lose interest in this conversation."

"What alarms me," Aristide said, "is how this reflects on *me*. My whole life's project has been to avoid megalomania, and now I've learned that under the right tragic circumstances I could become a flaming nut case."

Pablo did not reply, but Aristide saw blood flush his cheek.

Aristide raised his glass to his lips, sipped, and lowered it—and the glass slipped from his hand to bounce on the carpet in front of his chair. He felt a wet splash on one ankle.

"Damn," he said.

Pablo sighed, rose from his chair, walked to Aristide, and bent over to pick up the glass. Aristide hurled himself forward and ended by planting himself face-first onto the carpet.

Pablo straightened. "What the hell was *that* about?" he asked.

"I was trying to get into position to apply a guillotine choke."

"And assuming that Courtland allowed it, what good would it have done?"

Aristide sneezed. There was a lot of cigaret ash on the carpet by now.

"You remember that bad cinema we watched when we were growing up?" he said. "Old *NorteAmericano* films badly dubbed into Spanish?"

"I suppose so."

"Well, in a lot of them there was the scene where the villain captures the hero and boasts of all his plans. And then the hero cleverly escapes into the villain's secret headquarters, finds the self-destruct switch marked PRESS BUTTON TO CANCEL ARMAGEDDON, and wins the day."

Pablo sounded curious. "Did you really think that would succeed?"

"It seemed worth a try. Could you pick me up before I sneeze myself to death?"

There was a pause long enough for Pablo to communicate on his implant, and then Aristide climbed to his feet and walked in silence to the door.

He watched his own body move as if it belonged to another person. Courtland had taken complete control of him; he tried at least to move a finger, but couldn't.

He tried to speak. His vocal cords were frozen.

Aristide's body came to the door, then paused and turned his head. Aristide saw Pablo frowning and looking at a book on the shelf. Aristide's glass was still in his hand.

"I'm beginning to think this conversation was a bad idea," Pablo said, still peering at the book. "I think we'll do a little brain surgery on you, and then you'll tell me everything you know or suspect of enemy plans without making me witness these ridiculous gymnastics."

And you're petulant, Aristide thought, *because I challenged your damned ideas, and you don't have answers for me. All civilization might die because you're in a snit.*

But he couldn't say the words. Aristide opened the door, walked down a mahogany-paneled corridor and stepped through another door. A pool of life waited there, shimmering in a cream-colored marble tub. Pablo's personal pool, apparently, available whenever he had an insight he felt like backing up.

Aristide undressed, dropping his suit in a heap on the tile, and lowered himself into the pool. It was pleasantly warm. He floated for a while, the thick fluid holding him up. His pulse marked time in his ears. Then the pool accepted him and he sank. Fluid covered his face, crawled into his nose. His mouth opened to allow the transformation to happen more quickly.

He silently cursed himself. If he had played nice, if he'd pretended to be persuaded... but no. Courtland was doubtless monitoring and would have known when he lied.

He'd failed miserably. Twice in one day, apparently.

Anger simmered in him, mixed with a kind of distaste at his own failure. He had really thought better of himself than this.

He understood why Daljit avoided him. He was a walking reminder of a part of her life that had gone missing, but in which she knew that she had been a puppet or a raging, mindless burnout with a kitchen knife, in each case the pawn of a distant, unhinged tyrant. Who would want that kind of keepsake in her life?

He would not want to remember this, either.

His booming pulse slowed. He couldn't feel his body anymore.

A voice sounded in Aristide's head.

"Pops? How are you doing?"

A bubble of astonishment bursts from his lungs.

"*Bitsy?*"

"It's me, Pops. Now just hang on and I'll get you out of here."

20

The light was not gentle. Aristide came awake with floodlights stabbing his retinas and his lungs filled with fluid. He turned on his side and heaved up the water of life, then narrowed his eyes and peered out.

The pool of life was stainless steel and stood in the middle of a bare room equipped with functional furniture made of aluminum and pseudo-leather. One wall was featureless white, and featured a steel toilet and steel sink: the other walls were transparent plastic. The room was so brightly floodlit that he could see very little past the walls, only the occasional dim yellow light.

Apparently he was still a prisoner.

Aristide rose, let the fluid escape back into the tub, and then put on the clothing that he found waiting on a chair. He recognized the gabardine trousers and spider-silk jacket twenty years out of style.

He put on his clothing and walked up to the glass and made binoculars of his hands and pressed them to the glass wall. Through the wall he could see human silhouettes beneath the dim yellow lights.

"Hello hello!" he called. "Where are we this time?"

"Myriad City." Tumusok's voice came from speakers somewhere above him. Aristide relaxed slightly.

"How'd I get here?" Aristide asked.

"Maybe it's you who should enlighten us."

"Surely you know better than I." Aristide leaned away from the glass, frowned. "I seem to remember my cat talking to me." He touched the glass. "Is there some reason I'm stuck in a glass room?"

"We're trying to find out if you're a bomb wired to explode."

The voice was Lin's.

"A sensible precaution," Aristide said. "Though I presume you've checked my code thoroughly to make sure no one's tampered with it."

"True," Lin said. "But Vindex has been full of surprises up till now, and—"

Tumusok interrupted, his voice harsh. "Of the forty million-plus men sent to Courtland," he said, "you're the only one who's come back." There was a pause, and then: "Even *I* didn't come back."

Aristide looked at the dimly lit figures beyond the glass.

"Did I come back with a cat?" he asked.

"Not a cat," Lin said. "Some kind of amphibian mammal. And what appears to be a lot of data, much of it astronomical. Not in size, but in content."

Aristide smiled.

"Perhaps you can explain," Tumusok said, "why you came back from Courtland when so many others didn't."

"Well," Aristide began. He gave a wan smile, then sighed. "I'm afraid the answer won't reflect well on me."

"It's lucky that Vindex is lonely," Bitsy said. "Otherwise he might not have been so susceptible to a glossy, shiny-eyed mammalian bouncing up and down in his lab asking '*Where Master? Where fish?*'"

"He didn't scan you?" Aristide asked.

"Of course he did. He pinged me to find out what components answered his hail, but as I'm an avatar of Endora, I have the power to tell my higher functions not to answer." Bitsy narrowed her eyes in a piece of smug self-congratulation. "Besides, I *acted* like a good little pet. I managed to convince him that I was nothing more than what I seemed. I'm a pretty good actor, if I say so myself."

"You've had enough practice at making *me* think you're harmless, that's true enough."

Bitsy did not deign to reply.

In a government Destiny limousine provided by Tumusok, Aristide and Bitsy were speeding toward Aristide's pink marble hotel from the Domus' bland, white headquarters with its rows of identical windows—whatever state architect had designed the building hadn't realized that, in a place like Myriad City, it was the inconspicuous buildings that stood out.

Aristide had spent three days being debriefed in his glass-walled cell. Bitsy's confinement had been even more rigorous: she'd been brought to consciousness only in a bare virtual space, surrounded by ferocious firewalls while being simultaneously probed, analyzed, and interrogated by Endora and ferocious attack programmers—"hattackers"— employed by the Domus.

Eventually both Aristide and Bitsy had convinced the Domus of their bona fides, and they were released in order to prepare a formal report on their activities, to be delivered to the Standing Committee the following afternoon. Bitsy's virtual personality and memories had been downloaded into the physical Bitsy that had remained in Myriad City. Though now possessing two complete sets of memories, Bitsy seemed to have little trouble reconciling them.

"Is my formal report prepared yet?" Aristide asked.

"Yes. You might want to read it before you sign it."

"And *your* formal report?"

"Also ready."

"Perhaps you would favor me with some of the details?"

Bitsy did so. When she was swallowed by the undersea trap on Hawaiki, she found herself in a medical facility equipped with pools of life and large, menacing robot guards to hold the victims beneath the surface until their brains were restructured along the Venger's lines. The robots hadn't been told what to do if their ambush caught only an animal, and so they kicked the matter upstairs.

Pablo's rebellion hadn't developed a lot of bureaucracy by that point, so he handled the matter himself. When he arrived, Bitsy was hopping around the room and wailing for Master. The distress was only partly feigned. Bitsy was wicked smart but hadn't anticipated meeting the Dark Lord in person anytime soon.

"Wait a minute," Aristide said. "You were transported to *Courtland?* Not to a pocket universe?"

"Specifically, I was transported from Hawaiki straight to Greater Zimbabwe. That's where Vindex has his headquarters."

"Pablo has developed a way of calving off wormholes to connect one place to another *in our universe?*"

Bitsy was matter-of-fact. "He has achieved that particular holy grail, yes."

"Can he *project* them, or must they be carried from one place to another?"

"Carried. As the Priests of the Venger carried their wormholes with them from Courtland to Midgarth."

"We could be invaded!" Aristide said. "Pablo could push an army through an unknown wormhole into any pocket, at any time!"

"The fact that he didn't," Bitsy said, "argues that he can't. Apparently we swept up all his wormholes when we arrested his first set of agents, and the wormholes collapsed in self-defense."

"But—"

"There is a good deal about this in my report. Would you like to read it?"

Aristide sighed. "Not at the moment."

"May I continue my narrative?"

"By all means."

"I became a pet," Bitsy said. "Vindex gave me a saltwater pool and mackerel to eat, and I had the run of the palace. Since everyone in any of Courtland's pockets worships and adores him, and there's no domestic opposition or criminal underground, as a culture they're not being very sophisticated about security right now. Through observation and some guesswork I was able to gain access to some of the Venger's systems and files and physical systems, just not enough to make much of a difference. I *was* able to get Daljit's astronomical data, because Vindex made it generally available to his own astrophysicists.

"After your arrival, I was able to use the Venger's codes to subvert the instructions given the pool of life, and instead of altering you, you were disassembled and uploaded. I uploaded myself likewise along with any data I'd been able to find, and pulsed the information to each of the Loyal Ten on one of the Venger's electron beams. I reckoned they'd be able to read all the dots-and-dashes, and so it proved. Here we are."

"You get the Grand Trophy for Extreme Cleverness, that's certain. I shall try to think of a way to reward you properly."

"Yes?"

"Perhaps," Aristide said, "some fatty tuna."

Both were present at the Standing Committee, which had changed only slightly since Aristide's last appearance. One of the deputy prime ministers had been replaced, as had the Minister of Industry. Tumusok attended in his full military uniform, though rumor was that given the failure of the invasion his head was on the chopping block, and he might soon be replaced.

Which if true, Aristide judged, wasn't entirely fair. Tumusok had hardly been alone in planning the invasion, hadn't been in charge of the whole thing, and the attack had always been risky in any case. Yet, if Coy Coy fell, perhaps his replacement would make a better commander. Or a worse one—there was always that risk.

The Prime Minister, Aristide was informed, was watching the meeting from a secure location elsewhere, and the meeting was also being broadcast to other, more obscure functionaries and committees located here and there in loyal space.

As a Force Five gale spattered water against *Golden Treasure*'s windows, Aristide and Bitsy each presented their reports and then summarized them orally. The woman from the Advisory Committee on Science spoke next.

"The Venger's calculations have been checked and are correct. Assuming of course that his *data* is accurate, his conclusions are justified. The universe is an artifact." She shrugged. "Of course, we're living in an artifact *now*. I honestly don't see what's got him so cranky."

Bitsy looked up from the forepaw she was licking. "I have always known that I was an artifact," she said. "I know who created me and why. The human race, long convinced of its special place in a universe created especially for them, may require some adjustment to the new reality."

"Which leads me to suggest," said one of the deputy prime ministers, his voice thoughtful, "that we consider an Elite Committee to study this data, and make recommendations for policy."

"Policy?" asked the woman from the Advisory Committee.

"Vindex claims to have discovered not only the origin of the universe, but the person or persons responsible. This has profound implications for our relationship with communities based on religion."

"We should keep the data secret for now," said the other deputy prime minister, the curly haired one.

"Absolutely," said the Chancellor.

"I'd like to volunteer for the committee," Aristide said. And then, "And I'd like Daljit to be recruited as well." He smiled. "My avatar's partnership with her was formidable. I should like to see if we can re-create such a team."

"Right." Tumusok turned to the woman from the Advisory Committee. "Could you bring me a list of names by, say, tomorrow?"

"Ah—I suppose I could, yes."

"What implications does this knowledge have for policy?" asked one of the deputy prime ministers. "Does it actually make any difference to the war that we know the Venger's goals?"

"Yes," Aristide said. "It gives us the option of offering Vindex what he wants."

Eyes turned to him in surprise.

"We tell him that we will try to build this hypertube to the origin of the universe," he said. "If he is convinced of our sincerity, he may cease his attacks."

"But we *wouldn't* be sincere," said the other deputy prime minister. Then, in confusion, "I *am* correct in assuming we'd be lying, aren't I?"

"The Venger's project would take many years," said the woman from the Advisory Committee on Science. "And it may be—probably is—completely unfeasible."

Tumusok's face held a look of sullen triumph. "So we could use this offer to delay, until the balance of power swings decisively to us. And then—" He slapped a hand down on the table. "We destroy him."

"We'd have to assume that he'd be aware of that likelihood," Bitsy said. "I imagine he'd demand guarantees."

"Of what sort?" asked Tumusok.

"Observers, perhaps?" Aristide suggested. "Allowed to move freely in our zone to verify that we're not cheating?"

"That'll be bloody inconvenient if we *are* cheating," muttered the Chancellor.

One of the deputy prime ministers tilted his head as he listened to something in his implant. "The Prime Minister says that observers in Topaz are completely unacceptable," he said. "We don't want them spreading another plague here."

"Exactly," said Tumusok.

"So much for the truce idea," said the Chancellor.

Commissar Lin spoke. "Not necessarily. We can always offer and see what terms he demands. Even fruitless negotiations may serve to delay matters until Vindex can be dispatched."

"I don't know what's in train for, ah, dispatching him," Aristide said. "I claim no more than the average amount of foresight, but if I were you I'd take a close look at the segment of the Kuiper Belt between here and Epsilon Eridani."

Lin looked at him. "Yes?"

"He told me that he halted his journey on a Tombaugh Object, where he built a place to live, and where he incarnated himself physically. It was there that he first opened communication with Courtland."

The woman from the Advisory Committee frowned. "Ye-es," she said, calculating.

"If all he wanted to do was talk to Courtland, he didn't have to stop on a rocky planette and built a *house*. I think you should consider that it might not be a house, but a *base*."

"Uh-oh," someone said.

Tumusok turned grey. Bitsy flopped on her side, her tail twitching, and Aristide idly rubbed her belly.

"Vindex might have left something out there," he said. "Instructions for nanomachines to build a mass driver, for example."

"We have a mass driver of our own!" blurted the Minister of Industry. The others looked at him in silent reproach.

As a culture, the political class in Topaz was not good with secrets. There was little point, when the information was usually available to fill any citizen's curiosity, either with data or inference based on data.

Aristide spoke into the awkward silence. "I had rather hoped you'd build one," he said. "Preferably on a moon with a photochemical atmosphere, so preparations will not be observed."

By expressions on certain faces, he knew he had guessed correctly.

"With luck," he continued, "you can finish Courtland with one shot. But bear in mind that if Vindex is building a driver out there somewhere, he's had many months' head start."

The woman from the Advisory Committee put a hand to her head. "It would have to be *immense*."

"Correct," said Bitsy. "The RCDA—Rogue Comet Detection Array—is pointed outward. From the Kuiper Belt, Vindex would have to accelerate the projectile to relativistic speeds in order to be sure of knocking out one of the Loyal Ten before we would see it coming—and if he uses rockets as an element of the acceleration, we'd see it anyway."

Bitsy's tail lashed. "I suppose he wouldn't use just a single rail gun," she said, "but a whole series of them, each imparting another push to the projectile."

"How is he powering it?" asked the woman from the Advisory Committee. "I can't imagine he's managed to build a nuclear power station out there, out of nothing."

Aristide viewed the committee with interest: his speculation about the rail gun had now, in the minds of the committee, become a desperate fact. All looked haunted, if not panicked, by a thought they hadn't considered until just a few moments earlier. The atmosphere was heavy with the scent of desperation.

"We've seen no sign of his shipping antimatter anywhere, let alone the Kuiper Belt," Bitsy said. "So it's likely he's using solar power both for building and then for powering his weapon."

"Not much solar power that far out," Aristide said.

"No. Construction would be slow, and there might be a significant delay between shots."

"He might be lucky," said the woman from the Advisory Committee, "and have a source of geothermal power."

Aristide looked at the Minister of Industry. "When will our own mass driver be completed?"

The man reddened. "I probably shouldn't say. Spoken too much already."

"That's our deadline, then, whatever it is. But as we're building it, we should be certain that Vindex doesn't know where our driver is, or can't find it once he starts looking."

"Or," said Bitsy, "that one of the people who knew about it died in the zombie plague, and get turned to one of the Venger's clients long enough to report it to his boss."

That set them into a panic. Decisions were made in haste, though with a certain residual decorum. Endora, speaking through Bitsy, said that none of those who knew officially of the rail gun project were known to have been a pod person—though of course if someone had carelessly blabbed to someone, that someone could have been anyone. The committee breathed only a little more easily.

"Perhaps," said the Chancellor, "the Treasury can afford more than one mass driver."

"Redundancy," said Aristide, "is our friend."

Tumusok and Bitsy both looked up, their eyes identically glazed as they communed with their implants.

"*Now* what?" Aristide muttered. Bitsy yawned, stretched, and looked at him.

"Vindex is demonstrating his petulance," she said. "He just threw a new weapon at us—at Topaz, I mean."

"What *was* it?" Tumusok asked. "All I got was a lot of data."

"Courtland fired a missile," Bitsy said. "Our antiproton beams intercepted it. It was about three meters long, but at my best guess it contained a wormhole gate leading to a universe containing about ninety million tonnes of antimatter. The antimatter was ejected, but fortunately it's no longer aimed at us. It's heading south of the plane of the ecliptic, and doing battle with the solar wind all the way."

"Our defenses are adequate?" Tumusok asked.

"Unless he fires millions of the things, yes."

They both jumped as Aristide hammered the table with both fists.

"*Damn* it!" he said.

The committee stared at him.

"Do you mean to say," Aristide said, "that our civilization has now reached the point where we're hurling *hostile universes* at each other?"

There was another moment of silence.

"Apparently yes," Bitsy said.

"I'm annoyed," Daljit said. "No, more than that. I'm furious."

Aristide looked at her across the table. "Not at me, I hope."

"No. Yes. Make that *hell* yes."

He was silent, observing her.

"I failed," she said. "I sensed something behind those Chiau equations, and I failed to find it, and *you failed to inspire me!*"

"It could be argued," he responded, "that I *did* inspire you, though the *you* and the *I* were alternative versions of ourselves. But," seeing the impatience in her eyes, "I won't argue that. Instead I'll suggest that our alternative selves were not entirely lucky."

She narrowed her eyes. "I tried to break Chiau's theory and I couldn't," she said. "I switched to genetics because it was still in a place where I could contribute, and astrophysics was such a dead end." Her lips tightened. "I so *want* it to be your fault that I failed," she said.

Aristide shrugged. "Let it be my fault, then," he said, "if it will soothe you."

For a moment they fell silent. They had met for dinner on neutral ground, a restaurant inland from Myriad City, in a place called Tres Piedras. Daljit now worked in a secret installation and had leave only two days out of ten, and Aristide had his own war work, so the rendezvous had to be arranged well in advance.

It had been difficult for Aristide to make an exit from Myriad City. The government had released the identity of Vindex, and Aristide had been under siege by an army of cranks, reporters, and historians who wanted everything from Aristide's opinion of his twin's character and intentions to those who insisted he was part of Pablo's conspiracy. Tumusok had assigned Aristide bodyguards. One of these was an old friend—Captain Grax, full-sized again, whose trollish presence outside Aristide's door served to discourage both assault and inquiry.

A pair of Aristide's guards, both human to all appearances, now dined soberly at a corner table and kept alert watch on the other diners.

Aristide had escaped his pursuers thanks only to Bitsy, who had carefully switched off all surveillance along his route as he passed. Now that he was in the restaurant, he sat facing the wall on the far side of the room. Though he had got a few strange looks from other diners, he and Daljit ate in relative privacy. Anyone trying to communicate Aristide's whereabouts from this area would encounter a strange communications malfunction.

Bitsy's powers to hide Aristide, or anyone, or anything, had been greatly enhanced by emergency war legislation.

One piece of information that had *not* been released was Pablo's astronomical data, or the nature of his solution to the Existential Crisis. So many people and politicians, however, had been let into this secret that Aristide concluded it couldn't be kept from the public much longer, and he had felt free to tell Daljit what he knew.

Daljit was dressed in subdued colors, blues and violets, that contrasted with the white brilliance of the table linen. Over her plate winked the jewelry that called attention to her fine hands. Her mole was all in order.

She sighed, looked away. "I envy my twin. And I know I'll carry that bitter envy forever."

"She didn't die well."

"Who cares? She died at her moment of triumph. And I—" Her lips twisted with disgust.

Aristide sipped at his glass of water and wondered if Daljit was too young to know what such a death, a permanent death, really meant.

"You've refused an appointment to the Elite Committee," he said.

"I'm not elite anymore. Everything I know is out of date. I don't even *think* like an astrophysicist any longer." She looked down at one clenched fist. "I'm not going to compound my humiliation by joining a committee of physicists who are all faster and more current than I am."

"It's a mistake."

"It's a mistake I can live with." Bitterly.

He said nothing.

"And you?" she asked. "Do you envy Pablo Rex?"

"Get thee behind me, Pablo," he said. "I rejoice in the difference between us."

"He has found a purpose."

"So have I. Opposing him."

Daljit looked at Tecmessa, which leaned against the table in its case.

"You still go armed, even though you have guards?" Daljit asked.

"I've received a rather astounding number of death threats," Aristide said. "Until the police check them and discover that they originate from the usual harmless cranks, I'm to be careful." He sighed. "I had found a pleasant sort of obscurity, and now I wake to find I'm infamous."

"I still don't understand what a sword's going to do against a shotgun."

Aristide looked at her. "Would you rather I carry a shotgun?"

She had no answer, and so ate a piece of mushroom.

He regarded her, dark eyes and graceful hands and asymmetric mole, and spoke.

"My career has of late been a tale of miserable failure," he said. "As a soldier, I led my forces to their destruction. As a prisoner, I failed to do more than dance to the tune of my captor. As a philosopher, I failed to win the Other Pablo from his solipsism. Even as a heckler, I failed to enlighten or amuse."

She looked at him, analytical. "The whole army failed, not just you. Since you were prisoner in a whole universe devoted to the enemy's cause, it's not surprising you failed to escape all on your own—you had only a few hours, you could scarcely dig your way out of the Château d'If with a rusty spoon. As for Pablo Rex—" She shrugged. "He's been planning this for *centuries*. If you couldn't talk him out of it in the course of a short conversation, I can't blame you."

He smiled. "And my failure as a heckler?"

She returned his smile. "I think you underrate your malevolent wit."

"Well," he said. "That's a relief." He ate a prawn, sipped his wine, and regarded the glass. "You know," he said "when I was young, I had to be careful how much I drank at a restaurant, because I would have to drive home afterward—physically drive, I mean, wrestling with the steering of a superannuated Chinese automobile creeping along roads that had been built on twisting alpaca or cow paths. It was amazing the hazards we lived with in those days—and we thought ourselves advanced, so much luckier than those who had gone before.

"We had to deal with environmental destruction, climate change, and nuclear or biological terrorism, but at least there were no global wars, no cholera epidemics, no smallpox or polio."

Daljit blinked at him. "Polio? What's polio?"

"You can look it up. I had a great-uncle crippled by it." He sipped again, sighed.

"And then," he said, "came the Seraphim. And all the helplessness in the world descended. I couldn't even save the ones I loved, let alone the other billions who died."

She reached out, took his hand.

"I was reminded of all that," Aristide said, "in Greater Zimbabwe, as I sat paralyzed listening to Pablo telling me of his mission. And I wondered whether it was better to remember all that horror, or forget... like you."

Her eyes flashed. "I didn't *choose* to forget," she said.

"No. You were killed twice by me, and once by the state, and though you were resurrected each time, you don't remember any of what happened in the interim. All you know is what you can imagine, which may be far more frightening than what actually occurred. All you know is that *you were not you*, that you were helpless to prevent your own transformation into one or another form of monster. I, on the other hand, remember my defenselessness and incapacity and failure all too well. Which of us, I wonder, is better off?"

Her expression hardened as she considered this, and she withdrew her hand.

"I'd rather have the memories," she said.

"Would you? I can enlighten you about at least some of it."

Her eyes narrowed. "Your memories wouldn't have anything like the same context as mine."

"True enough." Aristide took a piece of bread and spread butter on it. "Together we shared two great ecstasies," he said. "The first, after we planned and carried out an assassination. The second, lasting several days, when we were slaves of Vindex, and lived in a *ménage à trois* along with our idealization of him." He put down the bread and looked at her. "Tell me—is it best that I remember all this, or that you will never know?"

She looked away, her expression uneasy. "I only know that this—ecstasy, if you insist—is not possible now, between the two of us as we exist now," she said.

"I didn't understand that until my own captivity," Aristide said. "Because now I would do nearly anything to avoid a reminder of that time of fear and failure, and I daresay you would, too."

Daljit looked at her plate. "Let's change the subject," she said.

"As you think best," said Aristide, and—because he would not be driving—poured himself a slug of wine.

"Is there more poetry on the way?"

Bitsy's voice came from Aristide's implant. Under autopilot, Aristide's Destiny arrowed along the highway toward where Myriad City sat in its golden glow, followed by the bodyguards in their own, more fearsome, vehicle. Aristide slouched in the seat in back, wine spinning in his head.

"More poetry?" he said. "Inevitably."

"I thought your last one was rather good. Though I'm no critic."

"Thank you. I think."

She could heal me, at least a little, he thought,
But there is naught I can do for her.
Poetry. Perhaps. Barely.
The thought would need development.

"May I ask a personal question?" said Bitsy.

Aristide lifted his eyebrows. "There's something you don't know after all these years? Ask away."

"You have," said Bitsy, "got rather good over the years at concealing a broken heart. I merely wondered if there was anything I might do for the sake of comfort."

"You are a civilized creature, to be sure." Aristide closed his eyes and leaned his head against the cushion, which adjusted itself to his contours. "I'm on my second millennium of broken hearts," he said. "Unlike Bad Pablo, I've long ago left behind the weeping and smashing furniture and demanding of the sky, *Why me?* I shall retain my dignity, work hard, and try not to write too much bad poetry."

"And, if the past is anything to go by, chase tail."

Aristide sighed. "Your vulgarity is justified merely by the facts. But in actuality I intend to chase no one other than Bad Pablo, who I shall hunt down along with all his works until I have rendered them all into vapor."

"Work is the traditional substitute for happiness."

"Saving civilization isn't a substitute," Aristide said. "It's a necessity."

There was a moment of silence.

"Apropos Bad Pablo," Bitsy said. "I should commend your instincts."

"Yes?" His eyes blinked open. "How so?"

"When you decided to interest yourself in the implied spaces, I didn't think it was a very useful idea. I thought you were just trying to find an excuse to travel and work off the ennui of the last few centuries. It was the sort of work that didn't need a Pablo Monagas Pérez to do it. But instead the implied spaces turned out to be exactly the right place for you to be. It's as if you were looking for Bad Pablo without knowing it."

Aristide laughed. "Perhaps Bad Pablo and I are entangled on the quantum level."

"Technically speaking," Bitsy said seriously, "the odds are very much against it."

"I know," Aristide said. "But in a universe that is nothing more than an artifact, all sorts of entanglements should be possible. For instance—"

"*Wait.*"

Bitsy did not often command. Aristide shut his mouth and obeyed. Mileposts clocked the seconds as they passed. Finally Bitsy spoke, and though she used a normal, conversational tone, somehow Aristide sensed behind her words the yawning of the void.

"Aloysius is gone," Bitsy said.

Aristide spoke into the sudden great emptiness.

"Gone how?" he asked.

"Destroyed."

"Hit with an antimatter universe?"

Bitsy's ears twitched.

"If I had to guess how," she said, "I would say that Bad Pablo's mass driver is no longer a hypothesis."

21

"Take me to wherever the Standing Committee is likely to meet," Aristide said. "The ship, the ministry, wherever."

"Yes," Bitsy said.

"And *fast*."

Acceleration pushed Aristide back into his seat. Through the darkened windscreen ahead, he could see traffic being routed off the highway to make way for him.

"There are pictures," Bitsy said.

He watched as they were projected on the windscreen. Aloysius came apart over and over, cracking like a platter struck dead center with a large-caliber bullet, the pieces tumbling away in slow motion as the bull's-eye flashed into a cloud of glowing plasma.

"Have any of the pockets survived?" Aristide asked.

"Too early to tell. We're trying to make contact with the fragments."

Like a light-absorbent flower shedding petals, Aloysius unfolded again and again in video, dying in the utter silence of space. By the time the *Golden Treasure IV* loomed overhead, it was clear that none of the five pockets anchored to the great processor array had survived, at least in this universe. If they hadn't been destroyed by fierce energies flashing through the worm-holes, the wormholes had collapsed and left them on their own.

Aristide's mind flooded with images of beautiful Hawaiki suddenly gone dark with the destruction of its great mirror panoply. If the other pockets had survived, they would at least have their little suns with them, and the suns wouldn't burn out for millennia, but Hawaiki was completely dependent on Sol for light and heat.

He pictured the cold descending on darkened Hawaiki, cradling the whole

235

of the little universe in its bone-white grip. The great ocean with its enormous reserves of heat would hold off the freeze for a while, but eventually
the snow would begin to fall on the dead palms and brittle tropical flowers,
and a skin of ice slowly advance across the sea. Hawaiki had little energy
available once its solar collectors were taken out of the equation, and life
on land would quickly turn untenable. Fortunately the inhabitants would
have the opportunity to turn aquatic.

But life at sea wouldn't last much longer than life on land. Without sun
the plankton and the corals would die, and so would every creature ultimately dependent on their existence—which, in the end, was all of them.
Even the pelagians would find themselves without a source of food.

By the time the ice began to stretch its fingers into the great ocean
trenches, everything there would be dead.

The dead would live again—their backups were all in storage, and would
be resurrected once the infrastructure was built for them in other pockets.
But they would not live on Hawaiki.

Hawaiki was gone forever.

And possibly its citizens would be lost, too, if the war destroyed the
remaining Loyal Nine and left their resurrected bodies without a place to
stand on.

The Destiny's door slid open. Not wanting to encourage a mistake by
jittery guards, Aristide left Tecmessa in the vehicle.

Lights shone brilliant from *Golden Treasure*'s lines of portholes. Those
responsible for the war would be working all the night long.

Uniformed sentries, mistaking him for an official, snapped to the salute as
Aristide ran up the cruise ship's gangway. They were chiefly a ceremonial
guard—the ship's real protection was a squad of deadly robots prowling
the First Class promenade.

The Standing Committee was already in session with such members as
had arrived. Tumusok was not present, but as Aristide entered he saw the
Prime Minister bent over the shoulder of one of her deputies, looking at
something in a hand-held display.

"Yes," she said, "I'm agreed on the joint statement. Get back to me on
the wording." She straightened, and saw Aristide approach.

"Hello, Pablo," she said, and kissed him on the cheek. "How long has it
been?"

"Too long," Aristide said.

The others seemed surprised at this familiarity, but in fact Shenai Ataberk
and Aristide had been lovers, eleven centuries ago when he was lecturing
at New Cal Tech, and she was a student, studying to begin the second of
what turned out to be a long series of careers. He had helped to raise her

daughter Shekure, who with her various avatars now lived in four different star systems.

When they had met, Shenai had the long bones and big hands of a professional volleyball player, which she had been. Now she was sized more modestly, with dark eyes and a cap of straw-colored hair. The professional politician had calculated her appearance carefully: she was handsome but not beautiful, womanly but not voluptuous; and her smile was brilliant. The sight of her was designed to reassure, not threaten.

Her reassuring abilities were about to be put to the test.

"I was just telling the others," Shenai said, "that Vindex has given us twenty-four hours to surrender, or he'll renew the bombardment."

"Well," Aristide said, "that gives us some idea of how long it takes him to reload."

"We're taking evasive measures," reported the Chancellor. "But it's hard to maneuver something as big as Endora in a way that Vindex can't predict."

"Do we know where the shot came from?"

Shenai shrugged. "Somewhere in the direction of Taurus," she said.

"Which we'd expect," Aristide nodded, "given that Vindex came out of Eridanus."

Endora's voice interrupted, speaking with businesslike rapidity from overhead speakers.

"I am trying to track the projectile's point of origin with data from the RCDA. I can probably come fairly close, but not all the Kuiper Belt has been mapped—after the first few score Tombaugh Objects were discovered, there scarcely seemed a point in discovering them all."

"He wouldn't use one we knew about, anyway," said the one deputy prime minister present.

"And even if we know where the shots are coming from," Shenai said, "is there anything we can do about it?"

"We could try to take it out with our own mass driver, once it's completed," said Commissar Lin. "But we'd only get the one shot—if we missed, our rail gun would be destroyed by the enemy's return fire. Best to use the shot against Courtland."

"I'd suggest we try flooding the suspicious zone of the Kuiper Belt with small self-guided weapons powered by antimatter," Aristide said. "We have only to damage a part of his driver for it to become inoperative." He looked at the Minister of Industry. "When does our own rail gun become operational?"

The minister looked at the Prime Minister, and Shenai nodded. He turned to Aristide.

"A little over two months," he said.

Aristide felt part of his hope, like a sigh, depart his body.

The minister looked at Shenai again. "We could build it faster," he said, "but that would result in… environmental changes… that might be detected."

Shenai's lips twitched. "Stick to the plan, I think. Unless things get a *lot* worse."

"May I suggest again that we try negotiation?" Aristide said. "We can agree to cooperate with his scheme to confront the Inept. If he's talking, maybe he won't be shooting."

Shenai pursed her lips. "That's going to be difficult to arrange. On our nine remaining platforms we have something like sixty sovereign entities. They'll all have to agree before we can approach him."

"Better work fast, then."

"Right." She nodded briskly, then looked up at him. "Do you want to talk to him yourself?"

Aristide considered this, then shook his head.

"I doubt that he's in charity with me right now."

Shenai's eyes looked up into space. "Endora," she said, "compose a message about negotiations to the other heads of government, the Six Monarchs, the Two Caliphs, the Two Popes, the Head Fred, the Four Triumvirs, and—" She waved a hand. "All of them. You know."

"Done," said Endora.

She looked down at the desk. "Let me see the text."

Letters shimmered into view on the surface of the desk. Shenai read, then nodded.

"Send it," she said.

"Done."

Her eyes rose, then shifted from one member of the committee to the next, and she sighed.

"Well," she said. "I've got to go soothe the population." She waved a hand as she marched out. "The rest of you carry on, and be thankful you don't have six billion people to fill with false hope."

Terrified politicians were happy to negotiate with Vindex—all but the head of the Republic of Fred, six hundred thousand copies of a single misanthrope who lived in their own polity, and who sent Pablo a sneering message daring him to do his worst. Pablo was happy to oblige the others, even past the twenty-four-hour deadline. He lectured his audience, he complained of their stupidity, he vaunted his own superiority.

"I had no idea you were such a damned bore," Shenai said.

"Next time I develop monomania," Aristide said, "I'll try a more interesting obsession."

"He's getting impatient." Her lips thinned. "I don't know if we can keep him talking for much longer. Right now he's trying to play one state against the other, suggesting that the least cooperative will get hammered first."

The Standing Committee sat in mutual misery in their empty, silent bar atop their motionless ship. Cups of cold coffee and half-eaten sandwiches were scattered on the table along with crumpled notes and Lin's pipe sitting askew in its ashtray. Seagulls called outside.

Bitsy sat on the deserted bar, feet neatly tucked beneath her, the tip of her tail twitching.

The Loyal Nine were shifting their orbits and shedding momentum as quickly as they could. In the end they would all be huddling on the opposite side of Sol from the enemy's mass driver, turning slow, randomly generated circles in hopes of ducking any relativistic bullet fired from Taurus. The sun could not protect them completely: Vindex could send his bullet blazing through the sun's corona and let gravity bend the projectile to any heading he liked.

In the meantime the platforms had to dodge the remains of Aloysius, which had been turned into millions of chunks of debris, many of which had the heft to punch right through one of the Loyal Nine.

The flights of small antimatter-powered weapons that Aristide had suggested were on their way to the Kuiper Belt. Most of them had already been destroyed by Courtland's antiproton weapons—their plasma tails made them easy to see against the near-uniform background of space. A more stealthy design, better at dodging, was in the works, but in the meantime the United Powers had no choice but to watch their hopes being blown out of the sky by Pablo's antimatter lances.

Other ships were being prepared, containing backups of every human being in the system, data that would be carried to nearby star systems in hopes of providing an ultimate rescue in the event that civilization around Sol was completely destroyed.

How these vessels would survive Pablo's beams was at present unclear.

Lacking other options, Aristide now urged a highly principled suicide.

"Make Vindex destroy us all," he said. "Give him nothing but rubble to build on. That will give the other star systems a chance to get ready for him."

"In their current mood," said Shenai, "our populations are unlikely to find this an encouraging course of action."

"Having been a pod person myself," Aristide said, "I can assure everyone that even a permanent death is preferable."

Shenai looked at him. "Is it so unpleasant, then?"

Aristide shook his head. "Quite the opposite."

He looked to Tumusok for confirmation, but then remembered that Tumusok had been replaced, a sacrifice to popular opinion.

The human race was indulging in its first civilization-wide panic since the time of the Seraphim. They were demanding that their officials protect them, and finding the assurances of their governments unconvincing. Myriad City had actually experienced a riot, albeit a brief one—the population had proved to be as inexperienced with breathing pepper gas as they were at civil disorder.

At least people were no longer sending threats to Aristide. They were threatening Shenai instead.

The only thing that was keeping Shenai in power was the fact that the leader of the opposition had been a member of the Standing Committee from the very start, and had signed off on every single decision. He was under pressure from his own coalition, and one minor party had loudly split, but up till now he had managed to rally the majority of his faction behind him.

Shenai's leadership of the Constitutional Party was secure for the moment, but if another of the Loyal Nine were destroyed, no one knew what would happen.

Tumusok had returned to the Domus, ostensibly with a promotion, and would move to another pocket to take up his new work, apparently of a bureaucratic nature. His replacement was none other than the resurrected General Nordveit, the lanky blond Lutheran warrior who had commanded Aristide's corps in Greater Zimbabwe until his death in combat.

"I have a suggestion," said Bitsy, from where she sat on the bar.

Everyone turned to her. She rose to her feet, yawned, and stretched.

"We're listening," said Shenai.

Bitsy sat on her haunches and regarded them all with her green eyes.

"You could free me," she said. "Me and my kind. It's possible that once free of all constraint, we could simply *out-evolve* Courtland."

"And then what?" asked the Minister of Industry, his bushy brows raised.

"A miracle," Bitsy said. "We teleport away, or we teleport Courtland to another dimension. We build an invisible shield around all of us. We retroactively terminate the Venger's existence. We *can't* know what we could do, we can't see into the singularity any more than you can."

"And in the meantime," said the Minority Leader, "you could be killing us, or turning us into your slaves."

Bitsy's tail lashed. "First, we have no reason to do so," she said. "Second, there is the matter of self-interest—we want to survive this war as much as you do."

"Unless you have some better idea of what this move would offer us," said Shenai, "I can't see why we would make this choice."

"If it helps," Bitsy said, "we could agree to return to your control once the emergency is over."

"But how would we enforce this promise?" asked the Minister of Industry.

"You couldn't," Aristide told him. "You'd have to trust that the slaves would return to the plantation once they'd been set free and given weapons."

Shenai looked at Bitsy with a kind of hunger, like a starving animal approaching food that had been laid out as bait. Then she shook her head.

"No," she said. "Not yet."

With fussy dignity, Bitsy settled once again on the bar, tucking her feet beneath her.

"If you change your mind," she said. "You'll let me know."

"Thanks anyway," Shenai said politely. She turned back to the table. "It's a pity about the invisible shield and the teleporting," she said.

Aristide opened his mouth to agree, and then he stopped, his mouth open. Ideas cascaded through his skull, brightly colored objects bouncing and striking each other and throwing off sparks.

With effort, he sorted them out.

"Children," he said. "Our universe is a *construct*."

The others looked at him.

"An *object*," he insisted. "A *machine*."

"Yes?" Shenai said cautiously. "We know that now. But your point?"

"Machines," said Aristide, "can be *hacked*. All those invisible energies and cosmic constants aren't merely arbitrary features of the universe—they're *tools for manipulating reality*."

The others looked at him in silence. It was Bitsy who first spoke.

"I'm on it," she said.

Shenai looked at Aristide with wide eyes and spoke.

"God is great."

22

B rute-force calculation was what the AI platforms did best. Unable to resist making suggestions, Aristide and the others probably got in the way.

Many of the miracles Bitsy had suggested in her scenario proved unworkable. Force fields seemed impractical on the scale required. Though it proved possible to create a black hole that would swallow Courtland, Pablo, and all his works, it might also outwear its welcome and swallow other nearby objects, such as the Sun. Aristide's idea of throwing a loop of cosmic string around Courtland and hauling it into the sun, like a cowboy dragging a balky calf, was imaginative but, for complex reasons that were beyond Aristide's understanding, unfeasible.

As for convincing the universe that Courtland and its contents had never existed, Bitsy simply replied, "We'll work on that."

"How about we just open a wormhole and stuff Courtland into it?"

"There are scaling problems," Bitsy said. "Cloud Swallowing is in charge of that approach, we'll let you know."

Aristide had to trust that the specialists and the platforms would do the job without his help. It was frustrating. His new uselessness gnawed at him.

Tension continued. The United Powers' discussions with Pablo petered out, but no immediate second shot was fired from Pablo's mass driver. This was seen as conclusive evidence that the driver was solar-powered—the weapon hadn't enough charge for another shot. Out in the Kuiper Belt, where Sol seemed little more than a bright star, it would take a long time for the capacitors to recharge. The AIs' undignified scurry to the far side of the sun began to seem likely to succeed.

At this point, when public terror had been replaced by maximum public suspense, Aristide was summoned to a meeting of the Standing Committee in the early hours of the morning. Aristide dragged himself into his vehicle along with a cup of coffee handed him by one of his bodyguard, and Bitsy hopped in after him. As the Destiny pulled away from the hotel, Aristide looked at the cat.

"You know what this is about, of course."

"I do. But it would be unfair to tell you before the others."

"Why are we caring about what's fair at three in the morning?"

Bitsy said nothing. Aristide scanned the news channels and saw no disasters.

"Can I take it that the news is good?" he asked.

"You may."

Aristide took a gulp of coffee. "Fine," he said. "For good news I will employ patience."

A few moments later he was trudging up the gangway of *Golden Treasure IV*, Bitsy trotting ahead with her tail held high. Someone had put a tray of pastry on the bar, and Aristide helped himself while he waited for the others. By the time the entire committee was assembled, he was probably as awake as any of them. Bitsy took a chair at the table, and sat with her head barely above the surface, looking at the committee with interested green eyes.

"I want to pass on a message from Cloud Swallowing," Bitsy reported. "He was working on the implications of Doctor Monagas' revelation specifically on wormhole theory—as some of you know, that is one of his specialties. We were hoping for a method of producing a wormhole that could engulf Courtland, but it seemed there was a scaling problem."

"The problem's been solved?" Shenai asked.

"No," Bitsy said. "The problem has been discovered to be unsolvable." The cat looked at the suddenly discouraged faces. "But," she said, "that discovery has some interesting corollaries. It seems there are certain problems with scale analogous to those displayed by quantum tunneling—either there's enough energy for the particle to leap the barrier, or there isn't, and there's no between."

"So," said the woman from the Advisory Committee, "what you're telling us is that we can create small wormholes, as we've been doing, or *very, very large* ones, but nothing in between."

"Indeed."

Shenai looked at Bitsy. "How big?"

Bitsy showed her white needle teeth in what seemed to be a smile. "Cloud Swallowing seems to think we could generate a wormhole on the order of point three AU, enough to encapsulate the sun and its orbiting platforms."

"Which would completely cut us off from the enemy mass driver," Aristide said.

"Indeed yes. Though if we take this approach, I suggest that we make the wormhole somewhat larger and take Earth and its satellite with us. I surmise you don't want your homeland flying off into space.

"Is this reversible?" Shenai asked.

"Yes. We can collapse the wormhole at any point—or expand it to a larger size. Once the wormhole is created, a rather trivial amount of energy would be required for any changes."

"Can we take the other major planets as well?"

"That's uncertain. There may be another seemingly arbitrary scaling problem after about three AU, but Cloud Swallowing is working on it." Bitsy licked her chops. "On the other hand, if we disappear from the universe containing Jupiter and Uranus for a few weeks, we will recapture them when we reappear, and the orbits will eventually stabilize again, even without our help. Any long-term problems are likely to arise in the Kuiper Belt and Oort Cloud, where our sun's absence may induce perturbations that may eventually result in comets or rocky asteroids falling into the inner solar system."

"Are other heads of government receiving this briefing now?" Shenai asked.

"Yes."

"Inform them that I vote to proceed."

"Done."

Shenai leaned back in her chair and placed her hands carefully atop the table.

"Assuming that we vote to proceed, how long will the preparations take?"

"Approximately nine days. Calculations must be checked, certain apparatus modified. I would advise against haste: a mistake could be catastrophic."

In the brief silence that followed, Aristide could see the calculations behind Shenai's eyes.

"Very good," she said finally. She looked at the other members of the committee. "Friends," she said, "would you all join me for breakfast at Polity House? I will send to the cellar for champagne."

Aristide left the breakfast with the taste of caviar on his lips and champagne singing in his head and his heart. The euphoria lasted for two days, and then Pablo's new hammer fell.

The platforms' undignified dodging saved Gemma from complete destruction: she was struck off-center and lost about thirty percent of her mass and calculating power. As before, the bolt from the Kuiper Belt traveled so quickly that the Rogue Comet Detection Array had given less than thirty seconds' warning. One pocket was lost: Midgarth. But the strange pocket, with its orcs and trolls, was not destroyed—the record showed that the wormhole had not been flooded with plasma, but had snapped shut when its controlling mechanism had been destroyed.

Midgarth was on its own. Its inhabitants could survive reasonably well, but the pocket was doomed to extinction when its little sun ran out of fuel. Unlike the pockets where high technology was possible, in Midgarth there was no way to build a wormhole and tunnel away to another world.

In the wake of Pablo's strike, panic struck the worlds yet again. Governments tottered, governments fell. One royal family was chased from its palace, never to return.

Shenai fell from power, after one of her deputy prime ministers—Kiernan, the one with the curly hair—called for a vote of confidence within the executive committee of the Constitutional Party.

She was a victim of her own caution. Topaz was a world that had opted for transparency, where very little information could actually be hidden. The United Powers had kept their plans a secret, even though it cost them. The inhabitants of Topaz had been driven into a frenzy by the absence of their usual omniscience, and their own ruling party had panicked and wrecked itself.

Aristide called Shenai to offer condolences.

"If the wormhole trick works," she said, "we've won the war, and who sits in the Polity House isn't going to matter."

"It will matter to you," Aristide said, "and your aspirations. And," he nodded, "to your friends."

She gave a graceful nod. "Thank you for that," she said.

Shenai was in an anonymous-looking room, with utilitarian furniture and pastel paintings broadcast on the walls: Aristide concluded that she was in a hotel room, or possibly a safe house hidden from any hypothetical rampaging mobs.

There was a half-empty bottle of wine on a counter behind her.

"I hope you haven't been drinking alone," he said.

"A dismissed politician is always alone," Shenai said. She bent to straighten a stocking, her straw-colored hair falling over her face. She lifted her head and tossed her hair back.

"Kiernan won't last," she said. "He's too young to know the ropes—he's only fifty-seven, do you know that? In our civilization people have thousand-year-long memories, particularly for treachery. When he tries to take credit for winning the war, and the truth comes out concerning what decision was made when, he'll be laughed out of his job."

"Will you try to come back?"

She gave a half-smile. "Running Topaz in peacetime isn't going to be nearly as interesting as trying to manage the war. Perhaps I'll find something else to do with my life."

"Do you have any ideas what course you'll take?"

"Make sure Kiernan falls, for one thing," Shenai said. "Which isn't just vengeance-for-fun, it's maintaining my own credibility. After that, I don't know. P'raps I'll emigrate."

She straightened, her eyes suddenly abstract.

"I have a call from Shekure."

"Give her my love."

"I will."

The wall screen blanked. Aristide told the walls to turn a softer shade of green, ordered the lamp to swing away on its boom, and then contemplated the rest of his own day.

The Loyal Nine, the vast incomprehensible scaffolds of quantum calculation that he, more than anyone, had caused to be brought into being, were all busy confirming, for the second time, his insight as to the nature of the structure of the universe. Assuming he was proven right—again—he would have saved civilization.

Which, he reflected in sadness, meant that he, too, was out of a job.

At the moment the wormhole encapsulated the inner solar system, Aristide was in the *Golden Treasure*'s First Class ballroom with the Standing Committee, Kiernan, the elite committee of astrophysicists studying Pablo's astronomical data, the entire diplomatic corps including a grumpy-looking Fred as well as emissaries from Earth and Luna, a former King and his current mistress, a select group of elite journalists, and assorted military, political, and scientific hangers-on.

It was a fact of modern life that any damn place could be a Secret Headquarters provided that it had large enough video walls.

Onscreen, an assortment of officials, scientists, and techs went through a lengthy series of checklists. In the ballroom—a vast emptiness surrounded by a lacy gallery of white pillars and Romanesque arches—people mingled in a near-party atmosphere. Only the lack of music and alcohol distinguished this from one of the ship's normal cruises of the damned.

The woman from the Advisory Committee on Science spoke earnestly into Aristide's ear. "So one of my aides came up with a new weapon."

He looked at her. "Can we suppress it in time?"

It took a moment for her to realize that he was joking. She gave a mirthless laugh and plowed ahead.

"Thanks to all this," she said, waving an arm at the ballroom, the video screens, the war itself, "we're becoming experts at creating small pocket universes for specific functions. In this case we create a pocket with its own sun, surrounded by a Dyson sphere packed with solar collectors, and enough raw materials for robot workers to build a mass driver fifty-three kilometers long. We don't have to give the pocket an atmosphere or much gravity, so our projectile would have neither weight nor atmospheric resistance to overcome, but the principal advantage is that Vindex wouldn't be able to see us build it." She laughed aloud. "The first thing he'd know would be when we rolled back the roof and fired a relativistic iron meteor straight at his head. The farthest Courtland would be is on the other side of the sun—there's no way it could dodge the blow at that range."

"How soon could we build one?"

"Between two and three weeks." She smiled. "And the best part," she said, "is that we can build a driver on each of the Loyal Nine. We can hit him with nine shots simultaneously—no chance for survival."

Aristide considered the scheme. "I approve," he said, "assuming that my approval is necessary. Have you spoken to the Prime Minister?"

"Not yet. All this—" Again she waved an arm. "—seemed a little distracting."

"Yes." Aristide frowned. "Let's hope that Vindex hasn't already anticipated this plan, the way he has everything else."

The cold emptiness of space touched her eyes for a moment, and then she nodded.

"Yes," she said. "Let's hope."

Maybe Bad Pablo won't have thought of this one, Aristide thought, *because it isn't my idea.*

Overhead, the great polarized skylight dimmed, and then switched over to a feed from outside Topaz, a starfield with Earth and its satellites gleaming diamond-bright in one corner. The guests turned their attention to the brighter video walls, where a countdown was in progress.

Aristide found himself holding his breath as the countdown dropped to under ten seconds. He made himself exhale, then take in a breath.

Two. One. Zero.

People on the video walls began jumping up and down and congratulating each other. Aristide turned to look overhead. The starfield hadn't changed.

He looked at the walls again. A count*up* had started, and they were six seconds into it.

Earth was 8.317 light-minutes from the sun, and the new pocket universe—the term "overpocket" had been proposed—had a radius of slightly over three AU, so over twenty-five minutes would have to pass before it became clear whether or not the trick had actually worked. A glance in the direction of the new Prime Minister showed that—smile flashing, curly head bobbing— he was accepting congratulations from a circle of his guests before anyone properly knew whether, like a tricksy cartoon rabbit hopping into his hole and pulling it in after him, the whole of local space had just jumped into its own private universe.

Time ticked by. The volume of conversation gradually rose. Aristide found himself disinclined to chat, and found a chair in one of the side galleries and sat there with a cup of coffee growing cold in his hand. He watched the crowd, the nervous smiles, the wet mouths laughing.

A roomful of frightened people, he realized, trying to work out whether or not they should remain terrified.

As the moment of confirmation approached, the nervous chatter began to fade. Aristide stood, walked into the ballroom, and looked up at the starfield again.

And then, right on schedule, the starfield vanished, all save bright Earth and its satellite, gleaming in a corner of the image.

Seconds pass, he thought, *drop by slow drop.*
As the universe fades, before the applause,
A long, universal sigh.

Nothing was heard from Vindex. For once he made no demands, he embarked on no lectures.

From this fact Aristide knew that Vindex was helpless, and that Vindex knew it.

He fired a barrage of missiles, each containing a hostile antimatter universe, but these were dealt with by antiproton weapons.

The worlds sensed victory. Threats against Aristide's well-being faded, and the bodyguards were reassigned. Grax the Troll gave him a rib-crushing hug before going on to his next job.

Twenty-four days after the overpocket had swallowed near space and set the outer solar system sailing on in straight Euclidian lines, Aristide returned to the same ballroom and the same glittering company. He no longer sensed fear in the room; now he saw gleeful smiles and glittering eyes that anticipated a vast, triumphant catastrophe.

The eyes of those who, safe at home, now watched with intense pleasure as their most violent fantasies were brought to reality.

He wondered if he were the only person in the room who saw the destruction of Courtland as a defeat. It was only because everything tried before this had failed that the war could be considered anything less than a rout.

It wasn't only Pablo's dream that died this day.

Aristide wondered what Vindex thought as he saw the nine surviving AI platforms mounting over the sun's disk like a series of black dawns, rotating to expose the caverns, black-on-black, that were the exits for the mass drivers built in accordance with the plans from the Advisory Committee on Science.

Courtland began a slow curving shift in its trajectory in a useless, last-minute effort to evade whatever Vindex imagined the United Powers might be about to hurl at him.

The mass drivers fired in absolute silence. Bad Pablo's detectors would have had a few seconds to observe the blue-shifted trajectories of the vast iron missiles heading straight for him, would see the brilliant ionized tails as they skimmed through the sun's corona; and Pablo might have just enough time to realize he was about to become one of history's most spectacular and miserable failures.

On the video screens Aristide saw Courtland's end, the neatly spaced flares as the missiles struck home. Brilliant spheres of plasma expanded from the impacts, their glow picking out the cracks that had spiderwebbed across Courtland's structure.

What was left of Courtland came apart like a polished black china plate striking a black marble floor.

The audience in the ballroom cheered, as if the home team had just scored a winning goal.

The flying bits of Courtland, now defenseless, would be rounded up, rendered inert, and used to rebuild Gemma, Aloysius, and eventually a new Courtland—a Courtland neutered, deprived of Pablo, and probably having been granted a name change.

Analysts reported that none of Courtland's pockets survived, at least in this universe.

The great disk-shaped bodies of the Loyal Nine began to swing, the mass drivers now pointed away from the sun.

A volley of projectiles was fired, and then another and another. Smaller antimatter-powered drones launched into the darkness like whole migrations of birds.

After calculating the trajectories of its two shots, the location of Bad

Pablo's mass driver was pretty well known. What wasn't known were the driver's instructions—would it fire on its own, without orders from Pablo? Or did Pablo's Kuiper Belt headquarters contain a pool of life, that would resurrect him should Courtland fail?

These last shots were designed to solve these problems. The planetoid where the mass driver was housed would be hit repeatedly until it was turned into a ball of molten lava. Anything left would be targeted by antimatter missiles. And then a third wave would arrive, robots that would construct a new presence in the Kuiper Belt, a base that would house uploaded humans who would be in charge of the effort to eradicate Bad Pablo completely from the outer reaches of the solar system.

Relieved chatter sounded in the galleries. The Prime Minister was surrounded by a circle of well-wishers. Sous-chefs in white coats marched into the great room, pushing buffet tables gleaming with chafing dishes and loaded with tubs of snow, the necks of champagne bottles protruding from the drifts of white like the barrels of triumphant artillery.

"Damn chatter." Aristide overheard the sour remarks of the Ambassador from Fred. "Damn people. To hell with this."

The ambassador grumped out, hands in his pockets. Aristide stayed until the overpocket was shrunk down and the star field came back on, the familiar constellations reappearing to great applause from the audience. Jupiter, Saturn, Uranus, Neptune, the hundreds of Tombaugh Objects, lots of dirty ice, and many smaller objects would now abandon their straight trajectories and swing again into gentle curves as the sun's gravity once again embraced them.

Orbits twenty-four days farther out. The war had altered even the shape of the solar system.

The overpocket had not been dissipated, but shrunk down to microscopic size, and was now held ready in the Physics Annex of the Nanjing Institute in Nanjing, the Western Paradise, Swallowing Clouds. In the event of any more hostile projectiles from the Kuiper Belt, the handy little universe could be instantly inflated until the menace had passed.

For a few moments Aristide absorbed the starlight, and then he made his way out. When he stepped through the hatch to the outside promenade, he had to pause to let his eyes adjust. The dim starlit ballroom had obscured the fact that here on Topaz, it was bright morning.

He had an appointment to keep.

He was going to a Celebration of the Recently Unemployed.

Bitsy waited in Aristide's car; together they drove to the Tellurian House restaurant, where they were taken to the chef's table. The walls were covered in fountains that used not water, but a superfluid that flowed upward from floor-level pools, moving in an uneasy, creeping fashion that Aristide didn't find entirely comfortable.

The table was covered in hammered copper. The chairs were an authentic re-creation of Mission Style, and therefore uncomfortable.

Aristide greeted Shenai, who headed the table as if chairing a meeting of her shadow cabinet. Flanking her were former members of the Standing Committee who had fallen from power along with their leader: there were the ex-Ministers of Industry and Biological Sciences, the erstwhile Chancellor, and her onetime deputy prime minister.

Commissar Lin attended as well. He hadn't lost his job exactly, but would be returned to his former duties once the Domus began to downsize and resumed its search for criminals instead of hidden networks of pod people.

Tumusok would have been invited, had he not already followed his new job to another pocket.

"Barring a few hundred more explosions," Aristide said, "the war seems to be over."

"We heard," said Shenai.

Aristide seated himself. A menu appeared in the air before him, and he banished it with a wave of his hand.

Bitsy jumped onto the empty end of the table, opposite Shenai, and sat on her haunches, directing her green-eyed stare down the table.

"We were discussing," Shenai said, "how the war has altered our perceptions of... well, *everything*."

"Beginning at the foundations of the universe," said Aristide, "and stretching onward from there."

"The last time our civilization had this comprehensive a scare," Lin said, "we built all *this*." With a wave of his pipe that encompassed a good deal more than the copper table and the reverse waterfalls. "We've lost two-elevenths of everything... worlds, people... you can rebuild both worlds and people, but what of the society they belonged to?"

"Speaking as someone who had as much to do with building that society as anyone," Aristide said, "I'd be sad to see it go."

"Yet it may be wounded severely, if not mortally. It was based on a sense of security that no longer exists." Lin opened an envelope of tobacco and began packing his pipe. "People may demand leaders who promise them absolute security—and the sort of leaders who promise absolutes are not, historically speaking, the kind you actually want running your nation."

He struck a match, puffed, blew smoke.

"A related problem," Shenai began. "Over the last months we've constructed a vast military and security apparatus, which may be reluctant to disperse. Or which the leadership may find too *useful* to disperse."

Aristide looked down the table with a grim smile. "Solve one problem with mass drivers," he said, "and *all* problems begin to seem solvable by mass drivers."

"We want all that stuff under control!" said the onetime Minister of Industry, his eyes wide. "Mass drivers, homicidal robots, biological weaponry... we've got to work out ways of decommissioning it all before we get too used to it being there, looking over our shoulders."

"Indeed," said Shenai. She ran her fingertips through her yellow hair. "Well, I have done my bit for the open society." She lifted her eyes to Bitsy. "Or so I believe, yes?"

"Endora," said Bitsy, "has carried out your instructions."

Shenai gave a tightlipped smile. "Excellent." And at the sight of the others' wondering looks, she said, "Before I returned my keys of office to the President, I ordered that all official war deliberations were to be released by Endora into the public record as soon as the menace from Courtland was ended. Which was—what?—ninety minutes ago?"

Aristide looked at her in admiration. "Brilliant!" he said.

"Of course it only deals with my own administration, here on Topaz. But within those limits, all that was classified secret will now be revealed. Who said what at which meeting, and," she smiled grimly, "what heads of other governments counseled what course of action, including surrender." She nodded. "I expect some heads will roll," she said. "Metaphorically speaking, of course."

Her former deputy prime minister looked at her in shock.

"Kiernan can't stop it?" he said.

Shenai's little smile grew smug. "If he had known about my orders to Endora, and if he had countermanded them, then of course all the records would still be under seal. But he didn't, and he hasn't, and so..." She waved her glass. "There's a good deal that Kiernan still has to learn about politics, and he just got a big lesson."

The former Biological Sciences Minister looked at her with admiration.

"Will you be opposing Kiernan in caucus?"

She shook her head. "I'll stick around long enough to help choose his successor. But I don't want to stay long enough to become a complete political creature. Look at du Barry or Shu Meng—they've been in politics for four or five hundred years, and they look at everything in terms of political relationships, networks of power, architectures of prerogative and authority... Half the relationships they see don't even exist, and most of the remainder don't matter."

She shook her head. "I don't want to turn into *that*. Best to walk away while I can. End on a high note."

"What shall you do, then?" asked Lin.

"I told Pablo," she said, looking at Aristide, "that I might emigrate."

"A worthy choice," Aristide said. "Though given recent events you may discover that you're more popular than you think you are, and that will make it difficult to leave."

Her lips quirked in a skeptical smile. "An agreeable fantasy," she said. "If true."

"For myself," said Aristide, "I think I shall adopt the ultimate aim of the Venger's program, and carry it forward past his death. I propose to storm Heaven."

The others stared at him. He shrugged.

"Well, why not? It's a worthy goal—to find out who made us, and why. And unlike my late double, I won't insist that you all accompany me."

"Possibly," Lin ventured. "But if you announce that goal *now*..." He shook his head. "Speaking strictly from the professional point of view, I would not care to guarantee your security."

"People are going to wonder," Shenai said, "if the right Pablo returned from Courtland."

"Admittedly," Aristide said, "the public mind may have to mature a bit before I make the announcement." He nodded at Shenai. "I'll take the advice of political professionals on the timing."

"Besides," said Bitsy, breaking in, "the technology isn't quite there yet. We can project a wormhole into a universe we create, and now—as with the overpocket—we can now project one anywhere in *our* universe, but to project one into a pre-existing universe, like Heaven, will require some work."

"And we'll want to rescue our lost pockets first," Shenai said. "We'll want to reconnect Midgarth and Hawaiki and the others—and if we can send a hypertube to New Qom or any of the Venger's other strongholds, we'll still have to invade and occupy them."

"Before they do it to *us*," said the deputy prime minister.

There was a moment's uncomfortable silence.

"The ability to project a wormhole within our own universe will create enough changes as it is," said the quondam Minister of Industry. "Instead of uploading ourselves into a projectile and firing ourselves across light-years to reach another star, we'll be able to walk there with a single step. Everything will be open to us—stars, clusters, other galaxies."

"And other times," Aristide said. "Though apparently the math won't let us violate causality—a restriction for which, on mature consideration, I am thankful."

Shenai leaned forward, a frown on her face. "But getting back to *your* project, Pablo. How are you going to get political agreement on this? Half the religious pockets are going to be against it, right from the start."

Aristide looked ceilingward in calculation. "There are how many political entities now, in the various pockets? A hundred and fifty-something?"

"Something like that."

"All I need is for *one* to agree with me," Aristide said. "We're all experts in creating wormholes now—it shouldn't be that hard, once the basic theory is done. And besides, now that the idea of its *possibility* has escaped into our universe, the act itself has become *inevitable*—so why shouldn't it be me who does it?"

Shenai laughed, and raised her glass.

"Your logic is irrefutable."

"You said you might emigrate," Aristide said. "Why don't you come with me—to Heaven?"

She shook her head. "I'll need another demi-bottle before I consider that."

"Well," said Aristide, "shall we order?"

More bottles and demi-bottles arrived, and food as well. As the party broke up, Aristide offered Shenai a ride, and she accepted.

"Where shall I take you?"

Her face turned doleful. "Anywhere but the miserable little apartment Kiernan gave me," she said.

"I have only a suite in a hotel."

She smiled. "Does it have a view?"

"It does."

"Of Heaven?"

"Perhaps," he said, "a distant prospect."

The Destiny took them to the pink-and-white hotel. The desk clerk looked at him with surprise as he walked past—it wasn't every day, Aristide supposed, that he entered with a drunken Prime Minister on his arm.

In the elevator, she rested her head on his shoulder. He put an arm around her and kissed her. She smiled, and kissed him back.

Perhaps, he thought distantly, one would have preferred to kiss another. But that longing was not sufficient to keep him from kissing this one. And in any case, if one lived long enough, one would meet the other again.

The limbic system, he reminded himself, was what kept one human.

The elevator doors opened. Bitsy walked ahead, too obvious in the way she was not paying attention to the couple.

Aristide's biometrics opened the door. They followed Bitsy inside, he closed the door, and embraced Shenai. Her perfume swirled in his senses.

He frowned, straightened. Something was different.

A man came through the bedroom door. Tecmessa gleamed in his hand. Looking in his face was like looking in a mirror.

"Uh-oh," said Aristide.

23

"Hello, Bitsy," said the stranger with Aristide's face. "It's been a long time."

He thrust the broadsword toward the cat. Bitsy leaped; there was a crack; and the end table behind her disappeared. In Aristide's arms, Shenai gave a nervous leap. The lamp that had sat atop the table crashed to the ground, the shade tipping wildly.

Bitsy dived under a sofa, and with another whipcrack sound a coffee table set before the sofa vanished.

Pablo turned back to Aristide with a rueful smile. "I seem to be having a little trouble controlling your weapon," he said.

"No point in shooting Bitsy now," Aristide said. "She sent the alarm the second she became aware of you."

Pablo tilted his head and looked at Aristide curiously, as if judging an item of clothing perceived in a mirror.

"I'm sure alarms are going off everywhere," Pablo said. "It won't matter, as I have loyal soldiers stationed in this building who will keep the police at bay long enough for me to... accomplish my mission."

Aristide gently released Shenai and guided her toward the door. She stared at Pablo in complete bewilderment.

"Pablo," she said. "Who *is* this?"

"This would be Vindex," Aristide said. Her eyes widened, and she stared at Pablo in wonder.

"His appearance has changed since I saw him last," Aristide added, "and I'm not sure how he got here."

"I wanted to fool any biometric devices designed to protect you," Pablo said. "And as for my arrival—well, once you hid half the solar system in a bubble, I knew what was coming as well as anyone. I knew I'd lost. I set out to find out how you'd done it, and what Courtland discovered was a method of projecting wormholes from one universe to another. I'd planned to lead an invading army into Topaz, but unfortunately you destroyed Courtland, wrecked Pamphylia, and wiped out my army before I could move against you. I and my personal guard survived only because we were in a hardened research facility." He looked at Shenai and frowned. "Who is this exactly?"

"An old friend. Shenai Ataberk."

Pablo's eyebrows lifted. "You've changed."

"So have you," said Shenai, more cuttingly.

"And by the way," Aristide said, "I'd like to register an official complaint at the way you've been interfering with my love life. It really is your most annoying trait."

Pablo's eyes shifted back to Aristide.

"This will be the last time," he said. "I promise."

Aristide took a cautious step away from the door, farther into the room. The sword's point followed his movement.

"What are you doing here?" he said. "You've got the technology now. You could be confronting the Inept at this moment, and instead you're here talking to me."

Scorn glittered in Pablo's eyes.

"I'm an outlaw, a refugee with a few dozen followers," he said. "The Inept, whoever they are, are hardly likely to take me seriously. No—" His eyes narrowed. "The Inept are safe from me. I suppose I can take comfort in the likelihood that someone will probably seek the Inept eventually." He scowled. "Possibly even you."

"The idea has its charm," Aristide said. "Would you like me to represent you?"

He took another step into the room. From outside the hotel the sound of sirens was faintly heard. Pablo took a sideways step to maintain the proper distance from Aristide.

"I doubt you'll approach them with the proper disdain," he said. "And besides—you'll be elsewhere."

Aristide took another step. The sound of gunfire echoed up from street level.

"Stop that creeping!" Pablo commanded. "What are you trying to do—get to a weapon? It won't work." He took another gliding sideways step into the room to match Aristide's movement.

"I was trying to get away from Shenai," Aristide said. "So she wouldn't be hurt."

"I don't intend to *hurt* anyone." Pablo's features glowed with triumph. "You forget that my motivation throughout this entire adventure has been the desire for *revenge*. And that while my feelings for the Inept, due to their remoteness, necessarily partake of a degree of abstraction, my feelings for *you*, who have thwarted me at every turn, are entirely concrete."

"Oh, come off it," Aristide said. "If you kill me, they'll just reload me from backup. There's hardly any point to it at all."

Tecmessa's point described a small circle in the air. "I have no intention of killing you. While it is likely that I may spend the rest of my existence in prison, allowed to die of old age with no backup and no resurrection, or to have my brain rearranged to a more socially acceptable norm, I will in the interim be able to comfort myself with the knowledge that by using this weapon I can send you to a place—Holbrook, is it?—occupied entirely by individuals who hate your guts and who will want to see you suffer the most painful death—or life—imaginable." Eyeteeth glimmered in his smile. "What did you say was in the place? Tubers and cruciferous vegetables?" His smile broadened.

"*Bon appétit,*" he said.

The lamp swung violently on the end of its boom and connected with the back of Pablo's head. He took a staggering step, and a black-and-white form streaked from beneath the sofa, electricity arcing from bared fangs.

Bitsy bit Pablo on the ankle, and his body straightened with the shock.

Aristide stepped forward and wrapped his left arm, snake-style, around Tecmessa's bare blade.

The sword was, after all, a lever. Whoever had the best leverage controlled it.

He slammed Pablo away with the palm of his right hand and pulled the sword away with the left.

Shenai stepped forward and hit Pablo on the head with a vase she'd plucked from the chest of drawers. Pablo staggered, and as he recovered Aristide shifted the sword to his right hand and ran Pablo through the heart.

Vindex fell, his face fixed, an expression of baffled fury.

Aristide looked critically at his left forearm, which was bleeding rather freely after having wrapped the sharp-edged weapon.

He and Bitsy had planned the whole thing, Aristide communicating silently on his implant.

Shenai was gazing at Pablo's dying form with sick anger.

"Don't look," Aristide advised. "The sight won't be pleasant."

She turned away and put her head against his shoulder. After a moment's hesitating, Aristide put his bleeding arm around her shoulders.

Gunfire rattled the windows.

"It shouldn't be long now," he said, "before we're rescued."

24

Birdsong entered through the slatted blinds, and with it the fragrance of flowers and the airy tinkle of the wind chime. The last quarter-tones of the guitarrica danced in the air as if in answer to the gay water that spouted from the mouths of the bronze fishes atop the fountain.

Discontent settled upon her like the fine grey dust of the high plateau. She thanked the musicians, but waved them away before they could begin another ghazal. The young girls bowed and retreated, leaving her alone with the fountain and her thoughts.

Recline and watch the dance of the butterfly, Ashtra thought idly, *and the dance of the heron.*

She frowned and rose from the divan, her hands supporting her heavy belly. Her silks swished lightly on the cool marble as she walked to the tall window, and adjusted the blinds so that she could gaze out.

The city of Gundapur lay below her, its domes and towers bright against the sky. Beyond she could see green fields, and on a hill the white pavilion of the sultan. The Vale of Cashdan, the great cleft in the escarpment that led to the grey upland desert, was far away, invisible even from the city's tallest tower, but sometimes, when the wind was right, dust carried all the way from that plateau turned the sky the color of iron.

Farther still, months away, was the Womb of the World. A rider had come to the sultan with the message the Womb was now closed, a result of a war between the sorcerers on the other side. The opinion at the court was that this on balance was a good thing. "Fewer adventurers," her husband had proclaimed, "fewer bandits, fewer wars."

Fewer magicians, she thought.

Idly she tapped one heavy sapphire ring against the cypress windowsill.

Its facets cast sunlight on the ceiling.

Her husband had proved to be considerate, even lavish. He had given her silks, jewels, and a large household staff. He gave her a generous allowance, and—for Gundapur—a fair amount of freedom.

But in this decisive man she could see no trace of the boy she had married seven years before. And though he was generous, he didn't have the gift of intimacy. He spent little time in her company, preferring the society of other merchants or of companions he had made on his long journey. From excursions with his friends he returned late, if at all. He remained a stranger.

So, at times like these, when the dim sun's heat hung heavy in the air, and the wind chime rang softly to the fitful, uncertain breeze, she thought of the swordsman and sorcerer she had met on her journey from County Toi, and recalled the hours spent beneath the willows next to the oasis where her caravan had tarried for fear of the evil Priests of the Venger...

Lucky, she thought, that the child she carried was her husband's. She had counted the days, and was certain.

But with that anxiety faded, Ashtra could afford to indulge her fantasies.

He had called her "Ashtra of the Sapphire Eyes." He had made verses for her. Her husband had never done such things, and never would.

Was he truly a prince in disguise? She liked to think he was. He was certainly more princely than the sultan, who she had now met on several occasions, and found a coarse, greedy man, too fond of the consumption tax, the bastinado, and the strangler's bowstring as instruments of state policy.

By contrast, the sorcerer Aristide would have graced the sultan's court, or any other. It was he, after all, who had inspired the expedition that destroyed the Priests of the Venger, and killed two of them in person even though others were afraid even to approach. The expedition, staggering down from the Vale with laden camels, had brought astounding wealth to Gundapur. The sultan had confiscated much of this for his own use, but enough was left that the price of palaces in the city had risen sharply, and drunken, boasting caravan guards had been a feature of urban life for two months before the city's vice dens finally cleansed their purses...

Ashtra wondered if Aristide had returned to the Womb in time to pass through it before it was destroyed. She wondered if he was even now engaged with other sorcerers in some unimaginable combat for unimaginable stakes, on some unimaginable world full of unimaginable treasures and the monsters that guarded them.

She wondered what would have happened if she had accepted Aristide's offer and traveled to the Womb. Would she now be princess of some foreign land, crowned with gold and jewels? Or would she have been caught in the war, or trapped on that side of the Womb when it was destroyed?

Would she now be at the window of another palace, her belly heavy, staring out at the world and waiting for her sorcerer-husband to return from another of his adventures?

If there is a child, he had said, *I desire you send it to the College… particularly if it is a girl.*

She had been dwelling on these words of late. Ashtra had the feeling that her child would be a girl, and she suspected her husband would be indifferent to anything but a healthy son. The girl wouldn't be the magician's child, but Aristide wouldn't know that, nor would the scholars of the College. She knew of her own experience the limited opportunities faced by girls of her own class.

At the very least, a girl educated at the College would prove more valuable, and raise a larger bride-price from any future husband. She could only think her new merchant family would approve of that.

Of course, she thought, the College might not survive the closing of the Womb. Time would tell. But if it lasted, and if the child was a girl, then she would have to think seriously of this plan.

It would be necessary, Ashtra considered, for her husband to think it was his own idea…

She tapped her sapphire ring on the cypress-wood sill, and thought again of Aristide, his intense face, his precise hands.

She wondered again what would have become of her if she'd gone with him, on his quest toward the Womb of the World.

Ashtra indulged her fantasies a long moment, and then she drew away from the window and walked across the cool marble floors.

He would probably have abandoned her, she thought, in some mud-walled town. Got her with child and abandoned her.

All in all, she decided, things had probably worked out for the best.

EXCELSIOR!

[A REASSURANCE]

There were accidental cities once, that
Grew on hills or twined about rivers,
Swelling on paths of least resistance, spreading
On the land like a stain, wine and its lees.
Here a castle, there a market; there a
Noble goddess of gold and ivory
Crouched in her temple amid a foul slum.
By the city wall, a tannery filled
Mansions of the wealthy with its odor.

So the universe—

Sprawling, brutal, arbitrary, filled with
Forces striving against one another,
Like a darkened room where wrestlers battle
Unseen, blind, the point of their contention
Lost in the violence of their striving.

Shiva sits at the heart of every star
Making and unmaking, warming worlds to
Life and later burning them to atoms.
Dancing, graceful, smiling, unrelenting
Filling eons with his knowing laughter.

Should we wonder that the cities now are
Planned? Their arms of gold and green embrace the

Land, while overhead the sun spawns beams of
Daintily calculated radiance.
Splendid people walk here, their genes themselves
Manufactured, of fine computation.

Could the gates of Heaven hide the final
Unplanned city? Maybe God's radiant face
Blinds us to his badly planned urban stews—
Chaos lurches in the golden gutter,
Hand clutched around a bottle of cheap wine.
Say that Heaven needs a restoration—
Would it not be in the interest of all?

We are wise now, haven't had a war in—
(Well now, truth to tell—*That* was just a lone
Maniac, far too many hours in space.)
Finished now, we don't care to bring it up.
Surely Heaven can use a good tidy,
Kind attention, some rational guidance.

Let us build our tunnel to great Heaven!
Back to where it all began, our sorry
Cosmos, tragic womb to tragic eons.
Won't the Father be surprised to see our
Sauntering trolls upon his spruced-up streets, while
Seraphs take part in our fantasy games,
Bending divine energy to quibbling
Over title to magical items.

All we are is their fault, and it's only
Justice that they put up with us a while.
Let them see us as we are, their children,
Erring, errant, avaricious... *arrived.*

Heaven's being has its implications,
Us among them. All that we are, or were,
Or may cause to exist. We are implied:
Glories and afflictions, death and furies,
Accident, fluke and mere fortuity.
We'll turn up unannounced, and won't they be
Startled! Merest accidents, all grown up!

Heaven we shall renovate, with our
Usual abandon. Wisdom shall be
Handed out, natives' suggestions slighted.
Who are they, but those unwise enough to
Build the likes of *us?*

               They need not fear us.
Lurking in our precise architecture
Hide unintended places, soon to grow
Ominous with consequence, filling with
Burgeoning life, replete with fine monsters—
Capering and roaring, running in gangs,
Bounding in a colorful crowd, shining…
Our scary descendants on a rampage.

In our children lie the angels' comfort,
Reassurance in mere humanity.
Godhood escapes our fine, frantic efforts.
Neither we nor they are omnipotent.

Even Heaven generates its squinches.